About the Author

Anna Cookson is a radio presenter, journalist, writer and dreamer of dreams. She hosts the Wake Up Call on BBC Radio Kent, which won Gold for the Best Speech Radio Show at the Aria Academy Awards and also Kent Programme of the Year at the Kent Press and Broadcast Awards.

Anna has worked across TV and Radio, as a QVC and Craft Channel Presenter and for a plethora of stations including Radio 1, Magic, Kiss, Capital, Heart, LBC and BBC London. She won a New York Award for her chat show, Girls Talk, which was also nominated for an Academy Award.

When she's not broadcasting or writing you'll find her travelling the world, running, painting, dancing and climbing the occasional mountain.

Also by Anna Cookson:

The Sound Of Your Soul

DANCING OUT OF LOVE

Dear Sara,
Thank you so much
for being part of
the party!
Happy reading!
✶ Anna ✶
xxx

Anna Cookson

Dancing Out of Love

Pegasus

A CIP catalogue record for this title is
available from the British Library

ISBN-978-1-91090-380-3

*Pegasus is an imprint of
Pegasus Elliot MacKenzie Publishers Ltd.*
www.pegasuspublishers.com

First Published in 2023

**Pegasus
Sheraton House Castle Park
Cambridge CB3 0AX England**

Printed & Bound in Great Britain

To you — and your own dance.

Acknowledgements

This book danced into life with the help of so many beautiful souls.

First of all, thank you to my husband, Ed, for encouraging me to write past my insecurities, to delve deep into my words and not let go, never give up.

Secondly, to Liz. I'm not sure I could have done this without you — you patiently read and suggested changes at a time when I was too scared to show anyone else in the world. I'm so grateful.

Next, to Goodey, a million thank yous for being on this magical journey with me. Your support means everything — it lights the way.

Special thanks to my amazing Granma, who passed before this book was published, but will always be my hero, my inspiration. I hope heaven has a library.

As ever, thank you to my incredible parents — for their love, support and willingness to help at every stage — and also to my mother-in-law Faith for her proof-reading prowess.

Massive big up and thank you to Juan Carlos Otero for sharing his flamenco flare — for checking my moves and my Spanish were authentic. You are a superstar (and a stunning performer).

Thank you also to Karensa and the good folk of Flamenco Mosaico for letting me gate-crash their lessons, and sorry I stayed undercover; I was too shy to tell you about the book!

Also, to my wonderful friends, for their enthusiasm, and all the community at BBC Radio Kent: you are brilliant.

Finally, to you, thank you for stepping into this dance with Kezia and letting my words be yours.

Prologue

Don't go down to the water, don't go down to the sea...
She's there, and she stares, with her long black hair trailing down to
the waves. Long, long hair flowing down to the rocks and the shells and
the glittering grains of sand.
The sand takes her tears and shines with them — pouring pain into the
ocean, loss into the ocean, hate into the ocean — as it groans with her
grief and surges with her sorrow...
And she sits and she sings and the sound goes around and around like a
bat that won't fly home.
Don't go down to the water. Don't go there at night.
She moans and she sings and the two cries catch each other, the way
the wind catches the sea. The songs scratch on your skin and latch onto
your heart. Slow, slow songs to break your heart.
Don't go down to the water, don't go there alone.
Her dress is white and her hair is black and she waits... and she
waits... and she waits.
She wants to die, and that's why she sings: long low laments and the
wind is ice, at the back of your neck.
Matías told me.
If you hear her, you'll go blind. That's what happened to Matías; for
three days he saw nothing but blood-coloured darkness, dripping with
sin and throbbing with shadows. He thought there was no way out and
maybe there isn't, always.
Don't go down to the water, don't go there at all.
She wants to curse you, and that's why she sings.

PART ONE

1

Castanets

One bead of sweat trickled slowly down her temple. Her head tilted back; her spine arched in agony. Arms out, bent like the wings of a swan.

She stopped. Then her arms melted up and over her head, where her hands opened — flowers blooming — and the petals of her fingers twirled as the branches of her arms stirred with a deliberate power. All around her firm torso they floated, swaying in the stream of notes that bubbled up from a single guitar.

Next her arms became wings again as she took them out to the sides and lifted one leg over the other, twisting into a deep lunge.

Kezia watched with her mouth open. Somebody mumbled, '*Olé*!' and the dancer turned — caught up and spun around in the web of notes — around and around, until she was facing the back of the stage, where she stilled and her hips moved — tick-tock — a pendulum flexing from side-to-side.

Pat leaned across to Kezia. "Been a long time since I could do that," his voice was gruff and lilting and his breath had a flat yeasty tang from the beer. Kezia nodded, half-smiled, but didn't take her eyes from the woman. *Snap*. Her castanets clacked out a syncopated rhythm that climbed in-between the guitar's flickering notes, weaving the two together in a musical double helix.

In the shadows, at the back of the stage, the man with the velvet jacket sat bent over his guitar lovingly, like a Madonna with child. He looked up as the dancer wound her body and the clicks together. When, at the front of the stage, she stopped, drawing one arm out in front as though she was holding a cloak, her other arm wide to the side, he clapped his hand over the strings. Silence.

The dancer's feet began a new rhythm then, sharp and strong, heel and toe, precise and slicing through the air. Faster and faster, crushing

13

her feelings into the floor. The guitar player picked up the new tempo, strumming out the chords now like clouds of smoke that built and built around her.

She reached for her skirt, which flowed in artichoke layers to the ground and gripped it hard in her fist, pulling it up so the curtain revealed her angry feet: stamping, stamping fast and hot. Faster they went and faster until her shoes were like sparks and her arms were like flames. The music got louder too, billowing around her.

Then suddenly, a loud crack. The final stamp — her head and her arms veered back in defiance. Full stop. The end. Her ragged breath highlighted this unexpected stillness and the audience didn't move either — they were caught in the web, as she was.

Until... her arms swam down and her smile broke out and she bowed, deep and slow and long.

A pitter patter of claps started and then built like rain. They showered the dancer and she bowed again and again.

"That floor must be reinforced. I was worried she might go through," Pat grinned and got up. "I'm going to the bar. Same again?"

He moved clumsily past wooden chairs and tables to where a huge puce ham hung dryly by a chalk board advertising a 'Menu Especial', in florid and slightly smudged writing. Glistening berry tarts were displayed on the counter, encased in burnished pastry. The back wall was a jigsaw of bottles: wine and port and spirits, in reds and rubies and blacks. There were horseshoes nailed above the bar and a crude drawing of a man in monk's robes holding a church in one hand and a crucifix in the other. He had a wide yellow circle drawn around his head. 'San Junipero', it said on his left and 'Serra', was written to his right. His big eyes looked thoughtful but his small mouth was petulant. Beneath the picture was written, in English, 'Always forward, never back'.

"Hopefully this is cheering you up a bit, Pet?" Having pushed his way back past all the other tourists, Pat put the glasses down, jerking at the last minute so a spit of red wine spilled onto the wooden table.

Kezia took a glass and wiped the drip off its side. "Thanks, Dad. Yeah. She was amazing." As she nodded towards the back of the bar where the stage area had been her cedar green eyes seemed to simmer. "I've never seen anything like that."

"I know!" Kezia's mum was also called Pat. Patrick and Patricia. They went everywhere together, Pat and Pat. They'd met when Kezia's mum went to nursing school in Newcastle and they'd moved back to London together. Friends joked they'd never been apart since. "Makes a change, right? It's not like the dancing you used to do, is it?"

Kezia laughed. "It's a long time since I did ballet, Mum."

"You were good at it, as a little girl — I remember."

"Until they told me I was too, what was it? 'Big boned'." She took the elastic band off her wrist and scooped her hair off the back of her neck into a ponytail, shaking her head to rid herself of the memory. Frizzy brown strands escaped, framing her face.

"Still, you loved ballet, you shouldn't have given it up because of that."

Kezia pulled more of her hair loose at the front to disguise her ears, she was always conscious of her ears sticking out. "I wasn't exactly going to make it though, was I?"

"Not the point. You should do the things you enjoy."

"And you can do anything you set your mind to, Kezia my girl." Kezia's dad wiped the beer foam from his lip. "Anything. And don't you forget it." His eyes shone with sincerity.

Kezia leant back in her chair. That wasn't how it felt.

"I think James would have liked it here, don't you?" Patricia was looking around. "Is there cheese at the bar, he loves his cheeses, doesn't he?"

"Pat!" Her husband looked up from his drink. "Come on now, love. That's not what Kez needs right now. Just needs to forget about it for a bit, have some time out, it's what this is all about. Right Kez?"

Kezia shrugged and nodded at the same time, not wanting to take sides. "It's okay." She picked up a flyer for flamenco which had been lying on the table and turned it over and over in her hands. "I mean... it's pretty hard to just forget about it all anyway." She folded the flyer in half and the word 'flame' stood out, the 'nco' hidden on the other side.

"Have you heard from him?" Kezia's mum couldn't help asking.

"He keeps begging me to talk, but I don't want to. I'm not replying to his texts, I came out here to get away." Kezia drew a line through the spilt wine with the flyer and watched the red soak into the words.

"Oh, but he's such a nice boy, so respectful."

15

"Pat, that's enough now." Kezia's dad put his hand on his wife's arm but she couldn't stop.

"She's twenty-five, you and I were married at twenty-five. I just don't want her to regret it, that's all. End up on the shelf. And James is so sweet. He used to call you his little sunflower, didn't he? Or was it marigold? I can't remember — but we want to see that happy Kez again."

"Well maybe if we stop talking about it, she will be."

Patricia looked anxiously at her daughter and rubbed her shoulder. "Yes love," she said. And then continued, "It was sunflower, wasn't it? It wasn't marigold."

"Look," Patrick held up his hand. "The whole point of this trip is to relax and unwind, so let's focus on that, shall we?" He looked at his wife, and then to Kezia. "What shall we do tomorrow. Another easy day?"

Kezia thought back to that afternoon, her parents asleep by the pool, deflated by the heat, their heads lolling. They'd worn flecks of oily tomato on their chins, lips pinguid with the sheen of tapas and their soft snores had formed a chorus with the flies buzzing insect halos around their heads. "Yeah," she said, unenthusiastically.

Pat and Pat started discussing the difference between tortilla and omelette and Kezia looked over her dad's shoulder, to where a faded photograph showed a strong woman with fierce disdain in her face, nostrils flared and head tossed back, leaning to the side and pulling up her long skirts aggressively. The picture was black and white but there was colour in the feel of it. Kezia wondered if it was dulled only by years and years of cigarette and cigar smoke. The woman was not looking at the camera but seemed acutely aware of its focus. Underneath the picture a label said: 'Carlotta de Santos'.

"That frame's not quite straight." Kezia's dad had turned to see what she was looking at.

His wife followed their gaze too. "Oh, look Kezia, see? She's rather stocky and she's a dancer. You don't have to be a waif you know. Maybe you should have a go at some flamenco while we're out here? You might like it, you—"

"No! No. No. No!" A young man with curly black hair was shouting at the other side of the bar.

They all looked over.

"I knew the food wasn't so good since Mando left, but I didn't think it was that bad," joked an American man with a moustache on the table next to them. His partner didn't laugh.

The shouting man stood up, flushed red and sweat shining on his face. "No. No. No, no." He was burbling and holding his hand out in front of him, fending off an imaginary assailant. His breath was coming in loud rasps.

"Matías, *qué te pasa?*" A girl with hair the colour of butternut squash stood up and put her hand on his shoulder. He groaned loudly.

"Do you think we should—" Kezia's mum began to ask as the Spanish word for ambulance flashed like a blue light around the bar and the man groaned again. He was sick on the floor.

"Okay? You okay?" A small, tanned man with a haunted face and skin so smooth he looked like a boy, came flying out from behind the counter. "Not sick?" he said in stilted Spanish, concern flaring urgently in his brown eyes. "Not okay?"

A portly man came next and batted him away, his double chins swaying with disquiet. "Sami, no." He took charge, leaning under the man's arm to support him as he convulsed his way to the exit, bumping into chairs and table legs until they were out into the fresh air — where they could hear him being sick three more times.

Seconds later a distant siren clashed with the shrill cawing of a crow, calling, calling and shredding the air with insistence.

2

Horse's Hooves

They'd taken the train from Almería. It was hot and slow. There were rough plants at the side of the track, aggressively leafy. The sticky passengers stretched, their hands unfurling above their heads, mimicking the foliage, and outside, through the open windows, the clouds looked like masks with spectral faces.

The train juddered and stopped. A dog barked belligerently and the sound scraped across the stifled afternoon, catching on ridges of airless atmosphere. Kezia's parents leant back in their seats and shut their eyes, smoothing the wrinkles of their eyelids, whilst their hands found each other and their fingers twisted together like roots.

Kezia rested her temple against the hard, hot window frame and looked out at the caterpillar body of the train curving round the bend. The path was compacted mud, the colour of milk chocolate, but thirsty — split in places, lacerated by the sun. Its parched lines paralleled the dry bark of the tree trunks further back, where the heat haze blended the leaves into the sky. She looked down again and there, on the path, outrageously, hideously, starkly: a pair of horse's hooves.

Hooves, no horse.

They were cut off, just after the hard part where the leg starts. Kezia recoiled and then leant forwards and the hooves shimmered in the sun.

The train pulled away but the image stayed in her mind the way dice hang from a rear-view mirror; she couldn't quite see past them. They were always there, rolling side-to-side, over the crisp grooves in the mud, rolling and rolling. Sometimes she thought she saw blood at the ragged part, other times the cut was smooth. She wished she hadn't seen them. She wished she didn't have to think about the hooves, rolling on the path.

They took a taxi from the station, a car like a wasp, yellow and black. The leather seats pushed heat into their backs as Kezia's mum chatted away to the driver, a woman with a very straight top lip and hair scraped back by an Alice band with a floppy floral bow on top. Patricia was talking so fast all she could do was nod, the bow moving up and down in agreement.

The metal silhouettes of bulls looked real as they glowered down from the roadside, horns turned up towards the sun. "So Spanish!" declared Patricia and the taxi driver nodded out of habit, rolling up the sleeves of her buttermilk yellow shirt. The wide road snaked past mountains banked up in the distance, resembling giant lizards with scaly backs. White houses like matchboxes fanned out on hillsides amidst tufts of trees and barefaced rock.

They drove through small towns with thirsty looking shops; pharmacies with dry cracked banners and boutiques with wide awnings faded by the sun. "Nearly there I think." Kezia's dad was sat in the back seat with her, smiling. "It didn't look too far on the map."

They went through a hotel complex of sinister tower blocks, large teeth eating the mouth of a bay, and on, through a park where men in sleeveless basketball tops lounged on benches while women in cotton summer dresses teetered on very high espadrilles. Then they swerved right and up, climbing. Ivory rocks and yellow grass and brown twigs all blurred past the window. Attenuated trees gasped up the hill. Red and yellow insects scuttled away and an old toilet seat was abandoned in a ditch, the foliage beginning to throttle its neck, claiming it.

Then the road began to flatten. Houses with terracotta tiles and proudly painted facades boasted balconies flush with flowers and elaborate names wrought in neat black twisted iron. There were guards over the windows and palm trees by the pools. 'Beware of the dog' signs pictured calm-looking Alsatians by extravagant gates.

"The sea is that way," the taxi driver nodded to her left. "The main beach is down that road, about ten minutes' walk. It gets crowded, you might prefer to go to *Cala Pirata*, it's nearer your hotel and not nearly so busy. There's a path, I'll show you when we get to your hotel."

The heat clung to them as the streets and the houses got smaller — everything seemed to contract — even the air. The buildings joined together and shuffled along in rows, connected by electricity cables, looped across. Signs for hairdressers, tattoo parlours and shoe shops jutted out and cats in doorways lazily licked their paws. Every street seemed to give way to a maze of alleyways, deeper, darker, cooler spaces Kezia could only glimpse — a flash and then gone.

They made their way around the side of the village square, where chairs and tables spilled from cafés and parasols protected wrinkled tourists from the tenacity of the sun. There was a solid stone church, two bell towers gravely protecting a central doorway with the statue of a man above, gently crumbling in his dress. Steps leaked out of the door and dripped to the ground. Everything seemed to be melting. Kezia wiped her eyes with hot fists.

They'd driven on, through wider shopping streets where beige buildings housed supermarkets and banks and plumbers and where date palms flourished in the middle of the road, adding the exotic to the quotidian utilities all around.

"Cala Pirata is that way." The driver pointed left and the bow twitched as she turned. They craned their necks, trying to see over neatly cut hedges and spongy olive trees. "You won't see it from here," she added, and they all leant back. To their right, houses banked up the hill; a Tetris puzzle of alabaster and lemon and dusky peach, with arches framing doorways and slices of roof just visible. Some had Grecian columns and chunky verandas, others were little more than cubes.

"So, are you from here then?" Curious, Kezia bent forwards to ask the driver.

"Kezia, always asking questions," her mum said fondly, and then waited, because she also wanted to know.

"No, I'm from Novelda, outside Alicante," the woman told them. "But I like working out this way." They pulled up at some lights and she scratched her arm. "It's very popular with tourists around here, nice beaches, slower way of life. We came here once when I was little and stayed for a week. I remember — I really wanted to go to *Cala Pirata* to look for the pirates, because it means 'Pirate Cove', but my parents wouldn't let me — they said my legs were too short for all the boulders you have to climb over." She smiled broadly, her top lip staying straight. "So we just played on the main beach and they fed me ice cream to shut me up about it."

Patrick laughed. "Well Pet," he said to Kezia, "If you want to go to the Pirate Cove we won't stop you, will we Pat?"

"Oh no, we think your legs are quite long enough," said her mum, pretending to be serious. "Unless of course you'd prefer to sit and eat ice cream, that sounds by far the better option to me."

Kezia raised her neat eyebrows knowingly at her dad because her mum always chose comfort over adventure. "How long does it take?" she asked.

"To get to the cove? Oh, about half an hour, forty minutes, something like that."

"And to the main beach?" Kezia's dad had wound down the window and was looking out of it like an eager dog, tufts of grey hair springing enthusiastically from his bald patch.

"It's about twenty minutes to the main beach in the other direction, just stay on this road and then go right at the square we just came through. When you get to a bar called Mando's — on the corner, you'll see it, it's got a big green sign outside and tables and chairs — when you get there, turn left and follow that path along, then do another right and it's about five minutes down the hill."

"I hope you're taking notes." Kezia's dad turned to her and grinned. "The bar sounds good anyway."

"Yes, very popular with tourists." The driver nodded. "They do flamenco performances and things but I've heard the food is not so good since the new management took over. It used to be run by a man named Normando, hence the name, Mando's. His wife was a famous flamenco dancer and she ran a school not far away, Carlotta—" she stopped suddenly, focusing on the road as a couple of girls in miniskirts crossed without warning, and losing her train of thought... "Right, we're not far from your hotel now."

All the hotels were on the far side of town. They drove past three squat 1960s blocks, balconies drawn in straight lines across functional rectangles. Next was a taller tower, with an oval of turquoise flaring outside its central atrium and the sound of bodies flopping into the water. There were a couple of gated establishments with thick pines cut into hedges, the intercoms gleaming silver, and further along, a campsite; a cartoon tent on a sign pointing the way. "Nearly there," the driver muttered.

Hotel Parños del Toro was at the end of the sweep. It had a smaller, more homely feel and it wasn't quite so square because all the windows were arched and all the paths were curved. There were multicoloured lights across a gazebo over the reception and a large plastic bull stood stoutly in the garden at the front, its head down as if it might charge.

"Ooh, *muchos gracias*," crooned Kezia's mum. "Look at this!"

They stumbled out of the taxi, fumbling with their bags as they took them from the boot, disorientated by the sun and the journey.

"So, if you want to go to that cove I was telling you about, go that way." The taxi driver pointed down the road to a wooden sign by a tiny path. "Down there and right at the end and then follow the markers. I think there are other paths as well but that's the only one I know about."

As soon as they checked into the hotel Kezia's parents checked out of life. They slept most of the time and drifted from meal to meal in a slow-motion trance. Kezia tried to relax, but without James, the old feelings of insecurity came back and, she couldn't help it, she kept thinking about the horse's hooves, stranded on the path; she blinked them away but they always came back, swinging, swinging from the corners of her mind.

She tried to swim, tried to read, but there was too much space, too much silence and she couldn't get away from the feelings. When she wasn't thinking about James she was thinking about Gary and other times it was like the bullies were still there, kicking the back of her chair: *boring Kezia, fat Kezia, no one likes Kezia. Boring, fat, boring, fat.* The words swung with the horse's hooves and they gathered momentum together.

After two days, she decided she couldn't face another afternoon torpor, she had to do something. "I'll see if I can make it to that cove," she told her parents, who nodded and went back to their snooze.

'*Cala Pirata*', read the elderly sign, frayed and gnarled, with the words just about decipherable in the weathered wood. Kezia traced them with her finger, liking the feel of the shallow script, wondering if pirates really did go there, in the olden days. James would have liked the history of it, but she'd come here to escape those thoughts, so she shook her head and set off.

She followed the direction down the side of a row of fluffy cypress trees and then sharply right. She pushed past branches, low and overhanging, she felt ferns skim her ankles. She looked down and noticed the arrows, red and yellow arrows, dribbled onto stone with thick paint, pointing the way along the path, pointing the way to the sea.

The heat clawed at her along with the branches, everything dry and scratching from the sides. Insects rustled and twigs crackled as she walked. She turned a corner and crouched to wiggle down a crag of mammoth stone, set into the hill with prehistoric ambition. It led to more boulders which eventually evened out to great slabs, and as she went on, the ground became sandy and blonde. Then the trees gave way to low shrubs and wild grasses. She could see now that she was in a small valley, a crease in the landscape, and as she turned another corner, out ahead, there it was: the sudden stillness of the sea. Vast and blue.

Gazing in wonder and not looking down, she tripped on an anfractuous root, so she focused back on the path again and the arrows smudged on the unruly rocks. There should be directions for life too, thought Kezia, telling you which way to go, because she knew as she turned left and right and left and right, climbed over rocks and skirted round boulders, that truly, when it came to her own life, she was completely and confoundedly lost.

3

Ocean

"You're brave."

A strange and terrible wind blew in from the sea.

"The winds are coming."

The grasses shivered.

"The winds are coming," he said again. And then, "They say she sings loudest on the nights of the *leveche*."

The sun was an apricot in the sky. Kezia blinked at it and then turned to see the man behind her. He gave a slight bow.

"I'm okay thanks." Kezia hugged her knees, conscious of her ears, as she always was when meeting new people. She had been sitting on the sand, picking bits of hard skin off her toe, feeling the warm wind, still trying not to think about James. The cove had come as a relief when she finally arrived, hot and grazed, and the cliffs around the edge seemed to hold her in. It was a horseshoe shape and she'd climbed across the rocks and sat in the centre, feeling protected, until now.

Dead seaweed lay in strips across the cove. It crunched as the man stepped forwards. The sleeves of his purple velvet jacket were too long and she couldn't see his hands, just his fingers, slender like crab's legs, with long fingernails. There were tiny blackbirds on each of the shiny gold buttons. A lilac handkerchief bloomed out of his top pocket and a Spanish greyhound stood totemic behind him.

"I'm making you awkward. Of course I am. But you must go, before it picks up — the *leveche* — the wind, blowing in from the south." The gritty air lifted the man's hair, long at the back, and he looked out to sea, placid and unblinking. The cove was growing hazy in the chalky light and the man's voice was precise and forceful. The accent ran through his English like the inseparable striations in stone. "You'll hear her before you see her. Don't stay. Don't look."

Kezia picked up a handful of dry seaweed and crushed it between her fingers, watching as it turned to powder. "What... what do you mean?"

"They say she comes at night. She comes and she sings. Sad songs to break your heart." The man stopped staring out to sea, and said, as if someone had prompted him, "I'm Darim." He held out the arm with the too-long sleeve. Kezia reached up and his thin fingers felt cold as she shook his hand. "I saw you at Mando's last night," he said. "You were there." When Kezia nodded, he carried on. "That man, after the dancing, the one who had the..." he chose the word carefully, "*Episode* — he heard *her*." Darim whispered 'her' and it carried on his breath like a wave. "You know the story? Of course you don't, or you wouldn't be here."

"We've only been in Parños a few days," said Kezia, wondering why she was excusing herself for not knowing something she could not be expected to know. The day was squeezing the ripe sun now, staining the clouds with an orange lilt.

"Yes, yes," said Darim. "Then you don't know. I'll tell you. Then you will go." And the dog sat down, as if expecting a story. "It all happened a long time ago, long before your mother or your grandmama or your great-grandmama was born. There was a woman, from the village, and her betrothed was to be killed. A heretic. His death warrant was signed, for sunrise. So she came here, to cry to the sea, and her grief spilled from her and out, out to the sea and up, up to the sky. She cried and she cried and the winds picked up and still she cried. The winds roared and she wept and the wind grew stronger until it swept her into the sea, and still she wept." As if telling the tale with him, the winds moaned agreement.

Kezia gripped the sand until it became a ball in her hand.

"'Take me,' the woman cried to the sea. 'Take me too.' She was ready to die. But then she heard a booming voice like thunder. 'There is a way. You can save your lover. But it will require great sacrifice.' The woman begged to be told, and this was the reply. 'We will spare his life if you will give us yours. Here is your choice: to roam these shores forever, to guard them and never die. To sit and sing for us, on the rocks by the sea. You will outlive him and the next generation and the next... for an eternity you will be ours... but his life we will spare. Or, you can have your life as it was before and he will taste the bitter fruit of mortality as soon as the sun does rise. It is your choice.'

"Thinking only of her love and not of herself the woman immediately agreed to guard the rocks and sing forever. In an instant she felt the weight disappear from her body, the sea let her go and she was pulled back, up to the shore and onto the rocks. Duly her love was spared, but the woman found she was unable to leave the cove. There was a force holding her back. So she stayed, and her love came to this place every day. He came with bread and fish and almonds. He came until he was a very old man. Then one day, as he was stepping over the rocks, he slipped and fell, smashing his frail body down, and the sea consumed him as he lay. His lover, weeping once again over his broken life, saved his bones and made them into a necklace. Years came and years went and still she did not perish. Still she sat, and still she sang. No peace could she get; she was doomed forever, to sing to the sea. For the life she saved and the life she lost, she sings. So you see, love never dies or gives you any rest. That's the price you pay for love."

The dog looked up and then rested its head back on its paws. Kezia shuddered. "Your stories are horrible."

"The truth often is, often is," said Darim.

Kezia frowned and the reeds hummed ominously.

"So you must go before the night comes. She curses those who come here now, jealous of their freedom to die."

"That's not true."

"As you wish, as you wish."

Kezia wrapped her arms around her knees. Her freckles had come out in the sun and her hair was tousled by the wind, soft waves down to her shoulders.

He turned to her, blinking slowly, like an old-fashioned camera taking her picture. "You are sad." It wasn't a question, but the dog's ears cocked up, as if he wanted to know why.

Kezia looked up and into Darim's eyes — they seemed to mirror the water: the depth and lightness of the ocean.

"His memory is the perfume you wear." Darim's statement hung, buffeted in the air, as the wind ruffled the sea. "Your heart is broken," he said after a while. "But I have news. All hearts are broken. Pain is the simple fact of being alive."

Kezia frowned again. "I'm just… unhappy with my life."

"That's very ungrateful."

"You don't know — you don't understand." She looked at the small blackbirds on his jacket buttons. She wanted him to go but couldn't say it.

"You came here to remember, or to forget?"

"To forget, I guess, but…"

"But you can't help to remember. He will not be worth all this… this *anguista.*" As he said 'anguista' he held up his fist and flicked his fingers out like a firework.

"How do you know?"

"They never are. They never are." He looked down at her. "You can sit and dissect the past, like pulling the legs off an insect, one by one, but it will not make you feel any better. All of this torture, for what?"

The wind eddied round them, lifting their hair and flapping at their clothes. Kezia crossed her arms tightly across her chest.

"Do not be cross. A beautiful woman must not go crazy over one man. There are many more. And they are all as irritating as each other."

"I'm not crazy," said Kezia, but she laughed as she said it. He had called her beautiful and she noticed his lip curling up in a smile too, like he was ready to kiss or sing.

"His memory is the perfume you wear," he said again, orating into the wind. "The feeling stays with you, even though you are apart. And that is because it is not about him." The winds whirred. "It is about *you.*"

The man made to go. "Come, Rollo." And the dog unfolded its legs, standing up. Then Darim turned and stared right at Kezia, eyes the aqua of ocean spray. "Go. Before it gets dark," he said. "And don't get lost."

A red cloud smudged the fading sun.

4

Raindrops

$\mathcal{R}$achel's hands were dry and cracked, the knuckles sore and rough. She gripped the pen and watched the lattice of lines bloom: tiny red threads. It made her think of the patchwork elephant Joe had as a child, sewn together with electric red cotton.

Hand cream, she wrote on the back cover of the spiral notepad on the desk, smoothing out the mess of creased pages. The front cover had come loose and detached in her bag and an array of errant shorthand characters undulated across the exposed first page, unlikely actors in a story she could no longer remember, something about an assault in Parson's Green… just another courtroom on just another day.

The office lights blared and blinked: bright squares in the ceiling, garish to the point of incivility. She took another swig of cold coffee and waited for the kick that didn't come. She thought about taking another painkiller, but she couldn't remember how many she'd already had that day. Too many, like every day, but the pain wouldn't come out. Like a shadow, it never left. The shadow stained everything, loomed over life with spectral certainty. Rachel ran from it, she tackled it head on, she hid beneath its folds, she tried every move she could think of, but still it never left. She took exercise, she had hot baths, she ate tofu in its blandest form, she did everything the doctor told her to do, but the pain never went away.

Rachel bit down on the end of her biro — frustrated — she heard the crack as the plastic fractured and she spat out a tiny shard of pen. It was late and banks of computers stared at her with blank faces, a sea of clutter washed up around them: cups and papers, books and wires, the flotsam of keys from lockers past.

The *London Echo* was all around her — an echo in itself — framed front pages lined the walls, competing for space, each headline shouting louder than the next: terror raids, Russian spies, floods. Next to them the battered air con unit choked its way through each day, bravely filtering the fug of twenty-seven journalists. One frail plant gasped pathetically on top of the cabinet, spidery limbs dangling fretfully down over the edges of its cracked pot. "I meant to water you yesterday," Rachel told it as she picked up a cup and went to the water cooler. She watched as the liquid soaked into the soil, disappearing the way her own pain was hidden inside her. "There," she said and the plant quivered in response.

The other journalists had gone to the Rose and Crown, and as usual, they didn't invite her. It was a familiar nagging ache and she buried it with the rest of the pain as she distracted herself with her inbox. Plans for a new car park in Islington. *Delete*. An octogenarian running a marathon. *Delete*. The Summer Opening at Buckingham Palace, press preview. *Delete*. Rachel exhaled very slowly. *"The news won't come to you, you've got to go out there and find it."* Rebecca, her tutor at university, insisted the bona fide stories weren't in the press releases — they were out there in the streets, real and raw and waiting.

"The news won't come to me," Rachel repeated and the pot plant trailed a lank limb very slowly in a waft of stale recycled air. It seemed to be pointing to the sign on the wall held up by three pea-sized dots of Blu-Tack; the fourth had dropped behind the cabinet a long time ago leaving the bottom right-hand corner to curl desperately towards the words:

A TEAM IS ONLY AS STRONG AS ITS WEAKEST LINK.
DON'T LET IT BE YOU.

The block capitals blared at her from the crusty paper and Rachel looked away, reaching for her phone as she breathed through the pain. She messaged Joe, who was spending the night with his dad. Typically, he typed straight back, telling her they were having triple pepperoni pizza, with a thumbs-up emoticon.

Dad wants to know, did your housing piece go?

Rachel sighed. *No*, she told him.

It was dropped for some breaking news about a panda being born at London Zoo, which Martin said would work better for digital.

Rachel found a picture of *Rambo* to send to Joe, a pink wriggling thing with specs of ice-white fur and eyes that didn't know how to open yet.

"Who isn't going to click on a picture of a cute baby panda?" her boss Martin had said, dragging a month's worth of investigation out of the newspaper template.

Aww he's cute, wrote Joe. *Dad says never mind, perhaps it will go next week. I'll see you tomorrow after school.*

Yes, sweetheart. I love you.

Joe went quiet after that, his attention back on the pizza. Rachel picked up the painkillers on her desk, turning the box in half circles absent-mindedly.

"Are you addicted to those things?" Andy had levelled with her one day, back when they were together and Joe was little, playing on the mat.

"No, I just... need them sometimes."

"Like an alcoholic needs a drink I bet."

"No." She'd tried to explain so many times before. He couldn't understand why some days she was fine and others not. There was no explanation. "The pain just comes and goes. I have good days and bad days." It was all she could say but it never worked.

"You just pretend you're in pain when it's convenient for you," he said petulantly. "When you don't want to do something."

"Believe me Andy, I want to do everything," she growled back. "On a good day, I can — and I do. Or do you not notice as everything just happens around you?"

He snorted and Joe cried out so she went to him and the matter was dropped, for now.

A notification flashed, jolting her back to the present. The email about Buckingham Palace had been forwarded back to her by Martin, telling her to go to the press day: ten thirty, tomorrow. Rachel doubled over briefly, steadied herself and stood up, reaching for her jacket, the leather one, the one that made her feel tougher than she was.

The lift was empty and she stared at her misty reflection in the dirty mirror. Her long black hair was caught up in a proficient bun, it needed washing, she thought, looking closer to see whether it needed dying again too. Her dark eyeliner was the warpaint she wanted but the mascara was conglomerating at the top of her lashes so she squeezed it gently between finger and thumb and it left a smudge like soot on her hand. She wiped it with a tissue then took a hard red lipstick from her bag and ran it over her dry lips, caked with previous applications.

At reception, Lyra was scrolling through Instagram absently, eyes distant, as if she was stroking a cat or brushing her hair. She was swamped by the ellipse of the huge glass desk, her name badge shining on her crisp blue uniform. "You're here late," she said, keeping one eye on the screen.

"Yeah, just looking around for stories."

"Oh yeah? Did you find anything?"

"No, and for penance I've got to go to the opening of Buckingham Palace tomorrow." Rachel affected a wry smile, even as the pain bit.

"Oh wow," Lyra looked up fully. "But won't that be amazing, all them chandeliers and stuff."

"Well, I guess, but it's been there a long time, it doesn't feel like news. It's no murder investigation, no bank robbery or drugs bust."

"Nah," Lyra said, shaking her head and looking down at her nails, which were painted with little rainbows. "I'd rather go there though, sounds much nicer and you might meet your Prince Charming." Her voice carried the grainy undercurrent of cigarettes, nightclubs and night shifts.

Rachel laughed. "If I thought that I would have gone there a long time ago."

Lyra grinned, teeth tinged blue from the energy drink she always had at this time.

"See you tomorrow then." Rachel pushed on the glossy revolving door, her face faintly reflected, showing just the dark line of her lipstick in a vague shape.

"Yeah." Lyra went back to Instagram.

It was raining slightly outside. Gentle, quiet rain. Huddled workers in sharp suits rushed through Golden Square, checking watches and making for the Tube. Tourists dawdled in their wake, swathed in transparent plastic cagoules, shimmering in the streetlights and ghostly.

"Excuse me?" one of the spectres asked, the hair matted onto her forehead. "How do I get to Carnaby Street?"

"Um, that way, turn left and then turn right."

The tourist repeated the directions as if learning the lines of a song and then looked relieved. "Thank you so much," she said as she rustled away.

The rain kissed Rachel's cheeks and frizzed her hair; an invisible veneer that settled on her skirt, slowly sinking in. Tall, solid buildings looked down at her as she left the square, cafés squatting in their paunches. A boy on a hire bike scooted past too close as she crossed the road at Brewer Street and she breathed out slowly after he'd gone.

At Piccadilly Circus she waded through the crowds, a medley of arms and legs and bags and elbows, all pushing, pushing. "Legbows," Joe had said sweetly, pointing to his knees when he was little and looking up to see if he was right. The memory gave her the familiar pang, just above the diaphragm, as she thought of Joe and Andy together tonight without her. Always without her on Tuesdays, and alternate weekends; that was what they had agreed. She tried to focus above the walking wallpaper around her to the sky above, the darkness cracked by the petrol glower of a cloud.

"If it was going to work, it would have worked by now." Andrea put it so succinctly, the way best friends do, but she didn't know Andy the way Rachel did. She wasn't there. Rachel let the memories slide and mesh, the same thoughts turning and jarring like a broken engine, as she wondered what she could have done differently, how the pain had changed her… it always came back to that.

"He wanted another child, and I…" She tried to explain it to Andrea, but it never came out right. It always sounded black and white when it wasn't, it was slippery with all kinds of colours she couldn't understand.

Rachel's eyes caught on the statue of Eros, resplendent wings above his bare torso, poised, pulling back on his bow and arrow. Below, at the base of the tiered fountain, a small man with a red guitar was singing as if he had just been hit by one of those arrows. Caught in the turmoil of it, he seemed insensible to the throng of people milling around him. Rachel stopped, resonating with the busker's anguish and transposing it for her own. As the song washed in, she felt her emotions shift, like silt. She reached into her pocket to find some change but there was only half a packet of chewing gum and a ragged tissue.

The rain got stronger. Rachel moved on. The drops glazed the pavements so they reflected the neon lights — each in its own square — like a comic strip. Umbrellas sprung up like jellyfish, to float in an ocean of heads, and Rachel fumbled in her bag for her own; the pink one Joe had given her on Mother's Day. The rain on the stretched fabric made a staticky beat and she walked with it, still contemplating the torment of the busker, as she arrived in Leicester Square.

The chalk portraits of famous people ran in the rain as if to illustrate the transience of notoriety. Their artists covered them, shifting from foot to foot, looking anxiously up to see if it would stop. Further along a man in a cap was spilling sounds, beatboxing loudly as his neck went forwards and back, one hand on his microphone and one foot on his speaker. Above, the trees seemed to conspire with each other, making music of their own, a swish of speaking as incomprehensible to Rachel as the boom of the mic below. She felt saturated with the rain and the sounds as she walked towards the blunt face of Leicester Square Tube. People were taking shelter under the glass roof that protruded from the nearby Hippodrome like a giant tutu. Two of them were hugging, another couple were having an argument; Rachel understood the gestures of friction.

By the Tube a man was holding out a free newspaper. Rachel didn't take one but she was trying to read the headline, when—

"Oi!"

"Oh, sorry." Rachel sidestepped the woman with the purple hair. "Sorry I wasn't looking."

"Too right." The woman pulled her denim jacket down and brushed her arm as if Rachel had contaminated it with contact.

"Sorry," Rachel said again, although the woman was already moving off, showing her umbrage in the slump of her shoulders. Rachel was left staring at a lamp post. She was about to head for the stuffy shelter of the Tube, but then she noticed the poster…

A dancer in a deep red dress wore skirts which billowed out like a waterfall of blood. She was leaning back with her hands on her hips and staring solidly at Rachel. In her stance there was power — defiance — a challenge. A flower in her hair. She was oblivious to the commuters and the rain and the stark difference of her vivid dress. She was in control, and right there Rachel felt a spark of recognition, like a memory that surges with a song. There was something in her face that felt like waking up.

5

Perfume

"His memory is the perfume you wear."

He'd said it the way smoke curls, softly.

Kezia shielded her eyes against the swirling sand as the wind whipped along the path tugging and pulling and tugging and pulling. The trees were rocking their heads hysterically and she felt the teeth of thorns, biting. The plants were ganging up around her and all the while it was becoming hard to separate the voices in her head from the voices of the *leveche*. Kezia was lost in thought almost half a mile before she was actually lost.

The sun's nectar had finally leaked away and it was too dim to see the red and yellow arrows on the rocks, which loomed larger now, like gigantic thrown dice. She had stayed too late.

"This way," said Kezia aloud and her voice was eaten by the wind. "Maybe…" But nothing looked familiar as twigs scratched and the air scratched and her feelings scratched. She was guessing now, this way, and that way.

"Don't leave Kezzie, we can work this out." James had called to her as she walked away from the park bench with the daffodils bold and innocent and the children playing on the swings. "Don't leave."

And here she was.

A shape like a hand made a grabbing loop out of the bushes, then hop, hop, hopped away. Kezia swallowed, and the frog was gone. She felt as though she was in a faulty television — all the colours and lines were fuzzy and the picture was flooded with white noise. The more it blurred and the louder it got, the more her thoughts blurred and the louder they got.

Lost in the looming night, Kezia tried not to wish James was there. *It's not him, I just don't want to be on my own*, she thought, but he was the only one she could imagine. She wished her phone battery hadn't died while she was sitting on the sand: her only source of help gone.

The wind went on and on, surging and sighing. It whipped up the weeds, and the trees and the earth until everything was hard and painful — sand in her eyes, sand in her mouth — it pushed her back and it kept pushing. "No," she said. "Let me go. Let me leave."

But the wind wouldn't let her leave. Inexorably it pulled at her hair and buffeted her face and tugged at her clothes like a naughty toddler. The whole world seemed about to take off, beating and flapping and beating and flapping; it howled around her and she tripped over a root feeling the pain like a scream.

Keep going, she thought as she hobbled on, *just keep going.* The spectre of the saint from Mando's bar flashed in her mind, 'Always forward never back'. *Never back,* she murmured as she pictured his drawn-on halo and pious eyes.

The voices in the wind sounded like James. "Don't leave Kezzie," he was calling. "We can work this out… We'll get through this."

Then it was her boss. "Come on Kezia. Come on… I've got to be honest, you need more grit… That's your problem Kezia."

Kezia pivoted, changing direction, and circling back again.

Suddenly a huge dark shape loomed in front, blocking the path. She stopped and the wind buffeted her from behind. It was a tree, solid at the base and stretching up to where a frenzy of branches drizzled down, tangling and untangling. It took Kezia a while to realise the way ahead was completely cut off by this tree. She stumbled to the left, no path. Then stumbled to the right. No path. She walked around again, wrapping her arms around her, chilly in her T-shirt and shorts. She looked up; the tree was a charcoal silhouette. The branches flung themselves back, reminding Kezia of the flamenco she had seen: the fluid anger, the feral passion. The tree shook itself into a dancer as she watched and the wind stopped talking and started moaning, a low guttural groan, a lamenting wail that started to sound like singing. She tried to separate the song from the wind but the voice was the wind and the wind was the voice — like two spotlights merging to form a single circle — sometimes she thought she heard them separate, but mostly they were the same.

"Kezia." She heard her name again and shook her head. Enough of voices, she needed to think. Which way?

"Kezia." A new voice rolled in the wind. She turned and turned but couldn't see anyone, felt as if the gusts were turning her, tugging and turning and tugging and…

"Kezia. Stop turning."

Suddenly, to her left, where there had been nothing but shapes and shadows, sand and air, suddenly — a man.

She screamed — high and short — and it was immediately lost in the timpani of the night.

Kezia did not move.

The man did not move.

They stood there together in the dark.

6

Atlas

James knew he would never be happy again. He moved through the rooms slowly, the high domes illustrating the chasmic dimensions of his despair. The gold gleamed at Buckingham Palace. Mirrors shone like lakes. Chandeliers dripped glass droplets from imperious ceilings: vast expanses of white stucco splendour. Corinthian colonnades loomed upwards, elaborate clocks ticked gilded seconds and candelabras eulogised Greek myths in lustrous bronze.

None of it felt real. There was a weakness in his legs and his hands shook slightly as he adjusted his tie. He thought of the daffodils swaying in the breeze on that final day when she said goodbye.

A light rain pattered on the windows, dashes and dots like a faint morse code. He listened as if there was a message there, waiting.

"Just be confident. You can do this. You don't need Kezia like some lucky charm, you can do this on your own." Hannah had given him the look she always gave him as she signed, head on one side — the big sister look — like when he was leaving nursery and she told him school wasn't that bad, like when he'd been worried about his exams, like when he'd finally left for university. She always had a way of coping, despite losing her hearing when she was only five, she had a robustness about her he never had. "You'll be great and it will go really well and all the tourists will just love Her Majesty's house and you'll wonder what you were worried about, trust me."

James tripped over his own shoe as he entered the White Drawing Room, flinging his arms out to steady himself and glancing around to check no one saw. He pursed his lips, looking down at the thick carpet leering with swirls of paisley and energetic flowers, flowing in a red so strident it stung his eyes.

The facts, he told himself. Stick to the facts — let's start at the beginning... *Buckingham Palace began life as a plantation of mulberry bushes*, they'll like that one, *they were planted by James the First in the early seventeenth century, to rear silk worms*. He pictured the hoary worms spinning great lattices of silk, tiny heads with grasping mouths.

The facts made him feel better, though the throbbing still pushed at his temples and the space behind his eyes... *The White Drawing Room is one of the most famous rooms at Buckingham Palace, you might recognise it from the Queen's Christmas speech and it's also where she welcomes monarchs and presidents from all over the world — most of the press shots are done here.* Gold grizzled from cabinets, candlesticks, fireguards and door frames; astringent gold, cloying gold. His head hammered as he tried to remember the date of the grand piano which collaborated with the rest of the room in its gold gilt. 1865, he thought and the angels painted on the side seemed to cheer the correct answer, holding up their arms amidst garlands of flowers. They were too happy, so James turned away and pulled on a pair of thin cotton gloves, walking purposely to the solid marble fireplace. The milky white stone was dappled with veins of grey, and he traced them, feeling a connection with the pressures of the past; the crush of heat deep within the earth and the shapes it left behind. There was no dust so he checked the ovoid urns resting on top, gently stroking their gaudy facades.

"James?"

James moved to the side and stabbed his thigh on the bony arm of a chair covered in silk the colour of sunshine.

"James, there you are!" In contrast to the formal setting, Chris was still wearing the beanie hat he used to disguise the gradual evacuation of his hair. The designer glasses were another distraction, and as ever, there were rhubarb circles under his eyes from lack of sleep. "I just wanted to check you're all right."

"Ah. Yeah, just walked into it." James, holding his leg, nodded to the offending piece of furniture, which displayed a haughty disdain in the curve of its gold legs. "Fine though, it's fine. And yeah, otherwise, I'm fine."

"You look pale." Chris' brow creased at the rim of his hat, like the line drawing of a bird in flight. "How's your head?"

James lifted his palm flat and tilted it back and forth, understating the hangover's foggy bite. "It's your fault you know?" he drew himself up in mock ire.

"My fault? Moi? That's the thanks I get? I take you out, I cheer you up, I pull you out of the depressive state you've been festering in — and you just throw it back in my face why don't you?" Chris laughed and pushed his glasses up his nose, as he did when he was worried. "Seriously mate, never seen you like this before, had to do something."

James opened his mouth but the words wouldn't come.

"It's all right, I get it." Chris nodded sincerely. "I get it."

James moved to check a mark on the burnished mustard frame around a portrait dominating the space above the fireplace. It turned out to be a shadow where the baroque swirls caracoled in the corner.

"Who's that then?" Chris ran his hand over his hat as he examined the lady in the flowing silk dress so white it looked silver: her tiny waist and fussy cleavage, her blue sash, regal poise and the small crown on the top of her head. "A princess?"

"Queen Alexandra," James recited without thinking. "Flameng. 1908."

"Where is Flameng?"

"It's the artist," said James distractedly. "Erm, Alexandra was married to Edward the Seventh, he's the one who completely redecorated the palace in white and gold and he made it a kind of hub for London socialites."

"Good knowledge." The Queen stared straight ahead ignoring them both. "Good thing you're 'Head of History' and I'm just a lowly Tweeter, isn't it?"

"Head of History," James laughed. "I like that. The job's a bit more admin than that, but you can't have it all."

"Okay, but I'm still going to put you on speed dial for anything I need to know later."

"Ha! Here's one for you. This room has a secret door, have you seen it yet?"

Chris clasped his hands. "That's so James Bond."

"Well?" James took a step away, holding his hands out for Chris to survey the room.

"My three-year-old would love his game." Chris looked around with relish. "And he'd probably be better at it as well."

"Yeah, I think Max would have found it by now. Do you give up?"

"Okay, I'm blaming lack of sleep." Chris rubbed the back of his neck as if he could purge the hangover by rubbing it away.

"See that?" James pointed to a long mirror wearing an elaborate headpiece of tassels and scrolls as part of its frame. "Look closer."

Chris squinted. There was a narrow gap between the mirror and the wall: the whole thing could hinge away. He went closer, leaning down so the tiny crucifix swung out from around his neck, seeming to hover in mid-air. "Amazing. Can we go through it? Where does it go? The Tower of London? The London Dungeons?"

"That would be telling." James stroked his chin conspiratorially, then conceded. "Actually, it goes to the Queen's private apartments, so when there's a function on here, she can just appear, like magic, like a ghost."

"Cool. I can't wait to tell Max. He's well into ghosts at the moment. I bet there are a fair few actual ghost stories around here as well."

"You can tell him about the monk on the terrace then." James nodded towards the window. "But don't scare him. He wears a brown robe and chains apparently. It's because there was a monastery on this site long before it was a palace and the story is that he died in a punishment cell."

"Ooh." Chris affected a shiver. "I wonder what he did?"

A mantel clock with a gold eagle perched proudly on top dinged delicately, the sound soaked up by the sumptuous curtains and continuous carpets.

Chris looked over. "Ah, I better get back. Don't stress, okay?" He smiled as he left for the media hub at St James' Palace, thinking about his friend as he strolled down the Mall. The flags shrugged in a bilious breeze and the rain flecked the orange beaks of the downy geese who came tottering out of the park in their mechanical see-saw gait, bottoms ranging from side to side. They seemed to talk to Chris as they emitted outraged quacks sporadically, holding their heads high on their pipe necks and puffing out their chests.

Alone again, James scrutinised a bronze statue for smears. Atlas, with the weight of the world on his shoulders and his smooth head bowed over. James' mobile hissed in his pocket and he pulled it out. Claire. He swallowed, staring at the screen, then back to Atlas. He put his phone away and walked briskly to the next room as if he could leave the problem behind.

The Picture Gallery felt longer when it was empty, the red walls seeming to close in on him with their patchwork of pictures jostling for space. They hung on chains like the damned, heavy in their fussy frames and dark with time and grandeur.

James stopped by a family portrait: Victoria and Albert surrounded by frills and flowers and cherubic children. The Queen was looking out of the painting, towards her subjects, as Albert gazed at her with loyal candour, reaching out to touch her hand, but only just brushing her fingers. Looking away, James winced as he thought he saw a spider. It turned out to be a bit of fluff scurrying along by the glacial skirting board, so he pinched it between his fingers and rubbed it until it became a tiny rope.

He worked the length of the gallery, checking for imperfections, until his eye snagged on a painting of a woman, stood deep in a room with her back to him. She was playing the virginals — a bright musical box — and there was a man with his arm on the instrument, listening: rapt. They wore bulbous seventieth century clothes, puffed sleeves, skirts and sashes. There was a feeling of focus, but it wasn't on the music. The light filtered into the room highlighting the suspense and the words on the lid of the virginals: *Musica letitiae co[me]s, medicina dolor[is].* James leaned in closer to read but there was no translation for the Latin and he couldn't reach for the meaning beyond the word 'music'. Instead, he looked to where the woman's face was reflected in a mirror on the wall and he could tell from the angle that she was looking at the man with the open mouth.

7

Lanterns

"I told you not to get lost."

The man in the purple jacket was standing very still. Behind his legs the dog's head was bobbing slightly as if agreeing with him.

"Isn't this the path?" Kezia looked behind her, conscious of the dead end. All the branches were moving left and right as though they were also trying to work out the way: left or right.

"That is the path." Darim pointed to the way she had just come. "But not the path to the village." His words were thin tissue paper, ripped by the wind.

"Oh."

"So you are lost." A blustery gust made a sound like a group of golf spectators when the ball rolls around the hole but doesn't go in. "You have come too far. It is too late. It is not safe in the dark. Come back with me now, we have room for you to stay — and in the morning, you can go home."

"No thanks," said Kezia, but her words were drowned out and Darim turned abruptly and started walking, neatly picking his way over roots and stones.

The darkness seemed to amplify once he had gone, like a bird puffing up its feathers. A leaf floated down and quivered across her cheek — she shrieked — and before she knew what she was doing, she was hurrying after Darim.

His steps and the dog's steps were very precise: small and fast. Kezia jogged to keep up. She could hear her breath ragged in her throat. They were just walking, not speaking. At one point Kezia's foot hit a rock and it trickled away, rustling in the undergrowth and down and down, navigating a hill she couldn't see. She looked more carefully at the path in front and the back of Rollo's legs, trotting behind his master.

After an indeterminate time, the roar of the wind eased slightly and the sigh of the sea cut through. The path was narrowing and it became lined with wooden fencing, then there were flagstones beneath their feet, and ahead, tiny pinpricks of light, fireflies, in the trees, dancing in dazzling shivers.

As they got closer, Kezia saw the fireflies were actually fairy lights, sprinkling their sparkle with the movement of the branches. They came to an arch made of twisted metal where a gate swung rapidly back and forth, slapping itself against the post in paroxysms of alternate joy and flagellation. At the top of the arch, a sign was swinging too, creaking up and down; a dissonant refrain for the gate's percussion. '*Escuela de Flamenco de Carlotta*', it said, neatly, and a bird had left a white stain above the 's'. Alongside the gate an intemperate hedge blustered its way round to the row of twinkling trees.

Darim caught the gate and held it open. "*Mi casa*. This way. Come on." Through the gate a garden opened out — it smelled of soil and lavender. Darim trod on the paving slabs as if they were stepping stones, taking care not to put a foot out of place. They were walking towards the statue of a lion, whose big eyes gazed up at the naked gladiator about to slay him — a dagger poised, just above his head — whilst his paw was on the man's thigh, the flesh bulging with the rip of the claws. "Mama had a taste for the grotesque."

Kezia glanced at Darim and then back at the statue, where the lion still did not have the upper hand.

"Papa calls him Aslan," said Darim. "Now come."

At the end of the garden to the right, before the trees, there was a dark shape — a shed with its eyes shut, the wonky windows blank. To the left, the house. Kezia stopped when she saw it.

"Mama's favourite colours were red and white," Darim said matter-of-factly, without looking back at Kezia.

The side of the house was painted in thick bands of red and white stripes, like deckchair print or an old-fashioned helter-skelter. The colours, faded by the sun, were still unapologetic. Lanterns swung solemnly outside, infusing the scene with a sepia tint. Three wind chimes donged like communion bells while shutters chattered open and shut and zesty geraniums penned up in window boxes knocked their heads together as if the wind had driven them insane. Ivy wove its way up part of the wall, clutching at the facade and flaming like the feathers of a green winged bird.

At the front of the house, a large terrace was surrounded by a low wall. They went towards it, past flower beds where shivering shrubs shook their scent around and the air smelt musky and warm. A black cat darted across the path, low to the ground, urgent, like the shadows themselves were slipping. Just when Kezia realised what it was, it stopped, turned to look at her and then melted into the garden.

There was a gap in the wall to access the terrace and Kezia heard running water — to her left was a pond, built into the grey bricks, where a bronze cast of Medusa spouted water from a widely grinning mouth.

"This way," said Darim, navigating his way past a large table and chairs. There were more flower beds at the base of the house, where long ferns with spiky fronds jutted upwards like swearing fingers. He tried a side door, but it was locked. "Okay. This way." They followed the wall around to the main entrance, past a jigsaw of planter boxes, ornate pots and long troughs.

At the front was a porch which looked like it was wearing a milkmaid's hat. Darim turned the circular iron handle in the blue wooden door. It was locked as well. "Rollo," he hissed, "*llave!*" And the dog, ears cocked, tail wagging, skipped off, around the far side of the house. "Useful being his size," considered Darim. "You can get in through windows." They waited, the trees swaying and sighing and the soft scent of calla lilies floating with the ghostly white flowers she could just make out to their left.

Rollo came back with a jangling set of keys in his mouth. They clanked as he set them down at his master's feet. "*Gracias,*" said Darim.

As the door opened and they stepped inside, the wind dropped a cadence. The relief was sudden, like the end of a bad dream. There were shoes all over the floor: black shoes, flip flops, boots. Through the porch was a hallway where a big wooden staircase rolled down like a tongue in a giant mouth. On the floor, an elliptical mat, tampered with time and frayed at one edge, was woven in deep reds, concentric ovals filling it like the rings of a tree. A clock in the shape of a cat had stopped and was silent on the wall.

Darim strode to the left of the stairs, Kezia following tentatively, down a corridor and through another door into the kitchen, where worn copper pots and pans hung on hooks above a pink Aga stove. In the corner next to it an old man in a rocking chair was snoring with a high rasp. He was wrinkled and mottled like a pistachio nut.

"Go to bed, Papa."

The old man's eyes became slits, but the only movement came from a grey cat, curled luxuriously in his lap, which lifted its head and yawned so widely its head split in two.

Darim sneezed a short and high-pitched sneeze, whipping the lilac handkerchief out of his top pocket just in time to cover his nose. "Papa," he said. "Do you have to let him in here, you know I'm allergic to Benja."

"It's too windy," the old man grumbled, laying a hand protectively on Benja's back.

"And tomorrow it will be too hot, and then it will be too... what? Always a reason." Darim sneezed again. "We do not have to be the depository for all the waifs and strays around here. Stop feeding them and they will soon find new owners."

"Your mama loved them so — so do I."

"The less said about that the better." Darim began folding his handkerchief neatly.

Unable to understand the Spanish, Kezia was trying to blend into the corner, where an apron was hanging over the door, but the old man's dim eyes alighted on her. "Carlotta?" There was a lift in his voice and in his stance, he moved forwards in the rocking chair and Benja stood up and jumped to the floor.

"No Papa," Darim said in English. "You know it cannot be Carlotta. This is Kezia. She got lost on her way back from the cove. The winds are higher than usual tonight. I told her she could stay — I'll put her in my old room. So, another one for breakfast in the morning."

Kezia raised her hand and tried to say hello but the word couldn't get past her throat.

"Not Carlotta," the old man said sadly, cradling his knees the way he had been cradling the cat.

"Papa. Go to bed now," said Darim gently. "It's late."

"Errrk. Belladonna." A parrot's voice grated and Kezia jumped. Sitting in a cage in the opposite corner, a red and green bird started to tread on his bar like he was walking up stairs. "*Bella. Donna.*"

"Shut up Pedro." Darim rounded on him and the bird leant back, moving his head down and his eyes up.

When Darim turned back to Kezia, he screeched, "Shut up Pedro," and ruffled his feathers, pleased with himself. Darim whipped his head back to Pedro who gave a little jump and then hid his head under his wing.

"Too clever for his own good," scowled Darim. "He speaks Italian, among other languages..." And he raised his eyebrows as if sharing a conspiracy.

Darim's papa began to stand up. "I need to go to the bar," he said to his feet as he struggled to hold on to the moving arms of the rocking chair.

"No. Papa." Darim took two swift steps so that he was close enough to steady him. "You don't work there any more, remember? And it's bedtime."

"Of course I do." He looked up. "It's my bar. Mando's. I am Mando." He pointed at his chest, shaking Darim off and shuffling towards the door. Kezia took a step to the side and the apron brushed her face.

"Papa," said Darim sharply. "Come back. Remember what happened? We had to give the bar away, remember? You got us into so much debt: giving away drinks, forgetting to charge for food, muddling people's orders... remember? We had to." And then, more kindly, "Please, Papa. It's bedtime now."

Normando turned very slowly. "Are you sure?"

"I'm sure Papa. We couldn't afford for you to do that any more. Not since... not since the accident."

Normando looked at him blankly.

Darim whispered, "The accident Papa. You know..." he glanced uneasily at Kezia.

Normando turned in a circle for reasons known only to himself, and as he came back to where he started, saw Kezia in the corner again. "Carlotta!" he exclaimed, joy in his face.

"Papa. No Papa," said Darim. "Come on. Come and sit down and then we'll all go to bed. That's it. Slowly." Normando shuffled to the chair, fumbled back into it and immediately started rocking contentedly.

"He gets confused," said Darim, still regarding his papa to make sure he was okay.

"Oh." Kezia stepped out of the corner. "I think… thank you for offering me to stay, but I think I'll go back now. The winds seem to be dying down. I think." She eyed the window. "I think I'll go back."

"You go?" Darim turned his head sharply to Kezia. "You go, you get lost. I do not rescue twice."

Kezia shifted her weight from one foot to the other. "I'll ring for a taxi."

Darim laughed. "A taxi? In Parños? There is one man who does taxi in Parños and only if you book two days before. No taxi."

"Well, at least couldn't I ask him?"

Darim shook his head. "Look. I need to feed the animals. I have work. It is dangerous now anyway. You go tomorrow, in the light. You will be safe here tonight. Remember what I told you, about the *ghost*?"

"I don't believe… in ghosts." Kezia stood on one leg and the door banged behind her suddenly, making her lose her balance.

Ignoring this, Darim said, "If you stay you can dance with us in the morning. I will give you a free class. Just one." Benja pushed back in through the rebounded door and sauntered past. Darim sneezed.

"I better call my parents. They'll be worried."

"Yes, yes. You call your parents. You stay."

Kezia remembered she had no battery on her phone. She took it out anyway. "It's dead," she told Darim.

"Ah. Use mine."

"Um, I don't know their number off by heart."

Darim stared at her. "Why?"

"Well, I've never had to call them without my phone before, so… so I could call the hotel?"

"Name?" Darim snapped.

"Hotel Parños del Toro."

Darim nodded, focused on his phone, then handed it to her. "It rings," he said.

Kezia waited for the young and uncertain receptionist to greet her in thick Spanish then asked for room three hundred and three, sure her parents would get the hotel to send a car.

"Oh Kezia. Oh love." Hearing her mum's voice cracking down the phone made Kezia well up, standing in this strange kitchen where the dejected copper pots told stories that weren't her own. "Where are you? Are you okay? Yes, we heard the winds. My goodness. Never known anything like it... Oh no, no please don't try and get back in the dark... No, no, need to... if you're safe, we'll not trouble anyone here. It's late. If it's a school, it must be safe. Flamenco! Sounds like an adventure Kez. I'll put you on to your dad."

Patrick took the phone. "What scrapes have you got yourself into now, eh? I don't know," he chuckled, then turned serious. "But they're looking after you, eh Pet, are they? Look, get some sleep and we'll come and get you in the morning. What's that? Oh, your mum's saying you should have that flamenco class while you're there." He started singing a dissonant refrain down the phone and laughed, his wife picking up the melody in the background too. They'd obviously had quite a lot of sangria.

Kezia gave up and handed the phone back to Darim.

"Okay. Come. I'll show you your room." Dazed, Kezia followed Darim back down the corridor, leaving Normando rocking silently back and forth, swaying wistfully towards Pedro the parrot but not really seeing the bird, who was sleeping now anyway. They walked past a square picture of the Last Supper where the colours seemed too garish, too happy for the occasion. Judas regarded Jesus warily whilst the other men took their bread and wine.

At the bottom of the stairs Darim turned to Kezia. "Your room is upstairs, second on the left. The bathroom is across the hall. The other bedrooms are on the other side of the house so you have it to yourself. We have only Sue and Java staying at the moment, there used to be more boarders..." He trailed off, momentarily lost in a memory, then snapped himself back to the present. "My other students come from the village, you will see them tomorrow too. I sleep down here." He motioned to a door by the Last Supper picture. "If you need me, knock. I sleep little. I sleep light." He nodded.

"Thank you," said Kezia, glancing cautiously up the sweeping stairs.

Darim shrugged and then looked at her more closely. "In your country, what kind of dance do you dance?"

"I don't dance," Kezia replied.

Darim's head retreated slightly. "Why?" the word flared from his mouth.

Kezia giggled, but he looked at her intently. "Well, it's just… I used to do ballet when I was little but now… I mean, sometimes I get drunk and dance round my handbag, that sort of thing, with the girls, but I have to be well away before that happens. You know?" She laughed again, nervously this time.

Darim stayed serious. "Why like this?"

"I'm… I'm embarrassed I guess."

"You should be embarrassed not to dance."

"I'd be rubbish anyway."

"No. Look at you." He stood back, admiring her. "No. Tomorrow, you dance. It will make you forget your… whatever his name was." And he flicked his hand, waving the name away. "Now I must feed the animals." He made abruptly for the door. "Don't worry my darlings, I am coming for you…"

At the porch, Darim slipped off his black shoes and shimmied into a pair of white wellies. He straightened up and pulled the door open, narrowing his eyes against the dying gasps of the wind. Then he turned with his fingers on the handle and said again, "Tomorrow, you dance!"

"I've told you," protested Kezia. "I don't dance."

"Then you don't live," he said, spinning around and marching daintily down the garden path.

8

Chandeliers

The ceiling arched above in a lattice of diamonds, white overlaid with gold like elaborate icing, each shape decorated with leaves and flowers. Angels frolicked in friezes below the cupola, footsure on a geometric border held up by columns: sleek and shiny and a startling royal blue. At the end of the room the windows curved with the rotunda and ushered in the dreary smudge of a cloudy day, multiplied and folded over by the long, vaulted mirrors.

The journalists shuffled in and gazed around with steady unconcern, empty eyes, like cattle staring at a horizon they would never meet.

Rachel let the images on her phone blur as she scrolled, conscious neither of the news nor of her surroundings, until James, in his palace-issue blazer, coughed and said, "So, um, Queen Victoria and Prince Albert loved music and we know they used to play and sing together all the time — in fact we are told they were some of their happiest times. So, um... this is the Music Room." A few eyes swivelled, one of the journalists scribbled in a notebook. "And look, you can see endless reflections in the mirrors... see? It gives the illusion the room goes on forever, look at it going back like that... it's a clever trick, playing with space and light." A woman wearing very high heels and a crisp white shirt drew in her breath as though she wanted to ask a question but was distracted by a footman walking by in a red jacket with gold brocade. "If you look up," James continued, and a series of ponytails and bald patches presented themselves as heads tilted towards the ceiling. "You'll notice in the pattern here you have the rose, the thistle and the shamrock, so, the emblems for England, Scotland and Ireland."

"Why not Wales?" a gruff man asked.

"Erm, because of the time it was made," James bluffed, forgetting what he'd read about Wales being a principality, not a kingdom, and the man looked bored again. "And, erm, the columns are very unusual in this room — very colourful — in the past lots of the columns in the palace were different colours to look like rare types of stone, but they were mostly painted over as the fashion changed, except in here. This blue is supposed to resemble lapis lazuli." James looked to one of the pillars for reassurance and it exuded extravagant solidity back. "Any questions?"

"Have you met the Queen?" a spry man with a blond quiff asked.

"Er. No. I've… seen her from a distance though."

The man nodded, disappointed.

"Okay. Shall we continue?" James herded his charges through the palace, stumbling nervously over his facts, trying to rouse their interest, until they came to the ballroom. "The most prepossessing room of them all," he quoted from the guidebook. "The largest room of the palace — it's big enough to hold eighty-four double decker buses."

A few eyebrows raised as the journalists looked casually up to the cavernous ceiling where crystal chandeliers hung majestically like sea creatures in an ocean of opulence. The coronation thrones sat in timeless splendour at the end of the room under a vast velvet canopy and huge candelabra were stationed like soldiers all around.

"This is where the Queen holds her state banquets."

"How many people can she have?" asked the woman in the crisp white shirt, fiddling with a loose stand of hair.

"They can seat over two hundred and you'd have about eighty staff serving them as well, so not a small occasion," James smiled. "They have four courses and five different types of wine, and at the end the bagpipers come out and—"

"But what—" she began to ask another question and then stopped as if she'd seen a ghost.

Shadowy figures in Victorian finery materialised against the sides of the ballroom, which morphed into rich silk wall-hangings. The lights dimmed and music started, faint and becoming louder, the wiry voice of the oboe, the muscular strains of the bassoon, the full-blooded tuba. The women wore wide sweeping dresses, extravagant waists pinched in tight and the fabric flaring off the shoulder. Their hair was in ringlets, tamed by chignons at the naked nape of their necks. The men were buttoned up in breeches with sashes and high-necked red coats and showy bright

52

tassels, like plumage. They began to dance. A circular dance, stately and slow, in and out and turning away and in, away and in.

Some of the journalists leaned forwards, a couple leaned back. One of them began to record the scene on his phone, craggy eyes rolling over the screen and back towards the apparitions.

"We ask that you don't film please," James interceded. "We'll give you official footage you can use at the end." The man pocketed his phone furtively and shrugged, keeping his eyes on the dancers. "What you're seeing here," James continued, above the music, "is the recreation of a ball Queen Victoria held in the summer of 1856, for the soldiers who had returned from fighting in the Crimean War. She wanted to thank them. Apparently, the dancing went on until the early hours and even Prince Albert, who wasn't a fan of balls, enjoyed it."

When the dance finished and the figures melted away, the background becoming a puddle of red before revealing white walls again, James told them, "We worked with a Hollywood production company to do this, so it really feels like stepping back in time." He had always imagined the soldiers in this room, still scarred by battle, with their smart uniforms and uniform dances. "It really brings it to life, don't you think?"

Two reporters feigned a waltz, bumping into each other and dropping their guidebooks. Others began to mill about; he was losing his audience. "So if you look up there," he pointed above the crimson throne canopy, hoping just one of them would listen. "See those winged figures? They represent history and fame." The two angelic figures reclined alongside a medallion showing the profiles of Victoria and Albert carved, indelible, as if to prove their own place in the annals of time and posterity. "But all of this didn't make Victoria happy, we know. In fact, after Albert died at the age of only forty-two, she hardly ever came here to Buckingham Palace and she called it her 'saddest of sad houses'." James felt that sadness like a stone in his heart, the vastness and extravagance of the room seemed to taunt him, as it must have taunted Victoria.

A tall woman came forwards, dark hair in a tight bun. "Is this room used for dances now? Does the Queen dance in here?" Rachel asked.

"Ah. No, it's just the state banquets and investitures now. Although, many people say the Queen does like dancing."

"*Dancing Queen!*" the man with the quiff blurted.

"You joke but that is supposed to be her favourite song."

The man grinned, scribbling in his notebook.

James ushered the group out of the ballroom and through the rest of the state rooms, recalling as much of the history as he could and pointing out trills and embellishments while they looked at their watches and took calls from the office about what stories they were covering next. It was a relief when they arrived at the gift shop and he watched as they rotated silver pencils, probed rubbers of the Queen's face, gaped aimlessly at the pink and white china and cooed over tables stacked high with fluffy brown teddies wearing puffy gold crowns.

Rachel picked up a mug with the royal insignia scrawled in indigo across it and wondered whether she should buy it for Joe. She couldn't decide whether he would like it or find it too twee: the pain blurred things. She was about to put it down... she wasn't sure how it slipped, but the next thing she knew it was out of her hold and falling to the floor with a cold hard smash. The low murmur of voices suddenly stopped. Faces turned to stare. Rachel put her hand to her mouth in horror. Then James was there. "Don't worry," he said, kneeling to pick up the pieces. "I'll get a dustpan and brush for the rest. Everybody, just keep away a minute. It's fine." He looked up at Rachel. "Don't worry, honestly."

It was his kindness that made the tears come. She could have coped if he'd shouted at her, she was used to that in the newsroom. "I'll pay for it," she muttered, fumbling for her purse as the teardrops melted her mascara.

James stood up. "No, no. It's fine." And he patted her lightly on the shoulder. That made Rachel cry more, feeling all the eyes on her, still.

A portly reporter sidled over and said, from the side of his mouth, "It's not the end of the world, darling," before slinking to the exit. He moved so quickly, rigidly and stealthily, there was something so crab-like and comic about it, that Rachael caught James' eye and suddenly they were both laughing.

"Okay," Rachel had found her purse, and a tissue, but she still had black smudges below her eyes. "How much?"

James shook his head. "No, I mean it, you're not paying. Here," he picked up a new mug and pressed it into her hands. "Take this one to the till. It's fine."

"Really? Thank you, erm, James." Her eyes brushed his badge just as she was trying to recall his name. "And sorry for the tears, I'm just a bit… tired." She hadn't been sleeping, it was the pain, always the pain.

"We've all been there," said James and she nodded, even though she knew he hadn't, he was a man.

"Thank you again." Rachel dabbed her eyes, making the mascara smudges worse. "Bye. Thanks for the tour as well, really good." She filtered away with the rest of the press, out into the dull summer evening where the yelps of children mingled with the throttle of exhausts.

James thought of Rachel as he swept the last shards of mug from the floor. When he'd seen her cry, it was like a chord tightened inside him. He focused on the shattered 'ER' and the broken bits of mug blurred momentarily. There was powder all around. Strange that something so solid can just turn to dust, he thought, finding the motion of cleaning satisfying and not stopping until all traces were gone.

He called Chris on the way back to the office, looking up at the stately columns of the palace entrance, lofty and precise and the warm colour of toffee. "Yeah, it went okay. They kept asking questions about the Queen and they weren't that keen on the stucco friezes. I guess that's what you'd expect."

Chris laughed. "Oh well, as long as they print some pretty pictures, right?"

"Right. How was it in the press office?"

"Busy. Lots of pre-promotion before we let the hoards in tomorrow."

"Mmm." James entered the quadrangle, feeling the crush of the puce gravel under his feet.

"And it's going to be fine. It's going to be good. Don't worry. You're such a stress-head."

James felt the smoothness of his blazer button between his thumb and finger. "Yeah," he said, unconvinced, not without Kezia. Nothing was good without Kezia.

"By the way, thank you for giving me a good reference for this job," Chris was saying. "Appreciate that, I'll try not to mess things up like I normally do."

James stared at the elaborate portico, trying to work out which Greek myth was depicted, as tragic figures writhed and wrestled. "Yeah, like the time you arrived at the airport without your passport."

"God," Chris groaned. "That is why I had to get married. Poor Sarah is like a PA for me most of the time. Have you got this? Have you got that? She has the patience of a saint," he chuckled.

"Sounds like we should have employed her instead, mate."

Chris groaned.

"Listen, I've got to go, just heading inside. See you tomorrow." James hung up and nodded at the footman by the door. The marble hall was cool and dim and the feeling enveloped him as it was supposed to do; a pressure change before the grandeur of the sweeping staircase and the high ceilings to come. He pulled his lips in like a drawstring bag, thinking about Claire, about the five missed calls. He'd tell her soon… he would. But now he did a final walkthrough, checking each of the rooms, feeling the unnatural quiet in them, how the stillness made the colours glow.

At the end, he came down the staircase where the statue of Venus leant arduously into a naked Mars, with his helmet and spear. She gazed rapturously up to his face; they would kiss, if they weren't made of marble. Even though James hurried past he felt the presence of their passion — he kept walking, conscious of the empty thud his shoes made on the compact carpet.

9

Feather

A small feather was caught in a spider's web outside the window. A white feather, tinged with grey at the base. It flapped and fluttered but it could not break free.

Kezia breathed in the sea air, leant her elbows on the windowsill and watched as a primrose butterfly scribbled through the morning. The winds of last night were just a whisper now and the day was bright and fresh. The sky was powder blue, the sun canary yellow and the sea was liquid glitter.

The scene dissolved the fear. The screams in the night. She'd lain awake unable to decipher the shrieks from the wind. It had become like one of those illusion pictures that's a young woman and an old woman at the same time, her brain kept flicking between the noises until she'd worried herself into sleep, a garbled sleep, patchy and uncertain.

The terracotta terrace below looked friendly now as it basked in sunshine instead of lurking in shadows. Enormous black bras resembling small parachutes hung drying on the washing line and the garish geraniums sat obediently in their pots like little red bonnets. A goat with a gaunt face stared blankly but unremittingly at her from where it stood next to the dilapidated shed, tied to a large nail by a fraying rope. Two crotchety peacocks pranced past and eventually the goat stopped looking and nibbled the harried grass at its feet.

Kezia went back to sit on the bed. The room felt different now too. It was whitewashed — the walls, the door, the bed — all white. The one curtain across the small window was white too, printed with little navy anchors which undulated with the material. A solid mat, the colour of the sea on a good day, was at her feet, where the patchwork quilt had fallen to the floor during the night. Opposite her, on a white chest of drawers, a tiny wooden ship with paper sails was going nowhere inside a glass bottle. Next to that, a conch shell, pale pastel peach and faint violet, the colour of veins; it was like a mouth, huge lips resting. She got up and stroked the outside of it tentatively, felt the dust over the smooth bulbous veneer.

Notes, gently strummed, drifted in through the window. A string of notes that curled around each other, weaving into a melodic fabric. When the tune was picked out above the chords, it reminded Kezia of the way a spider picks up its legs, jaunty and precise.

She went to have a look. Darim was sitting on the wall that marked the end of the terrace. He began singing, low notes, eyes shut, like an incantation. Then, without warning, he stopped, looked up, and said, "My heart beats strong in the morning. For you, for you alone I wake." One of the peacocks squawked. "Good view from that window isn't there? That was my room, as a small boy. I used to look to sea and dream of becoming a pirate." He sighed. "Oh, the fates, the fates of life."

Kezia didn't know what to say, so she looked out, beyond the garden, beyond the trees, past the boulders, to the sea. She could just make out the far end of the bay where they'd met, it curved round in a smile with rocks for teeth.

"So, Señorita Don't Dance," Darim intoned. "Breakfast is at eight o'clock. And then we see about Don't Dance." He turned back to his guitar.

Kezia slunk back from the window and tripped on the mat. She staggered onto the bed and felt suddenly tearful. It was only when the soft smell of eggs wafted in, that she realised she was starving; she'd missed dinner last night and she hadn't eaten since lunch by the pool. Next a cacophony of Spanish voices floated up with the aroma. Chairs scraped and Rollo barked, just once. She realised she had no way of telling the time — her phone screen stared at her in glazed blackness — so, she walked around the room a few times, gathering the confidence to go downstairs, wishing she had a change of clothes, and eventually, the hunger pressing at her, she left the room.

The sweeping staircase and the corridor felt strange and she forgot the way and ended up back outside the kitchen. She could hear Normando singing quietly to himself and Pedro gave a satisfied, "Erk. *Buenos días a todos.*"

Kezia turned and went back to the hall and through the porch with all the shoes. Outside, the warm air buoyed her and the tall trees seemed exotic and exciting. She went around the side of the house slowly, touching the red and white pigment on the plaster with the tip of her finger, looking across at the flower beds, noticing how the tulips made cups to catch the sun.

The glare was in her eyes as she approached the terrace and she had to look down to where the green paint was peeling off the iron table and chairs. Then suddenly the voices stopped, and she could tell that everyone was staring at her.

The goat made a sound like a laugh and a cloud went over the sun. Kezia blinked, faces coming into focus. At that moment Darim jumped to his feet, and in a contrasting slow movement, laid his guitar lovingly down on the wall. "Look what the wind blew in girls. Come, sit Kezia. Sit." He pulled out a chair and she sat down a bit too fast. She could feel the pattern of the metal hard against her legs. "Girls, this is Kezia." He said her name as if it was an exotic flower.

The faces were still staring, but Darim offered no more of an introduction. He sat back down on the wall and played a chord with such love that Kezia thought she shouldn't be looking. So, she gazed around, perceiving the clean light of the morning and the fresh feeling of promise.

A man wearing jeans and a baggy wool jumper, despite the burgeoning warmth of the day, opened the door of the shed at the end of the garden, yawned and stretched. He started pulling on a pair of boots, then trudged off towards the front entrance of the house.

Her foot brushed something warm and soft; it was Rollo, who had curled into a ball under the table. His pellucid eyes turned to inspect her casually, then he tucked his head back into his body.

When Kezia looked up, she saw a plate in front of her with a rough chip on one edge. On it, a faded hen presided anxiously over seven startled chicks and the aged glaze was cracked so they were trapped behind the lines like the contours of a map.

Darim concluded his playing with a theatrical flourish and stood up. "Eat!" he demanded, turning abruptly on his heel and walking off, Rollo uncurling from his hideaway to trot by his side.

As well as the eggs there was bread and jam and strange voluptuous fruit.

"*Hola*," Kezia tried, glancing down, though the sun was no longer in her eyes.

"The bread's straight out of the Aga," a girl whose short black hair framed her oval face like a pixie said, in English. "And the jam's good too, apricot."

Kezia looked at the golden jam which seemed to be glowing, then at the soft peaks of bread, blushing with their own perfection.

"And I'm Sue," said an older lady, as if the breakfast had just had its own introduction. "This is Java," she nodded to the girl with cropped hair, but she didn't mention a third girl, sat quietly, observing, not eating; her auburn hair ran down her face, half hiding it as she stared silently ahead.

"You're English?" Kezia blurted, then wished she hadn't.

"I am," said Sue, who had a round face, a round body and a round bob that puffed out like a halo. "Huddersfield — but now we live in Alicante. I'm just here for... a few weeks."

"I grew up near Madrid," Java interjected. "This was the closest thing I could find to running away to join the circus." She took a bite of the pale orange fruit and ducked her head as it erupted with sticky liquid. The yellow juice ran down her chin. "So," she said, mouth full. "Haven't you heard the rumours yet, or do you just like the thrill of it?" She swallowed, wiping her lips with the back of her hand and giggling.

"Java! She's only just got here." Sue gave her an affected nudge.

"Well, I bet he didn't tell her. Did he tell you? *'Her heart is broken and that's why she sings...'*"

"The rumours about the ghost, at the cove." Sue nodded her blonde bob in the direction of the sea. "I'm sure he didn't mention it, but people say—"

"People say all sorts of things. I want to know what he told her." Java was adamant.

The sun came back out and Kezia squinted. "He did mention it." She took a piece of soft, warm bread and found a knife by her plate, trying to remember the story she'd been told. It already seemed like a long time ago, before the winds and before the torrid night. "Something like a folk tale... about a lost love, a woman who didn't want her husband to die so she agreed to live in torment forever, or something. It was all a bit... messed up."

"Aha!" Java slapped her leg. "Well, that's not all they say in the village." She narrowed her eyes. "People say..."

"Java." Sue put her hand out. "There's really no need."

"People say…" Ignoring Sue, Java leant in, close to the table, speaking quietly and from the back of her throat. "People say…"

"Carlotta!" Normando came wobbling out of the kitchen, through the door Darim hadn't been able to open last night. He was clutching a tray with four lively glasses of orange juice clinking together.

"Mando, this is… what was your name?" asked Sue.

"Kezia," said Kezia as he put the tray down precariously on the table. Java and Sue thanked him and he smiled and shuffled back to the house. The silent girl stayed silent, looking down at her juice. "What's your name?" Kezia asked her, but she just wound her long auburn hair round her finger, staring.

"That's Darim's papa, Normando," Java gabbled, ignoring the pale girl sat opposite her. "We call him Mando. Do you know why they call me Java?" She raised an eyebrow. "My parents are nerds: Java is a programming language. Seriously? What kind of parents name their child after something to do with computers? So weird. Why do you think I ran away here?" She grinned. "You have to escape that kind of thing or you become weird yourself." Java crossed her eyes and laughed again.

"I still don't get why they would do that," mused Sue, reaching for more jam.

"Don't ask me. They thought they were being creative, artistic or something. Fact is, they don't know the first thing about creativity — which is why they work in tech."

"So are your brothers and sisters called things like Modem and Gigabyte then?" Sue winked and Kezia saw the silent girl's mouth quiver into an almost perceptible smirk.

"Ha-ha, very funny. I'm one of five. The other four all got normal names. I guess that's what happens when you're the youngest." She shrugged.

"Well, it's better than Sue," said Sue, adjusting her pink-rimmed plastic glasses. "More exciting. But that just sums up my life really, until now. I had to come here for a bit of adventure — fed up of being Sue the doormat all the time. 'Oh, Sue'll do it.' Cooking, cleaning, always clearing up other people's mess. I just needed a break. Let them see how they get on without me for a bit I say." Sue laughed and her breath smelled of stale coffee and old lipstick.

61

Kezia wanted to ask Java more about why her parents called her Java and she was thinking about how to say it as she picked one of the orange fruits and felt it dent in her fingers. She bit into it and the sweet tang shocked her mouth. Before she could swallow and frame a question, voices spiked from the other side of the house, near the road. An argument: sharp words clashing. Expletives like sparks.

Java rolled her eyes. "What now?"

They all listened.

It was Darim and a man with a stodgy voice, coarse from tobacco. They were speaking English but Kezia couldn't hear all the words.

"I didn't have to help you, Omar."

"Oh yeah? That's not what I heard. I heard your precious mama left all her money to a cat sanctuary. A cat sanctuary!"

"Leave Mama out of this."

"We'd love to. You're the one who makes everything into a performance. Just like her, are you?"

Darim said something inaudible.

"You need us. Don't forget that," the throaty man raged. "So no more stupid leaflets advertising for new students. No more!"

Sue touched Kezia on the arm. "They love each other really," she smiled reassuringly. "It's just their way."

"He's very passionate," Java added.

Kezia nodded, wishing she hadn't promised to wait for her parents so she could just leave.

The verbal fencing stopped and Java breathed out. "The wrong kind of gazpacho? Too much garlic in the olives? He should just let them get on with it, focus on teaching us."

"Yes, but I thought the bar was in the family long before this school was?" Sue said.

"That's right, but Darim shouldn't have given it away then."

"Harsh, Java, you know Mando couldn't have kept it up forever, so times move on, they have to."

"Okay, but he picked those clowns, didn't he? He could have picked, I don't know, someone like Hady who always dreamed of running his own café or bar — someone who would be grateful and put their heart and soul into it — someone who cared. But no, a pair of chancers he met at a party. What did he expect?"

Sue shrugged. "Apparently Sami has an incredible singing voice, that could be a real draw, along with Darim's playing, but he says he's too shy to sing at the moment, either that or Omar won't let him — wouldn't put it past him — but I think Darim's been tutoring him so I guess in time... Anyway, Hady was given the gardening job so he could work outside, you know that. It was what he wanted, after... what happened."

"What happened?" asked Kezia, but her mouth was full of fruit and her words were too soggy and quiet.

Sue carried on speaking to Java. "He wouldn't even be here otherwise — he'd still be in Lorca. Hady's dad is Mando's friend, remember, and it was the best they could both think of at the time. Mando told me Hady was totally shellshocked when he first came here. He's a different person now, apart from the nightmares."

"They are getting better too," said Java defensively. "Less often. So he's okay now. And he's here. And he could do it. Ever since he was a small boy he wanted to have his own bar, like his grandpapa did. I think Mando reminds him of his own grandpapa. He used to sit on a high stool behind the bar and help him serve the drinks after school, still in his school uniform. They knew everyone and everyone's business — I think that was why it was all so hard for him, all of the people that died, they all felt like family."

"So sad. So sad. I just can't imagine." Sue shook her head as if to shake the bad feelings away. "Do you think he'll ever go back there?"

"To Lorca?" Java thought about it. "Maybe, but he likes it here now."

"I wonder why?" Sue blew a kiss and Java pouted. "Anyway." She turned to Kezia. "Darim couldn't afford for his papa to be losing any more money at the bar, so it's not surprising he took on a bit of fresh blood. Things are... a bit tight money-wise around here." She fiddled with a piece bread. "Needs more pupils really. Everyone's getting scared off. He'll be glad you showed up."

"Oh no. I'm not here to dance." Kezia wiped her hands together, trying to get rid of some of the stickiness. "I just got lost, at the cove, last night. Those winds started and I've never known anything like it. Darim found me and brought me back here, just to be safe. I'm leaving soon. Nice of him to give me breakfast though." She took what she hoped seemed like a carefree bite of the bread and was momentarily distracted by how it dissolved in her mouth. She chewed, and swallowed.

Sue and Java looked at each other like they'd just placed a very clever and very certain bet. "Well," said Sue. "You don't want to be out when the *leveche* whips up that's for sure."

"It was terrifying," Kezia admitted.

"Like Darim when he gets in one of his moods." Java grinned, swinging her legs which were too short to reach the ground. "Oh, *hola* Tomi." A ginger cat with long wispy hair was limping past, juddering, unable to put any weight on its right front paw, which was bent inwards at an angle. He turned slowly to look at them with incisive green eyes. "That's Tomi," Java told Kezia. "He hurt his leg on the day—"

"Java, no—"

Java mouthed, "The accident." And Tomi meowed in corroboration. "He'll never be able to tell us what happened, we think he got run over when the ambulance came, or the police car, one of the two." The cat sat down as if taking a bow, and Java drew another breath, about to tell the story, but was distracted by the man in the woollen jumper, walking back across the garden. She held up her hand, trying to get his attention, but he didn't see her. Instead, he went to the shed and pulled out a spade. He started digging one of the flower beds, watched intently by the goat, whose ears framed her face like two question marks.

"There's Hady," Sue told Kezia. "He does the garden like we said. He lives in the shed. 'Handy Hady' Mando calls him and he does all the odd jobs too — useful as Darim is completely impractical. He's not so anxious now, we're all helping him, aren't we?"

"Me especially," Java smiled.

They heard the jingle of Rollo's bell and Darim strode around the corner of the house and over to the breakfast table. "You eat? Okay. We dance."

Kezia put her knife on the chipped plate and turned around to face Darim. "Thanks, um, so much. Thanks for having me. And thanks for saving me from the winds last night."

Darim bowed benevolently.

"And nice to meet you all too." She nodded back to the girls as Rollo came and put his head in her lap, gazing up at her, eyes gleaming. She touched the soft velvet of his head. "You too mister."

"Yes, nice," agreed Darim. "And now we dance. Your first class is free. Your first class will be *first class*." His lips twitched at his own joke.

"Oh, thank you. But no. My parents will be here soon, so... so I won't have time."

Nobody said anything.

"But thank you," Kezia said again. She took a sip of orange juice, glancing awkwardly around.

"Don't have time to dance?" Darim said it very slowly.

"No, erm..."

"I don't see your parents here?"

Rollo took his head off her lap and looked at her meaningfully. "Well, but they will be—"

"So, until then, you dance."

Kezia looked helplessly at Sue and Java but they just sat calmly watching as the silent girl sulked.

"You see, I'm the wrong... I don't know..." Kezia struggled for the word. "Build? Big hips." She rested her hands on them apologetically, conscious of her tummy, and her ears again.

Darim looked down at her waist. "No, there is no 'wrong' in flamenco. You are either in it or you are not in it. If you don't dance, you are not in it."

"Honestly, I used to do ballet but they said I was too... big boned. That's what my teachers used to say." Kezia laughed nervously.

"Without your bones you fall over. Did you think of that?"

Kezia clutched her elbows, not sure what to say.

"Flamenco is about your spirit, you do not shrink from that," Darim continued. "You have the perfect figure for flamenco."

"I'm sure I do not."

"Well, do you want to be weak or strong?"

"I..."

"Of course, you want to be strong. What else is there?"

"Umm..."

"You do not know your own power. So disappointing."

"I… I honestly can't dance."

"You do not understand. It is like saying you don't breathe. You don't dance flamenco, you *are* flamenco. For flamenco you only have to be who you are. Anything else is lying, and flamenco *never lies.*" Darim stared at her with piercing eyes; it was like being swept over by the tide.

After a while, she said, "You'd laugh. You'd all laugh. You haven't seen me try. Honestly…"

"You cannot always be thinking about what other people are thinking. Sometimes people think things that are not true. Have you thought about that? They tell you that you are 'big boned' and you believe them. They want to see you fail by not trying so it can make them feel better. Now you see how it works?"

"I don't know—"

"You should know that people will say whatever they like. They will say bad things anyway, so you might as well dance. You can be sad and criticised or happy and criticised. It is up to you." He cocked his head to one side. "You talk about being unhappy, so, I offer happy. If you do not take it, you will never know. You will never know how it feels to be free."

Kezia felt the sun like a tight grip on her skin.

"Remember," said Darim, "Regrets are like flies. They come and they come until there are too many to swat away." He let his words sink in, and then, for no apparent reason, the girl who had been silent all along started to laugh.

10

Lavender

ℋe liked to sniff the costumes. Taffeta. Velvet. Silk. He kept all her dresses in the basement and they hung like the dead, row after row: musty, dusty and lavender sour. The smell of high-end charity shop and desiccated time. Skirts bulged, chiffon puffed, dilapidated lace ballooned and draped. But there was one he never touched: the one she was wearing on the night she died. It was at the back, on a rail of its own.

"Mama was always the centre of attention." Darim looked mournful as he reached for the nearest sleeve and rubbed it across his cheek. The black gauze shimmered in the surly light of the bulb.

Kezia took a step backwards and crochet like a woolly spider's web brushed her arm; the surprise felt like pain. She was here because it had been easier to agree to the lesson and hope her parents would show up soon, than to fight the sea-stare of Darim's teal eyes.

"You can't dance in those." He had looked down at Kezia's blue and white scuffed trainers while waving his hand in the air, as if wafting an invisible handkerchief. "Come with me."

And so they were in the basement. A regiment of worn-out flamenco shoes lined the wall. "You are a size six, no? Here..." He picked up a wizened pair of shoes.

"How did you know?"

"It is my job to know. Try them."

The shoes felt soft and worn and the heel gave Kezia an unexpected lift. She giggled. "I normally wear flats, even for work. I'm not very good at heels."

"A woman must walk tall. Always heels. From now on. Please." In the small space between them Kezia could feel Darim's breath move across the still air.

"Darim," she said. "I like these shoes but I don't think I can dance."

"You will be good at it."

"How can you say that?"

"You have that look."

"I do not!"

"That's it! Defiance."

Kezia laughed and Darim stood very still, but his eyes sparkled. She wiggled her toes in the shoes.

"I would love to see you dance. You deserve more joy than you have." He shut his eyes and began softly singing. *"My love is like the mist at dawn, never will it stay..."*

In the damp cellar, surrounded by the extravagant dresses, Kezia forgot to breathe and started to feel dizzy.

Darim opened his eyes. "Stay and dance pretty Kezia," he whispered. Above, on a shelf, fascinators flexed like fireworks.

Spellbound, Kezia almost fell out of the basement, her eyes adjusting as they moved along the corridor, shards of sunlight slicing through the windows.

"We dance outside," he told her. "Today is happy weather."

Happy weather, thought Kezia, still following the man in the purple jacket.

"No one ever grumbled themselves into a better state of mind, you've got to *dance* yourself into a better state of mind," Darim declared as they got to the hall.

There was a statue of Mary on the other side of the stairs, standing on a rock. Carlotta used to cross herself every time she passed. Often, she would kiss the statue's feet. Dressed in a cornflower blue robe, Mary wore a white veil flowing down to the ground, her eyes were black and anxious, her arms held out at her sides. Darim had once asked why she was worried; he wanted to know, he felt sorry for her. "Her son was killed," answered Carlotta. "She is sad." Darim had looked again at the pale face with the small peach mouth. *Hail Mary, standing on a rock, the Lord is with thee. Don't be sad,* he thought. Even now Darim didn't want her to be sad, so he reached out to rub her flat feet, remembered how many times his mother had kissed them, and slowly pulled away.

As they emerged into the sunshine and rounded the side of the house, Darim marched off towards the kitchen door, leaving Kezia alone to watch the goat chew dolefully. She sat, crossed and recrossed her legs and looked across to the gate. A peacock shivered past, guarding the exit. By her side, flowers were exploding like flames, red and yellow, amber and gold. A colony of ants drew a line across the flagstones, their formation a wobbling arrow.

Then Java bounced around the corner knocking some petals from the flowers and asking to see her shoes. She was followed by Sue and they were both wearing long black skirts, making Kezia feel oddly bare in her denim shorts.

"Come on," said Sue. "We practise over there." And they moved past a trough of tangled plants with blooms like grasping hands, to a square space on the terrace. There was a room, in the house, with a special floor and mirrors — it was Carlotta's practice room — but no one had used it since the accident. They preferred to dance out here, as the birds split the air with their cries.

Three other girls arrived from the village, talking quickly to each other in sharp Spanish. They had hair drawn up into buns. They were cheating, it was in their blood.

Suddenly three claps rang out like shots and a staccato pang ricocheted around the terrace. Two fat pigeons stuttered into the air and the goat looked up and stopped chewing. Darim had re-emerged and was striding across the flagstones with such long steps he seemed to skate in from the side. "*A ver!*" he said in Spanish, and then, "We go." He swung around with a click of his heels, surveying them all for slightly longer than was comfortable, before speaking again. "Only six weeks until the competition!"

In response, some of the girls started swishing their arms in feint arabesque and warming up their hips in neat little circles. Kezia stood limply, her hands at her sides. She felt big and in the way.

"I always used to hide at the back," whispered Sue. "But it's hard in a group this small. Don't worry, just join in with what you can."

The other girls were now doing impossible stretches, scooping down and grabbing their ankles like giraffes drinking. One of them twisted her wrists in circles up to the sky, watching appreciatively as if she was taking a measurement. Another tugged the frills of her skirt until it sat flat on her stomach where she smoothed it with care.

"Flamenco says: 'Look at me! Look at me!'" They all looked at Darim, even the goat. "It's all about making your entrance. You need to stand up, like this, tall. Own your space. Command it. Your whole posture should demand to be the centre of attention."

Java tossed her head like a pony.

"That's it, Java. Like that. It's all about the attitude. That's the first thing you must bring. Attitude."

Kezia shifted from foot to foot.

"You need to be haughty," Darim continued, his voice floating high on the air. "Proud. Yes. You know your power but you don't think anyone else has seen it yet. Hold that in your eyes. Look at me. I need to see it. Yes. Like that."

Kezia squinted into the sun and hoped that would pass for haughty.

"Okay. Now posture. Bend the knees slightly. Bounce. That's your suspension. Keep it. Next tilt your pelvis forwards and imagine you are pulling on a very tight pair of jeans and zipping them up. Tighter. Next size down, really tight. Yes. That's it. Now, the arms." Darim swept his arms up over his head and at exactly the same time his foot stamped down hard. For a moment he just stood, his chest out and his face up, completely still. "Ready?" he broke the spell. "So, put your arms up like you are holding a beach ball. A big beach ball. Dramatic elbows, throw them out. Let's have some drama ladies. Shoulders down. Remember, you are defiant. You have seen too much, worked yourself almost to death and been jilted too many times. Know it. Express it."

While they held their giant beach balls, Darim removed his jacket and slung it over the low garden wall. Rollo padded over and sniffed the sleeve before dropping himself down for a nap.

"Now. Copy me." Darim moved his rounded arms forwards and back, rotating at the wrists and bringing all the fingers together as though he was grabbing flies. "Out… and in. And out… and in."

They fanned their fingers into the watching sun.

"And one, two, three and four… Don't forget, drama! Give me drama. Your arms ache from holding them up? Good. Let them. Grow strong. And one, two and three and four… and one… Okay enough. Now feet."

The girls shook out their arms.

"Feet and then we add the two together. But one at a time for now. We warm up the feet. Remember, the knees are bent, pelvis is tucked in. Connect your whole body with your stomach. Now, we lift the heel up and down. Up and down. We don't take the foot off the ground. We are grinding into the floor. Faster now. Good. Next, we lift the foot up and strike the ball of the foot on the ground. Notice I pull my foot back, not raise it up… so it goes down, and down, and down… That's it, and faster now too."

A trickle of sweat started mid-torso and Kezia scratched it away.

"Okay. Sevillanas. We go over the steps now. Follow, like me." Darim stepped forwards on his left foot at a slight angle, bringing the toe of his right foot to tap just behind the first. "Look. Pull your leg up like this, drop it down again, and slightly forwards, then tap your toe behind. I am exaggerating now so you can get the movement. It is very precise. *Ta taka ta dah*." He stepped back on his right foot and tapped the toe of his left foot just in front, reversing the movement, before swinging his left foot behind and stepping forwards on his right to repeat the whole thing on the other side. "It is light," he said. "Delicate. Heel just behind the toe. And we keep the knees bent, we are not tap dancing here. Relax into the movement. Feel the rhythm."

Kezia was getting lost in the steps, sometimes she fell in with the movement, but then it was gone. She stopped for a moment as Tomi limped stealthily along the low garden wall: a jarring prowl. His head rose to stare at her, eyes like cool water.

"Now," said Darim, shaking her out of Tomi's clear gaze. "Arms and legs together. Remember, the movements look big, but they are not. They are actually very precise." Darim faced the sun and pulled his hands up over his head, snapping his feet together in perfect synchronicity. Kezia noticed the sharp shape it made with his body — angular — like a carving. "See?" He did it again. "Like this. And then stop still. That is how you create drama."

They marked the steps with the arms and legs and Kezia felt as though she'd been asked to pat her head and rub her tummy at the same time; she couldn't make it all go together.

"Don't think so hard," Darim decreed. "Rollo does not think about wagging his tail, does he?" Rollo's eyes popped open and his head sprung up at the mention of his name. "Flamenco is an expression." Rollo studied Darim for a while and then went back to lolling in the sun.

On the other side of the terrace, quiet and with her hands in her lap, the girl with auburn hair sat very still, watching. Frogs jumped in and out of the pond next to her, but it was the dancing that had her full attention.

They went over and over the steps until the repetition was a kind of thirst. After a while, Darim called, "Rollo!" and the dog hopped up this time and yawned. "Rollo, *metrónomo*!" At which he trotted off spryly towards the house. He came back with an ageing black box, the loop of the handle in his teeth. "*Buen* Rollo," Darim cooed and Rollo seemed to be smiling as he sagged back down to the floor.

Tick-tock, tick-tock. The metronome kicked into life with a solid certainty. A satisfying, constant click. It set the pace now and it was like moving within the confines of a cage; they kept within its structured sounds.

Darim stopped dancing and surveyed his pupils, nodding. He went to fetch his guitar, then sat on the wall and started to strum, light and airy notes brushing the beat. He closed his eyes and raised his voice above the music. "As a flamenca, your heart cannot bear the pain of being alive. No. But you have no choice. You have to learn to stand what you see. For your men. For your children. You stamp your feet into the face of what you see. Yes. You learn to love the imperfection of it. To dance, even when it hurts. To dance *because* it hurts. And to dance because it hurts more not to." Darim's eyes opened and he looked directly at Kezia. "Your pulse will count the rhythm, even when you sleep."

Kezia stumbled at this and had to focus hard on Java in front of her to pull herself back into the moves. Self-conscious again, she wondered if her parents had come, if they were watching from the side of the house, so she turned around but saw only the girl, silently sitting.

They practised the steps until the dance became a trance, Darim staring off into the distance, playing the same chords over and over. He closed his eyes again and drew up his chest. He waited, and then, in a soft, raw voice, flecked with emotion as a sea breeze is flecked with salt, he began to sing. Darim's mouth didn't open very wide, but the sound that came from it was broad and felt as though it came from a long way away, a long time ago. The words were in Spanish and Kezia couldn't catch the meaning, but the song reminded her of the bark of a tree:

gnarled and strong, organic and enduring. It was a strong pain that caught in the throat; the song of an older man, a bigger man than Darim. There were condensed tears in the rasp of it.

Sue fell out of step and swore, glancing at Kezia who giggled, suddenly happy.

Darim's song flowed over the sunny morning.

"Darim, Darim."

Darim stopped singing, opened his eyes, but kept up the music on his guitar. Someone was running at full pelt across the garden, skidding down from the path by the house and arriving out of breath. It was the young man from the bar with the smooth face like a child. "Darim!"

Darim held out his hand, his palm flat. "You do not interrupt." Some of the girls stilled, others carried on dancing to the metronome's bald beat.

"Omar says come. Omar says now."

"I'm teaching."

The young man looked at the girls desperately, his face round and earnest, then back to Darim, and whispered, "He is *very* sick." Darim frowned and the man said again, "Very sick," then looked at the floor.

Slowly, Darim placed his guitar on the wall. "Rosa, come to the front, you are in charge while I go with Sami. You can practise the steps in pairs now, okay? Use the metronome. I'll come back."

Rosa walked to the front of the class as if she was still dancing, shoulders back, legs winding from side to side. Kezia recognised her too then, also from Mando's, she had danced the breathtaking dance where time had seemed to stand still and sparks come out of her shoes. Darim nodded at her as she took her position, then he picked up his jacket and swung it deftly over his shoulder, striding in short steps past the house and up towards the road.

11

Shoes

Kezia wasn't sure why taking the flamenco shoes off felt like a loss. "I better get my bag. My parents should be here soon." She felt springy as she went up the wooden stairs and the room looked different now, familiar, as she re-encountered it. The small backpack she'd had with her yesterday was hooked over the bedpost; it was the shape of an owl, the first present James had ever bought her and it stared at her with big owl eyes, round and questioning. Kezia folded up the patchwork quilt, which was still scrunched on the floor, and smoothed out the creases. She sat down next to it on the bed, picking up the bag and holding it in her lap.

Four and a half years. She'd met James at university and he'd been her first proper boyfriend. On the night they'd met the beats had encased the bar like musical scaffolding and she couldn't really focus without them getting in the way somehow. She was clasping a tongue-achingly blue cocktail and feeling intimidated by all the 'cool people', so when everyone started dancing, she sat nervously at the bar, trying to find a pose that said it didn't matter.

James had a wide face which made him look friendly, so she didn't mind when he sat down next to her. It made her look less alone too and she smiled her relief at him.

"Hello," he said, and then something else she couldn't hear over the insistence of the music. She just nodded and hoped he would keep talking so she could look at his hazelnut eyes.

After a while he appeared to ask her a question, holding his head at an angle and waiting for her to reply. "It's too loud," she confessed, and he nodded, holding his hands over his ears for effect.

"Do you want to dance?" he motioned towards the crowds.

"I don't dance," said Kezia, shaking her head. "Only when I'm really drunk. Which isn't now," she clarified, although she could already feel the blue cocktail fading the edges of the bar and the edges of her mind.

James laughed. "I'm a terrible dancer too. I look like a congested robot."

Kezia remembered thinking she hadn't said she was terrible, only shy. Funny how that thought stayed with her long after the night had stopped being a bright memory.

They decided to leave and Kezia slid off her chair, not quite sure why she felt as though it wasn't the end of the evening. James came back from the cloakroom with one arm stuck half inside his jacket. "Turns out it's quite hard to put on a jacket." His wide mouth did a lopsided grin and Kezia giggled. Feeling unsteady, she pulled the sleeve for him so it slid into place.

James had walked her to the bus stop and she liked that his eyes and his hair and his mouth were soft — and he listened and he didn't mind when she asked questions.

"I've been told I'm too inquisitive," Kezia confided.

"It's good to ask questions," James said thoughtfully. "It's how you learn. That's what I love about history. You get to ask lots of questions about the past and then try and answer them, like being a detective."

"Sherlock James," she said conspiratorially. She felt safe with him.

"Yeah," he laughed. "And there's just so much to discover. So much stuff, lying under our feet, even right now… Imagine, digging down and finding pottery and pick axes and beads and swords. Every artefact tells a story — tells us more about who we were — and therefore, who we are now."

Kezia murmured agreement. She hadn't been listening. She was too drunk to follow sentences, but it sounded deep, and she liked that.

"What are you studying?"

"Oh, me? I'm doing business studies." Kezia crinkled her nose, "My parents thought it would lead to a job. I wanted to do anthropology, but they said that would be no use unless I wanted to be a professor, and I don't. So, seeing as they are helping pay the fees…" *Boring Kezia*, she heard the taunts again, but James was thinking.

"Hmm, that is good because business will really get you a head start on any career. You can do anything with that."

Kezia smiled; she knew he had looked kind.

When they got to the bus stop, James looked as if he was thinking again. He opened his mouth to ask her something a couple of times, and then shut it and put his hands further into his pockets. When the red double-decker glided up, he said, "So nice to meet you." And there was a gap where Kezia was hoping he would ask for her number.

"You too," she said, teetering onto the bus, using all of her concentration not to trip. By the time she found a seat, he had gone, there was only the grimy light of the bus shelter and a cracked piece of pavement where he had stood. The bus pulled away and the streetlights became streaks, forming patterns in the night as she gazed through the window. Someone had scratched a heart onto the glass and there were two sets of rough initials. She wondered if she would ever see him again while puddles of London swam past, dark and not revealing themselves.

The white paint was rough and lumpy on the bedstead. Kezia realised she had been staring at it, lost in the past. She blinked, looking across to the tiny sails of the ship, perfectly intricate in their miniature bottle. *Ta ta tarka ta...* the flamenco rhythm sashayed into her mind. *Ta ta tarka ta,* and her toes started to tap out the tempo, her fingers click with the pulse. She let the beat replace her thoughts, sandpapering over them. Until...

"Kezia?" Familiar voices outside.

"Mum?" Kezia went to the window and found herself looking down on her mum's straw hat and her dad's rosy bald head.

"Ah. There you are darling. Are you all right? It wasn't too scary, was it? The winds!" Before Kezia could answer, she carried on. "Sorry we're late, we had a bit to drink last night and forgot to set an alarm, and we missed breakfast!" The blue bow on her hat swirled with the injustice.

"Stay there, I'll come down." Kezia took one last look around the room, suddenly reluctant to go.

"What a lovely spot," she could hear her mum saying. "Talk about landing on your feet."

"Unusual decor," said her dad, evaluating the side of the house.

By the time Kezia got downstairs, Normando had toddled out and was offering Pat and Pat a cup of tea.

"We couldn't trouble you for some breakfast could we?" Kezia's mum had taken her hat off and was fanning herself with it, the bow flapping.

"We should go Mum." But it was too late, Normando was smiling sweetly and heading back to the kitchen.

"Why darling? It's a lovely spot," said her mum. "Nice for us to stay a bit longer. We could do with a sit down after the walk." And they hugged her and told her they were glad she was safe.

"So where is your knight in shining armour?" Kezia's mum was wearing cherry lipstick and her sunscreen wasn't quite rubbed in properly.

"Here, mum." Kezia smudged it into her cheek and Pat nodded acknowledgement. "His name is Darim, I'm not sure he's around though, he left."

"Oh well, by the time we've had breakfast he might be back I suppose," said Kezia's dad as they settled themselves down at the table. There was a sheen of sweat on his upper lip. "Least we can do is thank him and pay for the room."

"And the flamenco class," Kezia announced, flushed. "He said it was free, but—"

"Oh, love. How wonderful. No wonder you look better. Not so pale is she, Pat?" Kezia's dad nodded abstractly, brushing away an inquisitive fly as her mum carried on. "So, what was it like? Did you do some of that stomping we saw, that looked really good."

"Well." Kezia sat down too. "I thought it was all a bit weird here at first so I really didn't want to do it, just wanted to get out—"

"Oh sorry Pet."

"No Dad, it's okay. I... I loved it actually. I mean, I didn't expect to, I thought I'd be rubbish, but he kind of talked me into it, into the moves I mean and I could do it."

"You were always good at ballet, I remember. You always had the timing when the other girls didn't." Kezia's mum was fanning herself again.

"But this was even better, this was even more... free, and when you get the beat of the steps it's really satisfying." Kezia smiled her old smile, the one with the dimples. And so, as the goat looked on, sitting contentedly on the grass, feet tucked underneath her, Kezia told her parents all about the lesson, showing them the arm movements and getting up to demonstrate some of the steps, laughing as she told them how she'd messed up and had to stop and start again.

They'd almost forgotten about breakfast when the pot of juicy jam arrived with the bread and two cups of tea. Pat and Pat rhapsodised over all of it — smothering slices with spread and wiping the sides of their mouths as they listened to their daughter.

"Oh Pet, we haven't seen you this happy in ages. Good for you." Kezia's dad took a gulp of tea and his eyes twinkled the way hers did when she was happy.

"Now then, where is this Darim, I want to meet him?" Kezia's mum sat back, brushing her hands together.

Embarrassed, Kezia tried to feign indifference, but she did want to find him, to thank him, to say goodbye and to tell him he'd been right, about the dancing. "Look, there's the gardener, maybe I could ask him?"

Still in his woollen jumper, Hady was digging a flower bed, watching as the soil turned over, and as Kezia approached, he stopped and leaned on his spade. "Hello," he said, in an accent that reminded Kezia of a woven blanket, warm and with many layers. His eyes were textured too.

"Hi, um, do you know where Darim might be?"

Hady nodded as if he had expected the question and gave Kezia directions to Mando's, making it sound very clear because, to him, it was. His English was good enough to understand as long as she glazed over the punctuation and let the words mesh together to form a meaning of their own.

"Thank you Hady," she said, and his smile was as comforting as his accent.

Kezia went back to her parents, who had already started nodding off in the breeze. Her dad snuffled like a rabbit.

"He's at the bar apparently."

"Right you are." They didn't move.

"Shall I just go over there then and come back for you?"

"Oh, good idea," said Kezia's mum, her repose now more imperative than her desire to meet Darim. "But he sounds lovely, you must thank him for us. We'll just stay here, it's a beautiful aspect." And, the balm of the sun soaking into them, they settled back down for a dose.

Kezia made her way up the track to the road, past an old wheelbarrow and broken pots in a lay-by strangled with weeds — she followed as the way widened towards the tarmac at the top — and turned right at the end by another sign for 'Carlotta's Flamenco School', this one a solid signpost, aged but steadfastly pointing.

The path was arid. Desiccated trees scratched their way up to the sky and little shrubs grew in thirsty tufts, while parched pine cones rolled across the ground. Petals hung deflated, like dead balloons. Cicadas chafed against the air and birds cawed like ripping cloth. The ants were overgrown and the flies buzzed like drones.

Kezia walked fast and her heart thumped like the metronome in her chest. After a while, solid stone houses began to squat at the side of the road: a canary yellow one, a powder blue one, a white one. A garage was set back from the road, with one lone petrol pump, and domed recycling points stood like robots. She hadn't approached the village from this direction before and nothing was familiar until she saw a car park over the road, just a clearing of compacted dirt, and opposite that, the bar: tables and chairs congregating on the pavement and an old man smoking a pipe under the sign that said, 'Mando's'.

She pushed through the doors; it was cool inside and smelt of polish and port. It looked bigger now it was empty. In the corner, reading a book of poems, was the young man who had run into their flamenco class. He looked up.

"*Hola,*" she said nervously. "I'm looking for Darim, is he here?"

Sami regarded her impassively, holding the book as if he might return to it any moment. "He left," he said.

"Oh, where did he go?"

"He has gone back to the school now." Sami started to read again.

"Are you sure? I didn't see him on the path just now, I came that way."

"Shortcut," he said, without looking up.

"Oh. Thank you." Kezia didn't ask about the shortcut, after last night she wanted to stick to the paths she knew.

Sami declined to acknowledge her as she left, and back outside, the man with the pipe had gone. It was even hotter as she returned, down the track, bits of grit getting into her trainers and flies landing on her skin. The thought of Darim meeting her parents felt odd and distracting and she tripped more than once. She almost missed the turning, recognising a dry tree stump only at the last minute and stumbling down the last part of the way.

As she approached the front of the house, the deckchair paint looked like a mirage and she could smell the musk of the red geraniums. The paving slabs pulled her closer, small islands in a sea of brittle grass.

She stared to the horizon and the calm, still ocean, preparing to leave this place forever. She wondered if her mum and dad were fuzzy with sleep, what they were saying to Darim, what she would say, as a final goodbye…

But when she turned the corner, her parents were gone.

12

Daffodils

He'd looked it up, the meaning: '*Musica letitiae co[me]s, medicina dolor[is]*', inscribed on the lid of the virginals. He told himself it was in case the tourists asked, but it was more than that. The image stuck — like when he looked at the sun too long and the circle stayed in his eyes, imprinting everything — it was snagged on his retina; the man watching the woman, the secrets within the layers of paint. 'Music is a companion in pleasure, and a balm in sorrow.'

"Excuse me, are these the real carpets?"

James turned, caught off guard. "Hello. Er, sorry?"

"Are these the real carpets?" The tourist looked up at him like a child, eyes wide and wanting to know.

"Real?"

"Are they the carpets *the Queen* uses?" Her voice was hushed now.

"Oh. I see. Yes. Yes, they are the same ones, we don't change them, no."

"Oh my. Fancy that." She turned to her small and expressionless husband who just rubbed his nose and nodded.

They were at the top of the grand staircase, bronze gilt cascading down the balustrade in elaborate floral swirls as it wrapped its arms around the hallway. Visitors filtered up on both sides, tripping as they gazed at the huge glass dome above, like a big eye, watching. Imposing portraits collaborated in the surveillance, looking down from all sides.

The woman frowned. "And, are these always here, does the Queen have these?" She pointed to the translucent plastic, flashing a reflection over the door.

"Ah no. Not the plastic. We just try to protect the doors." James began to tell her how King Edward the Seventh had entirely redecorated the interior of the palace during his reign at the start of the twentieth century, but the woman was already pulling her placid husband away and

81

into the next room, hastily rotating her head as if to see how quickly she could take everything in while the man dragged behind like a ship's anchor.

Another woman, who had been listening to the exchange, bubbled up behind them then and asked, intently, "Excuse me, are these the real stairs?"

"You mean? Er, what do you mean?"

"Are these the stairs the Queen uses?"

"Oh. Yes, when she has state visitors they come in this way. They are the real stairs."

"Wow." She shook her head slowly, looking down at the flush of sweeping red carpet.

"And that's Queen Charlotte up there, she—" James pointed to the portrait, but the woman was already gone. He smiled grimly, keeping his history to himself, staring up at the sad portrait. Queen Victoria's grandmother was in mourning: the anguish of tears palpable beyond the buttercream piping and lace of her flowing clothes, which seemed to move with the torment — an invisible wind that blew. She clutched a small Maltese dog who was sad and old and knowing, like a teddy who'd been cuddled through all her previous pain.

James looked down to where the statue of Perseus reigned, resembling a figurehead, in the middle of the landing. The Greek hero was holding Medusa's head over the stairwell, static blood dripping from her throat in carved curls, while the tourists chatted happily past, oblivious. James knew it was a copy of the original, which was in Florence, he knew it was from 1545, he liked knowing the details, ready to be asked. Although, no one did.

In his mind he endlessly catalogued baroque furniture, jade vases, antique clocks, as if he was studying for an exam. He knew each object like a character in a play, the patina of their skin, the stories they weaved into the rooms with the breath of the past.

And so the day dissolved under his dreams and occasionally the tourists asked questions he could savour, holding forth on the various kings and queens and architects of the palace, until the last of the visitors dawdled out into the London evening, clutching souvenirs and thoughts of dinner.

James stayed late, checking rotas and writing reports. He could have done this during the day, but he preferred to be out in the state rooms, making sure everything was going well, where the constant current of tourists distracted him from the ache of missing Kezia. It was a dull ache that intensified at the end of the day, when the quiet seeped in, and the grand interiors of the palace swept around him, amplifying the feeling like a sky that looks bigger after rain. He wondered what she was doing, who she was with. He fiddled with his phone but she hadn't texted.

It was still light when he left the palace, it was one of those July evenings where the summer scents soften and ripen so the air is rich and warm. The sky was a patchwork of ripped tissue paper, white overlapping blue, and the London Eye looped above as birds squawked a sense of freedom.

St James' Park was seething with people and ducks and shouts and half-eaten hotdogs. James focused his eyes on the calm water as he walked past the pond, rampant with lime-green algae; clumps like countries on a world map.

He pulled at his tie as he came to a clammy Trafalgar Square, nodding to Nelson, as he always did, squinting at the statue on the top of his long pole, before rounding the corner to the station.

There was a busker outside Charing Cross and she reminded him of Kezia. It wasn't the hair, which was dyed bright pink, it was the dimples. James had always told Kezia her smiled 'twinkled', and it did. He threw the girl a pound so he didn't have to look at her and it chinked against the dull pennies on the green velvet of her guitar case.

On the train the air conditioning shook him by the shoulders and he laid the *London Echo* on his legs as if the words might warm him. He glanced casually down at the crossword on the back page but couldn't draw his thoughts into the clues. It was the kind of day he would have suggested getting a takeaway and they would have eaten it together on the sofa watching mindless TV, easy and safe.

Kezzie, please, just let me know you're okay.

He typed message and then deleted the characters one by one. Don't beg, he told himself. So he tried again.

Hi, can you just let me know you are okay?

It still sounded needy. He stared at his phone and sighed, clicking the button on the side and watching as the screen went blank.

The late evening sun slanted over the city making everything shine. Skyscrapers flashed dull metal in sudden squares when the train picked up speed, catching the embers of the day. *I don't know who I am without you...* he let the thought flash like the reflections, never quite catching it.

"You haven't done anything wrong," Hannah had signed emphatically at him, but it didn't help. "This is about her, not you," she'd said. "One hundred per cent."

But her is me, James wanted to say. *If she's upset, I'm upset, we're not separate like that.*

"I think you should tell her about the ring," Hannah nodded as she signed it. "Maybe that's the problem, she wants more and she's not getting it."

James breathed out slowly, he wouldn't tell Kezia he was planning to propose, it would dilute the romance and the surprise. "No," he told Hannah. "I just need to wait for the perfect moment, then she'll understand, then she'll forgive me." Claire kept calling to say the ring was ready for collection, the ring he'd chosen so carefully, green emerald, to match her eyes, and the stone for May, her birthday.

He thought back to that day in the park. The blossoms had been out, a haze of pink on green. They'd sat on a bench and the daylight had danced through the trees. He'd wished he had the ring then, it was perfect, but Kezia's small mouth was drawn in and her vivid eyes wouldn't connect. "Come on Kezzie, talk to me."

Time slowed down. Even the children on the swings seemed to be in slow motion. She wouldn't tell him why she was unhappy, what was wrong. On the grass on the other side of the path, a gaggle of daffodils trumpeted with frilly mouths, yellow and happy. "They're nice," he pointed as they jigged in the breeze.

Kezia nodded but said nothing.

He asked her again what was wrong and she folded her arms like he should know. The more he pleaded, the more she pushed him away.

A child shrieked as it went down the slide backwards.

"If you're angry because I've been working so much — I've had to, we're getting ready for the opening, there's a lot to do. It'll calm down soon. It's important Kezzie, and I'm doing it for us, for our future, for our plans."

Kezia crossed her legs now as well as her arms. She focused on the lines of stitching on his faded red T-shirt. "Then why do I feel like you don't care about me? That work is more important?"

"Kezzie that's madness. I care about you more than anything else in the world. I can't do without you. I need you, Kezzie. Without you… I, I would fall apart. You know that."

Kezia looked up at a pink and white petal, falling from its bower in a helical swirl, with delicate power.

"We're good together," James said simply. "I can only be fully myself around you. I get too serious without you. I need you to cheer me up, make me laugh. You are my sunflower. You're still my little sunflower, aren't you?"

She looked at him; "I can't… I can't always be that. You're always stressed and it's always my job to make you feel better. But I'm tired." *What about me*, she wanted to say, but it felt too selfish.

"What do you mean you're tired?"

She wouldn't explain and the shouts from the playground peppered the silence.

"You know," James tried. "We should go on holiday together, after the Summer Opening — that's just what we need, some quality time. I don't know, Devon or Cornwall… or Spain, like we always talked about. That would do us good. We've not been ourselves — we could have fun again." He tried to put his arm around her but she leant forwards out of the way. "So why don't we?" His mouth had gone dry.

"Maybe," she said. Just, maybe. And then she got up and walked away and that was the last time he'd seen her.

The train made a mechanical whirr, jolting him back to the present and he watched Canary Wharf and its cohort of high-rise compatriots loom like a modern Stonehenge over the London landscape.

Soon they slipped into suburbia, houses vying for space shoulder-to-shoulder, parks gasping for air and roads weaving under the tracks.

As he got off the train at Lewisham, a man gripping an orange carrier bag, with a bull terrier squatting by his side, was shouting into the face of a stranger, gesticulating with his free hand. James edged around him, onto Lewisham Way, where the traffic backed up behind the buses, and the air was heady with fumes. He stopped at the supermarket to buy a microwave meal for one, choosing morosely between all the pitiful packets.

His keys felt sharp in his hand as he opened his front door, noticing again how grey his flat looked without Kezia's bags and cardigans to break up the colour scheme. The latch clicked shut behind him and he shrugged off his jacket, struggling with the sleeves. He noticed the picture of Gracie on the wall: the old family dog. "Just you and me again tonight," he said softly. She looked at him obediently, her fawn muzzle like a beard and her eyes shining and sincere. He started to reach out, and stopped. "And you are just a photograph," he told her. Gracie kept staring, loyal, worried.

James kicked off his shoes and headed to the bathroom. He sat on the edge of the bath, turned on the taps and poured a teardrop of green bubble bath into the tub, watching it foam into little kingdoms of cloud. It smelt of apples: searingly bright and synthetic. He dangled one hand in the water and felt the bubbles fizz.

When the bath was ready, he pulled off his clothes and eased in, feeling the warm water soothe him as it enveloped his skin. He shut his eyes, letting his legs float.

A noise like a rattlesnake came from the floor. He leant over the side of the bath, grabbing at his trouser pocket and pulling his phone free, in case it was…

It was Hannah, video calling. He sunk with the disappointment, back into the bath.

I need you, Kezia. James thought. *I'm not good on my own. I'm not good like this. See?*

Shutting his eyes again he imagined her in that dress he liked, the black one, him, on one knee with the ring, her hands at her face, she was crying, she was nodding, she was saying yes, yes, yes. He let the dream wash over him, the subtle warmth of hope, as he stayed in the bath too long and the bubbles turned to small flat islands on the surface of the water.

13

Kezarina

She was staring up at the red and white stripes and the thick and agile ivy, wondering what to do, when Java skipped out of the house. Kezia had been all around the garden, to the back where the shed was and to the right where the losing lion guarded the gate to the cove, then all the way past the cacophony of flower beds, to the left and up to the road again. She couldn't find her parents and she couldn't see anyone anywhere.

"Use my phone charger. You can give them a ring." Java plugged Kezia's phone into a socket in the hall and went off in search of Hady: "Because I need to ask him something…" leaving Kezia to stare at the picture of the Last Supper and wait for her screen to come back on again. Judas seemed to be sadder than Jesus, his face brooding and tortured, the gold bulging in his pocket.

Eventually her phone dinged back into life, so she tried to dial her mum with it still attached to the cable, but there was no reception in the house, so she pulled it free and went back outside.

"Surprise!" Kezia's mum was energised as she answered.

"What? Where are you?"

"Well, your knight in shining armour returned and told us everything…"

"Everything what?"

"How brilliant you were in class this morning."

"I was?"

"Yes, darling, and only your first one. Natural talent, it seems. He told us you wanted to stay for the next one but you were worried about the money. So we paid for you, and for your lunch as well. It's on us! We're just back at the pool now, you enjoy. You should have said you wanted to stay!"

"But I—"

"No, don't worry. Your dad agrees with me — we want you to have fun and take your mind off things while you're away, don't we darling?" She heard her dad concurring in the background. "That's what the holiday is for! Relax and have fun, how exciting. You'll have lots of stories to tell James when you're back, won't you?"

"But—"

"That man says you've got a natural flare for flamenco!"

"Are you sure? I don't think—"

"Now, now, stop doing yourself down, you always do this Kezia."

"Mum, thanks, but I'm done. Really. I'll start walking back now."

"You can't darling. We've paid now. Please, our treat. I'll pass you over to your dad, he wants to say something, here he is…"

"Kez, don't you remember when you were small, Pet, you used to love ballet? 'Kezarina the ballerina' that's what I used to call you. You used to pirouette around the house and leap off the sofa, it made you so happy. You only stopped because you thought the other girls were thinner than you and that was rubbish. So come on — we could see how much you enjoyed the lesson this morning, so go for it — and we look forward to hearing all about it later."

"Dad, that's so nice—"

"Just give it a go. For us. You've been through such a hard time recently, we just want to see you happy. What's that? Oh, your mum says you've got to live a little, shake things up. What do you say?"

Kezia watched a peacock strut across the grass. "Okay, okay. Yes, thank you, I'll see you later."

"That's my girl."

After she'd hung up, Sue emerged, looking tousled, as if she'd been asleep. "You're still here?" When Kezia explained she laughed and said, "Parents know best. I think they are right, you're on holiday, make the most of the freedom of it."

"Yeah, and well, I've just broken up with someone, so I think they wanted something to take my mind of it. They just nap in the afternoons anyway."

"Oh, we're doing palmas later — clapping — much better than napping, trust me," Sue chuckled, combing her hair with her fingers.

"You'll be glad you stayed, but are you okay? You don't have to talk about it if you don't want to."

"It's okay, yeah, I'm all right." Kezia moved her hand like a see-saw. "Sort of. It was my decision to end it, but it still hurts, you know? We'd been together since university, I thought we always would be."

They sat down on a bench and Kezia tried to remember when things changed, when she started to feel like she was resisting things, always pushing back. She couldn't think of an exact point or a turning, it was more gradual, like the temperature slowly going down. They were watching Java and Hady talking and laughing together at the end of the garden. "I felt," Kezia divulged, "I felt like he took me for granted."

"Oh. You're talking to the right person then. Why do you think I left? I was doing everything — all the cooking, cleaning, ironing, child caring, parent visiting, diary organising, homework doing..." Sue shook her head. "And what was he doing? Complaining mostly. It was a break or a breakdown for me — so I chose to come here — best thing I ever did, so it will do you good too, guaranteed."

"I feel bad now." Kezia crossed her arms. "James didn't make me do all the housework and we don't have kids, we weren't even living together, though we talked about it. It was more that he was always working, his job was more important than me."

"Well, that doesn't sound right either."

"And..." Kezia didn't want to tell her about Gary so she just said, "He wasn't there at times when I needed him and it kind of made me wonder where his priorities were."

"Good for you."

"I feel bad though."

"Why?"

"Well, he hasn't really done anything wrong..." He was like flour, soft, flavourless. His softness hurt her, it showed her the places she was hard, places she didn't want to see. "He called me Kezzie and I hated it, but I was never brave enough to say. You see? He hasn't really done anything..."

"Hasn't he? Put it this way." Sue shifted on the bench. "Does James want to break up with you?"

"No, he keeps saying..."

"I thought so, and why do you think that is? Hm? It's because he is getting what he needs out of the relationship: love, support, whatever. But you're not. It can't all be about what he needs, what about what you need?"

"I know but I don't want to be selfish."

"It's not selfish," Sue said passionately. "We shouldn't live in a world where girls have to be 'nice' and boys can do whatever the hell they want because of it. Like I said, why do you think I had to get away? You've got to think about what you need as well as what he needs. Actually, if you started getting what you need from the relationship then you wouldn't feel you had to end it — so he would get what he wants as well — which is for you not to end it." Sue sat back, satisfied, her hands folded in her lap.

"Honestly, he's not… it's not as bad as what your one is making you do."

"Ian," Sue laughed. "Doesn't matter."

"But also, I don't even know what I need."

"Okay, well, tell me again why you wanted to end it."

"We were arguing all the time before I left. It's like… like we can't let go of each other because it's so familiar and because we kind of grew up together, became adults, I mean. It's like we need each other to be part of our identity, with all our friends seeing us as one thing, one unit, but it makes me feel like I need to break free, to be myself, to find out how that feels for a bit. And he's always working and it's lonely and… it makes me feel not good enough."

A black and white cat Kezia hadn't seen before trotted confidently along the wall at the end of the terrace, stopping to sniff the air and then ducking down, continuing with its body low to the bricks. Sue bit on her lip, then said, "Okay, so he enjoys his job. What about your job?"

"I hate it," Kezia said quickly. "I work in sales for a company which hires out marquees for events. I thought it might be more glamorous than it is. I've never been to any of the events. I'm on the phone all day and I hate it when people say no to me, which they do a lot."

Sue rubbed her thumbs together with the fingers still entwined. "Could be part of the problem. You need to do something for you. Find something you love. Something that makes you the distracted one for once, see how he likes that. Honestly, you get busy and you'll be amazed how quickly things shift — he'll be showering you with attention. Ian calls me every day now I'm here and we talk, really talk, for ages. Before I was lucky to get a hello," she tittered.

Kezia giggled back. "Actually, he has been trying to get in touch loads since I came away."

"See! Look, if you're always trailing around after another person, then sooner or later you'll end up resenting them, because it's not about them, it's about you."

"Can't I just resent him a little bit?" Kezia looked to the horizon and then back to Sue.

"Ha! You can resent him all you like, just know it won't make you feel any better, trust me, been there."

The thick ivy rustled behind them, stealthily assailing the wall.

"I think… I think I'm just a bit bored as well," Kezia confessed.

"Familiarity breeds contempt." Sue nodded. "That's what they say. Well, if it's excitement you're after you've come to the right place." She raised her eyebrows and tilted her head towards Darim who was coming around the corner with Rollo skittering at his heels. He bowed to the girls, sashayed across the terrace and then disappeared into the garden as if it had swallowed him up.

14

Beer

James rubbed his hand over the brown leather of the armchair: dappled and dented like skin. The Phoenix was full of lively people in sharp suits; clumps of commuters burbling commentaries on their days, their deals, their dates.

"How come they've all got such perfect hair?"

"Hair is overrated my friend." Chris flicked his eyes up, pulling off his beanie.

James grinned. He tried to adjust his tie to be more fashionable and less like a schoolboy, but only made it tighter around his neck. "We'll just stay for one more, yeah? I'm sure you want to get back to Sarah and Max and Ava."

"Well, it's much more relaxing here." Chris looked around contentedly. "Ava's going through her screaming phase and Max is going through his ask-all-the-questions-in-the-world phase, so peace is not on the menu in our house," he sighed lovingly, then looked earnestly at James. "Listen, don't worry, Sarah's cool with me being out, we both just want to make sure you're all right."

"Thanks, that… that means a lot. Yeah, I'm fine, I'm good."

"James, you just tried to garrotte yourself with your tie, it's no wonder we're worried. Come here." Chris went to reach over but James batted him away and stood up.

"I'll get the next round in," he said, and attempted to loosen his tie himself as he manoeuvred round a chair, almost tripping on one of the legs.

At the bar James watched the amber surf crash against the sides of the glasses — the tides rising, the pints filling — until the foam quivered neatly on top. He held the drinks reverently as he pushed his way back to Chris.

"Cheers mate." A slug of beer spilt on Chris' trousers as James put the beer down, but he didn't say anything, just wiped it away. "So, have you heard from Kezia then? How is she?"

"No." James watched the head on his pint split itself into oblivion, "Well, not exactly. She wasn't replying to any of my messages... so I texted her parents."

"Her parents?"

"Yeah, we get on really well, they're actually really sound, and I... I just needed to know she was okay." James looked up.

"And they're all in Spain together, right? Where was it you said, Parños?"

"Yeah. Yeah, and they said she's all right. She's learning flamenco." He paused, regarding Chris desperately. "They found some nearby school and she's having lessons."

Chris pushed his glasses up his nose. "Flamenco? Are you sure? I didn't have Kezia down as the... well she's not really... I mean... dancing? She's not the right..." Struggling for words, Chris moved both his hands in a wavy parallel line until eventually he looked at his glass and said, "Shape."

James fiddled with his tie again.

"Sorry mate, I didn't mean to be rude, it's just... well, you've got to admit, it's surprising, right?"

James nodded, gulping back an unexpected emotion he couldn't quite define but that tasted of tears.

"Maybe she's having a good time, maybe this is just what she needed, to do something new and she'll come back realising she is violently in love with you and all will be well."

"I've just got a bad feeling about it."

"Yeah, but that's just you being negative. Don't read anything into it. Girls like dancing, let her have her fun. It's not like she's run off with another man, she's only on holiday — gives her a chance to miss you."

"I was going to take her to Spain, just feels like she's ruined it." James didn't mention the ring.

Somebody at the back of the pub started singing a football chant and a coarse chorus of voices joined in, loud and out of tune.

"That's rough," said Chris.

"The singing, or—"

Chris grinned. "Very good, no, you not getting to take her to Spain…" He leant forwards. "I know, why don't you go out there and surprise her? She said you don't care, right? Well, the big romantic gesture — that'll prove it. Go out there and — even better — dance with her. She'll love that." Chris pulled at the idea like it was a rope hanging in the air.

James swatted him away. "I can't dance."

"All right, go and take her for tapas then. Whatever. Just show her you care."

James drank deeply as he considered surprising Kezia. Her in a flamenco skirt, him coming around the corner, getting down on one knee, the green emerald sparkling in the Spanish sun — matching her eyes. "I have thought about it," he confessed. "I have. But I don't know mate. I just feel so powerless, I thought Kezia was the one thing I could count on."

Chris nodded sagely. "It's like that with women. Sarah wasn't sure for ages, remember? But I just kept hanging around and showing up and eventually she said, 'Shall we make a go of it?' as if it was her idea. Persistence, that's what they like — a bit of tenacity — that's why I think going to Spain might swing it for you."

"Won't I just look desperate? We've been together for long enough for her to *know* I'm in it for the long haul."

"Hmm." Chris mused, an opaque film of beer on his top lip. "I don't know. I think this flamenco thing might be her way of trying to get your attention. If she feels taken for granted for whatever reason… well, it just makes sense. She tells you she thinks you care more about work than her — and suddenly she's in Spain putting on a frilly dress. It just adds up, right?"

James thought about this. "It's my fault."

"James you've done nothing wrong. This is just about her needing you to prove that you love her. So go out there and do it."

James leant back in the chair, the hard leather at his back. There was a single candlestick above the fireplace and the wallpaper was ripped slightly above it, showing a seam of white like a scar.

"I'm going to the loo." Chris got up. "You think about it."

James shifted his focus to the back wall where a framed poster showed a woman in a helmet and robes brandishing a huge British flag:

It's Up To You, blared in bold letters below her and James recognised the wartime propaganda from A Level History. He frowned and turned to his phone, pulling up a new search and typing: 'Flamenco School Parños', double-checking the spelling from Pat's text.

There was a picture of Carlotta, staunch and feisty and with an ice-cold stare. There was an article saying she had been found dead. James shivered involuntarily. He looked to the next picture and saw Darim, thin nostrils flared, eyes large and lambent and his head turned at the angle of arrogance. He clicked for more and found a video which showed Darim dancing, chest-to-chest with a raven-haired girl, something unspoken in the arch of his back. It must have been a few years ago now as the footage was grainy. Darim was wearing tight black trousers and an open-necked shirt which billowed at the sleeves. His skin was shining where the shirt was undone at the top and his look was intense, his movements precise. He flowed with a grace and purpose James had not seen before and his focus was so exacting he was unable to lift his eyes from the screen.

When Chris returned, he didn't notice his friend sit back down. "Are you all right mate? You look like you've seen a ghost."

15

Shells

"*Palmas*!" Darim declared, striking across the garden, accompanied by the gentle jingle of Rollo's bell dancing on his collar. "*Palmas*. Come!"

He sat on the low wall as if it were a throne and began to play; soft notes like fine gossamer threads emanating from his guitar. The web of sound entangled the girls as if they were flies and, caught up in it, they came, one by one, to sit on a chair or on the floor.

Java and Sue, and then Rosa, with the other girls who lived in the village, Abril and Carmen, whose English was small but whose smiles were big. They lived to dance. Even the silent girl came, sitting quietly at the edge. Ensnared in the rhythm they began nodding their heads, swaying to the feeling of the notes.

"Without a heartbeat, you die," Darim pronounced. "Without a rhythm," he clapped his hands over his strings, silencing them abruptly, "flamenco dies. Learn the *palmas* and you will learn flamenco."

The afternoon was mellowing, a breeze stirring playfully in the sultry air. The sky was letting go, deepening into a languid haze. The garden stretched down to the trees and the trees looked out to the sea, parting their heads occasionally to show the white frills of it, in and out, in and out, making patterns of lace on the sand.

Darim rested his guitar on his lap and took up his hands together. "Soft," he said, cupping them like there was a secret inside. Then, "Hard!" His three middle fingers formed a plank to hit his palm with. All the time he was counting to twelve in strongly syncopated beats. "We go back to the basics, for Kezia." He looked at her intensely and she felt it like an electric shock.

"Two types. *Sordas*…" The word was like 'sawdust' to Kezia and the clap was muffled like it too. "Put your hands like this." Darim showed them. "You are world weary. You do not make a fuss, but the sound is heavy with your journey, with your heart. Feel it. Hear it. Tell it to me and just to me." Enraptured they clapped along. "You can make it fast, you can make it bright, but there is pain, always pain, just below the surface."

They clapped.

"Kezia. Don't think so much. I see it in your face. Relax into the rhythm." He lifted his hands to make his movements more visible, and then leant his head towards them. "I can't count the rhythm now because I just need to *feel* the rhythm. You can count if you want. But better to feel. Feel it!"

The late afternoon was busy with insects living a rhythm of their own, ripe in the glow of the nectarine sun.

"Okay, change." Darim was still clapping. "The second way please: *claras*. Here we strike back. We explode! 'Enough!' we say. So you make this air pocket in your palm, then three fingers over it. You pierce the pocket. Like this. Nobody is sleeping now, your heart is alive. You are awake!"

The girls watched Darim, his hands small and hard. While they were absorbed, Sami from the bar arrived and crept around the side to Darim, who said something to him very quietly. He looked thoughtful and then hurried to the path for the sea.

"Remember," exclaimed Darim. "The accent is on the three, six, eight, ten and twelve. Here we go. We can start slow. No matter, we speed up. One two *three*, four five *six*..."

Sue smiled a purposefully lopsided smile at Kezia. "Don't worry," she said. "I'm always getting lost. Just jump right back in again though, it'll make sense after a while. Like he says, don't over think it."

Darim clapped with little effort and much precision. *Clatter clatt, clatter clatt*. His movements were so tight but so loud. It was more than two hands hitting each other, it was a musical instrument: complete percussion. Kezia hadn't realised it was possible to clap like this. She'd always thought clapping was for concerts or cricket or being polite. She hoped he couldn't see her own hands stumbling over the count now that it was getting faster. She managed about one in every four beats despite concentrating hard.

"Stop! Like this. One two *three* four five *six* seven *eight* nine ten. Yes, keep up girls. Don't try to catch what my hands are doing. There isn't time to copy. This has to come from inside yourself. You just have to *feel* it." His hands were becoming a blur in front of his chest. "This is the foundation of your craft. Learn it. Clap. Come on. Clap!"

Kezia liked how the clapping was all around her now, she was in it and she was part of it — their own insect buzz.

"Java. Focus." Darim raised his eyebrows and Java pursed her lips. Following her line of sight, Kezia saw Hady, the gardener, turn away and bend down, suddenly very interested in a pink rhododendron.

Sami came back from the beach with two large shells, walking quickly up the path and sitting on the wall next to Darim. With a flourish he arranged the shells together in his palm — so they became the two sides of a castanet — and began to clack them together, finding the tempo, adjusting their position as he got used to their fit. The bulbous shapes, peach and clean, melded into his hands, became part of his own anatomy. Darim nodded and smiled and Sami's face glowed.

They were creating more than sound, more than beats, it was a story, and the narrative resounded around the terrace and cascaded through the air. Darim's foot lifted and came down with an involuntary stamp when the feeling was too strong. "Whatever is the problem," he announced, "flamenco is the answer!"

After a while, he opened his mouth, drew a long breath, and started to sing. His voice was once again rough and elemental, like the rocks by the sea. He hovered around the notes, as if he was locating the pain at the centre of them, drilling down. And the pain was his pain, he recognised it when he found it, the feelings striated through his body. Occasionally, he would just shout, like a spark flaring from a fire.

Normando came out with a whisk in his hand. He stopped in the dappled sunlight and nodded along to the rhythm, smiling faintly before going back into the house. A short time later, he emerged again with a chopping board and a courgette. He put them on the table, taking the whisk and trying to cut the courgette with it. The whisk rolled over the curved top of the vegetable.

Darim stopped singing. "A knife Papa. That's not a knife. Get him a... I'll do it." Exasperated, he jumped up. "Carry on, don't stop. Follow Sami, yes carry on." And Sami with his shells took the lead as they all looked nervously away from the old man and his whisk.

Darim glared at his papa, running inside and fetching a very small, very blunt, knife. When he came back, he said, gently this time, "Try this, Papa. Don't worry. Just try this."

Normando nodded, confused, then smiled affectionately at Darim. "Thank you," he said, patting him on the shoulder.

Darim returned to the wall, settled, and raised his voice to say, "Remember, remember what Mama used to say. Flamenco, it is the answer!" He resumed singing, tipping his head up, his shoulders back, and they clapped the afternoon into the evening. They clapped all sense of time away.

And for the first time in a very long time, Kezia wasn't thinking. She wasn't worrying. She was simply feeling the beats flood all of her: her only focus. And it wasn't until she stopped, cheeks flushed, the sky waning and the fairy lights starting to make dots in the trees, that she realised.

"How did you like it?" Sue drew her attention away from the glowing branches.

"I feel like my mind has had a holiday. All I was thinking about was the clapping."

Sue nodded. "Good huh? That's why I like it too. It's like the stress can't get in, or gets transmuted somehow, you clap it out of you."

Darim stood up, and turned towards the horizon, where the light was now just a faint luminescence. "Think of this," he said. "The sun does not really set at all. The earth turns and we turn with it." He seemed to sniff the air like one of the cats and then marched off, around the side of the house.

In her head, Kezia was still clapping out the rhythm, clapping, clapping out the rhythm. Tapping out the rhythm, tapping, tapping out the rhythm. The low moan of the wind was absent tonight and the peace was deep because of it.

"Are you going to stay? You could stay tonight," Java asked later, sitting cross-legged with her hands on her knees as the cloak of night wrapped the garden in its velvet allure. "You could dance with us again tomorrow."

Sue agreed. "Why don't you? What are you missing at the hotel?"

"Bingo night," groaned Kezia.

"Well then?"

Kezia thought about it. She would be disappointed in herself if she went back. *Boring Kezia. Never did anything exciting. Always took the sensible path. Scared of being taunted for going her own way, scared of the bullies...* and she recalled the defiance in Darim when he said, "People will say whatever they like... Remember, regrets are like flies..."

She'd text her parents. She would stay another night.

16

Condensation

Carlotta looked solid in her red polka dot dress, her arms like ribbons moving in a musical breeze. On the stage behind her, Darim, in a frothy shirt, black waistcoat and black fedora hat. The light was dim and James squinted to see the man's intense concentration. There was something fierce about his focus, a devotion entwined with angst which seemed to suffuse every cell of his body as he played. The video had been filmed by a spectator who'd held the phone the wrong way up, so there were two thick strips of black along the side of the screen. James pressed the home button to make it all disappear.

"It's just some people doing flamenco James, I don't get it." Chris moved back in his seat.

"But did you see *him*?"

"The guy with the mullet? Yeah, so?"

"He's…" James didn't want to say it out loud.

"He's a guy with a mullet. He's not a patch on you, James, if that's what you're thinking. He's not Kezia's type. You're Kezia's type. Everyone knows that."

James imagined the man dancing around Kezia, spinning and spinning as she watched the curve of his back, the passion of his poise.

"Hello! Earth to James," Chris shouted as he waved his hand in front of James' face, and his friend looked up, bemused. A couple of girls at the next table turned around. "Sorry," Chris grimaced. "Didn't mean to be so loud."

The girls exchanged a look and then went back to their cold white wine, one of them drawing lines through the condensation on the outside of her glass as she confided in her friend.

"Chris, someone died at the cove near where Kezia is." James found the article again. "It was the flamenco dancer. It's dangerous — Kezia should not be there." He looked up, rubbing the back of his head.

"Let me see?"

James handed Chris his phone and he scanned the page, fiddling with his crucifix, thoughtful. "James, I don't see that this cove is more dangerous than any other to be honest."

James looked down at his beer, glassy bronze, still flecked with foam.

"Look, I know you're worried about her," said Chris gently. "Of course you are, but she's in Spain not Sudan."

James tousled his hair and attempted a smile.

"Okay, enough of this." Chris picked up his empty glass. "Let's have one more pint and then call it a day."

James nodded, his thoughts turning back to the fervour on Darim's face and the smooth shine of his chest as Chris loped off to the bar.

The girl on the next table who had been tracing over her wine glass glanced at James shyly before looking back to her friend as if summoning the courage to speak. She had very dark hair in a very neat bob. "Do you work near here?" she said eventually.

James scanned the surrounding seats, not sure she was talking to him. "Me? Um. Yes. Over there." He tipped his head awkwardly in the direction of the palace as though that made it clear. "You?"

"We work in Pimlico. Do you know it?" The girl tucked her hair behind her ears. Big gold earrings rocked with the movement.

"Yeah," said James, trying to think of something else to say.

"I'm Elly. And this is Veronica."

"You can call me Vee," said the other girl, who had curled her long, bleached hair at the ends. "We're accountants," she added, like she was disclosing a great secret.

"Oh. Great," said James. "Er, that must be difficult."

They laughed.

"People always say that." Elly looked thoughtful. "But I love it. I love the order of it, trying to make everything add up and work out. I hate things being out of sorts. I'm a Virgo." The girls nodded knowingly.

"Oh," James said, pretending to understand and trying hard to think of a follow-up question. "Do you work together, or…"

102

"Yeah, we're in the same office." Vee put her head on one side. "Just decided in the week that we'd come out and let our hair down, didn't we?" She looked at Elly and they both sipped their drinks as if that was all there was to say about that.

James went to check his phone as a polite way to end the conversation, but Elly asked him, "What's your job then?"

"I'm, um, I'm in charge of the wardens in the state rooms for the Summer Opening at Buckingham Palace."

"Buckingham Palace! No way." Elly's earrings were rocking again.

"Do you know the Queen?"

They had both finished their wine now and were staring attentively at him.

James felt a pang of pride, like a bubble in his chest, and when Chris came back, he was telling Elly and Veronica all about the secret tunnels below the palace as they listened, sitting up straight like meerkats. "And when King George and the Queen Mother went down there, they apparently met a man from Newcastle living in the tunnels."

The girls put their hands over their mouths.

"What have I missed?" Chris lowered two pints and a packet of salt and vinegar crisps onto the table.

"James is telling us about his amazing job," Elly said happily.

"This is Chris, he works at the palace too." James took a beer as Elly and Veronica appraised Chris' balding head.

"And your name?" Elly turned back to James, and when he told her she held out her hand, showing the tattoo of a small butterfly on her wrist, drawn in thin lines, like an etching. Her hand was cold.

She nudged Veronica who reluctantly put her arm out as well. "I hate shaking hands," she simpered. "Germs."

"Ah, but we are very clean, especially for the male of the species." Chris made his most innocent face, sucking in his cheeks and holding his palms in prayer.

They laughed and decided to get more chardonnay.

"So where are your girlfriends?" Elly said as she settled back down and Veronica sniggered, as if it had been a dare to ask. "Oh sorry. I've had wine." Elly put her hand to her neck. "We've been out since five o'clock, haven't we?"

Veronica concurred and then they both stared at the boys, waiting for their answer.

"Well, my wife is at home with the kids," Chris said as they nodded, they had clocked his wedding ring. "And his is... in Spain, I guess."

"You guess? She's either in Spain or she isn't in Spain." Elly's brow furrowed.

"Yes, but she's either his girlfriend or she isn't his girlfriend..."

"Oh," they said together as James smiled through the sting of it, looking again at the place on the wall where the wallpaper had been ripped away.

"We can help, can't we?" Elly tucked her hair behind her ears once more.

"Yes, we're good at things like this." Veronica clutched her glass with both hands like she was offering herself communion.

"I... I don't want to talk about it, it's okay." James thought his voice sounded suddenly small. His cheeks blazed red. *Tomato chops*, that's what his mum always called him and he could feel the burn now.

"It's not okay," Elly sulked. "You're upset."

"Okay then," Chris said, with alcohol's exaggerated lilt. "From a female perspective, if a girl goes off to Spain and starts learning flamenco, is that game over?"

The girls thought about it while James narrowed his eyes at Chris who just grinned back and took a steady sip of beer.

"Yeah probably," Elly announced her verdict.

"I think so too." Veronica twisted the ends of her hair around her finger. "Yeah, it's the flamenco, isn't it?"

"Yeah, the flamenco."

"What about the flamenco?" Chris leant forwards.

"Well." Elly looked into her wine glass as if she was reading the runes. "She's finding herself, isn't she?"

"She's finding herself," repeated Veronica.

"And, when she's found herself, it's fifty-fifty whether she still wants you." Elly looked up with a deliberately sad smile. "It's the way of it," she added, pleased.

"So you might as well get drunk with us," finished Veronica, holding up her drink as they both began to giggle.

"Ahh, we've got work in the morning." James raised his eyebrows at Chris, signalling for them to leave. "Nice to meet you though," he added courteously as the lights in the pub dimmed just a touch, like a filter being adjusted.

"Shall I give you my number, in case you need any more advice?" Elly angled her head so she was looking up at James through her eyelashes.

"Erm." James could feel his cheeks burning again.

"You never know when, you never know — you just might need a woman's opinion." Elly reached for her plush leather bag and brought out a silver purse.

"Invaluable," snickered Veronica. "We are always on call."

Elly took a white and gold business card from her purse. "This is my work number, my mobile is underneath," she explained unnecessarily, handing him the card.

"Oh. Thanks." James nodded graciously. "I'll bear that in mind."

The boys stood up. "Bye then."

Elly swivelled her wine glass round and round, holding it by its stem. "Is that yours?" She was looking down to the floor where a jumper was curled like a sleeping cat.

"Oh, no, that's yours isn't it, Chris?"

Chris grinned. "I'm a disaster. I definitely would have left that there." He picked it up and dusted it off, clutching it to his side.

As they left the pub, Elly and Veronica waved an expansive goodbye before turning to each other, heads together, deep in conversation again.

The outside air felt cool as it hit their faces. "I think you've pulled mate." Chris looked sideways at James.

James exhaled, "I... well, maybe... she had nice hair."

"You should give her a call you know. She seems sweet. She liked you. No harm taking her on a date you know."

James' cheeks went a deeper shade of crimson. "I don't know..."

"Come on, what's to lose? Take her out, get to know her, it's just a date..."

"I know. I feel guilty."

"James, Kezia is the one who… Well, she's the one who has taken herself off to Spain, so it's not for you to feel guilty. You're free to do what you like."

"I don't really *feel* free like that, but look, I'll think about it." James patted the business card in his pocket. "I'll… We'll see. We'll see."

"Yeah, just think about it."

They walked in silent contemplation through St James' Park, the trees whispering like the girls back in The Phoenix and the squirrels darting, moving fast and changing direction without warning.

When he got home, James went straight past the picture of Gracie and dropped down on the sofa. He shut his eyes, letting the exhaustion come, blotting out the burble of voices still present from the pub: the soundscape rebounding in his ears. Elly and Veronica came and went, laughing and sipping their wine. Then there was Kezia. Always Kezia. The flash of her smile and her soft skin in the mornings. He let the images blur and sift until she was there in a knee-length dress in Spain, dimples in the sunlight, holding out her hand.

The sky flashed and the man with the intense stare appeared at her side, rude and in the way. He was dancing round her, passionate and closer, round her and round her, black leather trousers and black steaming eyes. He danced and she watched, uncertain at first, gradually becoming hypnotised, and he danced closer and closer, until she took his hand, and eventually, joined in…

17

Moonlight

Ta tah taka tah. Tak tak.

　　Ta tah taka tah. Tak tak.

The rhythm had made a groove in her brain: incessant and on repeat. Even now, in bed, her toes moved with the feel of it. That evening they had siphoned the colour out of the day and into their very existence: they came alive as the sun set.

Kezia rolled over and stared at a puddle of moonlight spilling silver gloss onto the floorboards. She wasn't sleeping, so she got up and went to the window… beyond the curtains the sea shone, reflecting the bright coin of the moon. Tiny boats, like punctuation, sat between the waves. She rested her elbows on the sill. "Darim," she said, liking the sound of his name out loud. "Darim."

She turned her head away, suddenly embarrassed in case she'd been heard, and on the floor, she saw the flyer she'd got at the bar, stained with the red wine. Picking it up, she unfolded its crusty sides to see: 'Carlotta's Flamenco School', in curlicued writing. Had she even read it before? The picture of two people dancing was unfamiliar, it wasn't Darim, although it may have been Carlotta, the head was angled away, a red flower in the black hair.

Kezia rested the flyer on the windowsill and took a step back, flicking her arms into the air. *Ta tah taka tah.* She swirled her wrists and it felt powerful even though she knew she wasn't doing it right. *Ta tah.* She moved her legs forwards and back trying to sweep them up in the right way and put them down precisely. She looked up at the moon and narrowed her eyes in defiance, drinking in the strong feeling.

"You're doing well Kezia. You're doing well. You've surprised me I must say."

Kezia tried to shake the memory away by focusing on her arms; up… and down. What was it Darim said about a beach ball? But the voice crept back in…

"To be honest, when you started, I thought you were too nice to be a good saleswoman."

And, as she danced, it came flooding in. That night. Gary. The kiss. The anger and the guilt — all of it — she couldn't escape, and so, she told her story to the moon, everything, step by step.

"You're too much of a good girl. You've got to prove you've got what it takes."

They'd both been working late. Him in his glass enclosed office, her at her desk, a big pile of papers to get through. James had already texted to say he'd have to cancel their date. The palace. Always the palace.

Gary came out of his office whistling. He was a gangly man with short blond hair who always looked a bit sweaty. His goatee beard hovered around his chin and his eyes were dove grey. He wore expensive suits and garish ties and the other girls in the office said he smelled nice. He bought his cologne in batches of ten at the airport.

Kezia tripped, remembering the look on his face, before finding the rhythm again and wishing, wishing she had just gone home, said no, and gone home, but then… that would have created problems for her too, just different ones.

"Just you and me tonight," he had said. "Want to make the most of it?"

She hadn't understood until he'd said they should go for a drink. When she seemed reluctant, he'd made it sound like a meeting. "There are some bits of business we need to discuss. Your progress. Might as well do it there as here."

It was James' fault. If he hadn't cancelled. If he had been there…

They'd found a table at the restaurant. There was a single cerise flower with a long stem in a white vase and a candle which had just been lit. Gary leant back in his seat and snapped his fingers for the waiter. She said she wanted a coke but he told her that would be rude and ordered pinot grigio for them both.

"That's your problem, Kezia. You need to lighten up a bit. Look, you're doing okay in the office, you work hard, but I've got to be honest, you need more… grit."

"Grit?" The silky music in the room jarred with their conversation.

"Look. We can't all be the blagger, swagger type, like me, right? I was a right Jack the lad when I started." His eyes glinted. "And it worked for me. I mean, look where I am now. We don't all have that, naturally." He paused for her to take in his greatness. "Still, there's a lot we can change about you, if we work together, and in time, I really do think you might make it."

"What... what do you mean?"

"How can I put this?" His eyes went up to the right, thinking, then back to her. "You'll never be one of the pretty girls. Take Claudia or Kate, for example, they can really work that. But that's not for you. I see you more as the girl-next-door type and that can really work, but we just need to change a few things — personality-wise — to get you there."

"Oh." Kezia rubbed her nose and then worried her freckles might show through her foundation.

"It's a compliment, I mean, when you started, I've got to be honest, I didn't think you'd last five minutes. A bit too weak, I thought, naive, yes. But you're still here, that's got to say something. And I can help you." He stared at her like she was a bird with a broken wing. "I was going to give the team leader role to Jon. I mean, he's younger than you and more inexperienced, but I see promise there. He's not as hesitant. He's got a natural confidence. He makes mistakes, yes, but he makes them boldly. That counts for a lot."

Kezia took a sip of her wine and it tasted astringent.

"Kezia," Gary said, looking at her with sympathy again. "There's a real sweetness about you and I like that. I really like that. We don't want to throw it out, but we just need you to be a bit more... real."

"Real?"

"Yes. I'm not saying we need to change everything about you — just a few fundamentals — then maybe that promotion can be yours after all." He touched her knee under the table so lightly she doubted she'd felt it. "Remember, good girls don't necessarily make good salesmen." He didn't correct the gender. "But I'm here to help you to loosen up, and who knows where that could get you."

They ate rubbery carbonara and Gary talked about himself for the rest of the evening. Relentless waves of anecdotes which put everyone

109

else down and paused only long enough for her to agree with him, cutting back in as soon as she started any response. He had nice eyes but he didn't say nice things. Eventually he looked at his watch. "Shall we?"

Gary made a big show of putting Kezia's coat on for her, and as they left, she felt dizzy with the drink and trying to process everything.

"Come here." On the way back to the office, Gary took her arm and pulled her into an alleyway. "Are you ready to start living a bit then? Show me you're loosening up? Show me you've got what it takes?"

There wasn't time to say anything. He came in close. He took both her arms and the cologne was intense and smelled like polish. She didn't understand and she didn't know what to do and there was no space to decide.

Back in the room, Kezia's arms fell down — she stopped dancing — suddenly unsure of the steps. She slumped onto the bed and looked at the last text from James.

Please Kezzie, just let me know you're okay. J x.

Her fingers hovered over the reply, but she was unexpectedly distracted when the flyer on the windowsill fluttered off and onto the floor again, seemingly of its own accord.

She lay back and pulled the sheet over her as a heaviness pressed down, a kind of concrete in her veins. Kezia closed her eyes, her phone sliding out of her hand and onto the mattress.

She dreamt of Darim. She dreamt he came to her in the night and sat on the edge of the bed. It was such a mundane dream, at first she believed it to be real. He sat and he told her it was time to get up. She was lazy, he said. Then, "But I like you." *You are lazy but I like you.* He looked at her for a long time after that, and in the dream, she thought, this means something, and then they were dancing on the beach in the flip of time and space that is normal for dreams. She felt self-conscious but she didn't want it to stop.

"I don't know the dance," she said in the dream.

And Darim said, "You think that matters? It only matters if you think it matters." And they danced and the sea was the rhythm as they danced and the sand was soft and pliable beneath their feet. Then the sky became dark, very quickly a bruised cloud drew in from the horizon, cloaking everything in its shadow, and a low howl started to come from the cove. "She is here," said Darim. "She is here. Run." So she ran and she ran back up to the house, in her bare feet, convinced Darim was behind her… and it was only when she got to the top that she realised she was on her own.

18

Graffiti

"*I*s she beautiful?"

"No, she's strangely ugly."

It was eleven o'clock and Kezia was in the bar with Java and Sue, the clack of the flamenco beat still in her head, but far off now, like a watermark. She had danced again that morning; she had let her feet stamp and danced away the feeling of the dream, although she still felt strangely warm and cold when she looked at Darim. She asked about the rumours, to distract from the feelings she didn't understand.

"*She will strike you down, she will strike you blind!*" Java was performing the stories, holding out her hands as she repeated what she'd heard from the village. "*Don't go down to the cove at night, you may never come back... you will never come back the same.*" She nearly knocked her drink over.

Kezia giggled, fiddling with her straw. "What else do they say?"

"Oh! The satin shines in the moonlight. Shines in the moonlight! White dresses and dirty skirts. They say you can't move in your tracks once you hear her, you're transfixed — fixed, fixed to the spot. It's the singing that does it... gets into your bones; it chills you, it freezes your blood and you're never the same again."

Omar barked an order to Sami at the back of the bar. They were carrying crates of beer round to the storeroom and the bottles clanked together in nervous percussion. Omar had to reach around his protuberant stomach to grasp the plastic handles, sweat glistening on his forearms, while Sami was struggling with the heavy load, but gritting his teeth, determined to be strong.

"How's Matías?" Sue's forehead creased with worry and the question creased the mood.

"Oh, I saw him, didn't I?" Kezia remembered. "He's the one that got sick when he was here the other night, right?"

Sue nodded soberly at Kezia. "He's the mayor's son."

"Well, he *is* blithering about a ghost apparently. Not making much sense. And he was there, he was there all right, he heard it. It was a dare, for his birthday, to go down to the cove on the full, full moon."

"Java. It's blathering, not blithering," Sue corrected, annoyed at her flippancy.

"Blithering, blathering, all the same to me." She smiled a crooked smile at Kezia. "English is a strange language anyway. You know what they say though, don't you?"

"No," Kezia leant forwards, full of curiosity.

"It was the ghost who killed Carlotta." Java folded her arms. "Yup, that she was drawn by the beautiful music, towards the singing, or she would not have been on those rocks." Java sat back looking pleased with herself.

"What...?" Kezia looked at Sue but she just sat straight-lipped.

"Yes Kezia." Java nodded seriously. "She heard the sad lamenting songs and she was cursed and doomed to die."

Kezia looked over to the photograph of Carlotta, hanging at an angle on the other side of the bar, shaking her skirts, her eyes focusing on the faraway distance.

Java noticed Kezia's expression and reigned herself in. "Oh, I'm not trying to scare you. It's just ridiculous that's all. Accidents happen — anyone could slip on those rocks — you don't need ghosts for that."

"And she had been drinking, Kezia, we know that too," said Sue ruefully. "They found the gin bottle there, so... well... as Java says, accidents happen. It doesn't stop the rumours though. Poor Darim, he loved her so much, adored her, he's not been the same since."

"Oh, really?" Kezia felt a surge of sympathy.

"He feels bad because he was in Morocco, so he wasn't there at the time. He believes if he'd been here then it would not have happened. She liked to drink, he was the only one who could control that temper of hers, but... But no use thinking what if."

"And is that why there aren't so many students now?" Kezia wanted to know. "Were they put off when Carlotta died? Sorry, maybe I shouldn't ask…"

"It's okay." Java shrugged. "Yeah, people are very suspicious, so it's hard. That's why we don't have enough girls for the competition. That's why we want you to stay." She held out her arms as if to welcome Kezia into the fold.

"And there isn't enough money now either, after Carlotta left all her savings to a cat charity," said Sue swallowing a hiccup. "So, the cash prize from the competition would help, but it's not about that really."

"Darim doesn't care about the money," Java intervened. "Just music, just dancing."

"Why did Carlotta leave all her money to cats?" asked Kezia, thinking back to the two black cats she'd seen chasing each other across the garden that morning.

Java raised her hand, wanting to be the one with the story. "Well, she loved cats, but that's not why. She had an argument with the mayor just before she died and she changed her will there and then. She was going to leave quite a bit to the village you see, for a children's play area or something, but she struck it all out in a fit of anger. No one really knows what happened, Mando tells one version of events, and the mayor another… but anyway, when they found the will, it was altered, and she'd written something like: 'You do not disrespect me and try to take my money', across the top. She was drunk, but it can't be undone now. She didn't do anything by halves."

"Yeah, we don't think she intentionally cut Mando and Darim out, she just didn't think, she got into wild rages, as we said."

"That's where Darim gets it from," added Java, looking thoughtfully at the fans spinning overhead. "There's a lot of her in him."

Kezia was about to ask another question, but Sue cut across her thoughts. "And how about you? Are you feeling better? Dancing helps, right? Nothing heals a broken heart like flamenco."

"Yeah. Um, yeah. I do actually. And I would never have come if I hadn't got lost, so I guess it's worked out well." A fly landed on Kezia's glass, alert to the sugar in her coke; she waved her hand and it zigzagged away.

114

Sue leant back in her chair. "You know, there's a feeling I get when I'm dancing that I never had before. A sense of space. A sense that I belong in my space. I'm not apologising for being there. I should be there. Did you feel that yet?" The fly circled Sue's head and she sat up, swiping at it with her hand.

Kezia thought back to when she was dancing in the puddle of moonlight, her emotions and her arms twirling. "Yeah, starting to..."

Java beamed. "You know," she said to Kezia, "You should stay for tangos this afternoon. That's when you really feel it and you really get your angst out."

Sue nodded. "She's right. So cathartic. If you've got heartache, I prescribe it for you — you need this."

"I don't know..." Kezia swilled her half empty glass, watching the melting ice swirl in a tango of its own. "I guess I should get back. I mean, all good things come to an end, right?" She felt an unexpected wrench, looking from one to the other, unsure.

"Well, what else would you be doing?" asked Java.

"Nothing, I suppose... but my boyfriend, well, my ex, he's not happy. He says I should be with my parents." James had been texting her again, he was worried, she shouldn't be there on her own, he said.

Sue sat up straight. "Oh yeah. Wants to keep you small does he, doesn't want you to grow? Doesn't want you to have fun? Pah! They always do that."

"I don't think..."

"Look, if he was off trying something new would you be telling him not to? Would you be telling him to go back and sit in his hotel with his parents or would you be telling him to go for it and make new friends and learn new things? That's all I'm saying..."

"Yeah, Hady and I encourage each other in our dreams." Java rested her head in her hands, wistfully. "We are going to run a bar like this together one day. That's what we want — a place where everyone can eat and drink and gossip together — it's going to be amazing."

"You said Hady came from Lorca," Kezia recalled. "But you didn't say why, what happened?"

"Oh." Sue adjusted her glasses. "Hady turned up here after the earthquake. Can't blame him, it was so awful, he was totally traumatised.

So, his papa called Mando and he straight away found a job for him, *outside*. Normando and Darim, for all their faults, would never turn away someone in need. I suppose they feel a bit like outcasts too, what with everything that's happened. Even before Carlotta died there was this feeling of us and them. I think people resented Carlotta's fame, her extravagance. They thought she was a bit of a diva, which she was to be fair, but a great flamenco dancer and a fantastic teacher — we miss her."

One of the crates crashed down a bit too heavily and they could hear Omar swearing at Sami. A few moments later, Sami came out and sat up at the bar sheepishly, drawing imaginary creatures onto the wooden surface with his finger, round and round.

Java was still thinking about Hady. "You see, he was actually in the earthquake," she told Kezia. "He still has nightmares, finds it hard to settle, to feel like everything is fixed around him. That church bell could have killed him, the one that fell. The whole bell tower came down, just crumbled." Java moved her hands to show the motion. "You can't forget things like that. He told me about it. All the rubble, bricks and dust, falling from the sky. After the first quake they all ran outside and they thought that was it, but it wasn't, it came back stronger. He says he can't understand it, a small boy killed, walking his dog. Out of nowhere. It doesn't seem fair. It's not fair. It shook everything — it shook his faith…"

The face of the child, white and unmoving, the sheen of death and dust. Horror in the glazed eyes, a cold seeping out of him already. He couldn't stay in Lorca. The memories settled on him every day, like the debris, that still seeped from doors and floors and ceilings, puffing out from every place like the breath of the ghosts who lived there now. His life, shattered. Nothing safe, nothing firm any more. He needed to get away, away from the smashing sounds and the screams. But they followed him. Every morning he woke drenched in sweat, ready for another day to try and forget it all, before the haunting came at night. But he didn't speak of it, not any more.

"At first he refused to sleep in the house in case it happened again, he thought it was going to fall on his head so he felt safer in the shed," Java continued. "Now he's just got used to it and he likes it. He likes to feel independent; it's his little home."

"Your little love nest more like." Sue poked Java in the arm.

"Oi!" She flicked Sue away playfully and carried on telling Kezia, "Hady works in return for food really as they can't pay him very much, there's no money, like we said. But he doesn't feel judged here, that's the thing. He said back home people were telling him to just get over it like everyone else. Well, he isn't everyone else and he couldn't. You've got to do things in your own way."

Kezia remembered the screaming she'd heard on the first night, the shrieks in the wind, the howls within the howls. "Poor thing," she muttered and was about to ask another question when Normando muddled into the bar in a blue and grey flat cap and a dirty white apron. He saluted the girls as he made his way to the back. "We're doing *patatas bravas* today," he said. "*Patatas bravas* with ham and my special tomatoes."

"Quick," said Java. "Before Omar sees him. He gets so angry when this happens. We need to get him back."

They stood up. "Mando." Sue was gentle. "Remember you cook for us now, don't you, back at the house. Not here. So let's go back now, shall we? We can go together."

He frowned at her. "But this is my bar. Mando's."

"Yes, but Omar and Sami are doing the work for you now aren't they? Just to make things a bit… easier."

"No, it's…"

Java took his hand and skipped around to face him. "You're the best Mando, come on, come back with us, please, and cook lunch there instead? We love it when you cook for us, we need you." She gave him a little hug and he patted the top of her head. It was enough. They ushered him towards the door — Sue and Kezia behind and Java in front — back out into the searing sunshine. Normando blinked and smiled and they all walked him slowly down the track to the house, Java pointing out geckos and goldfinches and the old man nodding happily.

It wasn't until they were close that they saw it. Kezia had been preparing to say goodbye, to wander back up the hill, to succumb to bingo and boredom. She was chatting to Sue as they rounded the corner, inching down the path, making sure Normando didn't lose his footing on the incline. They were just by the small lay-by, where the old wheelbarrow lay on its side defeated and the broken pots were stacked in cascading columns.

Java stopped in her tracks, her hand went to her mouth and she swore vehemently in Spanish. Normando looked around, confused, adjusting his flat cap on his head.

The ebony letters were large and dirty. They were sprayed callously on the wall by the front door, thick and dripping. They puffed out the word: '*Mentiroso*'.

"What does it say?" asked Kezia.

"Liar," said Java, stricken, a bright blue butterfly oblivious overhead. "I don't think we told you, but one of the officers in the village told everyone Darim tried to blame the mayor after Carlotta died, because they'd had that argument. They think he lied to protect himself. But it's not true. He doesn't blame her for it, as we explained, he blames himself for not being there."

"They believe it in the village simply because they want to," remarked Sue, still looking at the graffiti.

"They're jealous of Darim and they were jealous of Carlotta and they can't just leave it alone," added Java, Normando wobbling beside her as Sue took his arm to steady him.

Benja the cat sidled up to the wall and sniffed it, unimpressed. He settled himself down a few feet away and set about licking his thick grey fur.

Then Darim came out of the front door with a bucket of hot water and a sponge. Rollo looked like he was going to help as well, trotting with his head down. Benja stopped preening, stared with steady eyes for a few moments, then went careening off back into the garden.

Java ran over. "Darim are you okay?"

He put the bucket down and straightened his back, playing to the audience. "You can't get approval from outside of yourself. It has to come from inside. Always. This—" He gestured to the writing, which looked smaller now, with him beside it. "This serves as a good reminder, no?" He turned to confront the word, dipping his sponge very precisely into the bucket and scrubbing vigorously, but the letters wouldn't come off as he rubbed them with the soapy water.

19

Tangos

They lined up outside in the sunshine, bleaching their tangos with sweat.

The graffiti was smudged on the wall, a stain instead of a word, and Kezia wondered whether the dancing would feel like that for her soon, a memory that would fade but never come off. She looked around at the girls in the long skirts. Sue had persuaded her to stay — just one more lesson — and she wanted to study it all carefully so she could take the pictures home with her in her mind.

Darim had gone to check on his papa and the village girls were laughing about something, Carmen dashing back her sienna hair and Abril doing an impression of one of the local men, bowing her legs and sticking out her stomach, her cheeks flushed as she pointed in the air, gesticulating and embellishing her acting with words. She was more tanned than Rosa and her hair wasn't as jet black. She tied it back now as she finished her routine and Rosa peeled away, turning to Java who was talking very fast, like she always did, while one of the peacocks inched suspiciously past, its head cocked to one side, as if it was eavesdropping.

Sue smiled at Kezia. "You know, it's been really nice for me to have another English girl around. Java and Rosa are fluent, and the other girls are pretty good too, puts my Spanish to shame, but it's just been nice, reminds me of home."

"How long have you been in Spain?"

"Hmm, let's see, well Ian, my husband, got the job out here in... actually ten years ago now, so yeah, a while. The kids are Spanish really. But I still miss my friends, my family, I guess that's why I needed to get away and do something for me for once. I just threw my whole life, my whole self into Ian and the little ones and I had nothing left. They call it burn out but it was more than that, I was lost. So it's good for us all this:

they have to learn to manage without me and I have to find the part of me that's just me, and not connected to running round after them. We'll all be better for it I reckon."

"So how long will you say here?" Kezia asked over another burst of laughter from Abril and Carmen.

"Well, it was going to be until the competition, but we don't have enough dancers for that now." She looked at Kezia meaningfully. "So, actually, I've found it useful not to put a date on it, just take each day as it comes. Ian keeps asking but I think he knows I need this. Funny, if I'd known he'd be this good about it I would have taken time for myself years ago and never have got to 'the edge' as I call it — so it was me that was holding me back all this time, and I thought it was him!"

Kezia was about to reply but Darim came charging across the terrace. He shot his arms up in a fast flourish, arching his chest upwards. His stance was a challenge. The class had resumed.

"Knees bent. Arms up. Throw your elbows back. Shoulders down. That's it. Give me more attitude. Fierce." The vandalism had fuelled his zeal and the girls stood, staring him down. He lifted his chest even higher, peacock proud, and his arms came down and out like a display of feathers. "Okay, we go. In... and out. And in... and out."

They spiralled their arms and their hands until they ached. Then the flagstones echoed with the steady crash of heels and toes and heels and toes, striking down and down and down.

"Keep to the middle. Don't go to the side. Toes turn out. Better! Remember you are not tap dancing," Darim flicked the words off his tongue. "Let me tell you something. Flamenco did not start as dance. Flamenco started as work." He put his arms down abruptly. "No don't stop, carry on, carry on, and listen." The girls picked up the steps, waiting on his words now, not his movements. "The blacksmiths, the gypsy blacksmiths, in the forge, hot as they toiled, started to work with a rhythm. Down..." He mimicked hitting an anvil in time with their tempo. "Down, down..." Then he added clicks and claps between the motion, "See? And so they sang about their lives, they sang about their pain, and all to the rhythm of their craft. They sang about salvation, even as their work became their salvation. Now, this is our salvation!" Darim glided back into the dance, curved arms, curved back. Kezia watched the way he turned his head and hammered his feet and she thought of the flames of the forge — black hate, red love, all melding together — grief and passion and pain.

All the while the girl with the auburn hair sat watching, silently staring, sitting on the wall.

"Right. Remember, with tangos we kick our feet up behind, bend at the knees, the basic step is slow-quick-quick-slow. That's it, and then turn, with your arms out. Good Abril."

Kezia counted time, trying to keep up: *clack clack clacking clack clack*. She liked how much stamping there was, beating out the steps again and again — and again and again — until they were automatic; they were muscle memory, to be felt instead of thought.

"*Ta ta taka taka ta DAH. Ta da taka taka ta DAH!*" Darim's voice scratched out the sequence. "The beat will get into your veins; it will pulse in your blood. You will walk to it. You will wash in it. You will sleep with dreams that course to the rhythms of it, and you will wake with them surging through your insides. That's it. Stand taller Kezia. I know you can do it. Up, up. Now pretend you have a skirt, pretend holding it, like this. I will find you a skirt. But for now, like this."

They slammed down the rhythm with their feet. They beat until the blisters came and the sweat ran down their backs. They held their arms high and brought them down in front of their faces.

"*Olé!*" Darim cried — as if he absolutely couldn't help it — his hand springing into the air. "Now I want to see arrogance in the line of your jaw. I need to see the glare in your eyes, the one that says, I will eat you for breakfast, but first, I dance."

As they struck poses, their silhouettes spelled a new kind of alphabet and together they made sentences, words, stories. All afternoon they pounded the floor, down and down and down.

Kezia stopped noticing the effort of it — she felt light — and as again and again they repeated the movements she fell into the 'being' of it, like there was an intelligence in her body she didn't know about before. She heard the cry of a bird overhead and it didn't feel very separate to what they were doing.

The more she danced the stronger she felt too. She thought of Gary and the anger spilled into the steps so that each strike of her foot was a no — *no, no, no, you don't* — and as she thrust her arms up, she seemed to be pushing James away as well. If he wanted to work, let him, she was fine, she was powerful, she had other things to do. Up and out, she pushed the feelings away. It was like an enchantment, an ancient ceremony, her struggles leaving her body.

So when the tangos stopped, with a final, "*Opa!*" from Normando, who had come outside to watch, Kezia was completely refreshed, as if she had been diving through clear sparkling water. Even the goat seemed more content as it returned her gaze.

When Darim came and bowed to her, raising his hand with a twirl, there was a feeling like space in her heart. "So, Señorita Don't Dance, I told you we'll see about Don't Dance," he said with satisfaction and he smiled knowingly as he walked past her and away.

"I was all over the place in my first couple of days," said Sue. "You picked it up really quickly. Must be your young brain. You should find a class to go to in England."

Kezia beamed. "Thanks, it was so nice to meet you. Maybe I'll see you again before we go?"

They hugged and Kezia took off her shoes, reluctantly. As she made her way back across the terrace, she heard shouting coming from the kitchen. "You found it? You can't just go putting things into food that you *find*. What next? Mushrooms from the meadow? Flies from the forest?"

"But—"

"No buts Papa. No. It's not safe. You know that. You can't just start cooking with any bit of leaf or berry you find lying around. Promise me you won't Papa. Promise me?"

Darim turned, noticing Kezia at the door.

"Erm, sorry, to, erm interrupt," Kezia said, as Pedro the parrot ruffled his wings and focused his alert eyes on her from his cage. "But I should go now, and I wanted to say thank you."

"Thank yourself," Darim said abruptly. "You gave flamenco to yourself. A gift. Thank yourself."

"Oh. Well, erm, thank you for having me anyway. Here are your shoes." She put them on the floor. "And it was nice to meet you, Mando."

Normando was standing with a bowl in one hand and a sprig of inky berries in the other, looking dejectedly down at the shiny round fruit. He didn't respond to Kezia.

"So, you are leaving?" Darim cocked his head. "You don't really want to go." His words were succulent, as full of meaning as the berries were full of juice. "You should stay, stay with me and enter the competition."

Kezia laughed. "I've got work on Monday."

"You hate your job"

"How do you know?"

"Most people hate their jobs. Why would you be different?"

"Erk. Work on Monday. Work on Monday," rasped Pedro, marching up and down on the spot, his wiry feet gripping the round wooden bar.

"You, Kezia, can stay here free, as long as you enter the competition. Not quite six weeks, I can teach you in that time." Darim looked pleased with himself. "I told you we need one more, we are only five, Magdalena won't dance, we need six or more for the groups. But do not tell the other girls. I am not supposed to have favourites." And he looked at her intently, the same eager stare as the parrot.

"Who's Magdalena?"

"My niece. Long red hair. Long story." Darim waved the girl's existence away.

"She doesn't—"

"No. She doesn't speak either, but everyone else more than makes up for that."

"Erk leaf or berry, leaf or berry," said the parrot.

"Thank you, but I can't dance in a competition. I've done four lessons, that's crazy."

"Be crazy for once." His smile was dazzling. "You have potential Kezia. I see it. I see *you*." He paused. "And I will give you extra lessons, just me and you."

The ghost of Gary shivered down her spine. *Still, there's a lot we can change about you, if we work together, and in time, I really do think you might have what it takes...*

"I can't..." she said, stepping backwards.

"You are afraid?" Darim's eyebrows cocked.

"Um…"

"Afraid you might be… happy?"

"It's not that…" Outside the goat made a soft snort, flapping its lips.

"I am not him," Darim said, as if reading her mind. "You can be happy here — and what if you go home? Will you be happy then? Stay. Stay and lose your stupid job, so what? You'll get another stupid job. Ha! No matter because flamenco will change your life. Guaranteed," he finished with clipped certainty.

"I… I have to go," said Kezia.

"You will be back," Darim decreed as she slipped quietly out of the door.

"You will be back," the parrot echoed.

Unsettled, Kezia sat by the pond to catch her feelings, gazing idly at the frogs' backs, oily in the sunlight. "I should go," she told them, their red eyes like beads.

They reminded her of the frog at the garden centre all that time ago. James had just moved to his flat and he wanted some flowers for the balcony. He wanted Kezia to choose them so it felt like her place as well as his. It was March, the first vestiges of spring infusing the air with soft hope. The sky was baby blue.

They'd stood, looking at the banks of plants for a long time, loosely holding hands. He'd been admiring the colours and the textures and she'd been bored, wondering if they could get pizza after. They usually got pizza on a Sunday.

"So, what flowers shall I get?" James had smiled enthusiastically, "You choose."

"I don't know. I don't know anything about plants."

"Don't your parents garden?"

"Oh yeah, Pat and Pat love it. They've got really green fingers. Didn't rub off on me though… maybe it's not genetic."

"Well, how about these?" James walked over to where a saggy brood of yellow flowers spilled out of green foliage. "It says *Alyssum Montanum*, ahh, Mountain Gold, let's get some."

"They look nice," Kezia said noncommittally as the wind stirred, the Mountain Gold gagging in the breeze.

James picked a pot and put it in their trolley. The flowers flopped against the metal sides.

"Right. What next? Shall we see if we can get some red flowers? You like red don't you, it's your favourite colour, isn't it?"

Kezia's favourite colour was green. She didn't say anything. She didn't want to disappoint him. They meandered down the path, taking in the shrubs and the cacti. Kezia thought she'd like to only get cacti, then they would all be green and wouldn't need much to keep them alive. She turned to James, about to tell him, when he said, "Oh wow, look." A frog with stupid eyes and a fat back sat next to a fake pond where a fountain squirted intermittently. "Look at him!"

Kezia looked at him. His back bulged, his eyes bulged, his tummy bulged. Webbed feet stuck out from under him like he'd been splatted against the rockery and his nostrils flared. He stared an inane challenge. She didn't like him.

"Let's get him to sit by the back door. He'd look great. You can name him." The eyes, round and uncompromising, gaped from the thick head. "What do you think? Ned, or Colin, would be my guesses." James started towards the frog.

"He looks a bit stupid," Kezia managed.

"Oh." James stopped in his tracks, and turned. "You don't like him?"

Kezia looked back, helpless.

"Kezzie, if you don't like him just say." James was level with the frog now and they were both looking at her as though she was on trial. Two pairs of silly eyes.

"Well..." The frog would not look away. "Well, I just think he's... he's a bit stupid that's all."

"Really?" James was genuinely baffled, but the frog looked even more cartoon-like, defying the need for explanation.

"Just look at him."

A four-year-old girl came by, pulling on the hand of her adult and pointing at the frog. She was laughing and the man chuckled too. "Frog," she said, staccato.

And he said, "Yes," and they moved along.

"They liked him," said James, defensive.

"They found him funny," said Kezia, and it was a stalemate. The fountain played percussion to their stand-off.

"Well," said James eventually. "Well, we won't get him then." He was beaten, but optimistic once again. "Come on, let's go and find those red flowers, shall we?"

It's just a frog, they had agreed in the end. But it didn't feel like it was just a frog.

The pond croaked with real life, bringing Kezia back to the present. She shook from her head the image of the fake frog, sunk on its haunches, leering, and focused instead on the slippery bodies in front of her, alive and pulsing with every heartbeat. She heard the clunking sound of Normando's keys on his belt as he came out of the side door. For just a moment she thought they were castanets, clacking out a rhythm. His head turned and a smile lit up his face slowly, like sunrise. "Carlotta!" his voice was hoarse and he raised an arm, as if in a dream.

"No. Mando, it's Kezia," she told him.

He peered at her as if examining the hallmark on a very delicate ring. "Yes," he agreed eventually and ambled over to her.

"I'm leaving," Kezia said, kicking her legs against the wall.

"People do, people do," agreed Normando, whilst also shaking his head. "I came to Parños for one week, for work, but when I met Carlotta I knew, I knew I was never going back." He sat down next to her. "That was it. I quit my job and started the bar and made my life here… and…" His eyes glazed, looking past the frogs into days gone by.

"How did you know?" asked Kezia, but Normando wasn't listening.

"She was a great dancer," he said instead. "A great, great dancer." Then he stood up again and brushed the crumbs off his apron, humming an old and unfamiliar tune. He went back into the house, lurching to his own melody, leaving Kezia to stare at the frogs contracting and croaking in the water.

126

20

Leaf

"Kezia?"

Kezia's dad walked up the path to the house.

"Kezia?" his voice was thin as he shouted, because he never shouted. He pulled at the neck of his polo shirt, resting his hands on the protuberance of his tummy. His grey socks were sweaty in his beige sandals, freckled with sandy mud. He peered around the side of the house but didn't see his daughter, so he went back to the imposing front door and pulled the handle on the doorbell, feeling like he was flushing a huge toilet.

The door swung open slowly.

Darim frowned and cocked his head to one side.

"*Hola.*" Pat was slightly out of breath, he wiped his hands across his belly and then put them by his sides. "I've come for Kezia. Thanks... thanks for having her. So kind." He shifted his gaze, finding a tissue in his shorts pocket and dabbing his pink forehead.

Keeping his eyes on Pat, Darim tilted his body towards the stairs and shouted, "Kezia?" It was only after the long 'a' at the end of her name that he turned towards the stairs, as if pulled by the sound. Satisfied, Darim pivoted part of the way back, but instead of looking at Pat, he stood at one hundred and eighty degrees, staring straight ahead. For a while they waited like this, only the acacia trees stirring.

"Kez?" Pat's voice sounded like a dry branch cracking.

Darim turned to him. "She was leaving. You must have missed her."

"Oh. But I didn't see—"

Pat stopped mid-sentence as Kezia came down the stairs, clapping her hands softly to herself. "Dad!"

"There you are Pet! Are you ready? Come on."

"Oh, Dad I—"

"And we must thank Mister, er... thank you."

127

Darim smiled and took an elaborate bow. Then he spun around to face Kezia, blocking her dad out of the way. "Kezia. Remember my offer. Remember the competition."

Pat strained his neck so he could see Kezia. "You've had your fun now Pet, come on, all good things come to an end, right?"

"Wrong," said Darim.

"Dad... wait, I've changed my mind. I want to stay. I want to learn to dance. I want to do the competition." Kezia was tugging her T-shirt in agitation.

"What?" Pat scratched behind his ear.

Kezia just nodded and Darim held his lips in a straight line, as if stifling a laugh.

"Kez. We're so happy you enjoyed it, we knew you would, but you can't stay forever, eh? Back to life and back to work in the end."

"This is work," said Darim, addressing only Kezia. "This is work on yourself. The most important work you will ever do. I trust you to make the right decision." And he bowed again and withdrew towards the kitchen. Rollo looked between Kezia and her dad, anxious eyes full of understanding, before retreating after his master.

Emboldened by Darim's departure, Pat stepped into the hallway. "Come on then, Kez, let's go, eh? No more of talk of competitions and the like," he laughed nervously.

"I want to stay longer, Dad. You wanted me to — you both did — you said it would do me good and... it is." She was a child again, imploring.

"But only for a bit, Love, just a couple of lessons and that. I know things haven't been easy for you back home, I get that, but running away is not the answer. Never is."

"Maybe it's my gap year?" Kezia grasped at the idea. "Couldn't we think of it as my gap year? I didn't take one, remember? Not like most of my friends who went to Uganda and Chile and Thailand. We decided it wasn't safe, remember? Well, this is safe. And..." Kezia stared obstinately at a bush just outside the door, the leaves curling up in supplication to the sunlight, "And... and... I want to."

"Kezia—" It was her dad's warning voice, the one she knew so well. "We gave you the money for one more lesson. Now you've had—"

"Four."

"Four. Exactly. You've already had more than enough. Come on, there are flamenco teachers in London, aren't there? So, I tell you what, we'll find you a class back home. How about that? *Olé!*" Pat twisted his arm up into the air, trying to make her smile and soften, trying to win her round. When she didn't say anything, he added quietly, "What's this all about, eh?" and reached out his hand. She didn't take it.

"It would be free, Dad, until the competition. That's what Darim said because they need me, they need one more to do it. So we wouldn't have to pay. And there's prize money, if we win."

"What's the point of winning a competition and losing your job?" He was shaking his head.

"I just… I'm not ready to go home." Gary. James. All of it, but the words wouldn't come. She looked helplessly at a broken spider's web trailing on the plant.

"We know you're upset about James and everything, but I'm telling you, you can't run away, Pet."

"I'm not—"

"You can't *dance* away then." Pat smiled hopefully but still couldn't shift the mood. "I can't force you Kez, but think of your mum, she'll be so upset."

"I've told you, she encouraged me. She likes Darim, she wanted me to."

"Well, we both say it's enough now. I can hardly just leave you here, can I?"

"Dad, yes you can: go. I'll be fine. Look, it's fine." She motioned to the big staircase, the fraying rug, the statue of Our Lady. "I'll… I'll ring up and move my flight, it won't cost much. Please."

Pat winced like he was in physical pain. "I can't… I guess I can't make you…" From the other side of the house, the goat bleat plaintively. "How long?"

"Just over five weeks. Just until the competition. I'll tell work I'll use up the rest of my leave and you can buy extra days too. It'll be… fine," she said, knowing it wouldn't, but she could see him melting now, she was getting her way.

Pat took his wallet from his shorts pocket and looked inside. He pulled out all the euro notes he had. "Take these," he said. "And don't tell your mother." He shook his head, bewildered.

"Oh, thanks Dad, thank you." And she hugged him, aware as she always was that she was taller than him now.

"I'll see you, Kez. Let me know when you've changed your flights and we'll pick you up from the airport, okay?"

She nodded.

Confused and still shaking his head, Pat started to walk down the path.

She watched him, her heart hurting to see her dad sad — and suddenly sorry, in a rush of regret and guilt for getting her own way — Kezia was about to run after him, to admit she was wrong... but Darim sighed ostentatiously from behind her and said, "It is a hard life. We hurt the ones we love the most. Well done, Kezarina. You have passed the first test of flamenco. Spirit. You have shown you have got what it takes."

Pat's bald head was disappearing.

She didn't feel like she had passed. She felt hollow, uncertain now and slightly shaky.

Darim looked at her contentedly. She could smell him: leather and lime and the wood of his guitar. "The tempests of change blow cold but nonetheless enticing. Come." He led her back to the garden, as she was still wondering whether to go after her dad.

"Now, you dance for me. Simply do what you can remember, what I taught you. Make up the rest." He began to play and the music illuminated the air.

Kezia just looked at him.

"You dance, Kezarina!" he said and focused down at his strings as if to give her space. Kezia waited, and then, because she had been told to, hesitantly, she stepped in-between the notes and over her emotions, stumbling and then finding her feet again, each cadence a release she couldn't understand.

She was glad Darim wasn't looking but she felt the eyes of his essence all the same; he was with her like the wind, which is faceless, which you can't see or seize or stop — he was all around her. She hoped he couldn't sense her mistakes in the same way, but if he could he didn't seem to care.

When they finished, she felt calm and graceful, like a butterfly newly emerged. Darim lifted his head and the sun was golden on the hills and reflected in his eyes like a tacit promise. She smiled, letting her dimples show, and sat next to him on the low garden wall. Everything was still and smelt of roses.

They stayed like that for a while, until Sami came, demanding Darim's attention. "When is it time for my private singing lesson?" he asked, giving Kezia a sideways look.

"Tomorrow," said Darim passively. "At the bar."

One of the cats, a scrawny mass of haunches and claws tiptoed over to Sami and started winding itself around his legs. He leant down and stroked its forehead with one finger. Feeling anointed, the cat closed its eyes. "Darim is my teacher." Sami looked pointedly up at Kezia.

"Yes Sami," said Darim. "I am everybody's teacher." But the way he turned to Kezia then made her feel as if she was the only one in the world.

Sami hadn't seen, he was looking back at the cat, but when it slunk away, he joined them on the wall.

"*Palmas*," proclaimed Darim, and they began, slowly at first, feeling their way into the rhythms, making music with their hands. As before, the other girls appeared, joining in, until the staccato sounds echoed all over the terrace.

The way they fell reminded Kezia of her feelings, always jumping and never stopping still. She clapped and clapped until there were no conscious thoughts in her head any more. She clapped and clapped until it was all clapping and cadence and only the occasional awareness of the colour of the sky or the shaking of a leaf.

21

Smoke

The sun was ripe in the late afternoon: ochre and warm. The sweat dried with the ebbing day and the breeze came off the sea, whispering salty stories.

Rosa, Carmen and Abril went home, promising to be back early in the morning. "The competition!" Carmen exclaimed, smiling broadly, and nothing more needed to be said.

In the evening evanescence, the day slipping out of sight, they sat around the big table in the garden eating seafood paella with fresh salad and warm home-made bread. Normando shuffled in and out bringing serviettes and pepper and watered-down wine. Magdalena sat silently observing and Rollo was begging for scraps.

"Everything tastes so much better here," remarked Kezia, looking at her plate. "Food tastes so much better, and—"

"You were sick," Darim interrupted. "You did not know it but you were sick."

"Well, I suppose I used to survive on cereal bars and pot noodles… And now it's—"

"Real and urgent. Like flamenco. Like everything now. Now that you live." Darim nodded. He ate very little himself, preferring to nibble on small pieces of toasted bread and tapenade throughout the day. He drank sweet sherry and said it was enough; the music sustained him. "Next you will find *duende*. That is why you came."

"What… what is *duende*?" Kezia tried to pronounce it like he did, the 'd's important and the vowels undulating.

"Connection. Spirit. Truth. It is all that you are and all that there is — and you need to find it from within. Flamenco unlocks the door. It is the key, to *duende* and to freedom."

Sensing Kezia's perplexity, Java said, "I know. It's mad. But Kezia, it's like you've got a star inside you. You feel light and fizzy and as if you can do anything."

"You come alive," added Sue, with a smudge of oil on her chin. "It's a spark, yeah, you are white-hot in that moment. Radiant." She sat up straight. "You suddenly belong exactly where you are and you feel like you are part of everything that is. It's… it's the best feeling."

"You will find it." Darim stood up.

"Well, I already feel like I can be myself here. That's a good start." Kezia leaned back, as if to prove she was relaxed. "I'm not trying or pretending."

"Who gives you that permission?" Darim remained very still but his eyes effervesced.

"You do, I guess. You all do."

"Try again."

"Well, it's the magic of the place then, something about living by the sea, being outside all the time."

Darim laughed. "No. Try again. These are the things that change on the outside but you are the only one that can change on the inside. You. You are the one who gives yourself permission to be yourself. Only you. How can it be any other way?"

Kezia tried to think of an answer but he simply said, "Rollo, come," and went to feed the animals, the dog dragging himself away from Sue's chair, where he had been sure he was going to get a forkful of food.

"I'm so happy you stayed." Java turned to Kezia with her mouth full. "I'm so excited about the competition." She swallowed and grinned.

Kezia stirred the paella on her plate, it was satisfyingly soft. They told her about the competition, buoyant with the challenge of it, interrupted only when Normando dropped something in the kitchen and the clatter was followed by a throaty swear word. They laughed and the lanterns cast a mystical glow as the sea rolled up the evening and sighed it into night.

Sue and Java went to bed, but Kezia just sat and let the lilt of the ocean into her bones. She imagined the waves, lifting up to swallow themselves, separate, and then become part of the whole. The sea seemed to understand; she wasn't ready to go back, to her job, to James or to

Gary. She needed to be here; she needed the water to plunge its sound into the spaces where she kept the pain.

The jingle of Rollo's bell heralded Darim's return. "Not sleeping?"

"No, I'm just enjoying sitting here, listening to the sea. It's so calming."

Darim sat by her and they listened. After a while, he said, in a low voice, "I've always loved the sea and I find its presence necessary. The waves. I couldn't live without the constant rhythm of them." She watched the smooth outline of his face in the lamplight, the contours of his honesty as he told her: "I never had a constant, growing up. Never a constant school. Never a constant friend. Not even a constant papa, until Mando came along. Mama — Carlotta — she was always on tour and she took me with her. We moved around, until her hips started to give out, but we always came back here." His voice was quiet and cool, like the wind stirring in the trees.

"Didn't you want to be famous too? That's what Java and Sue say, you could have toured and had that life as well."

He smiled at her. "Always the questions, Kezarina, you get right to the heart of things." His shoulders relaxed. "Well, Mama put a guitar in my hands when I was nine months old. She had big dreams for me. But I saw too much of that world. I grew up in a showbiz den of fake flattery and backstabbing. I did not want that to be my life. What for? Money? Pah! We used to fight over it but I did not want that; it was her dream."

Kezia exhaled. "Yes. Yes, I work in sales and it's all so fake too, people say anything to seal a deal. It's part of the reason I don't want to go back, I don't want to become that. I don't want it to drip into me, if you know what I mean?"

"I do. I really do." His eyes met hers, and there was an underwater feeling, light reflecting somewhere inside her. "That's what I like about you, Kezia," he said, tilting his head to the side as he mused. "You are pure. I didn't see that much growing up. When you dance that really shows through, and that's what flamenco should be: raw, not calculated for adulation and praise. From the heart." He clenched his fist and brought it to his chest as if he might sing.

"From the heart," Kezia repeated, looking out into the shadowy garden.

Darim turned to her. "You know what I wanted to be when I was little? A pirate. I always loved pirates. I used to look out for them when

I was very small. I made myself a telescope from a cardboard tube and I looked and I looked; I wanted to run down to the shore and join a ship. I suppose I thought it would be a family." He blinked, thoughtful. "It's funny how things turn out."

"That's very sweet," said Kezia.

Darim shrugged. "I just think I wanted to run away because I was bullied at school. The kids decided I was different and that was a reason to hate me. Mama being famous — they did not like that either. They mocked my music, they mocked my dancing, they mocked the things that gave me joy. It took me a long time to see past that, to own my difference, to be who I am regardless. I suppose that's why I'm so passionate about other people doing the same, I know how it hurts if you don't."

Kezia breathed in deeply. "I... I do know how that feels," she confided. "I was bullied at school as well. Not at primary school, but when I got to secondary school. I went to a different one to all of my friends and it was hard. I wanted to learn and ask questions and that's not very cool apparently." She bit her lip in case she'd given too much away.

"No." He put his hand on her arm, a very soft pressure. "No, they try to crush your spirit because they can see it is strong. They are threatened by your light. I understand it, and it stays with you, it makes you unsure. Well, not any more Kezarina, here we want you to shine that light."

Kezia felt something shift inside her, a minute modulation, impossible to measure. He took up his guitar and began to play, softly strumming the strings. "I think it does not matter what you are, as long as you are free. Freedom is the only way to make your spirit soar, and we weigh ourselves down in a thousand different ways." His voice was dainty, like the lissom legs of a crab scuttling across the sand. "To find freedom you need to be healed from the past, trust the future and live completely in the moment." The guitar picked out the notes as his eyes picked out the stars. "*Olé*," he said reverently.

Kezia listened, trying to take it all in. "What does it mean, *olé*?" she asked.

"Ahh. It depends who you believe. What you want to believe. Some say it means 'God', from the Arabic; 'Allah', and others say it's from the Hebrew word, 'Oleh', which means 'to throw up in the air'." His eyebrows elevated with the meaning. "There is another story too, that it's from the Bible, that when Jacob was supposed to be marrying Rachel, he lifted his bride's veil to find it was Leah under there — and that's how the crowd tried to warn him by saying, 'Oh Leah'." His eyes arched to meet hers. "This I do not believe." He shook his head as if he had disclosed too much.

Kezia watched his fingers curl over the guitar and was thoughtful for a while, then she looked at him and said, "I've been meaning to ask you, why doesn't Magdalena speak?"

"Oh. You want to know? Only she knows the mysteries of her own mind, of course." He reverted to a sad refrain, minor chords, suggestive of sorrow. "But her mama left her papa for her flamenco partner. A younger man. Her papa considered this a matter of honour and he killed himself." Darim bowed his head towards his guitar. "A mortal sin." He looked up. "Magdalena blames her mama, blames flamenco, refuses to talk, refuses to dance. But she has always loved Mando, so she came here. She will not see her mama. She will not go back home."

A cat streaked across the lawn, running for a reason only it would ever know. "Oh no, poor thing, and she's so young."

"Yes. She is not yet seventeen. So you see. We look after her as best we can. She will not be helped and she will not speak and she will not see her mama. Being obstinate runs in our family it would seem." His lips curled but it wasn't a smile.

"Has she ever spoken to you about it?"

"Enough questions now my Kezarina, now you need to sleep," he said, still playing his mournful lament, and when she hesitated, he whispered, "Go."

She went upstairs, and after his confidences, it felt suddenly personal, being in Darim's childhood room. Kezia imagined him as a pirate, black belt glinting below an elaborate white shirt, and the image stayed with her as she fell asleep, drifting away in a ship of her own. Outside, Darim kept up a gentle refrain, scanning, scanning, scanning the horizon.

**

It was the middle of the night when Kezia smelt burning.

The moon was high and the night had the world to itself. A black smell woke her up.

For a moment, she wondered where she was, but like a child's magic picture book where the colours come with a sweep of water, she remembered the evening of *palmas* with the strawberry blush of the setting sun and the goat chewing happy consternation.

Burning.

She sat up and sniffed. It was definitely burning. Even so, the house was quiet.

Curious, Kezia wobbled out of bed, still steeped in the haze of sleep. She slid slightly on the rug and had to catch her balance on the chest of drawers. The burning smell got stronger.

She put on her shoes and trod carefully across the wooden floor in the dark, but as she got to the door and turned the handle, it would not open. She turned and she pushed and she turned and she pushed but it would not move.

She was locked in.

Trapped.

22

Ladybird

ℛachel walked slowly through Soho. Lights, buses, faces, figures flashed from a simmering soup of purpose and pleasure: everything moving, there and then gone. She tried not to hurry and the streets seemed to speed up around her, cars veering unnervingly past, e-scooters whipping round corners and people plugged into headphones blurring with their own internal sound. The razzmatazz rattled her; she folded her arms across her chest as if to shut it out. Rachel used to like the noise and the pressure of the capital, she could get lost in it, give up her soul to the chaos, but now… She thought about going home, but something was calling her, calling her on.

Great Newport Street was a jumble of dark brick and neon flare. A man strolled by wearing ankle length trousers and a thick fabric hat; he affected a staged boredom, his eyes unfocused as he passed. She checked the address again and looked for the numbers on the buildings. A woman fell laughing out of a restaurant, catching herself on a lamp post and swinging around. Her friends followed, tripping in circles like baby ducks.

Then she saw the heart — a red heart outside the door — decorated with white swirls and declaring: 'Bar de Tapas y Fiesta'. Rachel hesitated and somewhere a siren bled noise into the night. She hadn't found anyone to go with (Andrea had parents' evening), so she had decided to go on her own… it felt strange, but she was here now, she might as well go in.

The darkness inside swelled like relief, a chasm to wear like a cloak, but the floor was sticky and it made the shadows feel tacky too. Everything dirty. There were men laughing in corners she couldn't see. The music cascaded over everyone, fast and frenetic: Spanish pop running with an energetic drum and a trumpet creating squiggles over the top like a child with a bright felt-tip pen. A gaggle of stooped ladies in sequinned tops stood by the bar, impervious as a painfully enthusiastic saxophone joined the fray.

"Excuse me? Is there flamenco tonight?" Rachel leaned towards the bartender, a wiry woman in a black vest-top who kept her eyes firmly on the two beers she was pouring at precisely the same time.

"What?" she screamed.

"Do you have flamenco on tonight?" Some of the sparkly ladies looked over and Rachel felt self-conscious, and drab.

"Yeah. Seven thirty." The bartender looked up briefly then grabbed the beers which slopped white froth over their sides as she handed them to a man in a red checked shirt.

It was seven sixteen. Rachel looked around for somewhere to sit, but all the chairs were taken by glossy people who looked comfortable in their bodies: talking, laughing, holding hands. She ordered a margarita and stood at the back, trying to seep into the sides of the room, bearing the weight of being on her own and fidgeting with a menu she'd picked up from the bar. The tapas spoke of sharing so in the end she folded it and left it on the side. Rachel let the drink distort the pain the way it did — sliding the puzzle pieces around into a different and better configuration, displaced but not forgotten.

She'd just finished texting Joe when a bald man in a light blue T-shirt caught her eye and looked at her for a second too long. She'd forgotten what that felt like. She scurried to the ladies and stood in front of the mirror where she could see the endurance on her face, the careworn lines tracking her torment. The cranberry lipstick was too harsh but she put more on anyway. The mascara had clumped her lashes into irregular shards, like thorns, and they disgorged a kind of ash onto her face; she wiped it from the puff-pillows under her eyes and the concealer came off too, showing the grey of her skin underneath.

When Rachel got back to her space by the wall, the man in the blue T-shirt had gone. In his place, a couple kissing passionately, leaning out of their chairs and smoothing hands over thighs. She thought about leaving, but then, the low thump of brash pop stopped abruptly and a light sprinkle of guitar washed across the room.

A woman in a blousy polka dot shirt — red and black like a ladybird — and a skirt with a volcano of frills, came to a space between the tables and looked around. Rachel expected the crowds to hush. They didn't. They carried on talking with mouths full of stringy tortilla and mushy meatballs, shouting each other's names with spiky insistence. Only the tables nearest turned to acknowledge the woman. She shuffled, the music became louder, and she stood up straight. As Rachel watched, suddenly her hand went up and her chin turned to the side. She embodied the air of a clenched fist: defiant. Then, slowly she began, turning and swooping like she was diving into the dance. She stayed insular and in control, she was oblivious to the drunks in the front row, she occupied her own space and she was in the dance completely: it had taken her over.

Every move seemed to tell Rachel something she needed to know, something she had forgotten. There was no sense of apology, instead there was a wholeness about the woman dancing. She was in command and the feeling cracked like fire and flared like memory.

When Rachel had first met Andy, she had been strong like that. It had been on her terms and he had come to her, he had chased and she only needed to be who she was; it was enough. With every stamp she thought how that had eroded. Somewhere along the way, in news and nappies and Network Rail, she had lost herself and he had noticed and he had gone. "Stop blaming yourself," Andrea had said. "A decent guy sticks around through thick and thin and sleepless nights and whatever. He doesn't get out as soon as life gets busy and you're both tired. That's part of it. They are the bits you are supposed to help each other through."

"But would he have stayed if I was stronger?"

"Stronger? You do all that you do and you're in pain most of the time."

A man tried to talk to Rachel in a voice like sludge and it jarred too much to even look at him. "Sorry, I'm just watching…" she said and felt the pressure change as he moved away.

The woman arched her neck and Rachel felt that power swell in herself too.

There was one holiday… they'd been to Spain, Barcelona, the sun and the smiles flowing with the sangria. It was right at the start. She'd wanted to see some flamenco but Andy had said no, it was boring, so they'd been to the bullfight instead, and she had glazed over her repulsion as the beast snorted out its distress, because the love was strong enough to blank it all out; it was then. She just wanted to see him happy. *Finally,*

I'm seeing flamenco, Rachel thought with grim satisfaction and was sad when it ended in a burst of brio and a torrent of taps.

She left quickly, as if running after a past self. There was something rekindled in her now — a passion from the past — something that told her she could do it. She had seen it in the woman and she felt it inside now too. She remembered when chasing a story had burned like that, when journalism was fresh and exciting, overflowing with potential and power. Each story, a dance of its own. *I will get my scoop,* she told herself. *It's not all press releases and antique palaces, not any more. I'll get noticed by the national press when I tell the world a story they have not heard before, front-page news that'll get everybody talking.* The thoughts energised her and she walked quicker now, back to a Leicester Square fizzing with bright lights and dull people. Her body felt as fluid as the notes which still reverberated in her head, changing the way she moved, changing the way London looked; it was a strange and far-off feeling and it was the closest to happy Rachel had been for a very long time.

23

Croquettes

Kezia turned the handle backwards and forwards and backwards and forwards, worried she would screw it off. She shoved the door with her shoulder. She kicked it with her foot. Then she heard the slap of a door closing somewhere below and ran to the window. Outside, there was only Rollo, sniffing the base of the ivy.

"Rollo?"

Rollo looked up, eyes shining in the moonlight.

"Rollo. *Llave!*" Kezia pronounced the word carefully, trying to sound like Darim.

Rollo kept looking at her, keen but unsure.

"Rollo. *Llave!*" The dog's front two feet went up in a little skit, but he didn't move off, just stayed gazing at her, panting slightly.

The burning smelt even stronger now and seemed to be coming from the kitchen. "Rollo. *Llave!*" She shouted this time and Rollo galloped away, but she couldn't tell if he'd gone because he'd finally understood or because he didn't like being shouted at.

Peering down at the thick trunk of the ivy, Kezia considered climbing, but the paving slabs looked so hard and smooth and far away. Her stomach tingled aversion, her legs felt weak. She glanced back at the door, panicking now, and rushed to pull on the handle again, then back to the window, where the smoke was in the air…

And there was Darim. On the terrace. Calm and looking up at her. "Kezia. What are you doing? Why are you shouting?"

"Oh, thank God. Can't you smell smoke? I can't open my door. I think it might be coming from the kitchen."

Darim sniffed, then spun around and darted towards the nearby door, and as he opened it, black fumes fanned out into the garden. Pedro the parrot made a noise like the garden gate.

A moment later, Darim returned with Normando, who was bent over with eyes wide, finding it hard to breathe. "Don't panic. It's fine now. Come. Sit." Normando was shaking as Darim sat him on the bench and steadied him with a hand on his shoulder. "Breathe Papa. That's it. Nice big breaths. Good." Normando visibly relaxed and smiled weakly up at his stepson.

After a mumbled conversation in Spanish, Darim pivoted back to Kezia. "It's fine, thank you. He put some croquettes in the oven and forgot about them, he fell asleep. Ham and cheese," he added, as if it mattered.

"Croquettes? It's two in the morning."

"Yes, well, time does not dictate appetite does it, Papa?" Darim stroked his papa's back protectively. "Go back to bed Kezia. It's fine."

"I'm locked in."

"You can't be. The door is old. It must be stiff. You have to push."

"I did." Doubting herself, Kezia went back to the door. It wouldn't open.

When she returned to the window, Darim had gone and Normando was on his own looking dazed and coughing occasionally. Then she heard the key in the lock and Darim was there, shaking his head. "It's Papa," he said sadly. "He doesn't know what he is doing." He turned and went back downstairs and Kezia followed to see if Normando was all right.

The old man was sitting with his mouth open.

"You locked Kezia in Papa. Locked in! *Estás como una cabra! Una cabra!*" Esmeralda the '*cabra*' looked up suddenly, as if to refute the accusation. "You locked Kezia in. Do you understand?" Darim said loudly.

"No." Normando rubbed his head, looking back at the goat.

"No, you don't understand? Or no you didn't lock her in?" Darim tilted his head forward.

"I did not lock her in. Of course I did not lock her in. I don't understand what you are talking about. Is this a joke?" A half smile lapsed across his face, hopeful.

"It is not a joke, Papa,"

The smile melted away.

"You shouldn't even have keys any more. I told you to leave them on the hook. Hand them over. You've probably lost them now, haven't you?"

"I haven't. They're just… Oh…" The old man fumbled at his belt. Nothing. He looked even more confused.

Darim sighed ostentatiously. "No more of this Papa. Please."

"But—" Esmerelda let out a little bleat and Normando fidgeted with his hands on his lap.

"No more," said Darim.

"Erk. Belladonna, belladonna." In the kitchen, Pedro the parrot dipped his head and body down and up and down and up as he chattered.

Normando gazed blankly ahead.

"Bedtime now, eh?" Darim pulled him up by the arm. "And for you too Kezia. Off you go. Tomorrow, we dance."

Kezia nodded. "Goodnight." But just before she turned to go, she noticed a single tear roll down Normando's cheek, following the etched line of sadness past.

24

Tapestry

𝔖he sun was white in the mornings. The sea was light blue. It stretched out, like the day ahead, and time was soft, with no hard edges. According to the clock, it was always ten past nine, the hands stuck in a perpetual arabesque. They took the lessons when Darim was ready. They ate when the food came. There was always enough time. More time, than before, in London, when Kezia had counted the minutes and counted the hours. She had lived in a grid of appointments, moving from marker to marker, always trying to get to the next one. Now, all the lines were rubbed out and there was nothing to aim for, but instead of taking her out of time, it put her back in time. Back into the moment. Tick-tock. Nothing stopped and nothing started because it was always now. The clock was not in charge, she was. Before, the hours were absolute and she rushed to meet them. Here, time came to Kezia and she was getting used to it. She fell into nature for the flow of the day. She learnt to read what the sun and tides were telling her, learnt to let each moment lead to the next.

Two weeks passed. She thought about James and her old life and it was the feeling of seeing a reflection in the water — the familiar made unfamiliar. She didn't recognise the memories any more, they seemed far off, distant and faded. Too predictable and safe. With Darim you never knew what was going to happen next. He lived with a sharp intensity which saturated the seconds and erased the need for clocks.

One day, he came to her and asked, did she feel it yet?

"I don't… I still don't know what I'm supposed to feel."

"Then no. You don't."

An orange flower, livid petals scrunched around its stem, was rocking in the breeze. She stared and it blurred into a hand, beckoning. "I'm trying."

"No! You don't try *duende*. You *feel duende*. You know nothing yet. You have not touched the grief of ecstasy."

"Grief?"

"You will know when you feel it. Because as you feel it, you know that it is going to end. Grief."

A pang of jealousy was metallic in her mouth but she did not know what she was jealous for. The flower swirled. "What if I never feel it, never find it?"

"Then you don't," said Darim and started playing melancholic chords on his guitar.

"Can't you teach me?"

"Teach? No. I can teach the steps and the mood but I cannot teach *duende*. You are the only one who has access to your own soul. You need time. That is all. You need more time."

"And the other girls... Carmen, Rosa, Abril, do they... have they found it?"

"You do not compare. You do not give your power away like that. It is only you, as far as the cosmos is concerned, only you."

She wanted to ask him more but he leaned into his guitar and the moment was over. The fine grains of his stubble caught the light and glowed gold. His mouth folded down in a studious bow and his synergy with the sound was so strong that Kezia wasn't sure whether his hands were creating the music or the music was moving his hands. He was wrapped in the rhythm, sometimes licking his lips as if he could taste it.

Maybe he could. Everything was so visceral here, so alive. Kezia was aware of her senses in a way she had never been before, and because of the dancing, she was always hungry; so the simplest of foods — an olive, a tomato — was insanely piquant. She would shut her eyes, to savour the flavour. The world was increasingly vivid and — equally because of the dancing — her body was changing: she liked the way her waist felt as she pulled the skirts around it. She was stronger. Supple. Powerful.

As well as the skirts she was given three dresses and she liked the red one the best. The red dress with the wrap-around tie and material down to the floor. It was silky and she could pull the ribbon in tight. The dress said things she couldn't. Darim liked her in the red one too, she

146

could tell by the way his eyes followed the shape of her in it, and she stood in his gaze like a fine drizzle.

But she couldn't just look the part. So she practised alone in her room. She moved the mat away to dance in her bare feet and she liked the way the floor wasn't smooth; the planks were gnarly and bumpy and real. Every day she practised the exercises, stretching each of her fingers to the base of her palm in turn, flicking her wrist, and starting again. Her arms throbbed from the hours they spent in the air, her shoulders heavy. *One two three, one two three, one...* It became addictive, a way of not thinking about her life. If there was dancing, it kept her thoughts at bay.

But at night, the dreams came. Clenched dreams. She ached, and she couldn't tell where. The feelings haunted her sleep... Like the feeling of helplessness when Gary pressed up against her. His lips had smudged her cheek and then he had kissed her, heavy on the mouth. She'd gasped. "There's more where that came from," he had said, his voice a growl. "And I look forward to more with you, Kezia. It's going to be fun."

Kezia had just stood in front of him, his hands on her hips, stroking with two of his fingers, gripping with the rest.

"It's going to be fun," he said again. "And remember, our secret, okay? If you do get promoted, you don't want the others thinking this was more than... a little bit of extra coaching."

Kezia had put on a smile. It was a holding position until she worked out what to do. Inside, she was panicking. She tried not to show it.

"Trust me and you could go far," he'd said to her and kissed her again, heavy and hard.

The next day in the office she went through the motions with her eyes down. He walked past her desk often and on purpose, she smelt his polish smell and noticed his hands. Big wandering hands.

The other girls swooned over him and flirted and Gary looked at her and rolled his eyes behind their backs. She had a feeling she'd already played it too far, that she couldn't go back, even though it was a game she didn't want to play.

There were dreams of James too. Dreams that didn't know she was here. He was taller than in real life and happier. He wore his favourite grey jumper and jeans and he kissed her on the forehead. She felt disorientated by the dreams. She rolled over, and out of bed, trying to create a new rhythm for the day. She moved gently, warming up, light movements to brush the dreams away like spider webs.

The only man she wanted to think about was Darim. The way his top lip curled, the way he moved, entranced by the music, the muscles in his arms when he rolled up his sleeves. He was like a tapestry to Kezia; she wanted to be the one to unpick him, his rich thoughts and layered feelings, his textured temperament.

He used to go off on his own sometimes. He'd stare out to sea. He said he liked the cool feeling of the spray on his face, his eyes squinting against the sun. He said he missed his mama and he would talk to her in his head. The sea became the sweep of the taffeta — the dresses — rustling as she went, like audible perfume, scenting his memories with sound.

Other times he got into dark, dark moods. Nothing could touch him then. He would strum searing, painful melodies on his guitar, and Normando would nod and adjust his blue and grey flat cap and say, "Leave him be. Best leave him. He'll come out of it when he's ready. Just wait. You'll see."

And he did. He would come bounding back, clapping his hands and telling them to get up and start practising for there wasn't long until the competition, and they'd get to their feet hesitantly and only relax when they were banging out the beats or the *'compas'* and it was clear the mood had shifted. He seemed to clap his way out of it, hands moving so fast they blurred — clapping and clapping and moving the feelings out of his body, out through his hands.

After dinner, when the evenings stretched out long and hot, she waited for him, curling her legs up to her chest, gazing into the garden, and waiting. Sue and Java chatted on and on and she added the occasional comment, but as soon as he came, she went over, to sit on the wall by his side as he fondled his guitar.

Once, she'd asked him if he could teach her Spanish. He laughed. "You are learning Spanish," he said. "All the time. It will come." And it did. Slowly, she started inserting Spanish words, like bricks, into the walls of her sentences, clumsily, but they fit. Gradually, her patterns of speech and grammar shifted, in tropism to the Spanish sun.

"You learn flamenco and everything else is already learnt." Darim clicked his heels. "I will give you extra dancing instead."

So the next day the door opened and he was there in faded beige corduroy trousers and a pale blue shirt. "Time for your special lesson today, Kezia," he said. "I want to see you sweat. You will feel it with every pulse in your body. We will go from the top."

Kezia put her hands in the air and felt a very subtle temperature change.

"No. Like this." He arched his back, his arms at right angles, framing his body. "Turn your face towards me, that's right. Up a bit. Now, don't smile. Fume. Silently. Steadily. I am your husband and I have left my smelly socks on the floor again, and the toilet seat is up and I'm at the bar when I've promised to help with dinner... Good, and raise your eyebrows, even better. You're suspicious of the world, but you know you need it too. Next turn your arms, backwards, and to the side, yes and down. Okay. *Uno, dos, tres, cuatro...* you dance." Darim conjured the counts and she marked them with her feet. Her hands were roaming above her head, and sweating. She hadn't known hands could sweat, but she was learning.

"Stop." His eyes found hers with an insistent ardour. "Not like that." He took her arm tenderly and moved it down, like an artist painting with her body and then he tilted her waist into place to show the movement she had to give. "Like that. Now, do it again."

She faltered, then took up the steps again. "Yes, that's it. Feel it. Live it. Breathe it." Darim was clapping out the rhythm. "Passion, Kezia. You must have passion."

Exhilarated, Kezia stamped down harder and he danced alongside her now, talking in her ear. "*Y, uno, dos, tres, cuatro...* Years of torment and worry, let it out. Stamp it out. Hear the beat, cleave to it. It is your saviour. It will set you free. You want to be free, don't you?" He was moving faster and faster. "*Uno, dos, tres...* come on Kezia. *Uno, dos.* No, not like that." He showed her again, his movements those of someone who has danced from the time of learning to walk. She was hot and the turns baffled her, but they repeated them time and time again until they were deep in her muscles and sinews.

"I can't," she said breathlessly after a while. "I can't." She looked down to where there was the stain of a knot in the floorboards. "What if I will never be good at this?"

Darim stared directly at her. "Ahh life. Why are you so cruel? Why do you play such a cat and mouse game with our destinies?" He tipped his head to the side and added, "What if you are already good at this?" He let the sediment of the statement settle.

"I... I can't be. Shouldn't I leave it to the people who are really good? I look at people like Rosa, and I think, wow, I'll never dance like her, so what's the point? It's embarrassing. Really."

"But do you want to dance?"

"Yes."

"Then you would deny yourself just because you think someone else is doing it better? Maybe you're learning faster than her, learning more than her, because she grew up with it. It's like breathing to her, so sometimes she doesn't feel it. I know. I know when someone is just going through the motions. I know when someone is present. Anyway, even if she is the best and goes on to win a million trophies, on a day like today, when there's nothing to be won, it's just dancing. You do it or you don't. You gain from it or you don't. It's the same, for you and for her, and you will both get out of it what you put in. So forget good or bad, it just *is.*" He pressed his lips together, then said, "I tell you again because you have to learn this: you will never dance well if you care what anyone thinks. Art cringes under scrutiny. It flourishes set free. You have to set yourself free." She remembered what he'd said, that night on the terrace under the stars... *To find freedom you need to be healed from the past, trust the future and live completely in the moment.*

He stood back, as if watching the memory flicker through her. "You think I care what people think? Do you know what they think? They think I blame the mayor for Mama's death. I do not." He steadied himself on the chest of drawers. "I do not. I only wish..."

Kezia bit her lip as he stopped, narrowing his eyes against the sun streaming through the window.

"She had a rare gift, you know," he said eventually. "Mama had a great passion for her art... but she suffered for it too because the soul does not care about fame, only the head. And you will never make the head happy, too many thoughts." He shook his own head, as if to prove it. Then he took Kezia's hand very gently. "She will never be forgotten,

150

she was the people's flamenca and ever will she be. Now, with sweet sorrow and living hope, shall we dance?"

So they danced again and she saw the emotions contorted and controlled in the shape of his body: the way he turned, gradually, and swivelled at the waist, transmuting the pain into power.

25

Strawberries

"You're sad." James' sister carved the words slowly with her hands, letting the signs stain the air. The rain rubbed its nose on the window, sliding sluggishly down the glass. Thick rain. It had been raining all day, clouds like cobwebs casting shadows. Hannah got up and put the light on. It wasn't dark yet but her small flat seemed drab even with the curtains drawn back as far as they would go.

James shrugged and prodded a potato on his plate. It slid ungratefully away from him, gliding in gravy.

"What is it?" his sister insisted, reaching over and lifting his chin with one finger to force him to look at what she was saying. "There's something you're not telling me."

James shook his head vaguely, pulling back.

"I made you gravy especially and you still haven't smiled. You haven't even said hello to Lucas."

"Oh, where is he?"

Hannah pointed. By the sofa, a sleek brown hare flumphed along next to the wall, ears like two giant leaves, haunches round and velvet.

James turned towards him. "Hey Mister…" Lucas inclined his head, nose twitching, one leg quivering, before hopping over to be stroked and closing his eyes in satisfaction.

Hannah watched and the rain crushed all other sounds outside. After a while, she said, "James, most people can't sign, which means I've had to get by reading body language most of my life. Are you going to tell me what's the matter or am I going to have to pin you down and tickle you like when we were kids?" Hannah had a pronounced nose and empathic eyes like James, but her face was rounder, her cheeks softer. Her long hair, the same mahogany brown, was tied in a loose ponytail, stray strands decorating her face. "Is it the palace? Are you working too hard again? Do I need to tell you to chill out?"

James rubbed the back of his neck, still stroking Lucas, then he pulled himself up to the table.

"Is it like your thesis?" Hannah persisted. "When you wouldn't stop working, even on Christmas Day so we had to tie you to a chair to make you play charades?"

"That's not true!"

"You don't remember? 'I'm just going to do half an hour', I think that's what you said. And we said, 'No, it's Christmas Day, you're going to play with us', and annoyingly, you were better than me, and I sign for a living." She raised her eyebrows and tilted her head in a classic Hannah pose.

James let his shoulders sag. "Okay, okay, but no, it's not work this time. It's Kezia." He heard the deliberate thump of Lucas moving away.

Hannah sat patiently.

James picked up his knife and fork but made no move to eat. Then he put them down. "She's in Spain, learning..." He wasn't sure how to sign 'flamenco', so he mimed the dance as Hannah sat back, crossing her arms and shaking her head with a smile. James continued. "Her parents said she's going to stay there, even after they come back. So you see... I think, well, I don't want to say we're over, but I don't know what to do."

"What has she said to you?"

"She said she needed space and she won't pick up the phone," he was signing fast. "What can I do? I need her, Han, I've built my life around her. She's... everything — I told you I was going to propose — and now..."

Hannah nodded like an ancient sage. She put a large forkful of salmon and broccoli into her mouth, chewing slowly and purposefully. Lucas hopped closer and drummed his back foot as if impatient for her to finish. Hannah glanced at him and then back to James, swallowing. "I hate to say this, but I think you're going to have to back off for a bit and see what happens. I know it's hard," she added, watching her brother wilt, "but let her come to you."

"I can't just do nothing, it's killing me. I can't. Chris thinks I should go out there, surprise her. You know, romantic, prove I would cross oceans to be with her, what do you think?"

"It works in the films," mused Hannah. "But I don't know. Speaking as a woman, when I say I want to be left alone, I usually mean it. At least, in that moment I mean it. Even if I change my mind soon after. It has to come from me." She put one hand out to touch James' sleeve, breathing out heavily, before pulling back to sign again. "I'm sorry Tomato Chops." She used his old family nickname, a tomato and then a face, but seeing how serious he was, immediately rushed around the small table to fling her arms around his neck.

James just sat there as if it wasn't happening and when she pulled away, he forced his lips into a meagre smile.

"Look, maybe right now she's getting the chance to miss you." Hannah tried to catch his eyes. "And when she realises she misses you, when the gloss of sunshine and…" she affected a dance, clumsy arms in the air. "When the gloss of the dancing wears off, she'll come back and you can start again. But you're going to have to be prepared for that not happening as well. You've kind of got to forget about her for a while."

"I can't do that."

"Get a dog?"

"Come on Hannah."

"Get a new hobby?"

"I'm too busy with work."

"Okay, but the job is going well, right?" Hannah signed hopefully. "I saw the review in the *London Echo*, by someone called Rachel something-or-other and she seemed to rave about it, especially the holographic dancing in the ballroom, she said it was like, what was it she said? Like, 'time travel to the opulence of a bygone age'. That was my favourite room too, I really felt like I was at Queen Victoria's party wearing one of those amazing off-the-shoulder dresses." She pulled her hands over her arms, miming the outfit.

James looked abstractedly at a small crack in the white veneer of the table. "Yeah, it was a nice review," he said sullenly.

"Oh James, cheer up, it's your dream job, isn't it?"

"Pretty much, but it feels empty without Kezzie to share it with."

"I get it, but—"

"I need her."

"Uh, stop. Stop with the 'need', you don't 'need' her, you want her, but you're fine on your own. You always were before. A few dusty history books and you were happy enough I seem to recall."

"I just can't remember life before her any more. It's like…" He dropped his hands momentarily, then started again. "It's like when I met Kezia my life started properly and now… now I don't know."

"Okay, so things don't look like you expected or wanted, but that doesn't mean it can't still be good, James. You've got to trust life a little bit now, there are other women, other relationships… fun, excitement…"

"Not for me." He shook his head, reminding her of a younger James. "I only want Kezia."

"You're so rigid in your thinking. You always have been." She kept her eyes on him whilst bending down to pet Lucas.

"That's not fair. There isn't another Kezia. She's unique. She's… special. It's not like you can just pick up a catalogue and replace a person, is it? It doesn't work like that. She's the only her."

"Yeah, that's true," Hannah conceded after ruffling Lucas' fur. "But at the same time, you don't always get what you want and you don't always get *who* you want either. I'm not saying she won't come back to you — I hope she does and I like her too — I'm just trying to cushion you, just in case, that's all."

"Maybe there are some things you can't be cushioned from." James rubbed his forehead, messing up his hair. "Anyway, I am trying… Chris and I went out the other night and this girl gave me her number," he told her petulantly.

"Excellent… so, have you called her?"

"No."

"Do it. What have you got to lose?"

"I'm not ready."

"So you're going to wait until she's found someone else, are you?" James thought about that.

"Text her now. How long has it been?"

"Four days."

"Definitely text her now or the whole thing will go off the boil. Text her and in return I will bring you dessert, how about that?"

James put his knife and fork together politely.

"Well?" Hannah moved her head from side to side. "Are you going to?"

"Ahh look, I'll think about it, okay? But only if I get dessert." He smiled.

"That's better." Hannah smiled back. "I got us summer pudding. I only just remembered to take it out of the freezer. It should be defrosted enough by now though." She stood up and Lucas bounded away.

James went to help her collect the plates.

"No, no, don't worry, you stay there, I'll clear this. You go and have a chat to Lucas over there, he's a good listener."

So James went to where the hare was now crouching in the corner, and tickled the silky space between his ears, listening to the rush of the rain.

Hannah picked up the plates and took them into the narrow galley kitchen, laying everything down carefully next to the sink. She was still thinking about James and Kezia as she opened the fridge and took out the dessert. She slid the domed summer pudding out of its box and onto a faded brown chopping board crisscrossed with cuts. She picked one of the frozen strawberries off the top, cold and heart-shaped and vivid with its own perfection. She popped it into her mouth to see if it had defrosted, wincing as the iciness spread, biting then fading, leaving a sweet taste and just the memory of the cold.

26

Tortilla

 She sea was flat and endless. It dragged dank slime over pebbles and rocks. The morning sun slanted over the cliffs, which huddled close, surrounding the cove, undulating all around and up, up to where the pine trees twitched. A bird squawked, out of sight.

Kezia picked up a desiccated piece of driftwood and wished she hadn't asked.

"You want to know if Mama saw the ghost?" Darim's mouth was small, clamped, and he glanced to the biggest rock in the cove, the one they said she sang from.

"Well people say… so I just… just wanted to hear your side of things."

"People like to talk, Kezia. You know that. It doesn't make the things they say true."

Kezia's shoulders hunched apologetically. She looked out to where the horizon was a fading line, blue blending with blue.

Then, "I believe she did," he said resolutely. "Just maybe I'm wrong, but… I think so." His eyes found the edge of the sea and rested there too. "And I wonder, was she happy, in some strange way, maybe she was happy to see the ghost. Finally see the ghost she wondered so much about. I think… I think she would want to be connected to it now, because now, when people talk of the ghost, they talk of her." Darim shifted to inspect the sand. "And she would want people to talk about her, to be remembered. All Mama ever wanted was to be loved. To be adored." A whisper of sunlight fell across his face. "The heart decides what it cannot decide," he said, enigmatically, appraising the dried-out carcasses of bedraggled seaweed,

"I feel like I'm getting to know her, even now," said Kezia quietly. "You all keep her alive, it's… it's really nice."

Darim closed his eyes and nodded. The grasses hummed. Then he looked up and focused intently on her. "You seem happier now," he said. "How is your heart?"

"Um…" No one had ever asked Kezia that before.

"How does it feel?" Darim cocked his head to the side.

Unsure, Kezia hugged her knees, observing the water, watching the waves peak and dip.

"You have to feel it, Kezarina. Really feel it. Is there pain there? Does it hurt?"

"Maybe…" She was afraid to give the wrong answer.

"Your heart should feel like a lamp," he pronounced, taking her hand very delicately and holding it between his two palms. "Your heart should feel warm and it should glow, it should be full of light. But Kezia, sometimes you have to shield your heart. A good lamp comes with a lamp shade. It must be protected. You have not been protecting yourself, Kezia. This James, this *anguista*…" Darim shook his head, gazing back out at the ocean.

Kezia did not know what to say, she focused on the feeling of his hands and the slight pulse in his palms. Then she looked up and studied his face, his concern wrought in frown lines across his forehead. She hoped he would turn then and kiss her, but he just stared out to sea, his eyes like frosted glass.

"Heart lamp," she whispered, putting her free hand over her heart.

"Yes," he said thoughtfully. "Your heart will shine again Kezarina. It will…" he trailed off, letting her hand go. "Come," he said. "We must dance. It is time."

So they got up, shaking the sand from their clothes, watching the dance of the light on the ocean, and all the while, that sense of luminescence stayed with Kezia, as she followed him back up the path, wondering if she should ask more about the heart lamp.

Back at the school, the other girls were already assembled, talking and laughing in the late morning sun. They practised the sevillanas in readiness for the competition — just four weeks to go now — and Darim watched with quiet satisfaction. "Yes," he said, under his breath, as they turned together, twisting in synergy and at the right time.

158

He clapped out the beat and they made their moves ferocious and fast. "You are the lion," he declared. "You are the gladiator! You are the dagger!" And Tomi the cat hobbled past, like a little lion who had fought a gladiator himself.

When lunchtime came, they collapsed onto the chairs and benches and waited with anticipation for the Spanish omelettes they could smell cooking in the kitchen. Normando was beaming when he brought them out. "You must be hungry," he said, setting down the plates as they reached for the cutlery and sliced the perfectly round tortillas.

Kezia took a mouthful, and blinked as the flavour spread in her mouth.

"What?" Java was chewing, her eyes casting around in confusion.

"Umm," said Abril, "This is…"

"Sweet?" said Rosa, taking another dubious mouthful.

"It's… yeah, this is… not right." Carmen rubbed her nose as if to reset her sense of smell.

"What is it?" Darim was loitering near the table. "What has he done? Papa, what is in the tortilla?"

Normando wiped his hands on his apron defensively. "Well, just eggs, and potato, and tomato and onion and salt and pepper, of course," he said. "Lots of salt because I could see you all sweating in the hot sun today. Hard work, dancing."

Darim marched into the kitchen. Seconds later he shouted, "Papa!" and before Normando could turn around, was back out in the sunshine. "Are you sure you put salt into the tortilla, because the sugar is open on the work surface and—"

"No. No, it's not."

"Papa. Taste it."

Normando's hand shook as he took up a fork and pronged the tortilla, directing it very carefully to his mouth. He chewed. For a moment, his lips trembled and they waited… ready to rally round for his upset. Then, unexpectedly, he tipped his head back and laughed, loud and braying. With relief, the girls began to giggle too.

"Sugar!" exclaimed Normando over and over. "Instead of salt!" His chuckle was lively and catching and soon all of them just couldn't stop laughing as the peacocks sauntered by, and even they seemed to be smirking.

With gleeful mirth the girls ate the tortillas — every bite setting them off again — commentating on the taste like ardent food critics. Only Darim stayed serious, contemplating the scene as if he had created it.

After lunch Kezia went to the back of the garden, past the lion and the gladiator, to the trees at the back, to call her friend, Lucy.

"Dancing?" Lucy's voice sounded far away. "Wow, that's, erm, different." Her snigger was muffled.

Kezia turned to the horizon; the denim sea, far, far away, like the memory of a dream being slowly forgotten. It was the wallpaper on her new world.

"I just didn't imagine you doing that." Lucy cut into her thoughts. "You and me always joked about being eternal wallflowers. Don't tell me you're jigging around at the front now?"

"I'm not jigging."

"Then what are you doing?"

"Flamenco." The view started to look more like something from a picture book than something real.

Lucy paused, Kezia imagined her combing through her curly brown hair. "Okay, well… as long as you're okay… You know, James misses you."

"We're not together." Kezia thought her own voice sounded unreal now too.

"Well, if you came back, you could be."

"Lucy…"

"He loves you, Kez."

"I… I need *this* now, Lucy," said Kezia as she looked out to sea. *I don't want to be boring Kezia,* she thought, *not this time.*

"Stop running away from your life by pretending you're someone you're not and come back. I miss you too. There's a new Bond film out, we should all go and see it."

Kezia saw Darim striding across the garden with a bowl of fresh food for Esmerelda. He bent down next to the goat and stroked her head as he set it down; he was talking to her softly and she was listening as if she understood.

"Kezia, I think you're being irresponsible." Lucy's tinny voice brought Kezia back to the call.

"But Lucy, isn't it irresponsible to be in a relationship that isn't right?"

"But James is such a sweetheart and you guys are good together. I just don't want you to do anything you'll regret, that's all."

Kezia watched the flowers sway as the bees tried to land on them. "I don't understand either. I just know… I have to be here."

"What shall I tell James?"

"Tell him…"

Darim had finished feeding Esmerelda, he looked up, and seeing Kezia, he called across to her, "Kezia, we dance!"

"I'm coming…" she answered, pointing to the phone to explain her delay.

"You're coming home?" Lucy was confused.

"No, no, sorry, erm, I've got to go now Lucy."

Darim clapped his hands twice. "We practise now. Come on."

"Who is that?" Lucy sounded as though she was craning to see around the distance between them.

"Sorry Lucy, that's my teacher. I've got to go. Just don't tell James anything. I'll speak to you soon, okay?" Kezia hung up, destabilised, doubt rising like spores blowing off a dandelion and slowly spreading.

As she went to join the class the memories came, more spores, clouding her mind… The disappointment after James hadn't asked for her number; that first night, tracing scratches on the window as the bus carried her away from a man she might never see again, his smile, his hair, his kind brown eyes…

"He goes to our uni, doesn't he?" Lucy had said, convinced they might just bump into each other.

"Yeah, but he does history — that's miles away from the business studies building."

"Hmm. We'll have to go and use their café."

Kezia had giggled. "What, every day?"

"If that's what it takes."

"We are going to have a lot of tea."

"And cake!" Lucy pointed in the air, pleased with her plan.

But James had been smarter than that. There was only one 'Kezia' at their university so her internal email was easy to find. Kezia would never forget the way her heart had jolted when she read his message. She had squealed and called Lucy straight away. "That's my cake out of the window then," her friend had said.

Those first dates, those first days, had been the best of Kezia's life. She couldn't sleep, she couldn't eat, everything tingled. She leapt on his messages and read them fifteen times before she could even think of a reply. She lost track of time when she was with him, they talked for hours and she made him laugh; it made her feel good. So why didn't she feel that way now? Why was she running away, bored, dissatisfied?

The next morning Kezia told Darim she should probably go home, Lucy was right.

"It is too soon," he said, as if that settled it. "You cannot leave me so soon. Your friend tells you that you have run away? No, you have come home. To run away is to leave *here*. Did you think of that?" He took her hand. "Kezarina, when we met, I could taste your sadness like the salt in the sea air. What were you going to do? Dwell on it forever, let it eat you from the inside until you became dry rotten wood? Until people avoided you and you hated yourself even more than you hated them?" And before Kezia could answer, he said, "But it is up to you Kezarina. It is your life, your beautiful life."

The notion bumped along roughly during the day, a pebble skimming over water, and it was only in the evening, when the sun went down, that she resolved again to stay, and it didn't feel like a choice, just the natural rhythm of the sea washing in and out... She'd never been brave like this before, never tried. Now could be different. *"You, Kezia, will be the star on that stage. You will burn, they will feel the heat all the way to Cadiz."* He'd said that once, after a lot of wine — she remembered it and the feeling stayed — so she had to try just in case it was true.

That night it was too hot to sleep. Her thoughts were patchy and thin: wisps like clouds, drifting. When she'd first arrived at the school, she had slept a lot, big blank dark sleeps that left her groggy and unsure. As the days went on, the more she slept, the more she realised how exhausted she had been, and she didn't feel awake until she started dancing — it carried her through until lunch — but there was always a siesta in the afternoon, curled like a cat, sleeping.

Kezia couldn't remember when it had changed, but now she was always electrified, the days saturated with the colours of flamenco, the sun painting sweat down her back like scratch marks — she was so alive. Too alive to sleep.

They had danced again that evening. Him and her all alone. She'd thought that was it, they would finally merge into the passion of it — closer and closer they danced... but he pulled away just as she thought they might touch and they stamped out a rhythm around each other as the light withdrew from the sky...

Thinking of this, eventually, Kezia fell into tangled dreams, turning and turning and going nowhere, her heart speaking but she didn't want to hear. The questions too came curling around her with suffocating insistence and she couldn't cut them down; she hit out, as she slept. *Are you boring, Kezia? Will he think you are dull? Can you dance like he wants you to?*

But there would have been more questions if she had stayed awake. More questions to entwine and knot like weeds, because she might have seen him — Darim — leaving his room, hurrying out, scurrying into the shadows in the inscrutable, impenetrable night.

27

White Wine

Elly's hair was perfect and perpendicular, like a helmet. Today she wore long silver earrings resembling icicles and a black scoop neck top. Her porcelain skin was dusted faintly with some kind of glitter and shimmering slightly in the restaurant's low light. James hadn't noticed her eyes before, they were grey, slate grey, and they stared as she spoke. Her lips were smothered in translucent pink lip gloss and she was telling him about her day… Some paper had got stuck in the printer and Arun, her boss, had to help her get it out. Then, on her lunch break, she had gone with Vee to the little deli around the corner in Warwick Square to get sandwiches — ham and tomato and very limp lettuce — and the man behind the counter had flirted with Vee, but he didn't ask for her number. In the afternoon there had been a long meeting on a topic James couldn't quite fathom and she had filled the time by texting her mum.

Behind Elly, on the wall of exposed brick, was an abstract painting of a bird. Lines whipped around the canvas and primary colours blocked out some of the shapes, among them, just one disconcerting eye, staring, revealing the creature in the chaos. James wondered distantly what Kezia was doing now and his thoughts curved like the lines as the eye glared at him harder.

"How about your day?" Elly had finished her narration and was looking expectantly at James, folding her pale arms on top of the white table cloth. The doughy smell of pizza permeated the air, with the comforting top notes of grilled cheese.

"Ah, well, a couple of tourists tried to sit on the thrones and wouldn't move when asked politely, so we had to call security."

"Oh!" Elly leant back in her red bistro chair.

"Yeah, happens quite often actually. But it was fine, as soon as they saw the boys in black, they changed their minds. We had to track them all the way to the gift shop though, just in case."

"Goodness."

"Otherwise, my day was pretty standard. I caught Hamish, one of my guides, telling the tourists it was the warden in the next room's birthday — so every ten minutes they got sung 'happy birthday' in various languages," James grinned. "Harmless, but I did ask him to stop, kind of ruins the ambiance for the other visitors."

"It is funny though—" Elly was about to say something else when the waitress, a harassed looking woman in her thirties, bowled over to their table, brushing her unruly hair out of her eyes. She wore a badge on her navy-blue polo shirt: *Chloe*, it said simply.

"Ready to order food now?" Chloe asked them in a bored, flat voice and they both looked down to the unopened menus in front of them, the brown leather embossed in a florid gold script proclaiming: 'Ludovico's.

"Um, five more minutes?" James asked and she nodded, peeling away from the table with practised ease.

Elly skimmed her menu efficiently and closed it neatly, while James was still on the starters. "It's a good menu," she told him, as he desperately scanned the page. "So do you know the Queen then? What's she like?"

James looked up. "Erm, no, I haven't met her, but... I suppose I might. She sometimes comes around to say hello." He wasn't sure if that was true, but it sounded good. "She goes to stay at Balmoral for most of the summer though, in Scotland."

"Oh," said Elly, disappointed, and told him about the time she had seen a programme about Balmoral. "They make their own whisky there."

The waitress reappeared then, rubbing a hand over her forehead. "Right, what can we get you?" she asked, hopeful it wouldn't be a wasted stop this time.

"Oh, erm," James looked back at his menu.

"I'll have the lasagne please," said Elly. "I like your nail polish, that colour really suits you."

"Oh, thanks," Chloe glanced down at her purple nails. "Thought I'd try something different, you know?"

"It really works," said Elly and they both focused on James.

"Erm, yeah, the er… could I have the, er, calzone please?" he said, reading out the first thing he saw under the 'mains' section.

The waitress nodded and collected their menus absent-mindedly. "And any more wine?"

"Yes," said Elly, smiling mischievously. "Let's order another carafe of the house white."

James didn't really like white wine but he acquiesced with a nod and the waitress, clutching the menus, drifted towards the back of the room where a grey-haired couple were asking for the bill by drawing in the air with imaginary pens.

"I love Italian food," Elly told him, as if espousing a great world view. "You can't go wrong, can you? Well done for choosing Ludovico's. It's the best there is around here."

James didn't correct her, but Elly had chosen the restaurant. He had texted her on the way back from Hannah's, on the bus with the rain streaming down the windows. It felt wrong, but in the end, he had promised his sister he would, so he knew he'd feel bad either way. He'd asked her if she'd wanted to meet after work, drinks, he was thinking, keep it simple. She'd replied almost straight away, telling him he needed to try her favourite restaurant… so here they were.

James hadn't been able to concentrate all day, he'd felt nervous and guilty, a heady cocktail of emotions — apprehension and anxiety, and excitement too, but just distantly, like a ship far out at sea with a light on.

Elly was smaller than he remembered, petite and graceful, but forthright as she sat up straight and told him what she thought on a number of topics, all chosen by her. She was so opinionated that whenever she deferred to him for what he thought, he was afraid he was going to get it wrong and start an argument.

"I don't know really…" he said, prefacing yet another answer as she asked him whether girls should always paint their nails. "Um, maybe not purple, or maybe if they want to…"

"Is there anything you *do know really*?" Elly jibed, and James laughed, bowing his head slightly, feeling exposed.

A group of teenagers on a table at the other end of the room starting singing 'happy birthday'. "I think Hamish is here tonight," said James wryly and Elly looked confused, then laughed, and James wasn't sure if she remembered or not.

Elly tucked her hair behind her ears. "Oh, by the way, I read that article about Buckingham Palace in the *London Echo*... that Rachel woman who wrote it seemed to like it, didn't she? She gave it a five-star rating." Elly smiled, pleased with herself for doing her homework. The icicle earrings glittered. "So when are you going to get me free tickets?"

"Sure, I can," said James, pleased to be able to offer something. "We'd just need to get you booked in. I've got some friends and family passes and—"

"Right, here we go." The waitress arrived carrying a plate in each hand and looking hotter and more flustered than before. "Lasagne?" she said, and as Elly raised her hand, she deftly crossed her arms, swapping the dishes and placing them down, before spinning off back to the kitchen.

James took a bite of the calzone — it was too hot and burned his tongue — he tried to chew it quickly, painfully, hoping Elly wouldn't notice his anguished expression.

"How's your food?" she asked.

He nodded, trying to smile through the twist of dough and cheese by keeping his mouth shut, then he swallowed before he was ready and felt a lump sliding down his throat. "Good," he said, although he hadn't really tasted it. "Yours?"

"Yeah, you can't go wrong with lasagne, can you?"

James made some agreeing noises, swallowed again, and grasped his wine to wash it all down. As he was gaining control of the situation he looked across at Elly and the shimmer of her skin made her seem unreal — like an avatar — with her perfect hair and disconcerting grey eyes. He couldn't help comparing her to Kezia. Kezia with her refreshing smile, her easy conversation and endless curiosity which bubbled up with her giggles and made everything seem fun. Kezia's hair wasn't as neat, but her thoughts weren't as controlled either. Elly shimmered in front of James again and he tried to reason with himself — she was beautiful and smart, and perhaps more importantly, she wanted to be with him right now. That had to count for something. *"Give it a go James,"* Chris had said. *"Just give it a go."*

"And… back in the room…" Elly put her fork down and snapped her fingers in front of his face. "Away with the fairies, were you?"

"Oh, sorry. Long day. On my feet all day, you know?"

"No, not really. Accountants sit down all day, so I've never had that. We just sit and we drink endless cups of tea, as an excuse to go and have a gossip in the kitchen. I do go to the gym twice a week though, and me and Vee do yoga on a Monday. Vee fancies the teacher, he's really strong."

"I… that's great," said James, deciding not to defend his own fitness regime in case it didn't stack up against the handsome yoga teacher. He just went running across the heath when the weather was nice. He decided he should start doing weights and he tried not to think about how muscular Darim might be.

Chloe, still flustered, dragging an arm across her face, came back to ask how the food was. They made the right noises and she nodded, not really hearing, continuing on with her endless rounds.

"So did you hear from her then?" Elly asked, staring steadily, "Did you hear from your ex in Spain? Vee and I decided she'd probably start texting after a while when she began to miss you, and so you'd have to tell her you've moved on." She looked at him expectantly.

"Erm," James felt weirdly wounded.

"That's the way of it." Elly nodded sagely, her bob rocking with the movement. "They come crawling back, but it's always too late. It's like they can sense when you're pulling away."

"Well… maybe sometimes, but…"

"No. Always," Elly said categorically. "I read a piece about it in *Marie Claire*."

"Oh, well… she hasn't texted so…" James rubbed his eye.

"It's okay if you're not over her yet," Elly said, cutting the last of the lasagne into neat squares on her plate. "We don't have to do anything tonight. Just when you're ready."

James didn't know what to say. A drunk couple on the table next to them raised a toast and the glasses clinked above their cackles of laughter.

"I think it's good to take it slow," Elly was telling him. "Much better, builds up the romance. Vee always jumps in straight away, but I'm not like that. Never have been. Vee calls me Lady Elly." She looked across at James, as if awaiting a compliment.

"Ah, right, good," said James. "But... erm... you're right. I, er, I'm not ready. I thought I would be. You're so pretty, and nice... but being here tonight, it's made me realise, it probably is too soon. I'm sorry."

"Oh no," said Elly, smoothing down her already smooth hair. "I didn't mean we can't see each other, I just meant... you know, that we wouldn't take it any further tonight."

James wasn't sure if she winked at him, or if it was a trick of the lighting. "No, I... Okay... but yeah, what I'm saying is I'm not ready at all."

Elly reached across and put her hand over his, her fingers were cold, almost lifeless. "We can give it time," she said, and it felt like an instruction. "I understand. I was the same when I split up with Tyler. I dated loads of people after that and they all understood. Then one day you wake up and you don't feel like that any more and... well, you start having fun. So I'll wait."

James looked down at his half-eaten calzone. "That doesn't feel very fair on you."

"I don't mind. I might date other people in the meantime, until we're serious, but yeah, that's just the way it goes."

"Does it?"

"Course."

"I'm... I'm not sure. Sorry Elly. I think it's better to be honest. I'm not up for starting something new. Not just yet. I don't want to mess you around. I feel like I already am."

"You're not, because you're not hiding anything from me. That's why I trust you. That's why I like you. Most guys are seeing three or four other people behind your back anyway, but you're different. I can tell." Elly took her hand away and picked up her knife and fork again. "Anyway, maybe you don't love her as much as you think you do, or you wouldn't be here with me."

James sniffed and it sounded louder than he would have wanted. "You've got nice hair," he said miserably.

"Thanks." She nodded thoughtfully, the hair falling out from behind her ears as if accepting the compliment itself. "Okay, I'm going to the

169

ladies, and when I come back, we are not going to be so serious and we are going to drink more wine. Agreed?"

"Yeah," James conceded, his face creased with concern. "Thanks for understanding."

Elly just raised her eyebrows, picked up her taupe leather handbag and made her way across the restaurant, towards a door embellished with a wooden stiletto.

Left alone, James took his phone from his pocket automatically. Still nothing from Kezia. Just a good luck text from Chris, with a thumbs-up emoji. James hit reply, hovered over the space, and then closed the message with a sigh. He went to check the news as a distraction, but his internet browser showed the 'Darim' search again, drawing him in. He clicked on one of the pictures — fixated on the look in Darim's eyes — and jealously burned. He tugged at his shirt collar.

"What are you looking at?" Elly, lips shining with freshly applied lip gloss, was standing over him, squinting down at the screen. He could smell her perfume: cherries and something citrus.

"Oh, nothing." James put his phone flat on the table, screen down.

"Who was that man?" She sauntered back round to her seat.

"No… no one, just, erm, doing some research."

"Then why do you look so guilty?"

"Do I?" His eyebrows strained together. "It must be the heat, it's very hot in here, isn't it?"

"Right." Elly poured herself another glass of the house white. "He's just Vee's type," she said, angling her chin at James' phone.

James looked down regretfully and Elly waited, sipping her wine.

"So." James exhaled. "That is the man teaching K… my ex, flamenco. In Spain. I was… I was just looking."

They grey of Elly's eyes seemed to deepen, from slate to steel. "If she's learning from him, you've got no chance." She laughed. "Just saying it like it is. Just saying it like it is, while we're being honest tonight and everything."

James felt suddenly exhausted. The couple next to them stood up to leave, searching under their table for a missing umbrella.

"Right. Um, shall I get the bill?" he said, finding it hard to breathe properly.

170

The woman held up a blue brolly, victorious.

"Sure." Elly drained the last of her wine. "I'll split it for us. I'm not an accountant for nothing you know."

"No, I'll get this, the least I can do."

"If you insist." She shrugged as James raised his hand to call the beleaguered Chloe who wound her way around the tables to get to them.

James checked the amount on the bill without really seeing it and followed the instructions on the card reader. Elly and the waitress were talking idly about Elly's nails this time: two-tone pink, with a small black flower on each of them. "Thank you, that was great," James said when the receipt came out of the top of the machine in a mechanical whirr. Chloe looked down to see if he'd left a tip, before smiling and telling them to come back again.

"Right." James put his phone in his pocket. Elly was already wearing her white denim jacket. They stood and processed to the door, passing other, more successful dates.

Outside the sky was indigo blue — deep summer sky — and there was a chill now, an edge on what had been a balmy day.

"Are you getting the Tube?" Elly was looking down the road, in the direction of the Underground.

"Yeah, I'll walk you there if you like?"

"Great, thanks." And as they moved off, she told him about her route home. They were going too slowly for James, who wanted to be on his own again, who was tired of trying, of reaching to say the right thing. It had never felt like trying with Kezia. It was easy, it had always been easy.

When they arrived at Pimlico Tube, Elly turned to face him. "Thanks James," she said, moving closer. "It's been a really nice evening."

"It has," said James, adjusting his shirt.

Without warning, she put both hands on his shoulders, focusing her eyes unwaveringly on his. "This is where you kiss me," she said.

"But I thought..."

"Shh," said Elly, resting her finger over his lips. "Shh talking now. Just kiss me. It'll help you get over her. I promise." The lemon cherry of her perfume was too strong for James.

"What are you waiting for Mr Palace?" Her eyes flashed grey, empty grey.

James removed her hands from his shoulders gently. "You've had a bit to drink," he said. "It — well — it doesn't feel right."

Elly pouted. "I'm not drunk. You'd know if I was drunk. Vee says I'm really loud," she sniggered. "Okay then, maybe next time. Maybe. See you then." And she headed towards the station steps, teetering slightly on her kitten heels.

"I'm sorry," James called after her.

Elly stopped, suddenly thoughtful. "There aren't many guys as honest as you," she said. "It's good… It doesn't feel good. But it is." Her eyes flickered to the right, considering something, then she said, "When the Queen gives you a knighthood, don't forget me, okay?"

James attempted a laugh and it came out like a rattle, but Elly didn't notice, she just winked, blew him a kiss and made her way down the concrete steps.

James stood for a while, to put some distance between them. Cars sped past, one of them beeping its horn aggressively. A man called to a friend over the road: raised hands and raised voices. He thought of Kezia, her warmth and compassion, compared to Elly's… what? She was nice. She was pretty. Should he have kissed her? The way she had said, "I'll wait," earlier had made him nervous: there was something missing, something relatable. James looked at his watch pointlessly and then headed for the stairs.

The thick air of the Tube enveloped him as he descended: warm, gritty, metallic. He remembered the night he'd first met Kezia, at the cocktail bar, her smile supplanting the fake people and the strident music. It had changed everything. When he'd walked her back to the bus stop he hadn't kissed her and she hadn't asked for it. The memory gave him hope, like he'd somehow passed a test. As he went through the barriers and towards to the escalators, skirting a sweaty man in Lycra, he knew what it meant. It didn't matter how nice or pretty or suitable anyone else was, because anyone else just wasn't Kezia.

28

Ghost Song

No one really knew why the mirror had fallen off the wall. Darim blamed Normando. Then he blamed Rollo. There were tiny shards of glinting silver fanning out on the floor between the kitchen and the hall. Kezia saw the other girls crossing themselves as they passed.

"Maybe she doesn't think we're training hard enough?" whispered Abril.

"Maybe she wants to tell us something else… about how she died?" Carmel affected a shiver.

Their Spanish was thick like coiled rope — wound too tightly for Kezia to understand — as they invoked the ghost of Carlotta.

"It's a bad sign. Like the laminitis," said Carmel pulling her shawl around her. "You know? The horse disease, over at North Farm? The hooves fall off. The legs go rotten and then the hooves fall off."

Abril clutched Carmen's arm. "The whole hoof?"

"The whole hoof. There were some near the railway track the other day, no one knows why. Miranda told me. Just one pair."

Hooves. No horse.

Kezia watched the girls, their words distant and obscure, like the shadow of the horse's hooves themselves, still swinging in and out of her mind. She moved past them, distracted, thinking about Darim. It was the scent of his skin, sweet and sharp, the stubble on his face, the way he moved with poise and precision. That morning he had come to her before breakfast…

The light was lemon yellow and Kezia was still in bed. He pulled back the small curtain with a flick of his wrist, looking down at her, vivid in black: black trousers, black shirt. She sat up, wiping the sleep from her eyes, remembering her dream from before and wondering if she was in it. *You're lazy, but I like you.*

173

"I bought you a gift," he said simply and she saw he was holding a small parcel of tissue paper. "Take it Kezarina, it is for you."

As she took the packet, the paper fell away revealing pink satin the colour of watermelon. It was a nightdress, a slip with straps, lustrous in the lemon light. "Oh, oh my goodness, it's beautiful, are you sure?"

Darim bowed magnanimously, the spark of a smile in his eyes. "You deserve it, because you… you are mi *favorita*." The word sounded hot when he said it. "So, shall we welcome the day with a dance?"

Moments later, the nightdress placed carefully on the bed, she was warming up, her circling arms a windmill generating wakefulness. The feeling of the gift moved within her, shifting like a droplet of water, flowing as she danced, and he watched her like an art dealer might evaluate a painting.

"Go faster, Kezarina," Darim said quietly. "Show me that you can. Let me be your red rag. I goad you into passion. You will feel it." And he began to count the beats.

The room became a bullring then and, whipped into motion, she stamped her feet and shook her head. The rhythm settled into her — ossifying her bones — making her stronger with every step.

"Better. Better." Darim stopped counting and joined her in the dance, free as the dappled sunlight spilling into the room. "It's good Kezia," he purred reverently. "Señorita Don't Dance."

She felt his voice, his presence, his spirit surround her as she danced. She felt her own spirit soar. They bashed out the finish and their eyes shared an understanding as they bowed together at the end.

"Admit it," Darim said to her. "I am the best thing about your life." He folded his arms in pure arrogance.

Heart still hammering, still high from the dance, Kezia reached behind her for the conch shell on the chest of drawers, curled up and reclining in the sunlight. She took it and she threw it at his head. Darim leaned to the side effortlessly and it thudded on the wall, dropping unceremoniously to the floor without smashing. The intactness of it seemed to prove him right. Kezia cursed in Spanish, and the laugh rushed out of them both.

***

Another week passed and still she waited for *duende*, waited for it to come. The harder she chased, the further it felt, like a ship endlessly sailing towards the horizon. When he was in a placid mood, she asked him about it again, and his eyes seemed to ferment as he said, "Go gently into it, feel your way. Don't force. Let it be, my little flamenca. Let it be." And he kissed her quickly on the cheek. The feeling fizzed.

That night, when she wasn't sleeping, she turned the memory of the kiss over and over in her mind and wondered if, that afternoon, the beat resounding as they moved in unison, she had come close to finding *duende*.

Darim had wiped his sleeve across his forehead and whirled among them, fierce and proud. "Castanets of the heart," he'd said. "Play! Feel it. Play!" He'd come to Kezia and they had turned with the steps. Towards and around each other. For one moment, he took her by the waist, their sweat mingling. "Yes!" he said to her. "This is what I want to feel from you — the passion, *señorita* — the fire!" Then he was gone, swinging out to the front of the class again as the goat regarded it all with a vague and prolonged stare. Was it *duende* or was it Darim she had felt then? The two motions mingled like the sweat.

She was still thinking of the fire in his eyes and how it fed her when she heard the door to Darim's room open to the terrace below. It was late. Maybe he couldn't sleep either and wanted to play his guitar? She often heard the mist of notes drift up to her room as she drifted away. She hoped he would play tonight, she wanted to see him in the moonlight, to trace the outline of his silhouette, to pay silent homage to the way he sat so straight, so purposefully. She went to the window.

The susurration of the ivy harmonised with the babble of the sea as if the night was talking to itself. Darim's door was open — just a crack — and a shaft of light streamed across the terrace. She could see his guitar, propped up by the wall but he wasn't there. Then she saw him treading carefully along the path into the garden.

"Darim, where are you going?"

He did not hear.

"Darim?"

She watched him disappear towards trees, where the fairy lights were timid sentinels.

Kezia went back to bed but the heat pricked and there were too many questions. Where was he going? Was he sad again? Did he need her, could she be the one to help? It was suddenly airless in the small room. She sat up and reached for her trainers, jamming them onto her feet, pulling them hard so she didn't have to undo the laces. Then she made for the door.

It was locked.

'Mando," she cursed. "No, not now. I need to get out. I need to see Darim."

She went back to the window. Maybe this time she could do it, she could climb down the ivy — she could almost hear Darim saying, "See, see how you've changed Kezia. The frightened girl at the cove would not have been bold like you are now, would not have climbed." But when she looked down her stomach buckled again, her legs went weak.

Then there was a whimper, and she saw the velvet head of Rollo sniffing around Darim's door. He looked up and without thinking she commanded: "Rollo, *llave*!"

He paused, and gave another whimper.

"Rollo. *Llave. Por favor*. Please…"

He trotted away nonchalantly and Kezia sighed. She sat on the bed, despondent and sticky, thinking of Darim and the torture of the loss he felt, the death of his mama… When suddenly a soft clinking came from the corridor; the sound of keys set down by the careful mouth of a dog.

Kezia moved fast. On her hands and knees, she groped under the door — the gap was wide enough for her hand — but the keys were too far away for her to reach. She could hear Rollo breathing. "Rollo… Good boy Rollo, push the keys, just nudge them with your nose, go on… you see my hand, here boy, here." She rippled her fingers but there was just the patter of his paws as he rearranged himself to lie down.

She swore, looking around for inspiration. There was her dress, the red dress, the one he liked the best, hanging in the corner. She took it off the hanger and laid it onto the bed. Then she angled the hanger under the door and slowly, very slowly, hooked the keys, dragging them towards her… until she had them in her hands.

As Kezia unlocked the door she fumbled, not quite sure if it was too late now, too late to find Darim, to ask him what was wrong. She crept down the stairs anyway and went the long way round the house in case Normando was in the kitchen making midnight churros.

Out onto the terrace and down between the flower beds she went. *Darim, Darim, Darim.* His name like a heartbeat. Maybe she would find him and they would kiss, in the moonlight, their first real kiss… but the garden was empty except for the gruff snores of Esmerelda and the occasional flicker of a peacock in the mottled light.

Kezia went instinctively to the gate, looking down the path to the sea. Had he gone to be with her, his mama? The foliage rustled, speaking the language of leaves.

Don't go down to the water…

A gulp of fear made it hard to swallow.

Don't go down to the sea.

Don't… but he had said to her, "Do you want to be weak or strong?"
She wanted to be strong.

Firmly she went and the flamenco rhythms went with her: *Ta dah taka dah.* Her feet found pace in the *compas*, her stride falling into the beat. *Ta dah taka dah.* In the end it felt good so she ran. Down, down, down. Down the path to the sea. *Darim, Darim, Darim.* His name pulsing still.

She only slowed when she got there. The cove was wide and empty and her breath was ragged and raw. She was alone; there was just the sand soaking up the sea's restless churning. "Darim?"

She ran over the wizened seaweed, right to the water's edge. She did not feel alone. A milky moon spilled white incense into the night. She looked up to the stars, the ones she could see and the ones she could not see, she felt them all, and she began to dance.

She moved in time with the ocean's persistent pound, painting her passions in the flick of each wrist, shedding emotions like soap in water and letting them lubricate her steps — she moved with them and she let them go — she danced in sorrow and in anger, she danced for James and for Gary. She danced in need of Darim.

As she danced the moon shone brighter, steadfast and sure, pure platinum. The stars became crystals and the sea coruscating cobalt; they seemed more than their essence — and so did she. She was herself but she wasn't herself. She was a bud realising it was part of a tree, and with that knowledge, opening. She was safe to sway, part of the tree.

And then. A rush.

A swooping up the middle of her that tingled and extended out along her limbs. A swell of energy, new and bubble-pure.

Duende.

She laughed because she knew it.

And so she danced.

There was power in her now, focus in her arms, fire in her hands. The wind was carrying her movements, moving faster and stronger, faster and stronger until...

Eventually, Kezia concluded, letting her arms finish the dance with a victorious sweep. The moon, the sea, the stars were all pulsating still — everything dazzling and vital. Maybe the steps had been wrong and the movements crude, it did not matter — she had found the music on the inside — and she was calm, satisfied. Infused with *duende.*

It lasted for two whole minutes.

And then, in the moon-drenched darkness, a moan began to tremor through the deserted cove. A steady, haunting, dreadful, wail. Low at first, and building. Kezia turned, feeling the momentum of her power ebbing like a swing vacated, slowing to a stop.

The wind... it had to be the wind.

She looked all around and the cove seemed to shimmer in the purple haze of night, shadows and shapes and rocks wearing the darkness like masks. The sound reverberated around, taunting, terrifying, as the stones glowered with spectral uncertainty.

A long shrill piercing strain arrested the night — and then tore through a torrent of notes — defying the wind cadence by cadence. This was a song that pulled at her with immutable sadness. A barbed wire of emotion that caught at her heart and snared at her senses — rooting her there with a dizzying surge of sorrow. The chill was a breath, brushing the back of her neck. The moan went through her, it got into her cells like a virus and it would not let her go... It was the sound of pain, the pallor of tears, the feeling of a funeral and the shudder of the soul... she was caught up in the melody and she couldn't move, couldn't breathe.

The ghost was singing.

The ghost was singing to her.

PART TWO

29

Sweat

She offered herself to him in the desert. Brown skin, red scarf. Her eyes, polka dot, hot and cold. It was over very quickly and it was dirty in the end. She pulled up her trousers and put out her hand for the money. Darim thought they might embrace, look up at the stars, talk about the things that had brought them both here, but she lied, like they always do, she used him, although he was supposed to be using her. There was no sense of completion, only a dull, cold, lonely ache.

When he came out of the tent, he wanted to wash himself but there was nowhere. He just stared at the bald dunes as they stretched out and out like his guilt: undulating and forever.

Eventually, when the cold got too deep inside him, he went back in and crashed out on the hard bed, not bothering to undress. The wind fought the sides of the tent as he fought his own feelings until the dawn.

In the morning the heat rose with the sun. The winds had stilled in the night and Darim dragged his hand across his dry mouth and felt subdued. The light was too strong when he opened the tent door and everything bleached out for a moment before the ochre dunes came back into vision, like the arched backs of slumbering dinosaurs.

He walked slowly, observing the slight give of the sand and the silence all around. It was all flawless, as if to taunt him — his feet spoiling the soft surface with rough dents.

He was sweating before he even started the climb, feet sinking back and back, sand invading his socks and shoes, his breath tumultuous in the solid stillness.

The Berber guides told him not to go too far, not to lose sight of the base because the desert all looks the same, if you're new to it. Even so, he had to get out, there were things he needed to talk to God about, and God was in the desert, the bible said so. Someone shouted to him from the camp below and he turned, mouth open, but the man just waved and shouted in an antique voice. "It is a long way up!"

The sky was searingly cerulean, untouched by clouds, empty of everything except itself and its full, full colour. There was only umber sand and the brilliant blue sky, like being on another planet. A large bird flew overhead, wings outstretched in a show of freedom and power.

He stood on top of the dune and the desert flowed as far as he could see, meandering gently into the distance, like slow, lazy water. Directly below were the small circles of the huts and the guides beginning to fetch water, boil kettles, get breakfast. Darim looked down at the ripples in the sand and thought it looked like the sea bed. "As above, so below," he said. "As within, so without." There were camels on the other side of the dune, looking for food and finding nothing. Their coconut-shell mouths opened and shut, chewing the air instead. He sang quietly to himself, sad psalms murmured into the sunshine.

The argument with his mama swirled in his head, like the dunes that circulated around him. The thoughts swirled and the sand swirled and the endless dunes went on and on forever. "When are you going to make something of your life?" Carlotta had rounded her shoulders in a bullish stance, both feet flat on the floor.

"The school is my vocation," he had said. "Flamenco is my heart. As it is yours."

They were standing in the kitchen, the pink Aga like an outsized marshmallow behind Carlotta as she pronounced, "I went out and I earned real money from it. You need to make money. You can't accompany me forever. You need to make a name for yourself, you are good enough."

"What I do now is good enough."

"No! I did the circuit and I toured for years. I did it by myself. For myself. You are idle, you only go out when I go." She frowned with an anger that furrowed her forehead and drove dark creases between her eyebrows.

"I like teaching," he told her, and he did. There was a satisfaction in watching the girls change their shape when he told them what to do, of seeing their rough movements hewn and streamlined. "You think I want the kind of life you had? You dragged me round enough to see how

181

empty it is. The fake friends. The endless clamour to be loved and the meaningless, vacuous people." He turned his head and spat to the side. "They do not care about flamenco. They only care about making money. That is not *puro*."

"I wish you cared more about making money. You are spoiled. You have taken advantage of my efforts — had it too easy."

"You don't have to live through me you know. Just because it is over for you. *You* wanted fame, *you* wanted fortune. But what good are fans? Where are they now?" He kicked a bag of Pedro's parrot feed, resentful.

"I am still a household name." She brought herself up proud. "What are you?"

"I am your son. Is it not sufficient?"

She held a disdainful pose, looking past his shoulder.

"Papa needs me here anyway," he muttered. "I have to help him at the bar. He is… finding it difficult."

"Pah! You hardly help when you are there. You sit in the corner playing your guitar. It is an excuse not to work."

"Errk. Sit in the corner." Pedro was climbing an imaginary ladder as he trod methodically on his perch.

"You would miss me if I left to seek my fortune," said Darim, looking at the bird.

"No! I would be glad," Carlotta retorted. "I want you to go, go and make some money and meet a girl and make something of your life. You stay here forever and you rot. You will become like the small folk in the village." She stamped her foot as if she was about to take up a dance. "You are stuck here. Stuck! I see your talent wasting like unpicked grapes withering on the vine. It is not good. You are no good."

And so he went. He took the boat to Morocco without a plan. It was a reaction — just go. When their passions collided, the energy spun him outwards; it always did. He just needed to let her cool down, let her miss him and she would be sweet again, when he got back.

If only he'd known.

The desert's mellow dunes swelled around him. There was music in the desert. He listened. The soft wind and a silent beat he could feel just by looking. He faded to his knees before the precious metal sun, the animosity of the argument still seething inside him. He did not want her life, he knew this. He remembered too much of it, how she'd taken him on tour and how he'd been passed from dancer to dancer while she performed. They'd all been bored by his infancy and nobody wanted to dangle puppets in front of his face to distract him from the fact he was a child, with nothing to do. He'd waited up, tired, for her to finish her set, falling asleep under the coats in the dressing room, but when she came back it was often with someone else and they would pour glasses of gin and disappear behind the clothes screen making strange noises. When he was older, he would walk the corridors where rows and rows of pretty chorus girls in dresses indulged him with chuckles and high kicks then vanished into doorways, always out of reach. So he took solace in philosophy books, reading until his eyes hurt, taking his mind away, escaping down rabbit holes of thought.

Darim kicked the edge of the dune, causing a small cascade of sand. "I do not want to tour," he said. "I've seen what it does to people." He kicked out again obstinately and a camel below dipped her head in deference.

He watched, and he liked how calm the camels were, it started to soothe him. So he stood, soaking up the colours in the desert — blues and yellows and golds — and they became more than colours, they infused into the music, transposing into tones inside his head. The song carried him to a different place. "She's wrong," he said after a while. "I do not need anything outside myself. I do not seek the empty fame that made her so sad, always drinking, never complete without applause. I seek to teach people, to set them free. Free! We all need to set ourselves free. It is my calling!" Elated by this revelation, Darim ran back down the dune, digging his feet into the skidding sand.

***

Darim rode back to Marrakech in a four-by-four, bumping steadily over muddy tracks, staring bleakly at the dry landscape like a wounded animal. Sweat fell down his face. He didn't wipe it away.

They drove into a sandstorm, the desert flinging its body into the air, whirling unnaturally, like it was possessed by *duende*. The driver inched forwards but eventually had to stop. So Darim got out of the car and danced with it, feeling the force of the storm, the sharp sand stinging his skin. The pain pleased him, it contrasted with the dull ache inside. When he brushed himself down and got back in the car the sand was still blowing up into the air, but the gusts came and went, like passion.

They drove on. Eventually they reached Marrakesh and the car pulled in at the edge of the main square. Darim got out and blinked under the ferocious midday sun, he could feel the burn as he paid the driver and slung his bag over his shoulder.

He looked around. Too many people. There were men in traditional dress with raging hats like lampshades and fixed-on grins, trying to seduce him for a photograph. Beside them were ladies poised with henna pens, pouncing to make their mark, to coerce him into paying for a pattern that would last a few days, and then fade. He pushed past them, drawn towards a symphony of shouts where the thin reedy notes of snake charmers filled the air. He wanted magic, but he was sad to see the hosepipe heads of the reptiles rearing so lethargically: dull and drugged. Next to them, monkeys the colour of smoke wore nappies and chain necklaces. They teetered along the arms of their owners with fear in their faces and were roughly dished out onto tourists; the humans shrieking with delight, the moneys shrieking in terror. They wet their nappies because they were scared. Darim looked away.

He tried to leave the main concourse, stalking around the edges of the square, eyes down to avoid more entreaties from the men who might grab at him. He did not want to buy a scarf or a shiny silver teapot, these things irritated him, they were useless. He allowed himself to get sucked into a crowd bulging with backpacks and he flowed with them, down an alley, to the souks.

The walls closed in and the darkness was like a sigh. A roof of reeds blocked out the light and metal lanterns with kaleidoscope colours clustered near the roof, adding a mystical tint to the leather bags, clothes, phone cases and mountains of trainers jostling from floor to ceiling. There was always something in his way. Carpets dangled from nowhere, shrivelled fruit overflowed from baskets, shattered minerals swept the sides and the ground was scattered with incense burners and wooden camels. Darim tried to get past them all. Their house in Spain was full of moth-eaten rugs and shiny lamps such as these. Just like Mama to love it here; it was hopelessly out of control, like she was.

Frowning, he found an exit and walked out of the main souk, into a side street. Here the air was redolent with spices — amber, tan and rich red powders piled up in prepossessing cones — saffron, turmeric, cinnamon, cloves. He breathed deeply and stopped to buy a pound of a sweet spice he would later forget the name of. The seller in his tasseled hat wrapped it in newspaper with an agile twist as he asked, "Where are you from?"

"Spain," said Darim.

"Mint?" The man nodded as if there was an obvious correlation.

Darim held up one hand as he backed away.

He called his mama from the hotel and her voice sounded vintage and distant. She didn't ask how he was but instead filled his mind with little irrelevant details about her life that descended like ladybugs, crawling with colour, but all the same. Her breakfast, her new dress, the cats in the garden. Eventually he broke in and told her he didn't like Marrakesh.

"Don't be ridiculous, Darimito. Everyone likes Marrakesh. There's something wrong with you if you don't."

Dispirited, Darim ended the call and wandered out into the hot dry street again. There was still sand in his hair from the desert and a thirst like dust inside him. He bought some freshly squeezed orange juice from a wooden stall and savoured the taste as the bits floated around in his mouth.

The sign for the hammam seemed to catch him off guard even though it had been there all along. The arrow pointed and he knew he would follow. *Cleanse me from my sin.* He craved clean, needed it now, so he drained the juice and walked purposefully for the first time that day.

"How sweaty will it be?" he asked the man in the kiosk. "I want to be clean, not sweaty."

"Not sweaty much. Very hygiene," was the reply, so he went in.

He didn't know what to do so he looked around at all the other men taking off their clothes and hanging them on the wooden pegs lining the wall. He unbuttoned his shirt very slowly, noticing the gritty feeling behind the collar.

The first room was bare and concrete, like a prison cell. There were blue plastic buckets in the corner and men sloshing themselves with water at a tap protruding from the wall. Darim did the same, distastefully at first, but was surprised at how smooth the water felt on his skin, like a silk blanket.

The next room was darker with benches around the edge, tiled and slippery to sit on. Darim wanted to be alone, so he went as far from the corner as he could — away from the three men chatting in subdued voices and occasionally erupting into low panting laughs. A man with rolls of fat like rubber rings was talking the most and taking up most of the seat. When he rubbed the back of his neck the sweat rushed down. That was the first time Darim saw Omar.

Darim sat and some of the sand shifted in his ears. He let the heat soak into him. It should have been boring, but he felt his body give in to an undisclosed need. The wall was warm and smooth at his back.

"She was everything I wanted in a woman… except mine!" Omar was holding forth in a loin cloth and Darim tried to shut him out and listen instead to the water dripping off the pipes. He told himself suffering was inevitable, and needed to be borne, as the men in the corner eroded his peace.

Then a sound like a drill stopped them all short.

It was followed by a heavy silence, enshrouded in a pungent miasma. As soon as the rabble in the corner spiked up conversation again, a lean man with shoulder length hair got up to leave.

After he had gone, the other men gushed into helpless laughter. "That guy," said Omar breathlessly. "He's always doing that in here. I've known pigs with better manners."

Darim focused on the pipes, dripping, in the corner.

"Bring your gas mask next time." The smallest man had smooth glowing skin. It was Sami.

"Diving equipment complete with oxygen," said Omar.

The third man made a dry chuckle.

"Seriously, he has to stop doing that," said Sami.

"Such bad breeding," retorted Omar with glee.

They looked across to Darim and he nodded, not sure what to say. He glanced again to where a black pipe wound, snake-like, across the room.

"You have to excuse him, I suppose," said Sami. "Because at least he provides us with the entertainment."

They chortled again while Darim acquiesced politely, hoping to go back to his solitude, but from that moment on, he was included in the conversation. He had no choice. They asked him his name and they wanted to know what he was doing in Marrakesh. He gave short perfunctory answers but the less he gave the more they wanted to know.

"You're a flamenco teacher? So, what, you dance, sing?" Omar shifted in his seat and his skin made a sucking sound.

"Yes," said Darim.

"Yes what?"

"Both," Darim said firmly.

"Do you play the guitar?" Sami seemed starstruck.

"Yes. It is... it is my first love. Although, I adore all forms of flamenco, of course, they are like different parts of the same body, for me."

"Oh. Then you must come to our party! You can play for us," declared Omar and his puckered friend nodded, choosing to say nothing, just staring at Darim ceaselessly.

"Yes!" agreed Sami. "Play for us."

"There will be music and dancing and food, and well, maybe just a little bit of drink. You can meet Richard." He arched his eyebrows at his companions. "You will enjoy meeting Richard."

When Darim left the hammam he had a scrunched piece of paper in his pocket with the directions to the party and Omar's phone number. The light was golden and the air was soft and fuzzy. He walked back to his hotel, conflicted. He did not want to go to a party with these people he had only met because of another man's flatulence. He did not feel like making friends. But then, the chance to play and sing for strangers, the chance to tell Mama...

He sat on a cushion on his balcony and sipped water that tasted sweet because of his thirst. He squinted up at the round disc of the sun, feeling lightheaded after the hammam, and made a decision that would change his life forever.

30

Fever

Her song, luminous in the moonlight, bright and sharp and pulling at me. Singing, singing and calling my name. Kezia. 'Don't go down to the water, don't go down to the sea...' She's there, and she stares, pointing with long fingers to deliver the curse. The curse, pulsing through me in screaming waves, burning flames, then deep, deep cold like a river. Her face is blurred. The memory ripples. She sits and she sings, 'Love never dies nor gives you any rest...'

The walls were going in and out like the walls of a heart. The room was beating and Kezia was beating with it. She was swimming in and out of dreams. Everything felt underwater and she had forgotten how to breathe.

I want to go with him. I need to be with him. There. Where the sky meets the sea. Just need to find it — Darim and me. "Now dance with me," he will say and he will hold up his arm like he does. Life will infuse its hot pain into us and it will be all we need. I will dance and he will cry, "Aye!" with his head to the side. The music will curl around us and we will know there is life to be lived between the notes. Inside and between them. Brand new I go with him. Without him there is nothing but empty space. I want to go. Boring Kezia. No more boring Kezia.

The thoughts rolled like marbles around Kezia's head. She thought she could see Carlotta performing, doing flamenco on a wooden stage, but then the goat came and was dancing too, on its hind legs. Carlotta's face turned into a goat's face and the goat was wearing her costume with worn black shoes. A giant tambourine came in from the sky and the Queen started to play it with her sceptre.

Eventually, Kezia fell asleep to have more falling dreams. Falling and falling until she woke up, writhing with the sheets wound around her. She thought they were ropes tying her down. She didn't know where she was until she saw the ship in the bottle, moving on the chest of drawers, riding the sea like she was.

"Did you hear her, Kezia? Did you hear her?" Voices. Kezia tried to inhale and the air caught in her throat. When she closed her eyes she was riding a roller coaster but if she opened them the room was spinning and it was worse. The heat burned her skin yet there was ice at her core and nausea spread up from her middle in palpitations that made her weak. She couldn't stop shivering. She reached for the tangled sheets and tried to pull them up, but it was too complicated.

"Did you hear the ghost? Tell us Kezia. Did you hear the ghost last night?" More voices. Darim in the corner.

White dress, she thought. *Ghost*. Her head felt heavy and her mouth felt dry.

"If you tell me I can try to find something to help, but if we don't know, then…" The rest of the sentence curdled in the clammy room.

***

She couldn't remember getting back to the house but there were scratches on her legs and arms. Rollo was slumped by a chair on the terrace and all was quiet, dark. His ears stood to attention but he didn't get up as Kezia sneaked inside and back to bed.

The patchwork quilt, usually superfluous in the sweltering nights, felt paltry and thin. She pulled it right up but it was no good, the cold was in her, she couldn't get it out. She was gasping and shaking, unable to stop… Until finally she drifted into dreams, but they were patchy, like being at the bottom of a shallow pool of water — she could see stuttering shafts of light above but she was drowning and she couldn't swim up.

In the morning, the gossiping of the birds flittered into the room with the cacophony of breakfast. Words scraped and cutlery crashed. There was a pressure behind her eyes and the sunshine hurt. When she went downstairs, Sue and Java were deep in conversation and Normando, who had finished making the omelettes, was sitting in a wicker chair, talking to himself, eyes beginning to close. He noticed Kezia and started to push himself up, but Darim jumped to his feet instead. "No Papa, you rest. I'll get it."

Darim came back with a cold, rangy-looking omelette. "You look tired," he whispered. "Eat."

She picked up a fork and pushed the coagulated eggs around her plate, picking off small mouthfuls and chewing them pathetically.

"Eat. It will keep your strength up," Darim scolded. "And we need to practise!" He went to fetch his guitar.

The omelette tasted odd — sweet — but she looked at Normando and couldn't question it. There was a throbbing, like a little pulse, at her temple.

"Got to keep your strength up for the dancing." Normando was fully awake now. "That one, he's a great musician." He tipped his head after Darim. "But he can't cook to save his life, good thing I'm here." He winked at her.

She took another small mouthful.

"I'll be off to the bar then." Normando set about struggling to lever himself up on the arms of the chair.

"Oh no, not... not today, Mando." Kezia put her fork down. "It's not your job any more, remember? You don't have to worry about that now."

Normando sank back down, his eyes milky, staring off into the distance. "I loved that bar," he said. "Good friends, good food, good conversation, that's what it's all about, right?" He turned directly to Kezia. "Talk to him, will you? Talk to Darim. I need to get back there. Can't be sitting round here all day, it doesn't suit me." He was like a child pleading to stay up past bedtime. Sadness dragged down at the base of Kezia's stomach — she didn't know what to say — so she nodded and quietly finished the omelette so her mouth would be too full to speak.

On the other side of the terrace Darim clapped his hands for the lesson to begin. Kezia stood up.

"Talk to him. Please, er..." He found her eyes but couldn't remember her name. "I miss it. I miss my friends there."

"I'll try, Mando," she said, the promise peeling away inside her head as she said it. Everything felt unreal. She touched his hand briefly before walking over to the class.

Kezia needed the flamenco to fix her. She craved the surge from last night when she had blown like the wind and stormed like the rain; she had been fury and tempest and sunshine and spring and her soul had bloomed with the urgency of nature. She had been there. So, even though she felt frayed now, she intended to find her way back.

Pulse. Step. Tap. They began. Kezia moved her arms and dragged her feet. She was heavy. Her body tired and unwieldy and her thoughts unwieldy too, thoughts of the ghost, the sounds in the dark…

"Kezia. Focus," Darim called across.

Kezia brought herself back in line. The sun stabbed and the glare from the flagstones was almost as dazzling. She stumbled.

"Kezia!" Darim's voice blazed too. She stamped hard and in the wrong place, suddenly conscious of his brown shoe lifting up at the toe and down to the floor, counting the beats, and the line of his jaw, and the flash in his eyes — everything jumping towards her, loud and hot.

Kezia had been expecting the world to come into electric focus again. Colours burning, passions thundering with her heels, but the shapes ballooned and buckled as the power slipped away and the sweat dripped down. The girls hammered their feet into the floor, whisking their skirts into a froth and it was too busy, dizzy — she couldn't keep up. One, two, three, four, five, six. One-two-three-four-five-six. Onetwothreefourfivesix. Too fast.

When Darim started his mournful singing, the rough quality of his voice dragged through her like silt. His face rippled, a mirage, and there was a girl, in a cloak, with long black ringlets, standing behind him saying, "He's mine. Mine. He is mine…" laughing and saying it again. Kezia blinked and the girl was gone. She wiped her eyes and tried to fall back in with the dance, but then she was there again, on Darim's other side, stroking his shoulder as he sang. Darim turned to kiss her, there on the terrace, and Kezia shut her eyes and opened them but this time she didn't go away. And the wall was a bobbing bouncy castle and the trees were pushing near and far like a pop-up-book — and she tried to remember which leg went in front but her feet wouldn't move and the fog was filling her and the girl was laughing again, tipping back her head so her mouth fell open like a mechanical toy and her hair was spiralling to the ground, growing, growing and choking the terrace in a dreadful ivy and that was the last thing Kezia saw before everything went black.

***

191

She heard a door bang and footsteps outside. "Help," she rasped. "Help me." But no one heard. No one came. Kezia tried to draw the bedsheets back but they clung to her, wrapping around her legs so she was a mermaid, washed up on the bed. She writhed and wriggled and eventually managed to push her tail off the mattress, so she could peel the layers back and kick off the knot at her feet.

Crouching like a crone and feeling for the wall to steady herself, Kezia made it to the window. She fumbled for the clasp — taking a shivering eternity to open it — the cool air rushing at her in a body blow. She looked down woefully, summoning strength. "Hello," she whispered, her dusty voice, inaudible even to herself. She bent her knees and held tight to the windowsill. "*Hola?*" It was louder, like twigs cracking, but she regretted the exertion as she felt a sudden thunderbolt in her body — all her impulses firing off without her — her diaphragm juddering and the waves of nausea coming stronger and stronger, over and over, until she couldn't fight them any more…

… she leaned over the window and was violently sick.

It took the full force of her energy. She had vague concerns for the plant, for the patio below, but there wasn't time and everything hurt too much to think. She was recovering, with little gasps, when it happened again. The noise of the illness was so loud in her head she didn't hear the door handle turn and she didn't see Darim stand silently there. She hunched over to be sick a third time and she was retching now because there was nothing left. The curtain was breathing in and out with the breeze and she heaved along with it until the tiny printed anchors seemed to still her own ship.

When Darim returned with a glass of water, Kezia was watching the room turn around her.

"Here, drink this."

The glass floated in front of her face and she wasn't sure if it was real.

***

It was dark when she woke and the moon picked out a shape beside her on the bed. Darim. He was naked from the waist up and the breath fell silently in and out of him with the innocence of sleep. He was little boy Darim, she thought, dreaming of pirates. She watched his eyes move behind closed lids and felt the seconds tick.

Her mouth was so dry it didn't feel like her mouth. She couldn't remember how to swallow. There was a boiled cabbage smell and Kezia thought it must be Rollo until she realised it was the dried sweat on her own body. She inched away from the sleeping Darim.

"You are awake," he said, not moving.

"Yes," her voice croaked.

Darim opened one eye, his eyebrow slanting above it. "Still sick?" he asked.

The waves were gone but the world still didn't feel solid and there was pain in places she couldn't understand. She felt empty and weak and everything sounded tinny. "I don't know," was all she could manage.

"You are pale." Darim turned his head to face her fully and Rollo barked outside and she wished he was here to take the blame for the cabbage smell.

"I need a wash," she confessed.

"Yes."

A laugh bubbled up from the empty pit of Kezia's stomach. She heard it come out but she wasn't sure she had made it.

"You laugh? Why?" Darim frowned.

"You," she said in her rusty, distant voice. "You are so rude."

"I speak the truth. That is not rude. That is polite."

"Polite?"

"Yes, polite. But you, your sickness makes you bolder. I see. It is how it works. You go down to go up. You are made weak to be strong. Yes." He traced the line of her jaw with certainty, as if he had it all prefigured, but Kezia was too delirious to make the words stand still and show their meaning.

A brightness flashed at the window as the sun rode on the wind in a bid to get through the curtain. Darim glanced briefly at it, then back to Kezia. "You heard her, Kezia. I told you not to go down there. I warned you."

Don't go down to the water... The words came back like some long-forgotten nursery rhyme. *Don't go down...* She tried to recall

193

what had happened that evening. "But I saw you go, I saw you leave your room. I saw—"

"What I do is not the same as what you should do," he cut in. "I know this place. All of it. I grew up here and I know where is safe, but you, you do not."

Kezia put her hand on her head, absent-mindedly pulling at her hair. "But… where did you go?"

"Night walks. By myself."

"Night walks?"

"I told you, I sleep little, I sleep light."

Kezia laughed, she felt drunk.

"I speak of serious things, Kezarina," he said. "You must understand — you got sick because you heard the ghost. We must keep you safe now."

Images of that night, the cove, came fast like the nauseous feeling, rushing through Kezia's mind. "The ghost was there… I heard… I heard her singing." She felt like she was living a fairy tale now, that reality had slipped and she couldn't put it back.

Darim unfolded his arms and then crossed them the other way.

"Did your mama see the ghost, before she died?" Kezia's voice splintered. "Do you think she did?"

Perspiration gleamed on Darim's forehead. He stood up, leaving an empty space on the bed beside her. She looked down at it — the dent and crumpled sheets — and the feeling was like finding a bird's egg fallen from a nest: broken and empty.

He began pacing back and forth. Kezia waited. Her thoughts billowed, smoke she could not catch.

Darim stopped, and pivoted to look at her. "Still you ask? Always the questions, even now?" There was searing pain in his eyes. "Well, Mama died at that cove. She fell. I don't… I don't know what happened, I wasn't there." He turned away from her then.

'So sad," said Kezia in her parched voice. "Your poor mama."

"Yes," Darim sounded impatient, he began walking up and down again.

"I'm sorry, I should not have asked." Kezia watched Darim. Her tears were hot and fast.

"You laugh then you cry?" He came back to the bed, standing over her.

194

"I can't help asking questions." She shook her head. "I didn't mean to upset you. I'm… I'm not right. I don't feel… right," she faltered, the mist in her mind mushrooming.

Darim sat back down on the bed and let her cry. After a while she rubbed her eyes and looked at him as if she'd suddenly remembered a nightmare. "Am I cursed now?" she asked.

He took her hand and let the fingers curl gently round hers.

31

Stars

The kasbah sat like a fat sultan, squat and opulent in the centre of a tree-lined garden. The tiled path wound a harlequin welcome through the grounds and bulbous beacons gave off a turgid light. As Darim approached, his guitar slung over his shoulder, it felt as though this was a fortress he should be escaping from, not trying to enter. Guests were sauntering confidently into the gaping mouth of the front door and he hesitated...

A man in blue uniform with shiny silver buttons called a greeting he didn't recognise and, too polite to back away now he had been seen, Darim went in, following a woman in a long flowing coat.

Mats woven with thick threads lined the whitewashed walls: geometric patterns in blue and red and brown. Stained-glass lamps threw drops of colour around like the ghosts of gems and geometric floors hosted smooth mosaics. Candles glowed. Voices bubbled.

Darim wandered from room to room watching insincere people hugging and kissing each other. *I do not like parties,* he thought as a couple screeched at a man with very flat hair and an impish grin. *Too many people too close together, too much fake fun.* There was a feeling of emptiness just above his navel, like a hole opening up.

He found an alcove and sat down. Sinking into the shadows he immediately felt better; he was able to hide. (It was like when Mama took him to her after-show parties and he would tuck himself away, taking notes on human behaviour, listening.) People came and people went and Darim leant his head back on the wall, inhaling the faint damp.

"Mister Darim. Mister Darim. You are here!" Sami had sensed Darim, sought him out. "You are here!" his eyes shone in wonder.

Darim stood and offered his hand and Sami clasped it, pulling him close, kissing one cheek and then the other; he smelt of sandalwood and spice.

"Omar. Omar," Sami called, without taking his eyes off Darim, and out of the melee, his brother appeared, large face beaming, glistening with the heat.

"Ahh. It is our pleasure and our honour, Mister Darim. Please. Come. We drink." Omar's larynx was audibly congealed with stale tobacco and cheese.

They took him to a kitchen table robed in a red checked tablecloth and overgrown with drinks. Bottles and plastic cups formed their own ecosystems, jostling to survive.

"You must drink," Omar said soberly, pouring Darim a shot of vodka and lacing it with sweet syrup and lime. "Tonight is party night, wouldn't you agree?" He pushed the cup into Darim's hands. "We drink!" But he did not make one for himself or Sami.

Darim was about to point this out when a man in a white suit and beryl shirt, with argan-oiled hair and prominent cheekbones, strolled over and placed a hand on Omar's shoulder. "And who is your friend?" he asked in a posh English accent, raising one critical eyebrow.

"Oh, this is Darim," said Omar. "You could say the winds of fate brought us together."

Sami snorted with mirth and Omar whispered something in the man's large ear at which he nodded like a savant. "Good," he said, his eyes, onyx, shining. He inspected Darim before putting his hand out. "Delighted." His palm was dry and puffy. "I am Richard. Welcome to my castle. If you play," he extended his neck slightly to indicate Darim's guitar, "there will be music later." And he bowed and moved along to tell someone else he was 'delighted'.

Darim followed Sami and Omar to a wide white courtyard with a two-pronged fountain gesticulating in its centre. Green plants were climbing the walls and archways led to cool corridors connecting other parts of the house. Food came in small glazed bowls shining like open mouths, passed around by young boys and girls in black. There were herby olives, shimmering like pebbles, snowy white peanuts and dates that tasted of caramel: dazzlingly sweet. Darim liked the tang on his tongue so he reached out his hand for more and always, in the background, there was someone bringing him a drink.

After three glasses of a thick red wine tasting of plums, Darim began to feel differently about the party. Sami introduced strangers and he paid his respects, forgetting names as soon as they were served. Faces slid past him too while jokes gurgled away and he laughed about things he didn't understand and wouldn't remember later. As the conversation wound around him, he thought of his mama; she would be proud he was here. The thought pleased him and he smiled at Sami, who blushed.

It was a gentle thrumming at first. Mellow and insistent. A low tone, dark as the rocks deep beneath the earth, picking its way up and down the string. The resonant pitch sashayed between the notes like confident hips swaying. The sound seemed to land somewhere at the base of Darim's spine: tingling. Seeing Darim's expression, Sami said, "The *oud*. It starts. Let's go." He tugged Darim's sleeve as other, more jangly instruments began to play — musical voices talking all at once.

There were layers of sound, layers on layers, meeting and merging, peaking and dipping. Darim needed to be with them so he walked quickly as they climbed a wide staircase onto a landing, then up a narrower set, to the top of the house. As he stepped outside the warm air blew towards him and the candles flared theatrically.

Darim gazed out, across the coral and umber buildings, the flat rooftops and the shadowy archways. There were spiky palms and glinting lights and other terraces where people were sitting and standing and talking in the balmy evening. Above them all, the sky was a flowing blue cloth, wearing the stars as sequins. He felt the insistence of the music as a landscape of its own, overlaying the tiles and the trees and the tiny twinkling lights.

The musicians sat at the far end in waistcoats and fezzes and focused faces. They were tight-knit and they interacted like they were sharing secrets. When they started singing, the air buzzed with palpable passion. Darim felt it in his throat and he wanted to join in.

He was momentarily distracted when Richard came past in his crisp beryl shirt, jacket removed and sleeves rolled up; he patted Omar on the shoulder and went down the stairs. Darim watched him go, then he heard scraping and turned to see Sami pulling a wooden bench closer, so they all three sat down, like they were waiting for a bus.

Afterwards, Darim couldn't remember how he got involved in the music. It seemed one minute he was visualising joining in, picking out the notes by pressing on his sleeve, the next he was in stride with the song, playing vigorously with the men in their circle.

And when it was over, he found himself back on the bench as if it was all a dream. There were more men with them now and they were talking about work. "So hard. So hard to find a job here." Omar's enunciation was rubbery. "You know, since I left Tariq's there's nothing I can do." He bowed his head, thinking back to the souks, the herbs and the sweet, sweet spices — old Tariq, bent double as he hobbled between the careful piles of cinnamon and paprika. "It's true that his beard was so long it swept into the stock and added an alchemy of its own to the blend." They laughed and then Omar drew his mouth straight again. "But since he sold up, I cannot find another job." He turned to Darim. "They closed the shop and the new owners are going to convert it into a guesthouse. I wanted to be a porter, but they said they didn't need me."

"Said he'd frighten the tourists," Sami teased, catching Darim's eye.

Omar stayed solemn. "It is very hard here. There aren't many jobs. I don't know what we can do. We have an elderly mother to support. I am... I am scared." He opened his hands in his lap, as if to display his honesty. Darim thought of his own fragile papa and his eyes misted.

"I work as a courier," said Sami. "But it's only when they need me so I don't work all the time. I want to be an entertainer in Jemaa el-Fnaa, but Omar says I would not make money."

Darim was thoughtful, looking into one of the empty bowls, terracotta and deep, deep blue. "Mama is a performer, she is a dancer. You can make a lot of money. But..."

They stayed silent, waiting for him to continue, but Darim just turned the bowl around in his hands.

"I would like to try," lamented Sami. "I love to sing. But you have to be lucky, to make it work."

"Luck!" snorted Omar. "We do not have the luck. Sami has all the talent but we do not have the money and we do not have the luck."

Darim looked between the brothers and sensed the sadness there. He took a sip of wine and then he had an idea. He swilled it around with the wine and felt a wave of beneficence run over him; a tangible swelling of the heart. The music seemed to urge him on as the candles glowed encouragement. "Maybe... I can help."

He didn't notice the way Omar and Sami regarded each other, he was thinking about home — all the problems at the bar, how he and Mama were not suited to the hard work. "We have a bar, in Spain, in Parños. My papa runs it but now... it is very sad..." He was hoping to match Omar's candour. "He is not well. He is not well... in the head."

Sami's wide eyes widened.

"He is forgetful," Darim continued. "He makes people the wrong orders, he gives too much away free, he forgets to ask people to pay. We are losing a lot of money because of him."

Sami put his hand on his chest and Omar nodded with shrewd understanding. Their expressions emboldened Darim.

"Mama is famous. *Carlotta de Santos!*" He said her name like he was announcing her on stage, hoping to impress, but their faces showed no recognition, so he continued. "Famous in Spain, anyway. But she will not dance at the bar, she says she will not do frilly flamenco for the tourists, she is too proud."

"So you cannot use her name and charge lots for the tickets." Omar was one step ahead.

"No." Darim said simply.

"And you work there too?" Sami wanted to know.

"Yes, well, no. I play there. And I help, I have to *correct* Papa's mistakes. But I teach and I am studying classical guitar, I am very busy," Darim added, lying, conscious of his mama's chiding and not wanting to sound lazy. When they didn't say anything, he added, "Maybe you could come and help, work at the bar. Maybe..."

Omar nodded as the music ran between them.

"We like Spain," Sami said wistfully and Richard strolled past again, shirt still pristine, holding up a hand in greeting.

"Actually," said Omar, "we have some contacts in Spain. If we had a base there, we could think of other ways for us all to get rich too. This could work out very well, very well indeed."

"Very well," repeated Darim. "I help you and you help me." Mama would be so proud, he thought, finally meeting people, talking money. He relaxed into the hazy feelings of rapport and forgot to ask about the details. Even as they shook hands, he wasn't sure what they were agreeing exactly, he just liked the feeling as the wine and the stars and the music formed a golden bridge between him and his new friends.

32

Spell

She danced in the morning as the sun came up and the beat went *duk, duk, duk* inside her head. She danced slowly, and for herself, making up the steps and marking them one by one. She watched as the sun rose above the sea and she emptied her thoughts of everything except the rhythm.

The sickness abated like a curtain rising. An imaginary audience was clapping the weakness away. She felt clearer and fresher than before, like she had been wrung out and was brand new.

While she had been ill, the face of the ghost hovered. Always there, always just out of reach of anything she could understand… and the song, a chill in her heart. Tiredness was the understudy of sickness and took its place, coming in long waves she could not fight. Tangled days and hours tangoed around themselves and she could not follow their syncopated tempos.

Thoughts of James pushed in like her stomach cramps — sometimes guilt, sometimes grief. When she thought of Gary the anger was heat. Feelings blazed until they burned themselves out, until she lay, quiet and exhausted, and listened to her heartbeat, churning.

Then that day she woke from bland dreams and she knew that it was over. The sky dawned clear and blue. The sun glistened on the flagstones after last night's rain and there was a slippery feeling, everywhere. So she got up, with a rush of blood to the head, and danced through the dizziness. She shoved the swollen memories to the back of her mind and danced, danced, danced.

When she was sure she was strong she looked outside. Darim was at the table talking quietly and patiently to the mute Magdalena and there was a stillness inside Kezia that had not been there before. Next to the window a spider web was wearing the rain like jewellery.

She washed the illness away, scrubbing the sweat from her body, and after that she went to join the class that had already started. She walked slowly past Tomi who had found a dry patch under a bush and was curled up, his paws over his face.

They were warming up, coiling their arms into the air and the sun shone golden optimism, emotions evaporating with the rain. "I am not cursed," she whispered. "A ghost is just a ghost."

She could see Rosa, lithe and supple, her silhouette cast against the trees. Abril and Carmen were by her side, perfectly in time with the movements. Behind them, Java, delicate, like a child, and the more robust shape of Sue. As Kezia got closer, they stopped, heads turned and eyes widened, mouths opening slightly, forming questions that would not come.

"All right, girls. All right. You've seen Kezia before." Darim commanded them to turn around with a sweep of his finger and they reluctantly faced the front, shuffling and tugging awkwardly on their skirts.

Kezia took her place.

"You heard her?" Java hissed.

Darim clapped twice, glaring at Java. "We continue. *Cinco seis siete ocho.* And up, chest up, arms up. Proud. Come on girls. Stop looking behind you. Look through me. Burn a hole in my heart with your eyes. Better, Java. Better."

Kezia joined in the exercises and it wasn't long before her arms began to ache: a familiar, satisfying, ache. It felt good — the beat in the bloodstream — arms and legs moving in the rhythm like they were carried by it, hips swaying in perfect time. She flexed and stretched and let the feeling flow — it was like a warm light streaming inside her, an ivory light, shining and getting richer, infusing her whole body. *Duende.* She had it... Spilling like a thaw after a long and seemingly irrevocable winter. She felt light. She felt free...

Then Darim clapped his hands: a double full stop. "Enough," he said, bestowing Kezia with a special smile.

They stopped for lunch, spicy gazpacho soup made with tomatoes Hady had grown at the back of the garden. Kezia ate very little, feeling dazed and thinking vaguely about Darim without his top on, but the girls wanted her back in the present, asking about the ghost in low whispery voices.

"You *heard* her?" Java looked hypnotised.

Kezia nodded. "I heard... well, I heard something. I think... I don't know, but I think it was her."

"But you got sick, straight away?" said Rosa, concern deep in her rock-pool eyes.

"I know it sounds cracked, but… it happened. I can't… I don't have another explanation. It all feels… quite surreal now. Like even I can hardly believe it."

Sue straightened her glasses. "We were so worried about you. So glad you're feeling better." She smiled, folding her arms over her chest. "And as for the rest, well, there's a lot we don't know about the world. Some things are supernatural, I believe. We don't understand them, but we know they are there."

"Did you see her?" Abril wanted to know.

"No, it was hard to see properly because it was dark, and there was only the moon, but I could hear… I heard this voice and it was so, so sad, like it might crush your heart—" Kezia put her hand on her chest as the memory echoed inside her, feeling the ghost of tears too.

"For real?" Java left her tongue on her front teeth after pronouncing the 'l' of 'real'.

Sue rubbed her arms and Carmen affected a shiver from her shoulders down to her spine. "But Kezia, what were you doing at the—"

Just then Darim returned, cutting Carmen off. "Two weeks until the competition. Come on, focus girls. Focus! No more talk of ghosts." He sliced his hand through the air as if drawing a line under their conversation.

"But Kezia has heard the ghost," insisted Java. "It's the most exciting thing that's happened to me — well, to Kezia, but you know… and I need more details to tell my friends."

"We don't want to put people off coming here, now do we?" Darim's small lips curled upwards, like paper left in the sun.

Across from him, Magdalena scowled, but as usual, said nothing. She had been affecting disinterest in the questions about the ghost but her stealthy eyes had followed Kezia's responses like a panther on the prowl, noting every detail, then pulling back, not to be seen.

"We concentrate on the competition!" Darim pushed down on his words like a stamp.

"What if we lose?" Java was annoyed at the displacement of her favourite subject.

"We will not lose. We will practise until our feet bleed but we will not lose. We will not." And Darim stalked off, towards the garden, Rollo skulking in his wake. He picked his way thoughtfully through the trees at the end and out of sight.

Kezia watched him go.

"How are you feeling now, Kezia? You still look a bit washed out," said Sue.

Kezia smiled weakly. "Getting there," she said.

"Bit of a shock, eh?" Sue put her hand on Kezia's arm, warm fingers sticky.

Rosa crossed herself.

"But what about the curse," said Java. "I mean… If Kezia has been cursed, doesn't she have to break it now? Rosa, what about the village stories, you were telling me once, remember?"

"Hmm," Rosa leant forwards. "Well, yes, I mean, I don't know, but it's what my grandmama told me. She always said to break the curse you have to bring the ghost an offering, something that was precious to someone—" She looked into the distance, pensive. "Something loved by someone, that was it."

"That's what they say," said Abril. "*A token of emotion for her empty existence* — and isn't there a spell too?"

"Yes," Rosa nodded fervently. "I was told there is a spell you have to say, and then you have to stand and hear her sing. She wants to be listened to by the living. So, you give the offering, say the words, and then you listen, even if it turns your heart to ice, you listen."

"Sounds stupid, I think," Carmen turned to Kezia. "And I bet no one has ever tried it—"

"Don't they think Carlotta might have been trying it on the night she died?" Java cut in, her voice hushed but urgent.

"That is… Well, there are rumours," Rosa conceded.

"Others say she was just drunk," said Carmen pursing her lips.

"Could be both, I suppose?" said Sue. "Doesn't always have to be one or the other, does it?"

Kezia watched a black and white cat pawing at a spider, which scuttled away down the crack of a stone slab. She thought about Carlotta, feeling a sudden connection to her — her strength, her pain. "What is the spell? Do you know?"

"I wouldn't try it," cautioned Sue. "We'll look after you. You don't need to be messing with that now do you?"

Kezia didn't answer. Her head throbbed, she watched Rosa twist her lips as she was trying to recall. "Sorry, no, I can't remember, it's a while since I heard the stories."

"I bet Normando knows, seeing as Carlotta was obsessed with the ghost; she's bound to have told him," Abril asserted. "I wouldn't ask him about it though, or Darim for that matter, it's still sensitive, for sure."

Rosa nodded sympathetically. "Sue's right anyway, I don't think we should interfere with the dead, I really don't."

Java looked disappointed, and was about to say something, when she saw Hady calling her to the shed, so she stood up, skittered over to him and they both disappeared inside.

Rosa, Carmen and Abril started talking in Spanish after that and Sue turned her attention back to Kezia. "Do you want to go home now, recuperate there? I mean, it's... well, we'd understand."

"I could leave, but..." Kezia looked to where Darim's black fedora had been left on the wall. "I feel like I'm just beginning to find *duende*, things are just starting to click and... um, there's the competition..."

"Don't confuse finding *duende* with finding Darim." Sue looked over the top of her glasses. "We all know that man's magnetism, but there is flamenco in the UK you know, and the competition, well, that's just a few girls dancing on a wooden stage in the village, and don't let him tell you otherwise."

Kezia fiddled with her spoon, turning it over in the bowl.

"I just want you to do what's best for you, that's all. Especially after one heartbreak, you don't need another, and it's hard to pin that one down." She tipped her head towards the hat.

Kezia's spoon glinted, reflecting the light. She sighed.

"What about your job?"

Kezia shuddered. "I'm going to tell them I'm not coming back. I can't face it; I can't face Gary."

Sue had listened sympathetically to the whole story one sultry evening, when Kezia had been ready and the mood had been right.

206

"Kezia, it's Gary who should have lost his job, not you. Stop blaming yourself when it is clearly his fault."

I know but—"

"You have to report it at least, before it happens to the next poor girl."

"I wish I was strong like you." Kezia pushed her bowl away.

"You're stronger than you think," said Sue. "Look, we can write the email together. I'll help you."

"Okay. But I'm not ready to go back yet, not yet." The cat had found another spider to terrorise and was swiping as it ran in crazed circles. "Anyway," said Kezia wryly. "You can talk, you're still here."

Sue grinned. "Yes, but I'm not young like you, I can afford to be frivolous."

Kezia stood up.

"Don't worry, my love. Things will work themselves out, they always do."

Kezia nodded, narrowing her eyes against the sun and feeling unexpectedly tearful again.

"Always." Sue reached out and squeezed her hand and Kezia sniffed, before squeezing back.

She walked slowly to the end of the garden, feeling the grass prickle under her feet. *Tah da, taka ta.* She let the rhythm lead her as the lavender swayed — *ta da taka ta* — and the smokey blue fragrance reminded her of her grandmother. She strolled past the fretful lion to the trees and she stood at the top of the hill, looking down as the sea rippled with the sun on its back, playing a percussion of phosphorescence. "I am not afraid," she said, out loud, to make it true.

"Good."

Kezia hadn't seen Darim, sat cross-legged at the base of a tree trunk, his guitar by his side.

"Oh," she laughed, embarrassed. "I was just—"

"I know," he said, not waiting for her to finish. "You are finding your power, now that you know — there is much to be afraid of."

"But Darim, you did not tell me there was a cure, you didn't say…" she stopped, suddenly remembering Abril's warning.

"Do not speak of these things," he said abruptly. "They are dangerous. My mama…" he bowed his head as if in prayer. "I do not need to tell you, Kezia, why I warn you against such things. You will make it worse for yourself, you will make it much worse."

"I know, I'm sorry, but Darim... then what can I do?"

"It is simple," he lifted his head slowly. "Just one thing you need to learn. Do not go down to the water again, do not go alone, do not go at night. You do not. Now you will understand."

She squinted out to sea. The light skipped on the surf.

"You must be careful," he said, striking a lachrymose chord on his guitar. "Sometimes the cure is more dangerous than the curse. Just because not all stories are true, does not mean that some of them are."

Kezia watched the waves roll in friendless collaboration.

"We care about you, Kezia. We want to keep you safe," he said, lifting her spirits like a soft wind with invisible power.

She was about to apologise again when her phone rang; a jarring jangle interrupting. She looked at the screen: James.

"It's James," she told Darim, hoping to make him jealous and ending the call without answering.

He blinked slowly before shifting to look at her. "You do not love him," he said dismissively. "He was your security blanket. He was safe. But that is not real protection. That was co-dependency and boredom. That is not what you want. Now you will change. Now you must live for the dance, barely existing outside of the *compas*."

Kezia didn't know what to say. She sat down next to him and watched as he stared out to sea. With James, you always knew what he was thinking, it was either obvious or he told you, but Darim was different; his kaleidoscope mind flashed many colours. *What are you thinking, Darim de Santos?* Her thoughts felt so loud she was sure he would hear them.

He turned. "Kezia. You think ghosts only haunt in the night-time? You think nightmares don't exist in the day?"

Kezia shivered involuntarily, "What do you mean?"

"Some things," he said, half smiling. "Cannot be taught. You have to work them out for yourself." And he reached across to touch her cheek, very slowly, like he was seeing it for the first time.

The moment lasted so long Kezia knew the only way to continue the conversation was to kiss. She edged closer. She held her breath. She looked into his eyes. She heard the air stir in the leaves… She waited.

But Darim snapped his emotions back like elastic. He blinked and took his hand away. He returned to his guitar, rubbing the smooth curves of the wood, then stroking the strings. After that he didn't look at her again, he just sat there, singing, singing, and suffusing her senses with sound.

33

Velvet

$\mathcal{I}$t was the little round terracotta bowls he kept thinking of, glazed deep blue, and the view across Marrakesh, with the square buildings crenelating and the sequin stars, sharp in the sky. The feeling too, his heart a balloon, swelling. He wished he could remember more, but the memory was misty, the words blurred with wine and song.

He stared at the path, the mud fraying around the hard edges of the paving slabs. He gripped his bag and felt the irritation rising. He knew every ridge in every stone and his nose creased with the contempt of familiarity. A bird made a stifled, hollow sound.

"Mama! I'm home."

The trees wrestled with a cajoling breeze.

"Papa?"

Five leaves cascaded down in a gentle ambush.

It was late in the day and half the house was daubed in golden light, the other half wearing a cloak of shadow. Sunlight slanted across the porch showing the places where the spiders spun their secrets and lighting up a leaf so it glowed like an ember. There was dust on the ledges and on the glass panels.

The key was stiff and took two tries to turn — twist and push, twist and push — he knew the knack. He shoved the door open and dry specks of blue paint left their pigment on his palm like a disease. He almost tripped on the mat and looked down to see tiny flecks on its bristly surface too.

Benja was curled up just inside the door, his legs tucked neatly under him. He made a thin wiry noise and stared pointedly at Darim with green alien eyes. Darim sneezed and waved his bag at the cat, who glowered his discontent as he tiptoed away. The desert grit rubbed as he kicked off his shoes by the mat.

Something didn't smell right, and all the blinds were drawn.

"Mama? You could at least have opened the blinds," he shouted. "Where are you? I'm home."

Light sliced through from an upstairs window, staining part of the stairs yellow. There, strewn at the bottom, was one of Mama's dresses, discarded in a puff of petticoats. He imagined her throwing it from the landing in one of her rages.

Darim chucked his bag down and walked towards it, kicking an empty glass which span towards the wall and fractured, the last of the gin dripping through the cracks.

The clock spat seconds from the wall.

"Mama? Papa?" He was still looking at the dress. Something was wrong.

Tomi was sat, half underneath the material, looking at him with the same foul expression as Benja had. "Tomi. Go. Shoot." The cat did not move.

Darim ran through to the kitchen, where Normando was dozing with a small tabby kitten on his lap.

"Papa, I'm back. Why is one of Mama's dresses in the hall? It reeks of gin in there too."

Normando opened his eyes and tried to fling himself forwards, out of the rocking chair, forgetting he was no longer a younger man — remembering only as his joints creaked and his body refused to obey. Stiffly, he looked down at the armrest.

"Stay there, Papa. It's fine. Where is Mama?"

"She was deciding which of her dresses to give to the charity auction for the village. But then Elena Garcia came and said she should just donate money instead, that no one would want her dresses." Normando pursed his lips. "She did not like that, she did not like that at all... She took it very personally, called Elena all sorts of names, even though she's the mayor."

"And where is she now?"

"The mayor has gone."

"No, where is Mama?"

Normando shrugged. "Just got to let her cool down." The little tabby cat jumped off his lap.

Darim marched back into the hall and up to his mama's bedroom at the back of the house. It was a mess as it always was. There were lotions and potions and shoes strewn about. There was jewellery on every surface and wigs growing like mould. Dresses crashed across the room — fated acrobats — on the floor, on the bed, one of them half out the window. Darim sneezed; too many of the cats slept in here. He noted the empty bottle of gin lying on the dresser and considered what his mama might do next. He knew she often went down to the cove when she was in one of her moods, like he did. So he went, pacing down the path thinking of how he would soothe her, what he would say.

There was an eerie stillness as he got there, the pines above watching like statues, the rocks stoic in their solidity. Clouds wrestled the afternoon sun, sinking the bay in shadows and he couldn't see her, couldn't be sure she hadn't gone to the bar for more gin. There was only the sea, sighing with the tide, in and out and in and out. "Mama?" he called, and his voice echoed around. *"Ama, ama, a..."* He followed the sounds rebounding around, eyes darting to cover every crevice. "Mama?" Darim's throat constricted as he staggered towards the stones on the far side of the bay.

Her head was facing away from him, her neck twisted at an angle. He rushed, tripping and slipping. "Mama!" His voice as dry as the desert. "Mama?" The body did not move. He was close now, desperate, struggling to breathe. "Mama, get up." He arrived and crouched down, studying her side for the rise and fall that must surely come. "Wake up Mama. Wake up!" Darim looked about as if someone might save him but the trees looked on, helpless, and the tumble of rocks above told their own story; another bottle of gin, on its side, halfway up.

Carlotta's hand was flung dramatically outwards, performing even in death. Her lips were slightly parted, seemingly singing a final lament, and her eyes were open but dull: a sightless stare. Even in death she was beautiful. Her blanched face was haughty, adamant you could take her life, but not her dignity. Darim knelt as though before an altar. He raised his hands to caress her, and then dropped them again. He tried to understand. She couldn't be dead. She must be there, somewhere, in that stiff body — his mama must still be there. She was the strongest person he knew.

He tugged at the fabric of Carlotta's skirt, inching it up, over her high heels and her firm ankles, and as he pulled, the red velvet separated from the petticoat, leaving a film of fine mesh behind. Her legs were not broken, but she would never dance again. He gripped the material and then let it drop. Turning to her head, Darim adjusted the clip in her thin hair which bloomed like gossamer around her frozen face. He swept it away from her eyebrow and his hand brushed her forehead; she was cold. There was a hard bead of brown blood at her temple.

Not knowing what to do he put his face closer, as if she might sense his presence. He met the faint aroma of jasmine, a dry smell like old paper, and something else… something acrid. The skin around her neck was sagging. "Mama," he groaned, shutting his eyes. He put his lips close and moved forwards — he felt the icy rubber lips of his dead mother — he pressed into them, they were lifeless, a latex mask. He had expected some Sleeping Beauty moment, for his mama to rouse with the kiss of life. He'd expected this to be over. She couldn't be…

She was dead.

Darim pulled away and began to weep. He clenched his fists, arms hanging by his sides. How dare she be dead? He looked her up and down and then reached out again and ran his hand over her long dress, her hip arching gracefully underneath. He smoothed the material where it ruffled over her leg and stayed there like that for a while, the tears dripping onto the velvet.

***

When Darim arrived back at the house, Normando was in the garden talking to an azalea. He didn't notice his son at first, he was so engaged in telling the flower about his recipe for Russian salad, but when he heard Darim sobbing, he broke off and ran sloppily towards him.

They processed to the hall where Darim laid Carlotta in state on the oval rug. They knelt reverently by her and that's when Normando realised — she was not drunk — she was dead. His face shattered in a howl and his heart shattered, never to be repaired.

They cried together. They cried for a long time. Rough, regular ticks ricocheted round — the clock's insensitive truth — but time had stopped for them now. They sat looking down at her pinched nose and cheeks chiselled by death and they stayed like that until Hady came and called the ambulance.

34

Flytrap

James was dancing with Kezia. He could smell the bright peach of her perfume, the faint musk of her skin. It was slow and intentional and he was using the steps he had learnt, his head at an angle which said he understood. Kezia was serious and knowing, keeping her eyes on his as they turned, weaving around each other like the brocade in the White Drawing Room. In a moment, James would reach for the ring. He would pivot with a fast flourish and land on one knee. He was taking his time; he was in control.

"Excuse me?" A man with a thick lisp interrupted James' reverie, crashing him right back into the crimson carpets and crystalline chandeliers of the palace.

"Yes. Hi. Hello." James adjusted his blazer.

"When is the Changing of the Guard?" The man looked at him expectantly, then rubbed his nose.

"You'll need to be outside by ten forty-five," James said, checking his watch. "So in about twenty minutes. It's a woman leading today, by the way, and that didn't happen until 2017, when it started with a Canadian, to celebrate the anniversary of Canada becoming self-governing."

The man wasn't listening. He was conferring with his wife and they scuttled off, determined to get through the state rooms in time to watch the guards in their red coats and bearskin hats.

Left to his own thoughts again, James was haunted by Darim. Images projected in his mind in the same way the Victorians waltzed in the ballroom: Darim dancing, Darim playing his guitar, Darim smiling and turning away. A spell he couldn't shake. For all the high ceilings and sweeping stairs, he couldn't find the space to get away from this man, a man he'd never even met.

On his lunch break he found more of the flamenco videos, he couldn't stop himself, he was making it worse and the knot tightened inside.

"What are you watching?" One of the wardens looked up from his cheese sandwich, pleasantly intrigued.

"Oh, nothing." James silenced the tinny beat, cheeks flushing, as the man took a big bite into the bread, mayonnaise spilling out like a dirty secret.

James watched the rest of the video without the sound. The pictures stayed with him, adding to the anguish, the feeling of Kezia being there, sunny and without him.

The afternoon passed slowly. The visitors took their time, musing over murals and gazing up at cornices where exotic flowers cavorted with posh coats of arms. They studied the tiniest details in the furniture, the embossed silk, the gold leaf or a delicately carved toe. When they asked, he told them what he knew of kings and queens and knighthoods, but as the day drew on, he began to think about that evening. *Beginners welcome...* he pushed the words around, indecision like a revolving door, turning him around in the dilemma. Should he? What if he was the only man there? He was still deciding what to do when he left Buckingham Palace and streaks of baby pink washed across the clouds. His watch said seven thirty, the class started at eight.

***

On the other side of the mall, in her office in Golden Square, where the computers lined up for battle and the voices flew with the urgency of news, Rachel was weighing up the same choice. The pain made her muddled and queasy. *It can't be an excuse or you'll never do anything*, she told herself, a mantra as old as the long skirt she'd found at the back of the wardrobe. It worked well with her block heels and she had been pleased, but now she felt silly — the idea going cold in her mind. The plant trailed its withering limbs down the cabinet. *What do you think Barney?* she asked it silently, smiling grimly to herself about what the others might say if they knew she called it Barney. It was seven thirty. She could make it if she left now.

Rachel had told Andrea how much she adored the flamenco and it was such a lyrical, rhapsodic exhortation that Andrea watched open mouthed and said, "Rachel, Hon, I've not heard you talk like this for… well, since you were pregnant. That's thirteen years, my love. You need this in your life. I know… why don't you go to a class? Yes! You've got to."

Rachel had laughed before she saw Andrea was serious. "No, no way, I don't dance. I can't… I'm a journalist, I *observe*. That's what I'm good at and that's what I know best. No, let's go and watch some together instead, you'd like it too and we can just get drunk."

"Yeah but…" Andrea folded her arms. "No, you need to do it, I think. There was something different about you just now, when you were talking about it. Come on, it'd be good for you to do something outside work aside from looking after Joe — it'll inspire him as well — and didn't the doctor say some gentle exercise might help? Make time. Just one class a week when he's with Andy, what do you say?"

Rachel had protested and the conversation moved on, the notion sliding away, but a few days later, Andrea sent her a link to a six-week course in Pimlico: *Beginners Welcome — Come and Join the Fun!* "It starts on Tuesday, Hon. Enjoy."

Rachel stood up, hoping for some breaking news, something to keep her in the office. Martin was in the corner having a quiet conversation with Piers, the political reporter, and everyone else was either out on a story or clocked off for the day. She checked her phone, then glanced at Barney who waved an aimless frond. *All right*, she told him, and made for the lift.

***

James tripped up the stairs at Pimlico Station, catching himself on the handrail and accidentally stalling a city worker in a dove-grey suit behind. "Sorry." He pivoted to see the man's thick-set feathery eyebrows draw together in a line at the centre of his forehead. "Sorry," he said again, straightening his jacket and moving on. He took the next steps two at a time, emerging onto the road, pursing his lips and starting a shuffling run down the street.

She will love me if I do this. Will she love me if I do this? James wasn't sure. He was getting closer and it felt like an exam, a vice tightening in his stomach. *Is this creepy or romantic?* Hannah thought it was romantic and she was a girl... but she wasn't Kezia. He stopped outside the building, cheeks burning red, deciding what to do. Pimlico Academy was a square hulk of geometric lines, scholastic and functional — a machine for learning in — with its name emblazoned in silver above the glass double doors.

Rachel arrived just after James. She stood behind him as she pulled out her compact to check her face and reapply another coat of searing red lipstick. When she looked up, he was still in her way. She stepped to the side. "Oh, it's you?"

James rotated to see Rachel properly — hair in a tight bun, leather jacket, assertive, assured — the kind of person who would be good at flamenco. Then he recognised her. "Oh, hi. Hi."

"Are you going to the class?"

"Oh, erm, no... sorry, I was meeting someone, but I think I have the wrong place." He looked up at the school and back to her. "Yeah, wrong place."

"Oh. Okay. Well, thanks... for the other day. I felt like such a fool, I can't believe I dropped that mug. Thank you."

"No worries." James wiped his hand across his forehead, displacing his hair. "It happens. It happens quite a lot actually. We budget for it."

Rachel laughed. "Good, well it's nice to know it's not just me with the butterfingers."

James nodded, not knowing what to say.

"Okay, well, I'd better go in then."

James didn't move so she walked around him. "Bye."

"Bye." He held up a hand and watched as the sliding doors opened intentionally like a Venus flytrap. He brushed his hair back into place, watching for just a moment longer before turning, admitting defeat and walking all the way back to the Tube.

***

Rachel didn't look at anyone in reception, she didn't want to see another person she recognised. A bunch of teenagers were sat on the floor like a clump of mushrooms growing organically towards the stairs and the receptionist's head was down, his thoughts buried in his phone. There was a sign at the end of the room with an arrow pointing down. 'Flamenco', it said. 'This way'. She gripped the soft fabric of her tote bag and walked towards it.

On the next floor a queue of people had started filing through a green door. There was a square glass window reinforced with thin metal wires in it, making a tiny grid, like graph paper. The ladies were buoyant and springy and not in pain, they clutched proper flamenco shoes and they all seemed to know each other. The last one in the line turned to regard Rachel, suddenly still, with watchful blue eyes and frizzy blonde hair. "Are you... coming to the class?" she asked, her voice tapering up as if there was a question within the question.

"Ahh. Sorry, I'm... lost," she told her, feeling it.

"Knitting's in room twelve." The frizzy lady nodded across the hall. "Opera is down the way, you'll hear it... and life drawing is at the very end of the corridor. That's all that's on tonight, I think. Reception's that way." She banged the door shut before Rachel had the chance to pretend to be grateful.

Through the glass mesh, she could see them all stretching and laughing and donning big wide colourful skirts. "*Vamos!*" A slight woman, standing very straight, walked placidly to the front and the pupils lined up in rows, taking their positions on the graph paper grid. Rachel ducked away before the teacher could see her.

On her retreat, hurrying down the street she texted Andrea and confessed.

What happened? she added. *I used to be brave, I'm sure I did.*

Life happened. Don't beat yourself up. You're so harsh on yourself.

Rachel put her phone in her pocket and considered this. She felt a sense of failure and relief, spinning like two sides of a sycamore leaf, rotating to the ground. *Maybe next week*, she told herself, but she knew from the look in the blonde woman's eyes that she would not be going back. It was just another place that she didn't belong.

35

Pine Cones

"Where are we going?" Kezia was struggling to keep up.

"To the forest."

"But I thought we were meant to be practising? You said, and the competition is next week—"

"This is practice," said Darim, striding ahead.

"Really?" Kezia skipped over a stone to avoid tripping. It was hot and the sun seemed to be peeling back the layers of nature, everything bright and raw. "How is this—"

Darim held up his arm to silence her, finger pointing to the sky. "Wait," he said. "You will see."

So Kezia wiped the sweat from her face and followed, as the sea far down below rolled in and out, in and out, patiently and forever.

When they got to the edge of the forest, Darim turned triumphantly and bowed, ushering her inside so that he seemed to dive from the end of the movement into the woods in a seamless sweep, disappearing from sight. Kezia laughed and went after him.

Brown and green. It was dim under the canopy and pleasantly cool; a damp dark, sodden with the scent of rotting pine. It smelt like Christmas, and mud. "I like it," said Kezia. After the midday glare it was like taking a cold drink. Only a few shafts of sunlight filtered through to the forest floor, puddles of milky yellow, shimmers like dreams. Further ahead tree trunks and shadows merged in a game of hide-and-seek.

When they came across a clearing of eight or nine pines guarding a sort of circle, Darim walked in as if it was an arena. "This way, Kezia, come in here. That's right." He helped her over a fallen tree trunk. "Now, look around you Kezia." And he raised both arms. "Look."

She looked. She was hoping he had brought her here to kiss, but she could never read him, she never knew.

"Look at the trees, Kezarina. Here they are. When the wind blows, the trees bend, when it rains, they get wet and the sun makes them grow." Darim lifted his hands to indicate the light. "They change, they *react!*" He prodded the air as if putting the dot on an imaginary exclamation mark.

Kezia looked again at the trees crowding in; they didn't look very animated.

"When the wind blows, Kezia, do you bend? Or do you try to stand up straight?"

"Um, I don't know."

"You try to stand up! I have seen it. You talk of things that make you angry, but you are not angry, you are only sad. You sit, like a wet tissue, so the anger does not shift and move around your body. This is not good. This is not healthy. You have seen much. You react little. This will not make you a good flamenca either, because you need to feel things and show them through your dance. The trees…" Darim swept his arm around the clearing. "Do not try to hide anything. They do not desire to be a rose or a fern, they are as they are and they do not apologise. I do not see that in you. Yes, you are bolder since your illness, but it is only the first step. I want more, I need more and I need to see it in your dancing." He nodded, agreeing with himself, "You are apologising in your dancing right now, as if the bullies are still around you, as if they are ready to take you down. But no, you must not apologise for being you. I want to see the real Kezia. Fire. Passion. Shake them off. Why don't I see it? Why don't I feel it seething out of you when you stamp your feet and toss your head? I don't see it because you are holding back. You do not hold back in flamenco!" Darim finished and sat down on a log.

His words stung the open wound left by Gary. Kezia turned away, ambushed by the memory. *There's a real sweetness about you…, but we just need you to be a bit more… real.*

"Yes, Kezia," he said softly. "You are upset, I see that. We want to turn that emotion into something more useful to you."

She stayed facing a tree. "But I told you, I found *duende*, I'm getting there."

Darim acquiesced, lowering his head. "There is more," he said and began inspecting the log.

"I am real," she said, moving towards him again. "I'm just… polite. It's important to be polite."

"Why?" He looked up, kindness and curiosity swirling in his lambent eyes.

"Why? For other people, so you don't foist your emotions on them. It's not fair."

"That is not fair on you."

Kezia shrugged.

"No, we do not shrug it off. We do not bottle everything up inside, or we get sick. Do you want to get sick?"

Kezia shook her head, but then reassessed. "My mum said it's not ladylike to be angry."

"Pah!" Darim stood up. "You never met *my* mama. You want to be ladylike? You want to be like a lady? Then you let it out! Be powerful. Make your mark on the world. Be strong, like a woman should be. You let it out, you feel better. Do you want to feel better or do you want to be like a small string of seaweed being tossed about by the ocean? *Be* the ocean Kezia. Be the ocean."

"I don't know if I can."

"It is the most natural thing in the world. But you have suppressed it for so long, you have forgotten. Did you cry as a baby? Of course you did. Did you scream when you were upset? Yes. So, you can. I see the pain inside you and it's got… how to say it? Clogged up. It thickens the blood in your veins and stops you from moving properly. So now, we start. We let some of that out. You scream." His smile was the lick of a flame, flickering across his face.

"Scream? Darim, I can't."

"Yes. Here. You scream. We are in a forest. No one will hear you. It is quite safe. Let it all out."

Kezia narrowed her eyes at him. He didn't move. A fly flew between them, buzzing vociferously. "I don't… I can't, I can't just stand here and scream."

"You screamed when you saw me on the night of the *leveche*."

"That was different."

"Why?"

"You surprised me. It was dark. I wasn't expecting—"

"There are lots of things in life we don't expect. They don't all turn up on a dark night in the middle of a storm. So, you need to scream for all of them. I told you, you will feel better." He got up and walked over to the nearest tree, looking at the gnarled old bark, tracing a line down one of the ridges with his finger.

"It would be weird. I'd feel stupid," she said to his back.

"Stupid not to."

"Why are you taunting me like this?" Kezia suddenly felt hopeless. "It's not fair. Yes, I have been upset, but I'm away from that now, and I want to move on."

Darim swung around, eyebrows arching. "Don't you understand, you can't move on until you purge it from your system. Until you purge *him* from your system. I still see him affecting you — I don't want that."

Heat pricked the back of Kezia's eyes and her mouth was pulling down in the tug before tears. "I don't want to think about the time before. I just want to be here with you," her voice wobbled. "Why can't we?"

Darim considered this. "Because your emotions haunt you until you shake off your ghosts." He put his head to the side, as if willing her to understand.

"But…" Kezia turned towards the edge of the clearing. A sapling tickled her ankle and a spear of light hit her face. "But…" The tears came. Glass tears. Pure and empty.

"Yes, cry," said Darim. "Next you will scream for me. Try now. Try it."

Kezia walked towards the trunk of a tree and collapsed onto it, letting it support her, heaving with the grief that came welling up now, the tears that would not stop, like a pipe that bursts when the constant cold is suddenly too much. She was only partially aware that Darim had moved and was hovering, just beyond her left shoulder. "Now," he said. "Now you scream."

Kezia inhaled a snuffly breath and, as much out of frustration as anger, she let out a guttural scream. It was mired in the mucus of crying, stifled by snot, but it was there.

The next scream was clearer. It came from the underside of her heart. The pent-up pain found voice in the sound. She screamed louder, picking up momentum now, and as the wails passed from her core to the outside, she could feel some of the emotion leaving with them, the hurt being absorbed by the family of trees in the forest.

Her last scream petered away and the tears came again, bitter rivers down her cheeks. She put her head against the bark and her shoulders shook. There was just her and the tree and crying for a long time, letting it out, aware only of the reassuring solidity of the wood.

"That is the passion that needs to come out when you dance," said Darim his voice as gentle as a falling leaf.

She turned, aware that her freckles would have flared up on her face, aware of her vulnerability and hating it. Exhausted, she sunk to the base of the trunk and twisted around so she was sitting with her back to it, the knobbly parts digging in.

She was sniffing and shaking but she did feel better now, leaning into the support of the hard tree. The forest soothed her; the timeless essence of nature, the branches reaching up to something they could not see. "I can't believe you made me do that." Her words were puffy with a laugh that never came.

Darim sat down by her side and smiled as if the emotion had left him as well.

She shut her eyes, giving in to the tiredness after tears. Her chest heaved in and out with the same urgency as the sobs but silently now, finding a new rhythm, as a stream follows gravity, finding new grooves for its flow.

She wondered what James would think and tried to picture his face, but it blurred and she noticed her thoughts about him felt smoother than they used to and didn't catch at her any more. "Gravy goes with everything." An old memory drifted. James drawing great circles with the Pyrex jug, drowning the salmon in a brown watery grave. *Grave-y*, she thought now, smiling, and letting the feeling of the branches brush over the words, over the memories, over the sky.

"You are a good pupil. You learn fast, Kezarina," Darim said softly. "But you teach me things as well. You teach me to be curious, I think… I think somewhere I lost that." The trees whispered, a rustling that surrounded them with secrets, shared and gone. "Your smile," Darim said. "Is pure sunshine. Now it will shine brighter, Kezarina." His face flushed with something like shyness. "Now," he said. "Let's go back. You are right, we have a competition to prepare for."

36

Handcuffs

There was an unbearable stillness in the house, tangible and thick. The clock stopped ticking. It throbbed its final second and froze inexplicably — never to work again — the horological equivalent of a heart attack. That last tick sounded louder for the lack of any others, but neither man mentioned it as they sat on the bottom step of the stairs and waited for the ambulance to come.

The blue lights flashed outside and the men in green uniforms ran towards them; everything fast and out of focus. Darim and Normando didn't move when they took Carlotta away, not wanting to leave the place where they had last seen her.

Then the police came with hard shoes and loud voices. They strode straight in and told them to stand, so they rose, unsteady, propping each other up. There was a faded image in Darim's mind, like a mirage: her face, white, a death mask — and he couldn't see past it or through it — it was there, everywhere he looked. He reached for the banister, needing to hold on as the hall felt like a ship, moving up and down.

Papa said something; he was talking to the police and they were asking questions too quickly, in long waves of words. He couldn't catch them or fix them together, couldn't focus long enough to make them stay in a sentence. They buckled and warped and all his thoughts fell through his brain like a cloud. He had to sit down again. The strength was draining from his muscles as the thoughts were falling through his head. Everything slipping, emptying, pulling him down and people, lots of people making noise.

The handcuffs snapped on and he didn't move, so they pulled him up and pushed him to the door. Then they were outside and he was hitting his head against the side of the police car and falling into the back seat, the leather nutty and hot.

The journey was a blur — roads, houses, dense patches of trees, everything flowing away from him — and it was still moving when they got to the police station. "Why am I here?" he asked, dazed, as they went in, but they didn't answer, just kept him walking past a series of dark corridors and airless offices.

Eventually they prodded him in the back to steer him left. There was a plastic table and some plastic chairs in the room and that was all. They sat him down opposite a man Darim recognised from the village. He was young and he was trying to grow a moustache but the hair was like thin strands of cotton. His father had supplied beer for the bar until Normando caught him under-delivering on the order. He had blamed the old man's senility, "He cannot count," he had said, but Normando was adamant and had cancelled the contract.

More police filed in, leaning against the wall, watching. The officer opposite opened a notepad then started drilling questions into Darim — question after question — and he was trying to think, trying to remember. What happened? He'd come home and she was dead and that was all but they were making it more than that and it was confusing. As Darim looked around, he started to identify more faces from the village, the taunting faces of his younger days, the ones who pushed him around, the ones who spat on his guitar. They were enjoying seeing him there, powerless in the chair, no famous mama. He stumbled over his words, a child again.

"Let's go over this one more time. You say you were in Morocco, and you came back to 'discover' Carlotta — your mama — at the cove: dead?"

"Yes. I told you." Darim shifted, sliding slightly on the plastic chair, the grief constricting his heart.

The officer with the thin moustache looked up from his notes. "And you had an argument with Carlotta just before you left. That is why you left?" He scratched his top lip and Darim thought some of the hair might come away. "That is what Normando told us. Is it the truth?"

Darim looked at his hands. "No... well, yes," he said. "We had the argument, yes, but that is not why I left."

"Then why did you leave?" a man behind him said with a smirk.

He didn't turn around "I wanted to travel."

227

There was a barbed laugh and the officer at the table wrote imperiously in his pad. "And you have your tickets, we'll need to check the dates."

"I... I don't have them."

The man looked up and frowned.

"I threw them away. I hate keeping things I don't need. It is clutter. It makes me feel unclear. Mama is a hoarder, she keeps everything. Well, she did... I don't. I threw them away when I arrived at the port."

"Handy," said the officer he couldn't see.

"And you went on your own?" continued the one with the notepad.

"Yes." There were dust motes in the air, just above the officer's head. "But I met some friends, when I was there, in Morocco. They will tell you where I was on Friday night."

"But not on Saturday? Not today?"

"Well, I came home this morning, earlier."

"Right," said the officer, dismissively jotting it down. "We'll need to speak to them anyway."

Darim looked uncomfortable. He had not planned to contact Omar and Sami. He had made a promise he didn't want to keep, about the bar, about giving them work. He had slipped away hoping they wouldn't recall the words woven in the wine-soaked evening — hoping it would be a swirl of stars and music for them as well. "Yes," he said, his mouth so dry the word stuck. "But you could just... you could just ask Papa. He will tell you what happened. I came back home and I found her like that. She had an argument with Elena, she was upset, she'd been drinking and she went down to the—"

"Trying to implicate the mayor of Parños will not help your case, Señor de Santos. Are you saying it was her fault? How could it possibly be her fault? Trying to *slander* others will only make you sound guilty." He pitched forwards, pen in hand. "You know some think you were after your mama's money... Couldn't stand her any more, could you? Decided to push her off those rocks?"

"No, and I was not there. I wish I had been there. I am the only one who knows how to quiet her rages, and I was not there. I... for that I am guilty." Darim hung his head.

The man rubbed his itchy top lip again. "We believe the best way to proceed is to double-source all of our evidence. I'm sure you understand, Señor."

Darim pinched the piece of paper in his pocket, Omar's number scrawled in scratchy biro, almost perceptible between finger and thumb.

"Señor de Santos?"

"Yes, yes," said Darim without knowing what he was saying yes to and taking his hands out of his pockets as if to show he was listening.

"So we will contact your friends. How do you know them?"

"We met in a sauna."

The man's eyebrows rose right to the top of his head. "A sauna?" he exaggerated, playing to the crowd, and the policemen at the back of the room tittered appreciatively.

"Well," Darim qualified, feeling the oppression of their laughter. "We met there and then I went to their party and we made music together and—"

"You made music together?" The officer cut him off, to the continued amusement of the others. "Okay, that is enough for now. Let him go. We will be in touch, Señor de Santos. Don't go running away now — if you do we will track you down and you will be locked up."

Darim only realised he was clenching his fists when the sweat ran down, like water.

37

Owls

𝒮he thrones stood side by side on the scarlet stage, regally inscribed with the monikers *EIIR* and *P.* A carmine curtain fell like a blood waterfall behind and the steps concertinaed down from the dais, taking the plush carpet to every corner. The opulence was oppressive.

As ever, Darim was there, magisterial and laughing, leaning back on the throne irreverently, stroking the fringe of tassels under the armrest. James blinked and the image faded slowly. He looked away, up to where the crystal chandeliers dived down like octopi, heads full of candles, tails full of gold.

"So have you heard from Kezia?" Chris was taking pictures casually with a huge camera he had borrowed from the office, enjoying the long lens and the feeling of power. For once he wasn't wearing his hat.

James' lips went flat together. "No mate."

Chris framed an ornate wall motif: a burnished bird stood on a tambourine. "I still think you should surprise her, just book a flight. Think about it, going the extra mile, literally, it would work." The bird held out its wings as if it agreed.

"What if she doesn't want to see me though?"

Chris swayed his head from side-to-side. "Well, then you're no worse off than you are now. But at least you'd know." He stopped taking pictures. James was looking down at his sensible black shoes, his hair falling across his forehead. "Mate, it'll be all right. Every relationship goes through its ups and downs. You just need to ride out the storm. You guys are good together."

"I think so," James said quietly.

"Tenacity, that's the name of the game, like I told you." Chris gripped the camera and was about to say something about Elly, when a torrent of tourists eddied into the room in a tide of guidebooks and selfie sticks.

"Wow, is that where the Queen sits?" asked a startled looking man in a cadmium blue raincoat.

James looked up, fixing a smile to his face. "Yes, they are called the Chairs of Estate and they were for the coronation of the Queen in 1953. That's hers there and the one with the P was for Philip, the Duke of Edinburgh."

"Can I sit on them?" asked the man, clomping over to elbow James and showing him the gap in his front teeth.

"More than my job's worth I'm afraid." James grinned back. "But come closer and I'll show you something." They padded towards the thrones. "Look, see that blue band around both sets of initials, there, like a belt?" He pointed. "That's called the Garter Circle, it's from the Order of the Garter; the oldest order of chivalry we have."

"Ha, and I thought chivalry was dead!" The man's raincoat crinkled with his mirth. "But they want it both ways now, don't they, the women?" He snorted. "They want it all equal opportunities and that when it suits them, and still to be treated like princesses; have their cake and eat it. But they know, deep down inside they want a man to sweep them off their feet and you can't change that, it's human nature, right?"

As the man was busy nodding self-righteously, James saw himself charging up to the flamenco school on a glossy white stallion, hooves kicking up the dust, jumping down and drawing his sword against Darim, the sharp steal glinting in the late afternoon sun...

He realised the man was looking at him, so he coughed and said, "Yes... and see how dramatic the canopy is, like the thrones are on stage? Well, that's because it was designed by the architect John Nash, and he had a background in theatre set design."

"Drama. Ha!" The man elbowed James again. "That's the other thing women want, trust me. They just *love* the drama."

Before James could say anything, a shrill voice called the man from the other end of the room. "Bernard, come and look at this." He smiled and shrugged and tramped over to his wife on very flat feet.

As he departed, two Japanese girls sidled shyly up to James. "Excuse me," they asked in perfect English. "We have a question." And they led James over to an imposing picture of the Queen in a white robe and a sweeping blue cape with four corgis stationed loyally at her feet. "What are their names?" One of the girls pointed to the dogs.

"Erm, Willow. Vulcan... Candy and Holly," James recalled, motioning very loosely because he wasn't exactly sure which one was which.

"Ooh," the girls said. "Thank you." And left the room, satisfied.

"You're too good." Chris had been watching from the corner. "How did you know someone would ask about the dogs?"

"Oh, they always do," James replied earnestly. "Honestly, I tell the wardens to learn all of the animals and any stories about them. Queen Victoria was especially fond of the monkeys on the piano in the White Drawing Room, stuff like that, people love it."

"Sweet," Chris mused, adjusting the settings on his camera.

"I guess it's the mix of the grandeur and the little animal faces that delights them, kind of out of place amongst all the austere furnishings."

"Yeah, makes sense." Chris looked back at the corgis and framed them for a shot, taking his time to capture the shine in their eyes and the wet look of their noses. "Right, I guess I better get back to the office. I've got enough pictures now. Good to see you mate."

As Chris left the room he glanced back at his friend, observing the sadness in the slump of his shoulders. He pursed his lips, feeling for the cross around his neck and sliding it up and down the chain out of habit. At the door he quickly checked the state rooms' social media accounts on his phone — nothing to respond to — before stepping outside, squinting up at the clouds.

It started raining as Chris wandered along The Mall, a misty, ghostly rain, hanging in the air and leaving a spectral film on lamp posts and traffic lights. He wished he'd brought his hat as it shivered over his head, damp and persistent. A squirrel zigzagged across the path, alert, athletic, eyes like black LEDs, and then darted up the gnarled trunk of a tree. Chris inhaled pensively, getting out a butterscotch vape and letting it percolate his thoughts. *He loves her, she loves him...* He remembered them all laughing together in a park last summer, Max lurching between them on stumpy unsteady legs, the sun high in the sky. *She just needs... reminding...* An empty crisp packet skittered across in front of him and the rain thickened, inhabiting the mist, turning it into a relentless drizzle. He didn't notice.

He was still deep in thought when he made it back to the office. He sat down heavily, ignoring the burble and banter, and stared straight ahead at his computer, not really seeing it.

"Are you all right? Did you get the pictures? Is it raining?"

Chris didn't answer at first, still staring intently into the mid-distance.

"Chris?"

"Oh, yeah, sorry." He turned to face his colleague, Kate, wiping a glaze of water from his forehead, like cold perspiration. "Yes, great, got the pictures, all quite photogenic over there. Sorry, I'm just a bit distracted, I'm worried about my friend." He rubbed the back of his neck.

"Oh, can I help?" Kate rolled up the sleeves of her cardigan. She always wore cardigans. Today's was dusky blue.

Chris adopted a philosopher's pose, hand on his chin. "No, no, better not. I guess... I'm sure he'd rather I didn't tell you. It's his own stuff, you know?"

Kate nodded. "Sure, well I hope he's okay." She turned efficiently back to her press release.

After a while, Chris made a noise a bit like a whale and Kate looked up again.

"Sorry, that's the sound I make when I'm thinking."

She laughed and shook her head. "Carry on then," she said, wafting a delicate hand in his direction.

Chris screwed up his mouth, his mind straining at the leash to help. He thought back again to that day in the park, the way the light tessellated through the trees and made shapes on their faces, the idle chatter and the warm feeling of flat lemonade. She just needs reminding. That's what Sarah and I always do when we've had a bad day or an argument, we look back at some of our old holiday snaps and we laugh at some of the memories, the stupid expressions and the drunken nights before Max and Ava came along. Chris scrolled through the camera roll on his phone and found the shots of the picnic. There they were, James and Kezia posed together on the blue tartan rug; James in a plain white T-shirt holding a bottle of beer and Kezia in a black and white blouse, sunglasses pinning her hair back. You could see Kezia's dimples and how proud James was to be with her.

233

He looked for Kezia's number, the plan forming somewhere outside his conscious mind, but there was nothing between Kevin and Louise.

"Chris, have you edited those Throne Room photos yet?" Ash called over.

"Nearly," he lied, as the idea took shape and he opened Instagram, momentarily distracted by a picture of a hot air balloon over Devon. He moved stealthily so that no one saw, feeling like an undercover agent and smiling at the thought of a reunion caused by him. "Just call me Cupid Chris," he muttered as he adjusted the filter on the image, making it lighter, evening out the dappled fingerprints of the leaves. "Even better," he purred. "Now..." He found Kezia's account — @Kezia_Duke — it was definitely her because she loved owls and the profile picture was an owl with brown eyes and a patchwork body: blue, purple and pink. "Now, what to say..." He chewed on his fingernails, thinking. After a while, Ash stood up, so he quickly grabbed the lead for the camera and jammed it into his computer to transfer the photos across. Scrabbling back to his phone he had a flash of inspiration.

Summer picnic, summer memories, he wrote. *Let's do this again soon @Kezia_Duke when you come back from your flamenco lessons in Parños.*

Pleased he remembered the name of the place as it would make him look thoughtful and caring, he added the hashtags; #summer, #fun, #picnic and #love. He let the word 'love' come and go as he deleted and typed it a few times, then he bit his lip and decided to go for it. He pressed send.

Quickly, he turned back to the pictures of the Throne Room, picking out the best shots, the ones where the crimson velvet looked the most lavish and the thrones the most decadent and august...

Something was wrong with his phone. It was buzzing so much it was moving across his desk. Chris wrinkled his nose and tried to apply himself to the sheen of the insignia, but the reverberations didn't stop, the notifications kept on coming. He picked the handset up to see he had fifty-seven 'likes' in one minute from people he didn't know, names from all over the world...

That's when he realised.

He knew what he had done.

In his haste, Chris had forgotten to toggle back to his own private account to send the post. He had just sent it from the royal account — to six and a half million people worldwide. His photo was next to a painting entitled, '*A Lady at the Virginals with Gentleman*', by Johannes Vermeer, where two people from the seventeenth century clashed, in their staid pose and muted colours, with the modern shot of James and Kezia.

Chris' mouth went dry as he darted at the image, missing his mark several times before he managed to delete it. "Oh God," his heart was a timpani, at the crescendo of an orchestral epic.

"What?" Kate looked up, adjusting her sleeves.

"Erm." Chris was holding his neck at a funny angle.

"What?"

"It's nothing. It's okay. I'm okay."

"Your friend again, right?" Kate's heart-shaped face was suffused with concern.

"Right," said Chris, chest still thudding. "Yeah, my friend." He looked back down at his phone. The post was definitely gone. He hoped Ash hadn't seen. He tried to focus back on the pictures he had taken, shaking slightly, unable to concentrate on the bird standing on the tambourine.

The post was deleted, but it was too late.

In an office in Golden Square, even as Chris' heartbeat was returning to normal, Rachel, who had been following up her feature about the state rooms and checking the royal Instagram account to tag online, had seen the shot and sensed a story. She had captured it before it disappeared, and when it vanished, she was even more sure. She studied it and she recognised James. *You again*, she mouthed, thinking about the flamenco lessons and wondering if it was all some kind of sign.

38

Cherries

Sami was carving a small Rollo out of wood, with firm, quick flicks of his wrist. The real Rollo was lolling by his feet, oblivious to his role as muse. The more Sami carved the more he thought about Darim and Kezia together. All the time together. He felt forgotten. He felt put aside.

A group of tourists lumbered out of the bar loudly, carrying the dregs of their final bottle of wine, the door swinging open onto the creamy sunshine.

Sami looked around the now empty room and then back to Darim. "I saw you. I saw you go to the woods with Kezia. Why? What's going on?"

"Private lesson." Darim stared impassively at Sami.

"You can't do that."

"I teach people what they need to learn, however they need to learn it. That is my job."

"You make her scream. I heard it."

"Yes."

Sami stared back but before he could say anything, Omar came tramping in from the back.

"Who is screaming?"

"Kezia," said Sami. "In the woods with Darim." And he went back to his wood, making Rollo's head smooth and curved.

Omar rounded on Darim. "What? Do you want to draw more attention to us? What are you doing? Are you crazy?"

"I was teaching her a lesson." Darim adjusted himself in his seat.

Omar frowned. "Well, we'd all like to teach her a lesson but—"

"No. Not like that. I was teaching her — a lesson," Darim clarified.

"A lesson in how to scream?"

"Exactly." Darim sat back and crossed his arms.

Omar rubbed his rubbery nose. "You need to be careful."

"Yeah," muttered Sami belligerently, concentrating on Rollo's wooden face, finishing two surprised-looking eyes.

"Screaming in the woods is the last thing we want right now." Omar's lip contorted in annoyance. "And anyway, that girl asks too many questions."

"Stop panicking." Darim crossed his legs.

"You don't get it, do you? She is too... present." Omar lifted both fists. "I mean, the other girls come and go and come and go, but it seems you two are always... together."

"She is my favourite. Yes."

Rollo had gained a paw but almost lost it again as Sami looked up quickly while carving.

"You are not allowed to have favourites," said Omar firmly.

"I cannot choose whether to have favourites. You either have a favourite, or you don't."

"Okay." Omar glanced at the door, but the couple holding hands outside looked at the menu and decided not to come in. "So you can't help it. But you can stop it."

"No."

"Yes. Just don't spend so much time with her. She is getting nosey. I can tell. She might end up prying into our little secrets. Pillow talk is cheap, it must not come to that. Maybe we need to scare her properly so she'll go crying back to England..."

"I need her for the competition," said Darim, picking a piece of dirt out of his fingernail.

"Well, you can just get another dancer to make up the numbers. Everyone round here thinks they can dance flamenco."

"But they cannot."

Sami whittled with deft, decisive strokes, giving Rollo a tongue, which hung giddily out of his mouth.

"She is distracting you from what's important." Omar stood over Darim, hoping to make an impression with his size.

"No." Darim did not look up at him. "You are distracting me from what's important. Flamenco is important. Dancing is my life."

"And how would you survive financially without us? Ha! You'd be ruined and you know it. You need us or your precious school would have gone under, and that is the truth."

"My school does not need you meddling in it. When we win this competition, we will have enough money to keep going on our own. We will attract more students too. It is not up to you who dances and who does not dance. It is my school and I will run it the way I like. Mama," Darim made the sign of the cross, "Mama would have wanted it that way. It is important the traditions are passed on in the right way. I do it in memory of Mama."

"In memory of your mama? That's rich. You use and abuse that one whenever it suits you, don't you? I guess she would have approved of that too." Omar arched his eyebrows and there was a small silence filled only by the slicing of Rollo's newly formed tail.

"Just don't forget, you owe us. If we had not stepped in to testify for you, you'd most likely be behind bars by now, you know you would."

"No, what good were you in the end? You could not account for the Saturday morning. No, it was Papa who convinced them—"

"Your papa thinks Carlotta is still alive. A credible witness, huh?" Darim began to say something, but Omar cut him off. "It's a shame your father could remember the argument you had with Carlotta but not when and how you came home. It's the loud things, I guess, the loud things people remember, like screaming in the woods." His smile emitted a dull malice. "You have to stop being so explosive, Darim. You seem to have forgotten so much. And think of this: where would this bar be too, without us? We helped you because your papa was too infirm to carry on. You need us, Darim de Santos. Or do you want your papa to go back to handing out free drinks to anyone who wanders in off the street? Not keeping the books. Not knowing who is taking money behind his back and in front of his front. Money down the drain. Bar down the drain. Is that what you want? No. You want to dance." He grimaced. "So you better do as we say. We do the business for you, fine, but we will not have anyone interfering, you understand? No silly little girls in flamenco dresses around here." Omar glowered over Darim. "You need us. We saved your bar and we saved your life and we saved your stupid pointless little school."

"That school," Darim stood up. "Is my heart."

"Then you better do as we say, or there will be no school and we will stop helping you pay off the debt your father accrued on this bar. We are your saviours. Do not forget it."

Sami put his sculpted Rollo down and looked innocently at Darim.

"So," Omar continued, his gruff voice hushed with the taint of conspiracy. "We are going to scare the girl off and you will help us. A bit of gentle pressure, that's what's needed, because there is no way she is going to find out what is going on here. Do you understand?"

A gaggle of expats came in and stood at the back of the bar. "*Buenas. Qué tal?*" said one of them awkwardly.

"Ahh yes, welcome," Omar fawned. "You want to eat, drink? Come in, do come in." And he fussed around them with menus and serviettes, fielding questions about the food.

Darim picked up his guitar and went to sit in the corner where he played quiet, unobtrusive strains, 'restaurant melodies', he called them.

When the people had eaten a vast selection of tapas and drunk four carafes of red wine, they went away blithely, singing a song about a black horse and a cherry tree.

Omar was in the kitchen and Darim came back to where Sami was sitting, rubbing the real Rollo's ears absent-mindedly. "Mister Darim," said Sami. "They liked the music, they liked it a lot. They give a big tip."

Darim nodded curtly, not wishing to equate his art to money.

"They talk about the horse's hooves they saw on the path. Did you hear them?"

Darim shook his head. "No, I was with my music."

"Well, they talk of the hooves. They are mine." Sami paused, pushing back his shoulders. "They are mine. I found them over by the farm and I took them to make special castanets — special hard sound." He clapped his hands together. "They don't know why they are there but I know. I wrapped them in newspaper and tucked them into the side of my bag... but when I got home, they were gone. They must have fallen out." Sami looked at Darim and said deliberately, "I was singing '*La Vio el Rey David*' on the way home and I must have got carried away..." He started to sing in a dazzling and enchanted voice, and he moved his hands as if to show himself getting over zealous. "I was lost in the music and I lost the hooves."

Darim frowned. "They were diseased. You should not be touching them." His lips curled in distain. "And what have we told you about singing in public… It's… Omar would not be happy. We need to protect that voice like we need to protect the rest of our secrets." Darim folded his arms, still smarting from the things Omar had said to him earlier. Then he began humming '*La Vio*', unable to resist the siren call of the song.

Sami pouted, before remembering something. "Mister Darim, look." He felt in his pocket and pulled out the small carving of Rollo. "For you," he said, holding it out tenderly in both hands.

Darim took it, admiring the details. "Look Rollo," he said, and the dog cocked its ears. "It's you." Rollo peered curiously at the piece of wood in his master's hands, and then sniffed it. "See! He likes it," Darim told Sami. "It's very good. You carve well." He looked up, Sami was staring strangely at him, pupils large and dilated.

"We will have our own private lesson soon, for the singing, won't we?" Sami moved closer to Darim. "I thought we were the only ones to have lessons together in the woods. I thought that was just for us."

"Sami — you know why — you know why we do that."

"And I am getting better?"

"Yes."

"You like my singing? Maybe one day I could sing here, with you, in the bar?"

"Well, yes, you'll have to ask Omar about that. I hope so."

"I hope so too," whispered Sami.

"Sami, your eyes…" Darim breathed back.

"Don't tell Omar," Sami said. "I wanted to try it."

"You shouldn't…" said Darim.

"I know." Sami's eyes were luminous like washed cherries. "I wanted to be beautiful, like the ladies."

"*Bella donna*." Darim seemed to lick the words as he said them.

Sami nodded and two large tears fell fat and slowly down his face.

39

Roses

She sits and she sings, sad songs to break your heart.

Rachel shivered. The office plant quivered. Someone shouted that the Fletcher verdict was due in any minute and Piers came back in from the rain, his camera slung over his shoulder, his glasses steamed up and his coat dripping.

Rachel focused back on the blog post, wiping her hair off her forehead, strangely captivated by *Parños and its Past*, written by an ex-pat who called himself Retired Ron. She was reading the folk story about the ghost; the woman who was condemned to sit on the rocks and sing forever, to save her love, who lived and died and left her there. Retired Ron was scathing about the story, he said it was told to children to stop them going down to the cove at night, because the path was treacherous and it was easy to get lost. She read on.

More recently it is said that the ghost of the famous flamenco dancer Carlotta de Santos haunts the bay. She died by falling on the rocks — but did she fall or was she pushed? Her house at the top of the hill overlooks the cove and villagers are once again scared to go there at night. Carlotta was a fiery woman with a big temper when she was alive.

"What are you up to Rachel, have you got five minutes?" Clive leaned over from his desk.

"Oh, just doing some research for a story I'm pitching to Martin this morning." She held his gaze so he wouldn't look at her screen and see the ghost stories.

Clive's bulbous nose was covered in tiny hairs. "Cool, if it's not urgent then could you turn the unemployment copy round for me? The ONS have just filed the latest stats and we need them online asap. I'm keeping across the Fletcher court case." He slouched back in his chair, evidently too busy to do it himself.

"Sure." Rachel knew it would be quicker not to argue. She found the information and nimbly translated the figures into something more readable, emailing her piece to Clive with a chipper, "There you go."

"Thanks," he said, breaking off his conversation with Piers about how long he thought Fletcher was going to get.

Rachel checked the time, eleven thirty-six, a good twenty minutes before her allotted slot with the boss. She read back over her pitch, printed simply on one side of A4, it felt good, but then, her intuition had been calling her ever since that flamenco poster in Leicester Square, when the dancer's eyes cut through the rain and something had resonated, something she couldn't shake. Her tutor had told her to follow her instincts, but was it journalistic nouse, or just boredom? It was hard to tell when the pain punched at her gut and left her fighting her body all of the time. Still, today was a good day, a no pill day, and today, it felt good.

"It's in. Five years," Clive shouted, unnecessarily, because everyone could see the verdict flash on their screens as well. There was a flurry of voices, and people allocating tasks.

Rachel let it go on in the background. She had expected five years. She was more interested in Retired Ron:

Cala Pirata is so-called because it used to be a smugglers' cove. Ships full of tobacco and cloth sailed in under cover of night and were taken furtively up the steep path to be sold on the black market. In 1892 a special royal guard called the Carabineros was stationed there to stop the smugglers..."

Imagining pirates in lacy shirts hauling chests of contraband up the hill, Rachel then wondered vaguely if she would be able to swim there, she always felt better after a swim in the sea, but maybe it would be too cold, too rough.

"Rachel?" Martin stuck his head out of the office like a puppet, calling her name efficiently before disappearing back inside.

Rachel checked her lipstick in her small compact mirror, swiftly applying more before she stood up and brushed down her culottes. She had been into Martin's office only a handful of times and it always made her nervous.

"So." Martin was standing by the window, gazing out at the rain. "What's the idea?"

Rachel took one step forwards and then stopped. "I…" He didn't turn around. "I was wondering about a feature piece. Something for the summer, for the bored London commuter, to spice up their evening read. A piece about flamenco." He still didn't look at her so she coughed and carried on. "There are schools you can go and stay in, live there, and pay for a holiday plus dancing. It's becoming really popular," she gushed, without really knowing if it was true. "Loads of people will be doing it by next year so we want to get in early, hit the trend." *Trend* was a buzzword he liked to hear.

"Not just middle-aged divorcees?"

Rachel looked down at her combat boots. "Um, no, I… no, couples are doing it, young professionals, budding Casanovas, all sorts. And er, yeah, the odd divorcee as well, I'm sure." She felt Martin move away from the window, so she looked up and smiled, hoping to get him on side. "Here's the thing, when the weather's like this, and you're doing a job you can't stand, and you're on your way home in a crowded train with someone's elbow in your face, don't you want a bit of escapism? Something to take you away? We could do a really nice tease on the front cover, and um, it would work really well for digital too." *Digital*, another buzzword.

Martin sat down at his desk, thoughtful.

Rachel realised she'd forgotten the printed pitch she was going to present, so instead she took another step forward and gabbled. "I've found a flamenco school in Parños. Flights are cheap this weekend. I wouldn't miss any time in the office, it's my weekend off."

Martin simpered, he valued a strong work ethic above all things. "Yes," he said quietly. "I enjoyed your review of Buckingham Palace, you're good at the lighter pieces. This could make a nice splash, a bit of colour, some viral video. Get someone to film you joining in with the other students."

"Oh, er, yeah." Rachel hadn't been planning to dance, just write about it, she shuddered recalling the class in Pimlico, the door shutting in her face.

"Do it." Martin decreed. "Donna will book the flights for you, just email her the details. Make it exotic and fun. Make it feel like the *London Echo* has the inside track on how to make summer sizzle." He glanced out of the window at the rain.

"Thanks," Rachel said, rather more breathlessly than she would have liked, and retreated from the office, shutting the door with a satisfying click.

Back at her desk Rachel clenched her fists, a small victory. As she hastily emailed Donna she wondered if she would be brave enough to dance this time, perhaps it would be different if she was working and she had an excuse not to be any good...

"Oh God," she said out loud, suddenly remembering. Clive didn't look up; he was busy with Fletcher and the prison sentence. It was her weekend to have Joe, of course it was. She felt a wave of guilt for forgetting, she was a bad mother, her moment of glory quashed. She grabbed her leather jacket and her cigarettes and headed for the lifts.

Rachel only smoked when she was stressed, which was most of the time. She checked the packet as she descended — one left — she'd need more; calling Andy always made her tense.

The rain was stopping when she got outside and the air smelt fresh, washed clean and brand new. She inhaled as she hurried to the corner shop to buy a pack of twenty and, even after all these years, still felt like an errant teenager as she took them and scurried away with a quick, "Thank you, thank you so much."

Golden Square was empty and she skirted the edge by the trees, stopping briefly to light up. *I'll call him after this one,* she told herself, *and then I'll have another.*

After Rachel had smoked two, she took out her phone, going over the conversation in her mind. She looked down at a bench but it was slicked black, stained with rain, so she kept walking, on and around the statue of King George, lording it over the rose beds in his Roman soldier costume; robe and crown and open-toed sandals.

"Oh, hi, Andy." As usual there was the dissonance of clanging, hissing and banging in the background. She hated calling him at work.

"Hey. Hang on Rae, let me step into the office."

She could imagine him wiping his greasy hands on the blue overalls he wore, almost smell the dark tarry tang of the cars in their state of repair, suspended, waiting for spare parts or *spare hearts* — as Joe used to call the engines. "Sorry to call you at work." Rachel focused on George the Second's bare paunch, protruding over his kilt-like skirt. "I've got a small favour to ask."

"Right." Metal sounds clanked, someone shouted something about a chassis and a drill started. Andy's footsteps resounded on the hard floor. Then a door shut and he was in the messy office, surrounded by screwdrivers, papers, wrenches, tape measures, broken speedometers and the odd miniature Mini, given as a gift. "If you want me to look after Joe this weekend, I can't. I'm off-roading with the boys. We've had it in the diary for ages, as you know."

"Ah, I'd forgotten about that. Yeah, I was going to ask… yeah." King George looked at her unhelpfully, his eroded mouth a straight line.

"Rachel, you know we try not to make last-minute swaps. It's not good for Joe." She heard him move a pile of folders and sit heavily in a chair.

"I know, and I wouldn't normally ask, it's just that I've been given a special assignment for work and — it's all a bit last minute — and yeah, just that really. I've got to go to Spain."

"Hmm." Andy didn't sound impressed. "Can't you take him with you?"

"No, I'm working, and do you really think Martin would pay for the extra flights?"

"Ha, not Martin."

"Couldn't he go with you? He loves his bike and—"

"He's not ready for that kind of terrain yet. It wouldn't be fair on the lads to keep having to wait for him and he'll moan if it rains, you know what he's like."

A pigeon landed on the king's head. Rachel reached for another cigarette.

"Look, I'll tell you what," said Andy with a sigh. "I'll take Joe and leave him with my parents when we're out biking. They'd like that. They haven't seen him for ages and they spoil him rotten so he won't complain. Okay? But do not make a habit out of this, Rachel, it's not cool. I make all my plans around our weekends — I always keep my Joe weekends free."

"So do I normally." Rachel gripped the cigarette packet. "I, I think this might be a big story, that's all," she blurted, and then wished she hadn't, willing him not to ask, and rowing back: "I mean, it might be nice," she grimaced. She hadn't got into journalism for 'nice', but then, she didn't think she'd be single right now either, or in quite so much pain. "Listen, thank you so much. I'll take him for the next two if you like?"

"No Rachel, that's fine."

The bird flew away, leaving a white stain on the royal head, just below the laurel crown. "Okay, thanks, I'll book my tickets then." Rachel was aware that Donna would already have made the booking.

"And Rachel?"

"Yes?"

"If there's someone else, you can just tell me you know."

"What?"

"Rae, it's obvious. You work for the *London* Echo, why would you be going to Spain for work? Hello? I'm not stupid and I'd rather you didn't treat me like I was."

"But it's not — it *is* work. I'm doing — okay, I'm doing a piece on flamenco, how you can learn it in your holidays. You can read it when it's done. You'll see. It's a summer series thing, and it might not be the scoop of the century, but I've got a good feeling about this, I feel like it might… lead to something. Not that you'd care," she added petulantly as old feelings surged into the present.

"Rachel, that's not fair. I do care. Of course I care." He breathed out heavily. "Go to Spain, get your story. I'll read it when it's out."

Rachel looked down at the bedraggled roses and felt herself tearing up. "I'm sorry. Yes, thank you. Thank you so much."

"I'll pick Joe up from school on Friday then," he said, practical as ever. "Just make sure he's got whatever homework books he needs with him, yeah? You can collect him from school on Monday and… and I'll see you soon."

"Hope so," she found herself saying, not sure if she really meant it.

"I better go. I've three MOTs in today and the owners get really shirty if we keep them in too long."

"Oh, yes, thanks again. Bye then."

"Bye." And the line went dead.

Rachel stood for a moment, contemplating a petal; the slight decay at the very outer edge, the crinkled brown encroaching on the pure pink. She let the emotions billow inside her. This was why she didn't like calling Andy, it stirred up too much. In her job she liked to pretend to be in control, but he knew… he knew she wasn't and he knew how the pain ruled her, grubbed her, wrestled with her every single day. He knew too much and it made her vulnerable.

She fumbled with another cigarette, fighting the urge to call him back, to try again to talk about the things unsaid. She puffed urgently, for a moment letting herself picture them all together, one Christmas when Joe was about three. There was the little fake tree with the cheap red baubles and the tiny table Andy had taken from a skip. There were cards over the fireplace and fairy lights around the mirror. They were happy then, weren't they? She'd been tired she knew that — she was tired all the time — more tired than now. She stubbed out the cigarette, no point remembering one Christmas or one birthday, one cake the shape of a train. It was all the other bits that were hard, when he wasn't there, when he was out with the boys and there was just her and the pain and a screaming baby. Rachel headed back to her desk.

Clive and Piers and a couple of the other journalists were heading to the Rose and Crown for lunch. She didn't look up as they filed past, a timeworn agreement to avoid eye contact; she would not see and they would not invite. "Five years, man, I can't believe Fletcher got five years," one of the younger ones was saying.

"He was being made an example of, that's what," Clive replied, and she knew he would continue to hold forth over his pie and mash, so this time, she was glad to let them all go.

The plant waved dreamily at her and, just for a moment, being pain-free felt like being in heaven. Then she focused back on her computer. There was an email from Donna; the flights were booked, she was going to Spain. Rachel smiled to herself, some sense of victory flowing back. She checked the place on the map again: Parños. She liked the way it sounded, like a piece of music, a stirring, heartfelt song. She didn't need to tell anyone she had chosen it because of the Instagram post, but she did believe in fate, she always had done, and this was too much of a coincidence to ignore.

The muffled beep of a message broke her out of her thoughts. It was Joe.

I don't want to swap weekends with Dad.

He didn't give a reason, but she knew he didn't like change and the guilt scratched.

I'm sorry, Joe. I've got to go away for work. This never happens usually, does it? I'll make it up to you on our next weekend. Your Dad is looking forward to having you. I love you and I'll see you after school x

Joe didn't reply straight away which meant he wasn't going to. Rachel sighed and found the website for the flamenco school, to book her place. There was Carlotta on the homepage, striking a pose with both arms drawn up above her head like the horns of a bull. Rachel leant in closer, studying her features, her insolent stance; no wonder the locals believed she haunted the bay, she was haunting Rachel even now.

The rest of the site was in just two colours: red and black. The ornate font was hard to read. The menu at the top said simply: 'Location', 'Testimonials', and 'Contact'. There was nothing about booking, boarding or prices. Rachel checked the map, it was a thin line drawing, low resolution, showing the school and the sea and the path back to the village. Next, she clicked 'Testimonials': there was only one.

Carlotta is the best flamenco teacher in the whole of Spain. I was so happy to learn authentic flamenco from a famous dancer. It changed my life. It was not an easy ride but now I feel stronger and more powerful in every way. Thank you for what you have taught me and I hope to come back and learn with you again next summer. Floriana.

Rachel chewed on the end of her biro, wondering what Floriana was doing now, and if she did go back and learn with Carlotta again, was she really changed, or was this just the usual holiday reimagining? She hoped she would find some similarly enthusiastic pupils to interview, but something about the website worried her, it didn't feel like the school was pulsing with life, it felt like it had died with Carlotta.

Only then did Rachel realise she probably should have inquired before Donna booked the flights.

Putting the biro down, she clicked 'Contact', and below the postal address of the school was: 'Darim de Santos: darim@carlottasflamencoschool.net'. She pursed her lips as she wrote the email, deciding she could always stay in a hotel nearby, if she didn't hear back. The school couldn't have closed if Kezia was learning there right now, and by the looks of things, they would welcome the publicity of her article. She pressed send — this was the right choice — and the plant waved, as if it agreed with her, just the faint arabesque of a frond, so subtle and yet so definitely another sign.

40

Butterflies

When Kezia woke, she felt cleansed and peaceful. She had been growing closer to Darim, closer to understanding his moods and passions and ever since their time in the forest there was a shared understanding between them, as if her screams had broken an invisible boundary.

After breakfast, she joined the girls on the terrace and Darim acknowledged her with a flick of his head. She knew that this time, it would be quick. She raised her arms, and like a dowser striking gold within a few paces, the rush was fast and rich, all her emotions free and flowing and her blood hot with the pounding liberation. She was stirring sensations, mixing as she moved, stamping as she shifted, thrashing down hard with exhilaration… down, down, down and down.

All too soon Darim was signalling for them to stop — folding in half in an extravagant bow — and Kezia looked at him unfocused; she was still in that place. He nodded, he could tell. "Kezia, stay. Everyone else go," he said.

She heard them clatter away and she remained, breathing.

Darim picked up his guitar. "More," he said. "You are there. Let me see more."

So she danced for him. She danced towards the sunshine and the sky turned milky white. She danced to a place of being outside her body. She danced until Rollo came begging for food and Darim laughed and said, "*Sí cariño*, okay…" winking at Kezia and striding away, Rollo bounding out in front.

Sue and Java were on the terrace drinking juice the colour of flames. The others had gone, but Magdalena was by the pond, watching, as the water spilled from Medusa's mouth.

"Teacher's pet," said Sue. "I wish I could pick it up so quickly."

"I don't know, I've so much to learn and it's so different to ballet." Kezia's cheeks were flushed, her eyes bright and happy. "I just want to make sure I don't let you all down. I want to be ready for the competition."

"You'll be ready all right, as ready as any of us are." Sue looked like a cherub when she sipped her drink through the paper straw, her mouth sucking in, her eyes looking up.

Smiling to herself, Kezia went to get her phone, her feelings like fire. She was dancing for Darim, she was dancing with *duende* — there was a new power inside her now. She came back to find Normando had made her a drink too. It tasted of plastic peaches.

Kezia relaxed with the sun hot on her back; soaking up the stillness as the geraniums swirled in a breath of air. After replying to a message from her mum, she scrolled hazily through Instagram, clicking 'like' on a post from Lucy: pub lunch and a pint of ale. She didn't miss The Tiger's Head, she thought, she would rather be here. Then… "Oh my God." She sat up.

"What?" Java craned her neck, trying to see.

"Ohmygod." Kezia said the words together, leaning forwards, squinting at the screen.

"What? Tell us." Java was nearly out of her seat and Magdalena got up fluidly and moved closer. Even the goat was looking at Kezia, a question in the slant of its head.

"Someone I don't know has tagged my Instagram with a picture of me and James." She swallowed as if ingesting something putrid. "And they are implying we should get back together."

"Who?" Java leapt up to stand behind Kezia and look over her shoulder.

"I don't know." Kezia clicked on the account. "It's… it says The Royal Collection Trust." She looked up, confused." I don't see why they would—"

"Let me see?" Java reached over and took the phone. "Where?"

"It's the last thing they posted." Kezia put her head in her hands, aware of Magdalena's steadfast stare.

"All I can see is an old painting of a woman playing some kind of piano." Java scrolled up and down.

"It's before that. You'll see it. It's me and him at a picnic we went to last year."

"I can't, it's not there, am I on the wrong page?"

Kezia took the phone back to show Java, but the picture had gone. "Oh, it was there, it was…" she felt suddenly weak. Esmerelda bleated as if finally asking her question.

"It can't have been on there anyway, Kezia." Java scratched her elfin face. "It's just a load of old portraits and stuff and it says they are to do with visitors to Buckingham Palace, why would they care about you and James?"

"Isn't that where James works though?" Sue pushed her pink glasses up her nose.

"He works…" Kezia tied her hair up into a ponytail, doubting what she'd seen even as she was talking about it. "Yeah, he works for the palace. But he wouldn't have. He wouldn't do anything like this. James hates social media and he's not on Instagram, doesn't even know how to use it."

"So he asked one of his friends to do it?" Java clapped her hands. "So romantic!" She skipped back around to sit down again.

"Honestly, it just doesn't feel like something he would agree to." Kezia checked again for the post, which still wasn't there. "Oh my God I'm going mad. It was there, I promise you."

"It's the curse," Java rolled the words around like marbles, then crossed her eyes as if trying to see them in her mouth.

Kezia could feel the chill seeping back into her, pressing with flat palms: clammy and cold.

"Do you think it was a trick of the light?" said Sue.

"It can't have been, can it?" Kezia stirred the last of her drink with the straw.

"It's quite a creepy account, all those old pictures, so yeah, maybe the ghost did it." Java chewed anxiously at a fingernail.

Confounded, Kezia checked and rechecked, holding her hand over the screen to shield it from the bright sky. All she saw was the post of the woman playing to the man in the seventeenth century, a cello lying discarded on the floor. Before that, a pope in a red velvet cape, slumped in a chair and clutching a swathe of white cloth; he looked pleased with himself, as though he knew the secret. Then there was nothing but old paintings and antique furniture. She hugged her knees, aware that Magdalena was still watching, long hair falling down over her face.

Normando came back to collect the glasses and he smiled as he held out his tray, happy to be of service; it was what he knew best.

Java leant across and hissed to Kezia. "Maybe we should ask him about the spell?"

"No." Sue shook her head decisively, whispering back, "Don't. Remember what Abril said, it'll remind him of *what happened.*" She let Benja jump up on her lap and walk in small circles before folding himself up with his head on his paws.

Normando put the tray down on the table and squinted into the sun. "You want to know about the spell?"

Sue looked exasperated and Magdalena stared accusingly at Java, haunting eyes full of depth and despair. Java looked away.

"I don't know why people always presume I am deaf." Normando sat down on one of the empty chairs. "I may be old, but these things still work just fine." He flicked his ears and chuckled to himself.

"Sorry Normando, we didn't want to upset you," Sue said. "We were told… it might upset you."

Normando looked pensive. "Well," he said. "You get to a point where you can't be any more upset. You could say it's like getting rained on, after a while you know you're not going to get any wetter because you're soaked through already." Normando hesitated and somewhere out of sight, Rollo barked at an unknown foe. "People talk about the ghost. People talk about the spell. Two different things, if you ask me. You may have heard the ghost." He turned to Kezia. "But that doesn't mean you need to get involved in any magic. It's not… it's not the right magic in my opinion."

"Why?" Kezia asked, her voice transparent, like the sun shining through a leaf.

Normando focused on the green paint of the table as he spoke. "Because it can take you over. Carlotta… she believed it. She had a book she used to read to Darim when he was small, filling his head with all the stories." His eyes misted. "It was full of all the ghosts, all the secrets of the cove. The pirates, the smugglers, the history if you like, but a lot of

253

it was fiction, I'm sure it was, just stories. It captivated Carlotta all right though, and it captivates Darim too." A black and white cat chased a tortoiseshell butterfly across the lawn.

"Darim loves to go to the cove," mused Sue. "The books we read as children are very powerful."

"Yes, and I do think he'd be reading it to you now, only, the mayor took it off Carlotta, accused her of stealing it from the library. I'm not sure that she did, just had it on a kind of permanent loan." Normando's mouth twisted in a wiry smile. "She did keep one page though, I found it — ripped out — fortunately the mayor didn't notice or there would have been a bigger row than the one there was. Carlotta took the words of the spell, the one you asked about. I found it on her dressing table after she died."

Kezia held her breath. An unexpected wind dragged across the garden and the hanging baskets rocked in unison.

Normando watched as a peacock by the azaleas lifted its feet judiciously — up, hover, down — clicking its head by degrees, dancing to a metronomic beat all of its own. "I'm sure you know that Darim thinks his mama died because of the ghost. Yes, there's those that do. But I was there. I know. She'd had a drink, she needed to let off steam, she went to the cove because that was her favourite place in the world. You can say anything you like about spells and sorcery, but it was the drink that got her in the end." Normando regarded them all urgently, a clear warning in his eyes. "She was a fiery one, she was always going to burn out before the rest of us. That's just the way of things."

"Where is that page now, Mando?" Java said, her voice hushed.

He looked at her as if struggling to adjust his vision. "I, er... I don't know. I can't remember. I know I put it somewhere, but it escapes me now... Let's just hope the mayor does not notice and ask for it back." He cringed, and Java reached across and took his hand.

Uneasy, Kezia turned back to her phone and checked again — no picture of her and James. Did she imagine it? She didn't trust reality any more and the thought of the spell was making her feel strange, like there was something she had to do, something just out of sight and out of reach.

41

Two

James shook his jacket off, one arm stuck in the sleeve. He wandered into the kitchen and filled up the kettle, watching as it boiled, breaking into clouds of steam. He reached up to the cupboard where he kept his special tin of decaffeinated tea. It was an old biscuit tin, from two Christmases ago, with an embossed country house covered in snow on the lid and a little family of Edwardians standing outside clutching presents: square boxes with elaborate bows. He poured the hot water slowly over the teabag and it leaked its colour into the cup like smoke.

In the living room he set the brew carefully on a coaster; the cork one that he liked but Kezia said was dull. The room felt square and quiet, like a waiting room. It was at times like these he missed Gracie and her big black eyes glistening with love. He put his phone down on the table and looked at it for a while, sipping his tea. Then he thought of Darim dancing with Kezia and he picked it up and made the call.

***

"Oh, hello James." Pat smiled, her eyes like polished pennies as she walked stiffly down a corridor smelling of steak and kidney pie and cool cotton washing powder. She wiped her free hand on her apron, which was splashed from doing the washing up. "I'll just tell Pat you've called."

In the front room, Kezia's dad was slumped in an armchair, his large tummy rising cheerfully, a packet of chocolate biscuits balanced precariously on top. The TV flickered, unwatched, dribbling a constant ribbon of breaking news across the screen. "Don't let anyone tell you I was asleep." He grinned, pulling himself up the chair with one hand and rescuing the biscuits with the other. "Who is it?"

"It's James, love." His wife settled herself down like a chicken on a nest. "So, how's the palace? How's the Queen? Have you met her yet? Gosh, what would you say?"

James hesitated, looking down at his tea, not sure which question to answer first.

"The weather not putting the tourists off then? Rain, rain, rain, I don't know." Pat moved her shoulders, inserting another question as if squeezing it in with the motion.

"No, actually, it helps, brings them in from the parks." James leant forwards, trying to remember all the other things she had asked. "It's good, yes, it's going well. Er, more visitors than last year. The wardens are behaving so that's a relief for me." He laughed tentatively, not sure whether Pat knew exactly what his role was. "I'm... I coordinate the wardens, you see."

Kezia's mum blinked. "Yes, Kezia mentioned."

"She did?"

"Oh yes, it's a big deal, James, love. We're very proud."

James felt a hot rush in his cheeks. "The new worksheets for the children have gone down really well too. And um, I haven't met the Queen yet, although I know some people who have. I did see the back of her once, as she got out of a car, in the courtyard, but I guess that doesn't count."

"Oh. Lovely. What was she like?" Pat pulled a cushion onto her lap and began stroking it as though it was a cat.

"She was..." James searched for a detail. "She was wearing a blue suit."

"Well, fancy that. Just an ordinary day at work then, oh, there goes the Queen! I don't know."

The TV burbled in the background, the volume rising and falling in a tide of information.

"So how was your holiday?" James tried to subtly swing the conversation back to Kezia.

"Oh Spain? Yes, we love Spain. Too hot though. Hotter than usual. We had to lie by the pool most afternoons, didn't we Pat? Couldn't do anything. Makes us floppy." She relaxed back in her chair, the cushion cradled in her lap. "Got up to thirty-four degrees one day, didn't it? That's too hot for us. It's a shame as there is lots to explore, it's a lovely

256

part of Spain, really rugged in places, but it was just too hot. Still, a change is as good as a rest." She looked across to her recumbent husband.

"And Kezia? She…"

"Yes love?" Kezia's mum focused her eyes and wrinkled her nose like she was trying to read something slightly too far away.

"She… she's okay, is she?"

"Oh yes. Yes, yes, she's learning flamenco. Got to do it while you're young, eh?" She hugged the cushion, her apron sagging at the front, then said gently, "She just needs to get it out of her system, James, love. We think… we think she'll see sense once she's had the chance to miss you."

"Do you?"

"Oh yes." Pat coaxed him like she would a small child. "Oh yes."

James felt unexpectedly choked. The news trickled in the background, something about the economy.

"And she's in a good place," Kezia's mum continued, looking at the pictures of pounds stacked up on the screen. "A lovely school, really great. Charming young teacher, very handsome. I don't know what he did but I've not seen her so happy in ages."

Kezia's dad shook his head at his wife, hauling himself up in his chair and sliding back down straight away. He held up his hand but she carried on blithely. "So nice of him to say she could stay, no fee you know, honestly, and such good manners, what was his name? Daryl? Darius? Anyway, it will do her the world of good."

"Let me talk to him." Patrick reached for the phone and the packet of biscuits fell off his lap. He took the handset, his brow crinkling with kindness. "Hiya James, look, Kezia cares about you, I know she does. Okay she's not really… showing it right now, but we all make mistakes, right?" He patted his stomach as if patting his past mistakes.

James focused on the circular edge of the coaster, his tea going cold now.

"She's just having a bit of a phase, that's all. She'll be back soon and you can begin to patch things up again. Just got to give it time."

James gripped the arm of the sofa. It was now or never. His voice came out dry and unrecognisable. "Mr Duke, I was calling because," he coughed, "I was calling because… I would like to ask for your daughter's hand in marriage…"

There was a surprised silence.

James wondered if he had been too formal.

Kezia's mum was pulling at her apron distractedly. "What did he say?" She was trying to decipher the clues, studying her husband's face as Pat moved his lips but said nothing.

The monotonous drone of *Today's Closing Headlines* went unheard from the TV. The newsreader smiled ominously, and for a moment too long, before signing off with her name and shuffling the papers on her desk as the credits rolled.

42

Lilies

$\mathscr{F}$rissons and frills, jitters and jolts, apprehension and hastily practised moves. The school was scatty with anticipation, excitement rolling in a crestless wave, on and on and through each day. Java bumped her head on a cupboard as she rushed to get a glass of water. Sue tore her skirt on a rose bush while hanging out the washing. Normando left Pedro's cage open and the parrot flew out of the kitchen enjoying his freedom and refusing to come back. Even Rollo seemed more alert than usual, skittering behind his master who was humming out the rhythms and tapping out the rhythms and calling out the rhythms everywhere he went. "Have you got this?" He would stop the girls on the stairs or in the hall and clap out a pattern for them to repeat. "Again. Good. Better, again!"

And so they lived and breathed the dancing, waiting for the competition, waiting for the hour to come. They rehearsed — all of the time — wherever they were, fingers twisting around the movements, mouths whispering the counts. Silently, discreetly, the steps seeped into their bones.

"Remember we can win. Mindset is everything. We go into this with the winning attitude. We stand on the stage like winners. Like this." Darim took up the stance. "They will see it in your faces and the judges will know." He nodded, as if it was already done. "The others will have the steps, yes, they will put their arms like this and turn their feet so." Darim gestured. "But they will not make you feel that they know pain, that they know sorrow, that they have lived a thousand lives and each one stained with blood and soaked in tears." He stamped and they jumped. "That's it! Wake up. We do not dance in a daze. No! I want to see it in all of your faces, in the sharp bend of your elbows, in the scuff of your heels. You need this dance. It is your air. Drink it."

Even at night, the strains pulsed through their sheets, never left them alone; they spun and turned and pivoted on a phantasmagorical stage, with stars for spotlights and the sea at their backs...

Thus, they were all dreaming about dancing that morning, each hearing the music calling as they turned out of sleep. Their feet were tapping before they hit the ground and they were singing the melodies as the sun carved its intentions into the day.

Only Hady was immune, outside and in the garden. He was picking lilies intently, admiring the sharp green leaves. The white flowers reminded him of his mother, it was the perfume she wore. The scent relaxed him in the still before the day and he was just deciding which job to do next when he sensed movement. He cocked one eye in the direction of the path. A tall woman in leather trousers and with a microphone sticking out of her bag was treading cautiously, making her way down through the trees. Hady didn't wait to find out more, he slipped quietly away — into the shed, like the breath of the wind — gone.

Rachel's black boots were too heavy for the weather, her shirt was damp with sweat and her make-up was beginning to run. She looked up as Pedro the parrot swooped above in a graceful arc. "Erk, belladonna, belladonna." He settled into one of the tall firs; a splash of paint in its branches. She rubbed her forehead, the sun percolating the pain. The heat helped, but the hurt was still swirling, swirling in the background, and she didn't notice Java pirouetting around the house, leaping across the grass, skirting the pots and tubs, the geraniums and the gazanias and jumping across the flagstones one by one. It wasn't until she bounced next to her that Rachel took her eyes from the parrot and blinked, not sure where this nymph-like figure had come from.

"Oh, hi."

Java screwed up her eyes suspiciously. "*Hola?*"

"Do you speak English?" Rachel wiped a trail of sweat from her neck.

"Yaha." Java nodded, looking her up and down.

"Oh great. Is this the flamenco school?"

"Why?" said Java, reminding Rachel of Joe when he was little.

Rachel peered ahead at the red and white stripes on the house, the ivy clinging possessively in patches. "Erm, maybe I've got the wrong place. I'm... I'm looking for Darim de Santos, is he here?"

"Darim?" Java's nose furrowed.

"Maybe I should explain. I'm Rachel from the *London Echo*." She held out her hand but Java didn't take it. "I… I emailed him about coming here to do a feature on flamenco. He should be expecting me," she added as she lowered her arm.

Java was staring at her open-mouthed.

"So, erm, could I talk to Darim about how it's all going to work?" Rachel tugged at the strap of her bag and felt for her bun to check it was still in place.

Java nodded, then clasped her hands together underneath her chin, eyes wide with curiosity.

"So, erm, is it that way?" Rachel pointed and then adjusted her bag again as Tomi the cat came limping down the path, dragging his useless paw and piercing her with a glacial green gaze.

Java began twirling her wrists. "I can't wait to tell the others!"

Tomi sat down in front of Rachel and uttered a long and plangent miaow. She took a step back. She did not like cats, especially cats that stared at her. As she steadied herself, she saw Java was waving to someone behind, further along the way.

It was Sami, clutching a vase he had made for Darim, carved wood, sleek and shapely. He slowed as he saw Rachel, the patina of the leaves forming a mosaic on his face, like a mask. Behind him, blundering and steaming slightly: Omar.

"Sami, Omar, a journalist has come to see Darim!" Java shouted, eager to be first with the news. "She wants to do a feature about the flamenco school. We're all going to be famous!"

"Well, I didn't say that…" Rachel took her bag off her shoulder and put it on the ground as if disarming herself of her weapons. The microphone fell to the side like a broken pendulum.

"Yes, you did," Java insisted. "We're going to be in the paper. It's the same thing."

Omar was frowning, his bushy brows coming together to form a hairy caterpillar above his eyes, "Hello. Miss, er—"

"Rachel," said Rachel, not holding out her hand this time.

"Miss Rachel." Omar bowed almost imperceptibly. "Madame. You are a journalist. I'm sure in your heart-of-hearts you know we are not news. We are a small and very humble flamenco school here in Parños and we do not wish to be the centre of attention. Please go and satisfy yourself with some proper stories and leave us all in peace. With respect."

"But Omar, this will be great for Darim," Sami interjected. "The lady journalist must write about the incredible Darim de Santos. It is only what he deserves." He stepped forwards and the shadows on his face shifted.

"No, no. Off you go. Out with you." Omar waved a stubby hand in a dismissive gesture, forcing a smile. "Goodbye."

Rachel hesitated. The shed door clapped open and shut and the ivy shimmered against the side of the house. Tomi shuffled to the side where he was petted by Java and, at the end of her rope, Esmeralda the goat was chewing moronically, eyes fixed steadily on her. The heat was making Rachel dizzy. "Honestly, it'll be a really nice piece. A shot of Spanish sunshine for our readers, to lift them on a dreary London day. Just a small piece in a small paper, really nothing big, nothing to worry about." The sweat traced another line down her neck.

"No," said Omar deliberately. "You should leave us in peace. Please." He bowed again, more fully this time.

"Shouldn't you at least ask Darim if he wants to see her?" Sami kept his eyes on Rachel, as if to keep her there. "It should be up to him," he said. "I'm going to ask him now."

"No." Omar stood tall, head held high, defiant.

"But Omar, this has got nothing to do with you."

"You are an idiot sometimes Sami, don't you know that?" Omar talked down to his little brother, pejorative in a manner ingrained, like water running through well-worn grooves.

"No. No, I'm going to ask him." Sami's response was similarly honed over the years: churlish and defensive.

Rachel's face contorted with unasked queries and the leaves rustled in the trees like the petticoats of a thousand flamenco skirts.

"I know what's best for this school — I know what's best." Omar rounded back to Rachel. "And if you know what's best for you, you will leave."

"But wait—" Rachel started.

262

"You may go." Omar held up a flat palm — cutting her off — but then stopped short as a symphony of breaking glass cascaded from the other side of the house. It rang out, leaving behind a silence which reflected the feeling of the smash: jagged and cutting.

Java, Omar and Sami shared a look between them and then made off, after the sound, walking quickly, leaving Tom staring at Rachel, until he too, turned and hobbled away.

"Right." Rachel picked up her bag and fiddled with the straps. "Right," she said again, and waited a moment, thirsty and unhinged.

The parrot squawked loudly, hiding somewhere above her. "Errrk, you may go. You may go."

And, almost in slow motion, scanning the canopy cagily, she began to walk away. *I'll get a drink*, she thought, *I'll just get a drink, and then I'll come back, and try again.*

***

Normando had dropped a huge crystal bowl full of salad. Tomato and lettuce were washed up on the terrace like a garden shipwreck, a colourful treasure trove, with jewels of broken bowl reflecting the yellow sun and the green plants and the red and white stripes of the house.

"What have you done?" Darim was looking at the beautiful mess on the flagstones.

Normando took his flat cap off his head, holding it with both hands. "I…" The tears came; more jewels, shining and real.

"No, no Papa. It's okay. Sit here." Darim helped the old man, speaking gently as he settled him on the bench. Then Omar, Sami and Java came around the corner, full of questions and concern. "Stay back," Darim shouted, sharp as the shards at their feet. "Don't stand too close, there's broken glass."

"I'll get the brush for you." Sami started edging around, towards the kitchen.

"No. I'll go. And don't come across until it is swept. Bits can cut in above your sandals."

Sami smiled lovingly at Darim's back as he went through the side door, emerging almost straight away with a dustpan and brush. The glass sighed as he scraped it across the stones.

"Darim, Darim." Sami put his vase on the table, watching him as he worked. "Darim, a journalist has come to write about you!" He laughed, his face flushed with disclosure.

"What?" Darim didn't look up. As he moved a large piece of crystal, the water seemed to run through it, refracting the cascade from Medusa's mouth, then morphing the sunset shades of the nearby hibiscus flowers. He placed it carefully by the pond.

"Yes," Java hugged her elbows. "And I saw her first. She wants to put you in the paper, so that people in London will know about flamenco and be jealous of us when it is raining."

The shards tinkled as Darim swept them into the pan. "I see... yes, she did contact me about that..." He raised his head to see Omar giving him a portentous stare, the gathering of storm clouds, the strong threat of thunder.

"And when you win the competition, she can write about that too," said Sami, hoping to catch Darim's eye, but just then Normando began pulling his apron off and was getting it tangled around his head.

"Papa? Let me help." Darim put the brush down and moved over, carefully extracting his father from the strings.

Omar sat down heavily on the bench next to Normando and Darim went back to his brushing. "Darim, we cannot have journalists here. Darim, are you listening?"

A splinter of glass skittered across the floor.

"And why not?" Darim followed the fragment, sweeping it deftly back into the pan. "Why should she not write about our school and the dance and my mama and spread flamenco throughout the world?" He stood, propping the brush against the low wall.

"It is quite simple," said Omar, slowly, as if calculating an equation. "And if you can't work it out then you are more stupid than I even gave you credit for. Flamenco is bad for the brain, evidently."

"But we could be in the paper!" Java skipped with a spark of frustration. "We might not ever get this chance again. My parents always said I'd never do anything good. Well, now I could show them. My brothers and sisters haven't been in the paper; I could be the first in our family, the first!"

"This is not some little game to prove your own self-importance," Omar barked.

Java jumped back, holding onto a chair.

"There's no need to get cross," said Sami softly. "Let's not get cross." In a conciliatory gesture, he took his vase off the table and held it out, the bulbous base curving up and out, like the head of a tulip. "Darim, I made you this…" He grinned and was suddenly shy.

Darim frowned as he took the vase, nodding his thanks and turning it over in his hands, finding solace in the smooth bulge of the wood.

"I do not like journalists," Omar scowled. "That woman sticks her nose in where it does not belong and we will not be left in peace. No journalists. Okay?"

Darim was still rotating the vase in his hands. "This is not for you to decide, Omar," he said quietly, feeling the stare he did not raise his eyes to see.

The click of paws on patio heralded Rollo as he came scampering out of the kitchen, wagging his tail erratically and looking fuzzy, like he'd just been asleep. Normando called him over, away from the glass, and stroked his head as the dog's eyes became limpid pools of love. Omar regarded them thoughtfully, then got up and went to Darim, whispering in his ear with slightly bared teeth. Darim flinched and tossed his head back and Omar growled something else, something final, before sitting heavily back down and folding his arms across his wide chest.

Darim retreated to the pond, crouching down to watch the frogs slide over each other, and Tomi limped close, to monitor their movements with him, peering into the murky waters, his expression somewhere between predator and prey. One of the frogs made a plump splash — deliberate and precise — and Tomi hovered his impotent paw, the signal of an attack that would never come, as the slippery creatures swam stoically below. Darim glanced at the cat. "The dance of life," he said faintly to him. "Has many turns, many partners, many steps. In the dance of life, you dance to many rhythms — and some of them are not your own. Not until you take them, and make them your own. You make them your own."

Tomi looked up and mewed, a miserable silken sound.

43

Lightening

𝒦ezia was having a nap when she heard strumming seething with a quiet passion outside. She blinked and rubbed her eyes. The white light came through the curtain and the smell of the sunshine told her the time. Noon. She floundered, adjusting her T-shirt, walking to the window and pulling the curtain across. Darim was on the wall.

His head snapped up and he studied her suspiciously. "Kezia," he called. "I need to talk to you."

His tone was off, she seemed in trouble. "Why? What's wrong?"

"Something is wrong," was the only reply, and Esmeralda gave a long, vibrato bleat.

Immediately she thought of the curse and a deep cold spread in her, the cold of a low, slow river in a crow-black night.

Darim rose and set off abruptly round the house, staccato steps, going the long way to enter through the hall, touch the worn feet of Our Lady and look briefly up into her anguished eyes. He took the stairs two at a time, pivoting in the hall and standing in Kezia's doorway as if poised to tango. "What is this picture of you and James?"

"What picture?"

"Do not pretend you do not know. Java told me about a picture from the Queen, of you two together, a romantic picture."

The mask slipped and for a moment she saw small boy Darim, wanting to be a pirate Darim, lost without a friend Darim. "The Queen? Oh, oh no." Kezia flushed, rushing to reassure him. "It's nothing. Someone put a photograph of us together on Instagram, but it's gone now anyway. That's all. It was there for a short time — I think — and I don't know why, but it's gone now."

"I do not believe you." He swallowed, his Adam's apple dipping and rising like a piston.

"Honestly. It's not there and it doesn't mean anything anyway."

"Show me. I want to see this picture of you and him that everyone is so interested in." His eyes strained and his teeth pinched his bottom lip.

"But I told you—"

He took a short sip of air, looking around to see Kezia's phone charging on the bed, the cable dripping off.

She followed his line of sight and grabbed at it, pulling out the wire. "Look, it was just a stupid photo — I'll show you, it's gone — just us at a picnic and it was taken ages ago."

"Us? You call you and him 'us' now?"

"I didn't mean it like that."

"You and him, Kezia. You and him. You know I do not like it — you and him." His voice was sing-song, almost sinister.

"But I didn't post it and I don't even know who did. It wouldn't have been James either. Probably just someone trying to be clever. Well, it's not clever and they must have realised because they deleted it." Kezia went to find the account, but suddenly, without warning, Darim's hand shot out to grab the phone — he missed — pushing it from her so it slipped and fell like a stone to the hard wooden floor, hitting at an angle and then falling on its side.

For a few seconds, neither of them spoke.

Kezia bent down slowly and turned it over; the screen was cracked, a tiny zigzagging line running across like black lightening.

Darim squatted by her side. "Oh Kezarina. I'm sorry." He reached out carefully and cupped her bowed head in his hand. "Too much passion is my problem. Always. Always too much from me, I am told."

Kezia stared at the phone as if something inside her had also cracked. He lifted her chin, imploring, his heart a jar he was about to tip over. "I was jealous of you and this James, this public photograph. I want you here, I want you to be mine."

In the next moment there was only his eyes. There was nothing else in the room, nothing else in the entire world, only his eyes, drawing her in. Then, very quickly, he took her by both shoulders and pulled her towards him, kissing her full on the mouth, pressing his lips deliberately onto hers. He kissed her with a softness she had not known and she gave in to the surprise of it. *The kiss, finally, the kiss.*

Abruptly he pulled back. "It is too much, Kezarina?"

Kezia put her hand to her lips as if to keep the kiss there. "No," she said, victorious, and it felt like a stamp, her foot down hard and in the right place.

He held his head to the side and smiled, taking both her hands and was about to say something when—

"Darim!" A rough voice bellowed from outside.

Darim exhaled, looking distractedly down at his knee. "It is Omar," he said candidly. "He is not… happy. He does not like that the journalist came…" He paused, before adding, "Bad for business."

"Business?" Kezia questioned, cautiously, her voice satin soft, hoping he would kiss her again.

"I must go." Darim did kiss Kezia, but quickly this time, just one second on the lips. "I go." He sprung up and left the room like a bird flying from a branch.

Kezia sat down on the bed, staring at her cracked phone, the taste of Darim still strong in her, the feeling of his lips like a force gripping. The smashed screen didn't work any more; she could see the bright icons laid out, but nothing happened when she touched them. She kept trying, but they wouldn't open, wouldn't function. She sighed, looking across at the ship in the bottle, static on its paper sea, not wanting to break away from the feeling of the kiss…

Eventually, when she heard another shout, she stood up and went to the window. Normando was dozing with Rollo on the bench, the dog's smooth head in his lap, and on the far side of the terrace, Sami was gazing up at the sky and wondering if he could one day be a famous singer.

Omar and Darim were a little further into the garden, by a camellia bush, the pink flowers bobbing in the breeze. They were gesticulating, rough tufts of sound drifting like spores, sparse and out of context. When Omar shouted again, he woke Rollo, who blinked and pulled himself up mechanically, shuddering, while Normando stirred, breathing the word 'Carlotta' through a snore before returning to the rhythm of sleep.

Rollo jumped off the bench and cantered over to the argument. Omar was staring intently at Darim now and Darim was looking out to sea as if he would weather the storm. Rollo ran around them both, one lap and then two. He stopped, planting his front feet firmly down and then lifting them in a little leap of distress. He barked and then rallied again. "Down Rollo, down, it's okay," whispered Darim.

"It is not okay," countered Omar.

A red cloud drew across the sun.

PART THREE

44

Hedgerows

His hand brushed her waist — their hips undulated past each other — their eyes locked. They danced with quiet rage and pent-up passion and the garden shimmied with them. The frisson in the flowers, grasses, leaves and the sensual breeze were all the music they needed. The beats were in their blood. Faster they moved and faster, weaving past each other, merging movements then pulling apart. Kezia and Darim dragged the darkness around them like a cloak, possessing its shadows, diving into its depths.

They didn't know they were being watched. In the bushes, craning his neck to see: James. He observed in agony as Kezia held her arms high; she was in control, her hands tracing circles. She moved towards Darim and their bodies rippled with a desperation that made his heart contract. He picked at the plant he was crouching behind, foliage dying with little pieces of him.

James had come because there was nothing else he could do. His mouth had been dry as he sat stiffly on the plane, his fingers knotted, turning his thumbs over and over, watching the plastic peeling away from the onboard safety notice in front. Ravines of clouds banked up outside and they seemed solid, but it was a lie; he knew he could fall right through them like they weren't even there. The air hostess handed him an inflight magazine and he leafed listlessly through pages of tacky perfume and snacks in neon packets. The journey had taken so long... but now he was here, he wasn't ready. It felt as though he was in the wrong scene of a play — he didn't know his lines and even Kezia was a different character. She had lost weight and was stronger, firmer. She looked more upright, more certain, and she didn't wear dresses at home. Only her ears were the same and something in her essence that he couldn't quite define in the dark; he knew her, but not like this.

Kezia and Darim were reaching the apogee of their dance now, feet hammering down and down, sweat silver in the moonlight. After an explosive finale they stopped; they were freeze-framed silhouettes, breathing heavily.

James looked away, the moment too intimate to bear. He studied the leaves around him, curled at the edges, glossy in the grey light, and when he looked back, Kezia and Darim were gone. The terrace was empty.

He stumbled out from his hiding place and stuttered uncertainly through the garden. A goat made the noise of a broken wind-up toy and a peacock sailed past, just a shape and then gone. The house was asleep, shutters pulled across, eyes closed. James noticed the red and white stripes, rusty in the pale light, and the hanging baskets, shifting in the shadows, not sharing their secrets. He stood helplessly, staring.

When a lamp blinked on downstairs he shunted backwards, straight into a metal chair, hitting his ankle in a sudden clash. He bent down, clutching it and trying to breathe through the pain, digesting the shout he had only just managed to swallow. When the throbbing waned, he stood, squinting to see, hoping it was Kezia in the room but there was only the man — Darim — looking at his reflection in a mirror. James stepped forwards, holding his breath now, as if that would make him somehow less visible.

Darim was singing sotto voce, a slow song, something sentimental. He cocked his head to the side and stared at himself like a cat sensing something new, sniffing the air. "Mama," he said plaintively. "You see what you make me do? This is your idea of making money I suppose, is it? You drive me to this and I never even got to say goodbye." Suddenly he stood up and James fumbled backwards, catching at the chair which scraped sullenly.

"Tomi? Tomi. What are you doing?" Darim called in searing Spanish. The door opened, light fanning out onto the flagstones. "Tomi?"

A ginger cat limped past petulantly, turning to look at Darim, who cried, "Tomi. Stop it." And promptly shut the door again, leaving Tomi to lick the side of his chest as if it were a wound.

James kept low, scanning the house for more signs of life. He was deciding what to do, thinking about creeping to the other side, when Tomi finished preening and hobbled towards him, staring, eyes like ice.

Just a cat, thought James, *just a cat,* feeling the frost of the disconcerting gaze. But when Tomi grew tall and mewed obstreperously and the goat replied in a desolate bleat and the wind caught the hanging baskets which swayed capriciously, his frayed nerves fractured and he darted away, involuntarily scrabbling and tripping and running and panting his way back to the path.

At the window, unable to sleep, Kezia was contemplating the patchy shadows in the garden. She saw the shaft of light illuminate Tomi as Darim opened his door and she saw his ginger fur turn to charcoal as the light retracted again. Then she saw a figure jerk and almost fall across the garden as it left. A fleeting phantom? It looked like James.

Hallucinating. Again. Kezia hugged her arms around herself. *James… James is not there.* She stared into the empty obscurity below, blinking and rubbing her eyes, her words just a whisper as she asked, "Am I cursed? Am I cursed?" Finally, she retreated to the bed, pulling the sheets up over her face in a cocoon of her own making. *Am I cursed?*

Kezia fell into a light and troubled sleep. James was everywhere, but camouflaged. He blended into walls, doorways, castles, ships and even a floral wallpaper. She was travelling with the dreams, too far and too fast, and when she washed up out of them, she was sweating. She heard something squeak and a muffled bleat, the dull thud of her heartbeat, then the clack of Darim's door opening. Kezia disentangled herself from the sticky sheets, unwinding from the bed and taking the few steps to the window.

A shape outside. Another one. *Real, or…* Kezia squinted to see. Too many shadows, too many shapes now; the ghost realm opened up to her. *Now I see them all,* she thought, *now they are part of my world.* The shape flickered away, just as James had.

45

Snake

$\mathcal{I}$t was early in the morning when James came edging back down the path. Desiccated twigs cracked and the air vibrated with insects. He was heavy and hot, and as he brushed his hair from his eyes, he tried to brush the image of Kezia and Darim out of his mind — dancing, dancing and getting closer…

He was nervous and he needed the toilet. He peered about before slinking off, into a roadside coppice where the trees were spindly but plentiful. They murmured, a disturbing wind rattling their branches as he edged over a carpet of crippled pine cones into the densest bit of thicket, hastily unzipping his flies, about to relieve himself when—

A smooth green hosepipe uncoiled from the undergrowth — rolling stealthily over the arid ground — sliding towards him, making a straight line for his legs. The snake had steely blank eyes and a purposeful head. It moved relentlessly forwards with the consistency of a conveyor belt and it hissed as if it hated James, who jumped backwards, tripping and landing on the dusty floor with his trousers around his ankles. He put his hands behind him and shuffled away, forming an awkward table with his body and his bare legs, but the snake was gliding closer — closer and closer — and faster and faster. James yelled, pushing himself to his feet, grabbing his trousers, pulling them up and running back to the path, running and running and not slowing until he got to a fork in the track, his breath ragged and his heart pumping.

He let out a long exhale and went to steady himself on a tree, flinching as a dry branch snaked towards him in a reptilian replica. As he withdrew his hand he saw the dirt, and it was all over: grit on his arms, grit on his crotch and grit on his face where he'd swept back his fringe. "This was not the plan," he said. "This was not the plan." And shuddered as he thought of the snake, so calm and calculated. He brushed his palms against each other, some of the particles flicking off, some too deeply embedded.

Then James' whole body lurched for a second time as he remembered the ring and felt for it in his pocket. Still there. It was somehow still there. Relief surged, and he swallowed, looking down and shaking his head before heading back to his hotel, to change. The streets were empty, everyone inside, away from the simmering, soon to be scalding sun, but eyes roved in windows and curtains quivered with prying people, curious about the man with the cheeks like ripe tomatoes.

The hotel lobby was a square cube of air conditioning, blue lights adding to the cool feeling. A low sofa hugged the wall, with a large crucifix above, dripping bright blood and painted-on pain. Opposite, on the vacated reception desk, a plastic bull with wide nostrils and wide eyes perched, watching.

"James?"

He turned quickly, conscious of the mud marks on the back of his trousers.

"James, wow, we meet again."

"Oh. Er, yes…"

"It's me again: mug smasher extraordinaire." She grimaced, looking up at him through husks of mascara, "We met in Pimlico the other day too. What a coincidence!"

Not wanting to talk about why he was in Pimlico, James said, "Thanks for the nice review." And tried to pick more of the grit out of his hands.

Rachel appraised him. "Are you okay?"

"I, err, well… I had a run in with a snake actually," James told her. "So I'm just a bit rattled. It wasn't a rattle snake," he added wryly, raising his eyebrows. "I don't know what kind, but it was too big for my liking."

Rachel chuckled bleakly, hunching her shoulders. "There are loads of snakes round here. I hate them."

"I know. It's all right, he came off worse," said James, feigning a karate chop.

"Don't tell me, now he's your belt."

"Ha! Well, actually, I just ran away, but I took a stumble so I came back here to change," he smiled sheepishly.

275

"Well, honestly, if I'd have met a snake, they would have heard the screaming all the way back at Buckingham Palace, no joke. So don't worry about it. But wait, let me buy you a drink, you look like you could use one and I still have to say thank you for being so nice about the mug too. That really… that really stayed with me, you know?"

"It was nothing, but thanks."

"I'll ring the bell, Luis will come."

As Rachel went over to the desk, James realised his flies were still undone; he pulled them up as fast as he could and settled self-consciously on the sofa, the ring box bulging squarely in his pocket.

Rachel smiled as she came to sit down. "I can't believe this coincidence — what brings you to Spain?" She leant forwards, feigning curiosity, accidentally knocking her bag with her foot so a packet of painkillers slid onto the floor, the branding a stinging shade of red.

James glanced at them. "Oh, well, my girlfriend is here actually, learning flamenco. I just thought I'd surprise her."

"Nice!" said Rachel. She didn't mention the mark on his face, or the box, which he was trying to conceal with his arm.

A rangy waiter hurried from a back room, wiping his hands on a little white apron tied around his waist. They both ordered orange juice and he scurried back behind a curtain of beads.

"How about you?" James asked. "Why are you here?"

"Well, I think this was meant to be, I'm actually writing a feature about flamenco!" Rachel told him. "You know, the tourist boom around dance. A taste of the exotic. Maybe I could talk to your girlfriend, ask her how she's found it?"

"Maybe." James nodded, catching the manic glare of the plastic bull on the reception counter: midnight black and staring.

Rachel was regarding him like a paint swatch held against a wall. "Erm, so how long are you here for?" she asked casually.

He swept the hair out of his eyes, feeling the slight grate of grit. "Oh, just a long weekend. You?" He tried to rub his forehead without her noticing.

"Yep, same, back to work on Tuesday. Luis told me there's a flamenco competition tomorrow so looks like I picked the right weekend." She nodded assertively.

"Oh right, nice."

The waiter came back with the drinks on a chequered tray. James thanked him in flaky Spanish, taking a quick sip and wincing as the sugar shocked his parched mouth.

"So, when are you going to drop in on your girlfriend then?" said Rachel, rubbing her hands.

"I was going to do it just now — then this happened." James indicated the dirt. "Not ideal... but I'll just make myself more presentable and then, yeah..."

They finished their juice, making small talk about the weather and Spanish food, and when the conversation dwindled James said, "Listen, thanks for the drink. I guess I'll see you around."

"Well certainly, if history is anything to go by!"

He smiled awkwardly and she watched him tread heavily up the stairs, the carpet swirling uncertain patterns of orange and puce, then she texted Martin.

Great news, one of the student's boyfriends is here and he is going to propose, I just know it. It'll make a really nice extra for the piece — romantic and feel good — I'll follow him down and get some pics.

She didn't tell him about her encounter with Omar.

Martin's reply was typically brief.

Good. Get video — more clicks.

When James re-emerged at reception, he was wearing a pair of chinos and a new white shirt. He didn't see Rachel as he left. She was stood outside, just to the right of the doors, smoking a cigarette: saffron ember smouldering as she lifted it to her lips. She watched him go, saw him feel for the ring once again in his pocket, gripping the box tight and walking on. She checked her watch; she'd give it five minutes, then follow.

Rachel felt a familiar roll of pain start from her stomach and undulate outwards. The heat seemed to crack at her. To take her mind off it, she remembered the good feeling she'd had about flamenco, how this was her time, this was her story. Too many coincidences for it not to be;

277

she had to trust it. As she contemplated, the pain subsided and she breathed slowly, looking for somewhere to stub out her cigarette. There was a metal bin on the other side of the door, reflecting the piercing sun in a blaze of white, like shining armour. She was just moving across when a short man with a nose like a tap accosted her. The tap was dripping. His voice was hoarse and thin, as if it was made of crepe paper and might tear if he spoke too loudly. "*No bajes al agua,*" he said. "*No bajes al mar de noche.*" His nubilous eyes sought out hers, and there was a stain on his blue polo shirt, just below the collar.

Rachel smiled and tried to remember a bit of Spanish. "*Hola,*" she said, and then, "*Inglesa,*" pointing at herself.

The man nodded, making a slurping sound with his mouth, before speaking again in a stream of Spanish, words pouring over themselves, fast and slippery. She recognised a few: 'woman', 'beach', and 'night'… but she couldn't put them in any sort of order as the meanings blended and merged and washed past her.

"*Gracias,*" she said to the man. "*Gracias.*" And backed away.

The man wiped his nose on the back of his hand and then wiped his hand on the side of his T-shirt.

46

Peacocks

Normando was dozing on the terrace, the sun combing through his cares. Benja was on the table, legs folded fully under him, his eyes closed in contemplation and his mouth curled up in a smile. Darim bustled out of the side door. "The kitchen is a mess Papa, will you let me clean it now?"

Normando's eyes fluttered open. Benja stretched one leg out in front of him and the old man looked at the cat as if he had just asked the question.

"Get off the table, shoo." Darim waved his hand at Benja who regarded him reproachfully and then skittered to the ground, skulking round the nearest chair legs with a portentous glare. Darim sneezed.

"Bless you," uttered Sue, coming round the corner and brushing her hands together in the rhythm of the sevillana. She nodded her hellos and sat down carefully on the bench beside Normando, who smiled sweetly at her thinking she was Carlotta.

"I'll go and clean up Papa, you stay there with Sue," said Darim and was about to depart when they heard Rollo bark three times — hard and imperative — then a low growl, then three more barks. Darim lifted his head sharply, at the same time and in exactly the same manner as Benja.

Rollo came careening round the side of the house, a message backlit in the shine of his ebony eyes. "*Bueno cariño*, okay," Darim translated instantly. "Someone is here. It's probably that journalist, back again. I'll handle this. Sue, you keep an eye on Papa." And he followed Rollo as the dog led him, running forwards and back, forwards and back, checking his master was always in his wake.

When they got to the front of the house, they saw James. He was at the end of the path and looking up at the ivy trailing around the open shutters, the jaded paint in its helter-skelter hues. "Who is it, Rollo?" murmured Darim and Rollo made his stranger noise at the back of his throat.

279

They surveyed as James adjusted his shirt and came forwards, still looking up at the house. He caught his foot on a flower pot and it tilted and rolled over, spilling the dark blood of its soil. They saw him bend to set it right, observed his expression as the calendula seemed to be shaking its head at him, one dull eye adamant, its petals like a mane of flames. "That is my plant," said Darim to Rollo as James put it down, stem still swaying.

When James looked up again, he saw them: Darim with his arms folded, Rollo's ears alert. They waited, statue still and staring. He tried to walk purposefully now, taking long, loping strides, almost falling forwards. Even so it seemed to take a long time for him to reach them, everything suddenly motionless and watching. He felt eyes everywhere. Esmerelda moaned mournfully, a thirsty, gnarled complaint, and one of the peacocks teetered daintily past. A leaf fell slowly from a tree, wavering slightly as it drifted, gliding to the ground.

James could see Darim, the man who had haunted his days and tortured his nights, the man who, only last night, had danced with Kezia too intimately, too amorously to endure. He didn't know whether to shout or fight or scream and he couldn't quell the nerves that caught in his chest.

Rollo growled, as finally, he drew close. Darim still did not move or speak, so the two men stood, examining each other, until James said, "Darim?" It was all he could manage.

"Yes." Darim arched his eyebrows and unfolded his arms. He looked smaller in real life, but more dynamic. He narrowed his eyes. "Who are you?"

"James. I'm James, I'm Kezia's… erm, I'm James. Could I see her? I'd like to see her." He rubbed his hair and some of it stuck up at the back of his head.

Darim looked at it. "Why?"

"Oh." James coughed. "I just… I just need to talk to her. There are some things we need to work out—" He faltered, turning to Rollo as if the dog might understand.

The ivy flapped against the side of the house. "She does not wish to see you," said Darim, his words like barbed wire.

James tried to draw himself up taller. "No, she can decide that. Let me see her."

Darim folded his hands together so the lattice of his fingers meshed. Slowly he said, "I am her teacher and I know what is best. She has a competition tomorrow, she needs to focus. I will not have her distracted before then."

James looked desperately at the house, the peacock strutting up and down as if on patrol. "Just if I could..."

Darim regarded him calmly, implacably. "No. She is mine now. I decide."

The words hit James so hard the world seemed to blur around him. *She can't be. No.* He felt his cheeks burning.

"You may go," said Darim coolly.

"But I've come all the way from England," James heard himself say.

"I do not care if you've come from Timbuktu. She is mine now and she will not see you." Darim felt his rage rising. "I have told you she is mine. You will go." He took a step forwards, the heat in his blood. He was shorter than James but stronger — he puffed out his chest.

"Look, at least let me talk to her. That's all. I just need to talk to her," James pleaded. "Where is she?"

"You will not make her love you with your impudence!" Darim snapped, then he smoothed down his shirt. "She has moved on and so must you." Rollo sat down as if he agreed.

James took a step back.

"That's it, off you go." Darim flipped his hand like he was flicking off a fly.

"I... Please."

"Go on, off with you. She will not see you." Darim's jaw clamped shut, he would not be moved.

James could feel the sweat drying on his skin. He looked up at the house trying to sense where she might be... "Kezia?" Before he knew what he was doing he was shouting, up and as loud as he could. "Kezia!" He felt like a madman, standing and calling her name.

"Go now or I will call the police," Darim bluffed. "You are stalking her. You must leave her alone."

"No, no I just want to talk to her, that's not—"

"I have told you, she does not wish to see you."

Without warning the patrolling peacock started rattling its entire posterior, beating and shaking and beating and shaking as it raised its feathers in a sail which blazed about its body, orbicular iridescent markings catching the sun and glinting like eyes.

James observed the refulgent reflections. "She will want to see me," he declared. "I'll call her. Honestly. She will."

"Fine." And Darim tapped his toe while the number rang out — unanswered.

As James put his phone away, a man in a woolly jumper and jeans who had been digging in the garden walked over, still carrying his spade. He stood behind Darim. "Is everything okay?"

"This intruder is just leaving," Darim said, and it was two against one.

James studied Hady, wondering if he should ask him about Kezia, but just then Sami clattered out from the house brightly and they all turned to see. "Darim, it is time for my lesson. Darim! Oh, who's that?"

"You see, we are busy," said Darim, swinging back to James pointedly.

"I don't need long, I promise. Could you just give me ten minutes?" said James, looking to Sami now as the least threatening of the three in his sky-blue T-shirt and yellow shorts.

"Long, little, it is all the same," said Darim. "We do not want you here and you will leave now."

Hady came towards James, rolling up his sleeves, the spade under his arm.

Confounded, James turned to go. He took a step... but then he spun back again. He couldn't tell Chris he capitulated, he needed to be the hero, to take them all on...

"It is that way," said Darim sharply, moving forwards too, his steps and his words clipped.

Then Rollo sprang up, his body tense and firm and James knew there was no way through. He held his hands up in defeat. "Okay, Okay," he said. "I'll go."

Rollo barked and the sound was dry and rusty.

James turned, wishing he was brave, retracing his steps — slow and sad. There was a sheen in his eyes that wasn't quite crying. He didn't look back, he couldn't, the shame was too much. He felt for the ring box in his pocket and wondered, if it was true, what he'd said: *she is mine now.* He shuddered. If he could only talk to her, then he'd know, but he couldn't go back, not now. His ankle nearly went over on a boulder of dry earth which disintegrated as soon as he stood on it, chalky and brown. He kicked the dirt off his shoe and walked on, scanning the way for snakes, his thoughts stinging like wasps, and he was so distraught, so distracted, he didn't see Rachel.

She was over in the lay-by, just off the path, where the cicadas sang in the tangled weeds. She was hidden by the old wheelbarrow and the broken pots, clutching her camera, willing Kezia out. "Go and get her," she had whispered. "Come on…" nudging a shard of pottery with her foot and framing the house the way she wanted to film it. The sweat dripped down her back.

When James walked past she took a picture, and another — clicks camouflaged in the insect soundscape — a part of the story, she just didn't know which part, not yet.

Then Sami came running along the track and Rachel ducked down again. "Yes," she said to herself. "Show's not over." And pulled back a bit more so she was definitely out of sight.

"Mister James, Mister James…" Sami caught his breath. "Mister James?"

James, ensconced in his emotions as he was, didn't notice Sami until he was almost parallel with him, still calling his name in a musical voice like wind chimes. "Mister James, stop…"

James rounded, automatically clenching his fists.

"Mister James." Sami cocked his head, blinked a few times, then skipped on the spot. "You are James!"

Hot and bewildered, James nodded, relaxing his hands.

"Mister James, you do not have to be unhappy. Darim, he lies." Sami stopped to assess the impact of his statement, but James just opened his mouth and didn't say anything, so he carried on. "Darim is keeping Kezia here against her will but I know she loves you and she wants you to take her back to England," he sighed happily. "Darim is a bad man. But she is not his favourite. I am." Sami looked up to the sky, feeling the sun on his face.

"What?"

283

"Kezia loves you." Sami bit his bottom lip and then started speaking very fast. "She loves you. She told me. She is trapped here. She is… *cursed*. You need to rescue her. You can save her. She needs you. Darim… does not love her. It is the curse."

"Curse?" James squinted at Sami, shaking his head in disbelief.

"You do not know about the curse? Of course, you have just come." And he launched into a jabbering account of the ghost and the cove and the beautiful, dreadful music.

"I'm sorry, I…" James began to back away.

Sami reached out as if he might grab James' shirt. "It is true. Don't go down to the water, Mister James, or it could happen to you, too." His eyes were round like a deer, imploring.

James shifted his gaze to the circus stripes of the house and back to Sami, who was smiling now so that his head became the sun above the blue sky and yellow sand of his outfit.

"It is true. Why else do you think she has not come home? She is trapped here, trapped by the curse. Only true love can set her free. You, can set her free."

James scratched his ear, floundering.

"You can save her still," said Sami, pulling his lips together, straining with seriousness. "Tomorrow. All you need to do is come to the village square tomorrow, at noon. She will be there, dancing in the competition. You can find her and take her away and she will be saved and you will be… happy." Sami beamed, his face hopeful and shining.

James nodded but kept moving away.

"She loves you." Sami waved his arms like he was throwing confetti.

James felt for his ring box, still there in his pocket.

"Tomorrow," Sami said. "And then you can get married!"

James nodded dumbly.

"And also, Mister James — that journalist is following you, see—"

But when he turned round, there was nobody there, just a butterfly fluttering over an old flower pot, its wings, stained violet.

47

Silk

𝒯he light was pearly white and Darim was sitting on Kezia's bed, looking at her. She thought he was another hallucination until she reached out and touched his leg and it was warm and firm with living. He looked tired and stern and his mouth was smaller than usual. She wriggled upright, pulling the back of her hand across her eyes.

"I'm sorry for your phone," he said, staring straight ahead.

Kezia was still blurry from her nap, she had dreamt she heard James calling, calling her name, and his voice was hot in her head. She looped her little finger around Darim's index finger. "It's okay," she said. "Accidents happen, right?"

"Accidents happen," he echoed sombrely. Rollo was asleep in the corner, the soft white hairs on his belly gently rising and falling. Darim watched him for a while, then said, "Temporal as this life is, the moment is ever more so." And he raised his eyebrows in a mixture of understanding and disbelief.

Kezia was about to ask him about this and was just adjusting her position when he spoke again, sharply this time, his words serrated, glinting steel. "Kezarina, did you ask him to come?"

"Ask who?"

"You know."

"No. Who?"

"This James." Darim pulled his finger from hers and looked away in distaste, "James. He is here."

"What?"

"That's right," he said, satisfied by her shock.

"That's the last thing I want. You know that."

Darim nodded curtly. "I should have guessed your old life would come back for you eventually," he lamented. "It always does, it always does."

"Where is he?"

"He came here to the house, I told him to leave you alone." Darim sounded pleased with himself now.

Kezia thought back to the shadow falling across the lawn last night. It was James. She sat silently for a while, brooding.

"You do not want him here, do you, Kezia?"

She looked up. "No, you know I don't." She took Darim's hand and let their fingers intertwine. "I want to start again."

Darim moved towards her and tilted her head to look at him. He leant forwards and kissed her roundly on the mouth. "You are my favourite," he said. "Those eyes, that smile." And he held her there, in his gaze, for a while.

When he pulled back, Kezia watched his expression carefully, his mouth still small and perturbed. "How dare James come here?" she said. "How stupid. As if that changes anything. It makes it worse. It makes the whole thing worse. It's the curse, isn't it?" She looked desperately at Darim. "It's the curse that's brought him here to ruin things for us, to get in the way."

"No," said Darim, and then quickly, "Yes."

"You don't know?"

Darim said nothing, dolorous on the bed.

"It must be. It's so unlike him... Look, Darim, I know you said I shouldn't ask, but please tell me — what is the spell to break the curse? You must tell me now. For us. I want to... I want to be free of the curse."

"Kezia..."

"I know, you said it is dangerous, but surely, surely, I've got to try. When my past comes back to haunt me and there are faces and voices everywhere still. Please. Please Darim."

Darim sighed. "Kezarina. That spell died with my mama. Only she knows where it is now."

"That's not true. Mando found it, he told us. He told us but he just couldn't remember where it is. You've got to help me find it."

Darim shifted uncomfortably. "Mando is right. It is lost. He probably burned it in the Aga by mistake or used it to line Pedro's cage, long since cleared. I would... I would have given it to you otherwise. But it is futile to hope in something that cannot be. I'm sorry, my Kezarina."

"Then… then what can I do?"

Darim thought about this. "Go — go and tell James you do not love him." There was fire at the centre of his eyes now, his look a challenge. "Yes!" He stood up swiftly, took her owl bag from where it was hanging over the bedpost and put it in her lap like a dog returning a ball. Then he strode across the room and plucked the red silk dress, the one he liked the most, from its hanger, laying it delicately beside her. "Put on your best dress: you must always dress for the occasion, Kezarina, always. This is your moment." He flung his head back as if it was his moment too. "Tell him you are mine. Do it for me. It is a matter of honour."

Kezia looked at the dress, the silk undulating in waves of polished ruby. "I do not want to see him, I don't—"

"What about me, Kezarina? What about our love?" He looked at her truculently, holding the pose as if counting the beats.

"But Darim, me seeing James won't change anything. I already told him—"

"Then you were not clear. Before, you did not know what clear is. Flamenco has taught you that."

"If I go running after him, surely he'll get the wrong idea, won't he?"

"Not when he sees you in your power!" Darim turned dramatically. "You will tell him this morning, and after, we dance!" He stood back, nodding to himself, then his narrow hips began swinging mechanically, left-right, left-right and he danced out of the room as though it was his stage, heels clicking across the floor. "Go and tell him, go and tell him," he sung as he left.

"Darim don't leave — tell me — why should I have to prove it to you?" Kezia shouted, but the sound just fell into the empty space of the corridor.

***

"Kezia, what's wrong?" Java put her head around the door and then catapulted inside. She had heard Kezia shouting after Darim and now she could now see her spirit was as creased as her bedsheets. "What's wrong?" She waited a beat and then leapt towards the bed, flinging her arms around her friend. When she pulled away, Kezia was too dazed to explain so Java just stroked her hair as if she was Rollo.

Soon they heard Sue's voice, anxious to find them, floating through the hall, light and loving. "Java? Kezia?"

"We're in here!" Java yelled, skipping up onto the bed and cradling Kezia's knees so that when Sue came in, she could sit at the side.

"Oh love," exclaimed Sue. "Are you poorly again?"

Kezia sniffed, shaking her head. "I am cursed though. I'm still cursed." She hugged her elbows. "I must be, or why has this happened? James has come here — here to the house — and Darim wants me to go after him and tell him it's over but it's obvious and he should know. I don't understand why he's angry with me. I feel... cursed." She folded her arms across her chest.

Sue made a clicking noise with her tongue, considering. Then she said, knowingly, "Darim is jealous. That's all. It's dented his pride James coming here, you know what he's like, he's insecure. He sees you as his project, his alone."

"Yeah," Java agreed. "Totally does."

"But honestly," Sue continued. "He'll have forgotten about it all in a minute."

Kezia rubbed her arms. "You don't think it's the curse then?"

"No more than love is always a blessing *and* a curse," said Sue, leaning back on the bedstead.

"Anyway, it's the competition tomorrow." Java pressed her hands into Kezia's knees. "So we need to practise, we need to focus on that." She affected a pout.

"But maybe I should go and tell James first, just so that—"

"No," Sue interrupted. "No, just because Darim says so? I don't think so. Do it for you, if you'd like to, but not because he tells you to. You are your own person, and you don't look like someone who wants to go running after a man you've already tried to split up with once." Sue was adamant. "And anyway, as I said, we know Darim's emotions blow like the wind. He's just in one of his moods."

"Another one." Java rolled her eyes.

Kezia's head throbbed. She rubbed her temples. She thought she heard James' voice, thin and reedy, outside, talking. "I'm still hearing voices." She shook her head as if she could shake them out. Java hugged her knees tighter and Sue put an arm round her shoulder as Kezia shut her eyes and heard James again. She shivered. Voices, always the voices.

"Don't worry, you're safe here with us," said Sue, in a sonorous, timeless way.

"Do you think though..." Kezia struggled for the words. "Don't you think I should at least try the cure? If we could find it? I asked Darim and he doesn't know where the spell is but... look I know Rosa said not to but I had to... I need that now. Don't you think I need it now?" Kezia sniffed and wiped her nose on the back of her hand.

Sue was about to answer but Java got in first. "Oh, I haven't told you — I asked Hady to talk to this guy, Ron, who he sees at the bar." Java rearranged herself on the bed, preparing to divulge. "He's been researching it you see — the legend — and he says it's correct, what the others said. The words you say are one thing, but you do also have to find something that was loved, something precious to someone, and yeah, you take it to her as an offering, and after that you say the spell. You say the spell and then you have to stand and hear her sing. You have to listen right to the end. Then — then — you have broken the curse." She nodded sagely, "No one has ever done it though. No one."

The spectre of Carlotta seemed to hang in the air and for a moment the room rippled with her presence.

"But we don't have the spell anyway," breathed Kezia eventually.

"Well, perhaps you don't need it," said Sue comfortingly. "Perhaps things will be all right anyway. We'll look after you and things will be just fine."

Java seemed disappointed.

"Are you sure?" asked Kezia.

"Yes," said Sue and gave her a cavernous hug. "Anyway," she added afterwards. "As Java said, we need to talk about what we're going to wear tomorrow."

Relenting, Kezia took both their hands and they began chattering about the competition and the costumes and the masks, as Rollo slept blissfully in the corner, giving the occasional little snore or swiping a dream rabbit with his paw.

When Darim came back, the girls were lying against each other, laughing. "What is this?" he demanded. "You lounge about? The big day is tomorrow. We must practise. All of you, get up!" And he spun out of the room.

"See? I told you he'd forget all about it," said Sue. "His mother was just the same. Come on then, let's dance."

48

Bunting

𝒪Masks. Burlesque masks. Feathered masks. Sequinned masks. Masks scratching the tops of noses and pinning back ears. They wore long crimson skirts and black velvet masks.

They hid behind the masks as they filed up the path, a flamenco troupe in disguise, each holding their skirt in a fist like a talisman of war. They kept looking straight ahead, resolute and proud, fierce, with heads held up and eyes flashing fire. This was how Darim had told them to be.

Darim, leading the girls, dressed as a bullfighter, a vertical mask covering one half of his face. He walked calmly with a hand on his hip and he nodded graciously to the animals as they passed. Hady was at the back like a bodyguard, keeping a steady distance behind, as Java turned to grin at him, swishing her skirts, showing off.

The sun beat down and they began to sweat as they started up the hill; a purposeful procession flecked with excitement and anxiety, hope and doubt, whispers and the occasional song.

Soon they could hear the noise from the village: the low thrum of a sound system stippled with car horns and organisational shouting. As they got closer, bunting appeared; frayed triangles in faded blue and yellow — strewn from trees and houses, tied between lamp posts — it flickered, as if excited. Then the people: rowdy men, skittish women and heady children unhinged with anticipation.

There were flagons of ale on small fold-up tables, sliced oranges on plates attracting flies and brightly coloured sweets like beads in bowls. There were barbecues pumping smoke into the fresh morning air and strings of sausages lined up. Bright burgundy grapes resembled tiny balloons nestled in huge wooden caskets, waiting for men and women with rolled up sleeves and rolled up trousers to tread them into a helpless pulp of purple. "That looks so fun," said Carmen just as a grown man in a grape costume waddled past, waving and smiling a big grape smile. Then another troupe of dancers crossed their path, all in traditional Spanish dress: white tunics and long raven skirts.

"They look professional!" squealed Java, adjusting her mask.

In the main square, the stage was waiting for them. Constructed from the back of a lorry, it filled the whole of one side, opposite the church with its steps cascading steeply down and its two solid stone towers reaching for the sky. There were fold-up chairs in the centre, set out in straight lines like an odd version of solitaire.

The girls drank freshly-made lemonade in paper cups while looking longingly at the vats of rich plum coloured wine. "After," said Carmen, "We will have a drink after."

They didn't notice Rachel, skirting the square in black leather trousers, weaving herself into the day like the invisible thread of a spider's web that only shows when the light is in the right direction. She was good at hiding. She took pictures from afar.

"Oh, did I tell you what Mando said?" Java stood up straight which usually meant she had gossip. Sue and Kezia shook their heads absent-mindedly, watching men in robes gathering by the church. "Magdalena's mama has gone to live in America, with her flamenco partner, but they haven't told Magdalena yet. They don't think it will help."

"Oh God," said Sue, "They really ought to tell her."

"Darim won't apparently. He's worried it might send her over the edge." Java mimed two hands pushing.

Kezia was only half-listening, she was going over the steps in her mind, waiting for the moment, sizing up the stage. *You're not into dancing*, Lucy's words returned to taunt her. *Aren't dancers kind of... I don't know, petite and graceful... Not like us.* The nerves bit. She tried to focus on what Darim had said. *Remember, we can win. Mindset is everything.* She did not want to let him down.

The procession started. Catholic priests in snowy white vestments began a low chant around the statue of a man holding a wooden cross in one hand and a small neat church in the other; he wore the brown tunic of a monk, tied at the waist with a rope ending in a crucifix, like a rosary. His ear was chipped and part of his foot missing, the paint peeling from his shoulder and cheek. He looked familiar to Kezia, with his wire halo and purposeful stare. *'Always forward, never back...'* The memory distilled in her mind as she pictured Saint Junipero at the bar, with the cross and the church too. At that moment the statue was hoisted high into the air by four burly men the shape of tombstones, broad shoulders hulking below shrunken necks and bald heads. They took a corner of the platform each and the drums started as they moved off, the priests filing behind, followed by some people with trumpets. The statue swayed as it was carried, regarded earnestly by women who crossed themselves in its wake, heads covered, joining the priests in resonant song.

The procession left the square but could still be heard as it wound through the streets. The church bells chimed midday; the peals infusing into the hot air with the lemon scent from their now warm drinks. To the left, a group of drunkards in sleeveless basketball tops propped up the bar, leaning on large barrel tables, shouting ragged swear words and lolling back in the sun.

When the statue appeared again — wobbling above the heads of the increasingly thirsty bearers — there was a large crowd behind it and everyone advanced into the square: some tearful, some bored and some children pulling on their parent's hands, hankering for freedom. The fold-up seats began filling with surly men defeated by the heat, their wives fussing around them.

People in black T-shirts milled around the stage, checking cables, hitting the microphone tentatively and nodding at the plump thud it made. When they had finished, a man in a suit with a clipboard ushered Elena Garcia, the mayor of Parños, up onto the platform. Elena looked around hesitantly, as if surveying a new kingdom, then smiled, satisfied. She stepped up to the mic and made a long, garbled speech, which not many people heeded, except a few comatose looking women at the front who were fanning themselves with makeshift scraps of paper.

"And now we will decide the Queen of the Festival!"

A few nervous teenagers — squeezed into dresses and with plastic flowers in their hair — congregated and swirled onto the stage, flouncing and curtseying and listening for the cheers of their family. Each one gave a shy address, looking apprehensively to their assembled relatives for affirmation. Some sang. Some recited poems. A few forgot their lines completely.

Next the mayor stood up from her seat at the side of the stage and walked along the line of girls. They held their breath, eyes bulging with the effort of pulling their stomachs in. After a feverish and fretful wait, Elena grasped the hand of a vigorous teen called Miranda with an abundance of dark curly hair and eyes like coal, and pulled up her arm. A cheer erupted, mainly from a large contingent of women in garish off-the-shoulder blouses and tight white jeans, their hair tied up to show big gold hoop earrings. Miranda fell to her knees and was then presented with a huge bunch of bulbous flowers and a silver plastic crown. She got up, went to the microphone and gasped her way through an acceptance speech, at which her mother sobbed, reaching ample arms up in happy adulation as Miranda told Parños this was the best day of her life, which it was. Miranda clutched the flowers closely to her chest as she took her seat next to the mayor, settling down righteously, ready for her first job as Festival Queen: to judge the dancing competition.

There was a short break while some very loud music blasted from the speakers and everybody got drinks and cured meats and cheese with slices of very neat bread. Even Darim didn't notice Rachel, just off to their right, photographing the apprehension and the angst in Kezia and her friends. He was pacing up and down, disturbed by the crowds and the synthesised music. "Stay focused," he said to the girls. "This is your moment — to shine — to light up that stage. We are on fourth." He flourished a small piece of paper printed with the running order and it made them even more anxious: stomachs tingling, blood rushing, thoughts whooshing. They were drunk on hope and worry. Only Hady remained calm, an island in a sea of skipping nerves, he said nothing as he looked over the crowds to the stage with a kind of placid optimism.

There were seven dance troupes in the competition and one dancing dog.

It turned out the dancing dog was for the talent show later that night — his owner had caused confusion by dressing him up in a flamenco costume: ruffles and a frilly little skirt. He looked disgruntled as he foraged the curb for scraps. There were also to be fire breathers, opera singers, a man who said he could eat his own feet and a magician who made doves appear out of hats. But they didn't need magic from where they were standing, the air was already electric. It was as charged as it was redolent with cloves and ginger from the stand selling gingerbread flamencas who kicked out doughy feet and wore thick bands of icing.

The girls pooled around Darim, the rock to their restless excitement. "Okay. We focus. We do not think about the others. They are nothing to us. Pah! We have our own style, our own spirit, and that is what I want to see shining through today, brighter than the stars." He nodded upwards. "Java, where is your mask?" Java pulled at the elastic across her neck and swivelled the plastic around from the back. "Good. Now Kezia — Kezia, this is your first time on stage, your first opportunity to show everyone who you really are!" His eyes were luminous as he looked at her, like the sea with the sun on it and the feeling lapped against her beating heart.

"*Olé!*" A drunken man wearing a grotty vest, holding a beer aloft, shouted from the makeshift bar of barrels and a gaggle of his pals snorted with laughter. Some of them pretended to dance, looking mockingly over, their dumpy bodies like bean bags and their mouths cracked with derision.

"We focus," said Darim again. "This is our time." And then quietly, "The power is yours, do not give it away."

The mayor came back on stage, looking bolder now, cheeks flushed with wine. She coughed then smiled, and her introduction to the competition was long and complicated by drink. They stopped listening as her Spanish lilted on and on... Finally, she smiled again and clasped her hands together. "We begin!"

As she retreated, a male group cantered onto the stage, posing and patting each other on the back. They wore red shirts that were already sweaty from the festivities and their suede trousers were too tight. Miranda, the new Queen of the Festival, was given the microphone: it was her duty to introduce all the dancers. She mumbled a name no one could hear and then ducked her head and went back to her special seat.

The men arranged themselves in rows and began to dance as soon as the last one had taken up his place. Their steps were inadequate so they compensated by posturing and by force. The stage didn't look as though it could hold them as they bashed through their bullish routine; the slats creaked and jumped so much that they were part of the dance, bending unwillingly to the beat. Darim looked perturbed by their rowdy rampage. "Lightly," he muttered, under his breath.

The performance became long and plodding and a little girl yawned in the front row, then, it stopped as suddenly as it had started. The glistening men stood stock still, right hands held high, sombre faces snapping into grins. Their friends in the crowd roared and clapped and whistled. Some people left their seats, doing a dance of their own to wiggle past the other spectators for beer or food or the temporary toilets.

"I just want to do this now. Get it over with." Kezia hugged her arms as if it was cold. "I've got butterflies."

"Two more, then it's us," said Java.

Sue nodded like a child who's just been told about an injection. Even the more experienced girls, Rosa and Carmen and Abril were subdued, sipping their drinks, gazing up at the stage.

Miranda introduced the next act, who were very young, mostly teenagers. They had the raw makings of good dancers, but they were trying to appear cool and their languid, distant attitude cut the urgency from the piece. Their teacher, down at the side, was thrusting mechanically, trying to transmute some life into her young charges, but with their friends in the audience, they were only ever going to appear lackadaisical and nonchalant.

They sauntered off the stage like it had never really mattered, and they didn't even stop to bow, unlike the first group, who had dragged their applause out for five vainglorious minutes.

"One more, and then we're up." Java giggled nervously and Sue looked slightly sick.

The succeeding troupe had at least five decades on the last — aged from their seventies to their nineties — yet they walked onto the stage with poise and grace. They wore old fashioned wrap-around dresses and their hair was pinned into formidable grey buns. After a look was passed from the oldest around them all, they began with such precision Sue was open mouthed. Up went the arms, down went the feet, bodies taught and toned. Their metronomic moves were baffling. They didn't put a foot out of place and their heads tossed like twenty-year-olds. They lashed down on that stage with almost a century's worth of pain and anguish. Darim smiled an old secret smile and murmured a sensual, *"Olé."*

"Oh no." Sue rubbed her stomach.

"We can't lose to them, they're old!" Java declared, but her voice betrayed her doubt.

"*Hopa!*" came the shouts from the crowd.

Suddenly it was over in a blur of clapping hands and standing ovations and the elegant ladies were being ushered off stage. They heard, 'Carlotta's Flamenco School', in the liquid tones of a dream and they looked at each other, uncertain. After wanting nothing but to get it over with, to have it done, Kezia now felt completely unprepared. Java pinged her mask back on.

"Remember, the beat of your pulse is the beat of the dance. Feel it. Just feel all of it," Darim proclaimed and they turned to him desperately while he waved them on, up to the stage.

The steps wobbled as they trod tentatively to the top. Kezia looked at the bright patchwork of spectators and then down at her feet. She needed to show him, to do this for him. Time seemed to slow as they positioned themselves where they needed to be, the familiar, unfamiliar in the boxy space. Kezia shut her eyes briefly and pretended she was on the terrace; she was sure she heard the distinctive screech of Pedro the parrot. The music started off to the side and the notes washed over her. She shuffled, trying to calm the creeping dread. Sue smiled and the fear showed through, but then Rosa frowned like Darim would have done and they all nodded an unspoken determination.

The beat kicked in and they stood to attention, ready to go.

The opening motions steadied them and, placated, they remembered who they were. Timidly at first, and then stronger and stronger, they moved — they were in — they were doing it; the crowd fell away and it was all at their fingertips. It just happened, seamless legs and seamless arms, sharp silhouettes and confident twists.

Delighted, Kezia turned fast and stomped harder. She began to enjoy the feeling of the stage beneath her and she travelled to that untouchable place where the dance is the world and the world is enough. She stamped out the rhythm, lifting her skirt with a clenched fist.

But then.

A face in the crowd.

James?

The central point in a whirlpool of faces. The only one in focus, sudden clarity in a mirage as she turned and turned and all was blurred, except him. She shut her eyes to shake him away, to come back into the routine... but he was there. She could feel it. His face near and far and near and far and she lost the beat — her foot one second out — she stumbled to bring it back in again, to pick up the pace and find the pulse of the dance, but she was hovering on the edge and she knew it. *Ta taka ta dah...* she clung to the steps, moving with the girls, but her focus was frayed... *James... how dare he be here? Not today... not now... The curse...* the thought shivered with her as she turned.

Darim would be scowling she knew. She was no longer in 'that place', this was not how to win. Anxious, Kezia tried to make up for it, to go in harder, but she stamped so savagely she came too far forwards, and Sue looked across, losing her stride too, suddenly unsure. Java was to their left and she shouted out the count to help them, which put the others off — and the whole spell was broken — the web they were weaving unravelled and became a sticky trap.

They fought their way out of it; Rosa, Carmen and Abril bringing Sue and Java back into the dance, but Kezia couldn't get there, she was too aware of James, too aware of Darim, too aware of the crowd of staring faces, each one a shadow she couldn't shake. Like a bad dream she battered through to the end, sweating and feeling the strain of the tears she knew would come, heavy in her chest and throat.

Then it was over.

They were being herded off the stage, they were wobbling down the shaky wooden steps.

"Kezia, what happened?" Carmen looked startled.

Kezia put her hand to her mouth to stop the tears uncorking and looked again for James in the crowd. Not there. "I'm not sure... I."

"Kezia, are you okay?" Sue put a clammy hand on her shoulder.

Darim was ahead with his arms folded, his lips a thin line.

"I've got to go." Kezia was pale behind her mask. "I can't see him. I've messed it all up. He'll be so cross."

"What?" Java jumped in beside her.

"I stuffed it all up. He's going to be so angry." Kezia was looking about frantically, as if she might bolt.

"No, it's not like that. We did it. That's the main thing. Who cares what he thinks? We did it. In front of all these people—" Sue took her mask off and her blonde hair was claggy with sweat, sticking to the sides of her face.

"We totally did it," Java added as Hady gave her a thumbs up and she ran to him.

"No, it… it should have been better than that. It should have been different. It's my fault."

The next group of dancers took to the stage and their music filtered over the square.

"Let's get a drink," Carmen said. "It's so hot." And the other girls blended into the crowds. Kezia was hesitating, looking at Darim, wondering what she could say, how she could…

Just then Rachel emerged, tall and imposing. "Kezia, did you know James is here? He's looking for you. What do you say to that?"

Sue and Kezia stared.

Rachel tried again. "James is looking for you. Shall I help you find him?"

"Who are you?" Sue was indignant.

For a second Kezia stood, still flushed with shame, still close to tears. Then, acting on impulse, she broke away, through the seats, weaving past gnarled old knees, mothers leaning back to pull their infants out of the way. She looked back and saw Rachel was following, coming down the row behind. Plunging through, Kezia made it to the other side of the square while Rachel tangled in the legs of a man with an apple belly and a refusal to be moved.

Kezia hurried, past the troupe of male dancers who jeered loudly, drunk on their own performance, cradling mugs of magenta wine, past people selling candy floss, bubbling out of bowls in pink clouds, and past a red bicycle, abandoned on its side and helpless where it lay.

She darted down the first shadowy side street she found and the world closed in around her. Cats slunk into doorways and an old lady teetered forwards, balancing on a cane. She ducked into a doorway, smelling pine and fresh plaster, knocking a wooden rosary hanging on a nail which swung backwards and forwards like a lethargic timepiece. She waited, watching as it slowed, her breath ripped and snagged. Eventually she peeked out, down towards the square.

The road was empty except for one white dog licking its hind leg, so Kezia rushed out and up, up, up the cobbled street, winding uphill as the noise from below receded gradually like a tap turning off. Rows and rows of houses stared at her from either side; window boxes like elaborate eyelashes, pretty doorways for pouting mouths. Washing hung across the street in a kind of prosaic bunting, stories told in the family flags of dresses, tops and trousers. She thought she saw Pedro the parrot swoop above, as colourful as the clothes, but free.

Kezia put her hand over her heart, her mouth tugging down as her bottom lip quivered. A black cat stared from a step with lemon eyes and she wished for Darim to comfort her but she knew he never would. He would be cross; she imagined his face fuming. She walked on, with an ache and a longing so strong, the feeling of failure subsuming her even as she tried to crush it with her steps. She walked and she walked until the emotion broke through the barrier of her spirit in a surge of tears. She let them come, salty and strong, as she thought about Darim, and the distance between them grew.

49

Whisky

Java got back to the house first with Hady, holding hands. Dappled light filtered through the trees and they smiled as Rollo came bounding out to greet them. They strolled round to the terrace, past Esmerelda chewing nonchalantly, to the pond and the soothing sound of water slipping from Medusa's mouth. Hady listened patiently as Java took him through it all again, step by step, move by move, beat by beat: the stage, the fear and the feeling of relief at the end.

The other girls drifted back, drinking sangria in disposable paper cups with striped paper straws and sharing more anecdotes from the day. The memories were already becoming indistinct — stained with sun and blurred with emotion.

"I knew those old ladies would win," said Java, in awe.

"They were the best. They were in a different league to everyone else." Rosa bowed her head reverentially.

"You're easily that good Rosa," said Sue. "I'm sorry we let you down. The nerves, I think. We hadn't done anything like that before. It's scary."

"It was so scary," Java agreed, leaning into Hady, his arms around her.

"They would have won anyway. Don't worry. They would. They have the experience. We will get there one day." Rosa felt for the tiny silver heart around her neck.

Carmen and Abril nodded, sloppy smiles attached to the straws in their mouths. "Next time we win. Next time." They giggled, not sure why it was funny.

Sue rubbed her arm where she had been bitten by a mosquito and it had come up red and inflamed. "Maybe," she mused. "Still. We did it."

"We did it!" Carmen and Abril echoed in chorus, raising their paper cups.

Then they saw Darim marching down the path, eyes darting around.

"Oh God," said Java. "Give me some of your sangria. Here he comes."

"We did our best," said Sue, still scratching.

"And, I'm telling you, we wouldn't have won anyway. No way. So it doesn't matter." Rosa sat down on the bench.

Darim's double clap was muted as he approached, the sound not as sharp as it usually was, his hands not as firm. "*Señoritas, señoritas…*"

"Uh oh." Java squeezed Hady's arm.

"*Señoritas.*" Darim's voice wavered, just slightly. "The moment — each moment — is part of your soul, it does not play to order. Now you know. It is not for other people that you dance. Never. I have told you this — now you see what happens." He hung his head theatrically. "It is not for other people that you live, or you lose your way." His eyes flicked up. "You have to learn. This is how you learn." And his arms rose and his head lifted as he spoke, heralding a new dawn: "Next time, you dance only for you. Only for you!" He dropped his hands to his sides again. "Where is Kezia?"

"She hasn't come back yet," said Abril, staring at the bottom of her drink.

"She hasn't come back?"

"I heard James was at the festival." Carmen rocked back and forth as she spoke.

"James," Darim said coldly, staring straight ahead, and before anyone could think what to say, Normando wobbled out of the house with a plate of bruised-looking pears, cut into pieces. They took the segments pensively and thanked him as he departed back into the shade with Benja.

"Perhaps we should go and look for her, check she's okay?" Sue suggested, nibbling on a khaki chunk of pear.

"I will go," said Darim affirmatively, looking at his watch. "Ten minutes, then I go." And he began to pace up and down, surveying the path and checking the time alternately. After only about two minutes, he slipped away, Rollo following with the gentle clink of his collar.

Darim went the long way round the house, past the frilly geraniums gossiping in their pots, past the acacia trees singing a thirsty song with wizened branches, over the stepping stones one by one, and in, through the front door to the hall, where the statue of Mary was there, always there. Her constancy made him feel calm. He stopped and knelt, kissing her small worn feet, he looked pleadingly into her anxious eyes and he whispered a private prayer. The floor creaked as he got up and walked across to his room.

"Now, what to wear for a search party?" he asked Rollo, who gazed at him in adoration. Darim held a blue shirt to his chest and sighed. "Oh no. Not the blue… although, *I am* blue." It put him in mind of a melody and he sat down on the bed and started to sing the sad refrain. Rollo came over and used the mattress as a ledge to rest his head on. "Ahh, but what to wear? What to wear?" Still humming, Darim stood and scrutinised a white pair of trousers. "We will find her, Rollo. This James will not win." Rollo's ears lifted like a puppeteer had pulled the strings. "Maybe she is talking to the journalist? We are not afraid of the journalist, are we? She will not find out what does not concern her, will she? Our secret is safe Rollo, is it not?" Rollo whimpered and pawed the ground with one leg. "We are not afraid, we are not afraid, we are not afraid…" and, repeating the words, Darim turned them into a little ditty to dance to while he changed and Rollo sat up straight with his tongue hanging out.

"Okay. Okay. We go." With a purple shirt and the white trousers, Darim chose his belt very carefully — snakeskin and gold — then he tied a pink necktie at an angle and donned a broad brimmed hat. "We go."

In the porch, he was just putting his embossed cowboy boots on when his phone spat at him from his pocket. It was Omar. Darim read the message and sighed. "We have to see Omar first, Rollo, we have to see Omar now. Quickly, then we find Kezia."

***

Omar was behind the bar, slouching on a stool, staring dejectedly at the naked ham hanging by the chalk board, and swatting the occasional fly. "Why is she still here?" he said, as Darim appeared in the doorway.

Darim clipped down the room with short steps and placed both his hands on the wooden counter. "Who?" he said pointedly.

Omar looked petulantly at him. "The journalist, Darim. We have a shipment coming tonight — as you well know. We *cannot* afford to have journalists sniffing about." He shuddered. "This is serious. This is not some kind of performance, it is not a new dance for you to practise until you might get it right. This is real. There are no second chances."

"It is the same with dance." Darim stood tall and his fingers curled and uncurled. "You are in the moment — that is all. That is all there is. If there was more, then we would not have lost the competition today." He looked down dramatically.

Omar flicked the edge of Darim's hat and it flipped and fell to the floor. Darim didn't pick it up.

"This is not some stupid competition, Darim. These distractions do not serve you, do not forget the school is only there to make you more legit. It is our mask, nothing more."

"That school is my life."

"Not any more, Darimita. We are your life now and you will do as we say."

Darim adjusted his cravat and said quietly, "No."

"Then guess who isn't getting paid?"

Darim turned away to retrieve the hat and brushed a seam of dust off its rim.

Omar spoke softly and deliberately. "Let me spell it out. That journalist is putting us on the map. No. We need to be off the map. Very far off the map. You know that. That is why we don't even let you advertise for pupils. That is how far off the map we need to be. What the hell will Richard say?"

Darim flinched.

"So, I say it again. The journalist must go — it is that simple."

Darim held onto the bar. "Where is Kezia?"

Omar shrugged. He poured himself a tumbler of whisky and swilled it round, looking deep into the glass like it might contain the answer. "At the festival…" He shrugged again. "With her English lover?"

Darim let go of the bar. He made a fist but didn't bang it down. "She does not love James," he said, under his breath.

Omar took a gulp of his drink. "I couldn't care less who she loves or who she does not love. Grow up Darim. This is exactly the problem. This has always been the problem. Your soft little heart must protect all the strays around here, it is what you do." He rolled his eyes exaggeratedly, arching the whole of his head. "Now you are too involved. That girl has been nothing but trouble since she turned up, you have not been focused, you are slack — that is how we ended up with her snooping around down at the cove. She is an outsider, and they are more dangerous. You know that and you know why. The school is supposed to be our line of defence."

There was a gravid silence, grazed only by a faint whimpering from Rollo.

"You will not let any little matters of the heart mess up what we have here. We've got it good. Girls come and go, but money… money never lets you down, so get your pretty little head around that." Omar downed the glass of whisky.

"I've got a bad feeling about tonight." Darim was looking at the picture of Saint Junipero, stern, and with the yellow disc around his head.

"Starting to believe your own stories, are you?" Omar lifted his hands and spread his fingers, making an 'oooo' sound, his lips pushed forward.

Darim whipped his head to the side, a martyred expression on his face.

"Look Darim, we just need to be extra careful. That is why I'm telling you, the journalist has to go. I'm as uneasy as you with all these people here for the festival. And for God's sake, make sure you lock Kezia in her room if she is still here, which I hope she is not. We do not want her wandering about. It will not end well."

"She will not get out," Darim sulked.

"Okay, go on then, go and get rid of the journalist. Frighten her. Tell her stories. I don't care what you do. Just get her to leave. As I said, we've got enough to worry about without her sort here as well, trust me."

"Trust you?" Darim drew back. "Trust you? Yes, because when you're in charge things never go wrong, do they? Matías, for example. Christ! He could have died."

"So what? He needed to learn. They all need to learn."

"Didn't you hear me? He nearly died. You want to be a murderer as well as everything else?"

"No, he brought it on himself. And in any case, then he would have learned the ultimate lesson, and no one would ever have disturbed us again." Omar exhaled, the stain of stale cigarettes and sugar on his breath. "Don't pretend you didn't encourage me. Revenge is sweet, huh?

The village who wouldn't let you in, all those people who bullied you as a child and who still bully you now. The village who derided your mama…"

Darim narrowed his eyes, a petrol gleam in his pupils.

"You wanted to play. And here you are," Omar intoned. "It is too late now." He laughed a chugging laugh, emitting more cloying fumes from his lungs. "Anyway, anyway, you are the one who screwed up the dose, Darim, and you know it. It was your fault."

"The berries are stronger than… Look, I didn't know."

Rollo, who had been moving his head from left to right, following their movements as though he was tracking a bird, gave up and put his head on his paws.

"Okay, it's done, it's done." Omar flared his nostrils like a bull. "Now we just need to make sure tonight goes off well. Don't bring the stash you already have over here as planned, leave it now, we can bring it all over together once the crowds have gone and things settle down a bit." He glared acerbically at Darim. "But keep it hidden for God's sake — from aged papas and traumatised gardeners and curious flamenco dancers. Jesus, you've got a right circus over there. Don't let anyone find it? Okay?"

"So far they have not."

"Yes, well, let's keep it that way. We'll have so much after tonight you'll have to be careful. Richard's contacts will be here next week. You can bring it over in bits in your guitar case as usual, but slowly, we can't rush anything at the moment. We need to stay calm."

"Calm," Darim repeated.

"So, go, go on then and find the journalist and put out this fire. I don't care how you do it — just put it out," he glowered. "Tell them they are all cursed if you have to, because if they aren't, then we are."

Darim pursed his lips and turned to go.

"One more thing — don't be late tonight. And make sure no one sees you coming down. Like I said, there are more people about, up late, drinking. Stay alert, look out for stragglers."

Darim lifted his chin in acknowledgement. "Come, Rollo."

"Our ship is coming in, Darim, we can't mess this up!" Omar shouted after him, reaching to pour another shot of whisky.

***

Darim took the shortcut around the back of the village to the square. It wasn't a path, more of a dotted line he had drawn as a boy, to escape the other children: a riot of weeds and brambles and rocks and scrawny trees. Thin green vines looped out of nowhere, branches swung in from the sides, snakes slithered away. He picked his way through the scramble of nature, tangling and catching his clothes, he lifted his legs high and placed them down in the gaps in the undergrowth. It was a dance to him, where the steps had to be precise and noiseless, as it had always been. Dance had always been his escape. He prayed silently to Our Lady, the words like beads — round and strong in his head — and he kept up the rosary as he pulled down his hat and tiptoed back into the central streets, where the bunting flickered like flames and the seats were scattered with drunks. "Kezarina," he sighed. "Where did you go?"

He sensed Rachel before he saw her, in the way he might feel a cloud before looking up. She was tall and wearing London clothes, too hot for Parños: tight black trousers and fitted white shirt. She teetered in her heels as she looked around like a rabbit, twitching and unsure. He watched her move tentatively over to where a man in a red baseball cap was selling toffee apples, the smooth syrup glazing the round fruit as he deftly wound the flat wooden sticks and stood them in the sun to dry. The man smiled at Rachel and tilted his hat towards his wares. Darim saw her shake her head, strands of hair detaching from her bun, the wisps decorating the nape of her neck. She leaned in closer to him and was talking in slow English as he wiped his hands on his dark blue apron. He nodded and scanned the square, searching, then pointed as he saw Darim, a fat finger, sticky and certain.

Darim walked calmly over to the stall, eyebrows raised, Rollo padding in his wake and the man, disconcerted, looked down at his toffee apples, his nose reflected in their bright faces: distorted and tumid. Darim folded his arms, and waited.

"Oh, hi," said Rachel, unnerved by his posture. "Darim, nice to meet you. Do you speak English?"

307

Darim regarded the toffee, turgid in the bowl. "Yes," he said and his eyes snapped back to Rachel.

"Oh good. I emailed you the other day, about coming to a class, talking to some of your pupils?"

Darim said nothing.

"But when I came, I wasn't let in."

"Omar," said Darim quietly. "Yes, I have friends who do not like journalists. Why should I let you come?" He stood straight, defiant, Omar's threats loud in his ears.

"Oh, because I'll write a really nice piece about your school; it'll be great publicity for you — free. I just want to show how enjoyable it is to get away and learn to dance, give my London readers something to desire as they face another drab day in the office."

They heard an apple communing with the gunk in the bowl as the man muttered, in Spanish. "Heaven knows you could use some good press after what keeps happening down there."

"How dare you, Alberto?" Darim's cheeks reflected the red of the naked fruit. "I cannot help our proximity to the cove, I tell the girls not to go there, that has nothing to do with my school, nothing."

"I've heard such good things about the school," said Rachel, gauging the tone of their voices and not wanting her chance to slip away. "I would be honoured to visit and write you an excellent review."

"An excellent review?" Darim considered this. "An excellent review for an excellent school. We deserve it." He narrowed his eyes as if Omar were in front of him. "Okay. Tomorrow," he told her. "You must come tomorrow. You will see how excellent we are. But not today, it must be tomorrow. We do no more dancing today. The competition… has made our girls tired. Come tomorrow and we will give you a good show." Darim was pleased; he would not need to tell Omar and the shipment would be done by then. "We are a humble school, we hope you will take us as you find us." He bowed.

"Yeah?" Alberto spoke in English this time. "Humble? And we all know why that is, don't we? We all know why no money was left to you — or us — why we didn't get the new children's play area we were promised? Will you put that in the article?" he growled as if preparing to spit, then turned back to his oleaginous confectionary.

Darim smiled at Rachel. "You see, some people, they want something for nothing. They think because my mama," he crossed himself, "was a famous flamenca, famous throughout the land, that *they* should be rewarded for *her* hard work. Let alone defiling the memory of her tragic death by making it about money. You have no right, no right, Alberto."

The man stayed focused on his viscous brown toffee.

"Let her death be a warning to us all," Darim orated. "Do not go down to the cove at night, do not go down to the sea. If her passing tells us anything, it is that. You think I do not mourn her death every day? Every day! Do you think I do not wish I had been there to stop her from going? Do you think that? I grieve the person. You grieve the money. Now tell me who is in the right here?"

Alberto's eyes became as large and shiny as his apples and he set about stirring his toffee with more vigour than required.

Rachel glanced down at the upturned wares, lined up like skittles on the tray, slowly oozing onto the greaseproof paper. She was deciding whether to ask her questions now, or wait until the morning.

Darim examined her profile. "You are in pain," he told her.

She looked up quickly but said nothing. An empty beer can rolled at her feet.

"You are in pain," he pronounced again. "Yes, we are all in pain, but you… you wear yours on your face, it is deep."

Alberto hid a laugh behind his hand.

"Look, I came to write about flamenco, so if you don't mind—" Rachel took a step away.

"You say what you like. You came here to get away from something. I can see that. Flamenco will help." He adjusted his pink necktie.

"I'm sorry but that is way out of line." Rachel was shaking her head, more hair coming loose from her bun.

"You need to dance. You need to be set free. Flamenco will set you free." Darim nodded and Rollo's little bell jingled as he looked up at his master. "Tomorrow you will dance."

The heat bore into Rachel as she squared up to Darim, her voice loud and flat. "I'm sorry, but you can't cure endometriosis with flamenco."

Darim angled his chin at her. "Well, have you tried?"

309

"No, because… because it's just another stupid suggestion from another stupid man." Dizzy now, Rachel felt nauseated by the saccharine fumes of the sugar.

"I am stupid now?" Darim said, shaking his head superciliously. "Then, you will not listen. Then you will suffer. Then you will not know. Come, Rollo," he said to the dog who lifted its nose high. "The truth, they always run away from the truth."

Rachel watched him turn and go.

Alberto grinned at her. "That's Darim. Eccentric like his mama." And he tried again to sell her a toffee apple. "It will make you feel better…"

50

Berry Tart

The ache crept across the back of Rachel's head. A deep dark pulsing pain, poking at her eyes and pushing down her shoulders. She bought a beer — poetically cold and shining with the assurance of quenching her impossible thirst — but the promise was empty, like so many were. She pressed the chilled glass against her cheek and wondered what to do. No story. Not yet… but plenty of clues. *Follow the scent,* her tutor, Rebecca, had always told her, *trust your instincts, they are usually right.* But her instincts had told her James was going to propose this afternoon. Perhaps he wasn't the type to leap up onto the stage… but afterwards, with candour in his eyes and Kezia all sweaty and grateful. She should have her picture by now and be writing a pithy top line. Instead, she had lost James and she had lost Kezia and the moment was slipping away. "Excuse me, do you know Kezia Duke?" she asked a friendly looking woman with two small children using her as a climbing frame.

"Kezia?" The woman pulled the smallest child off her shoulder as Rachel hoped for a glimmer of recollection. "Hmm, *no sé… no sé.*" The toddler started crying, its face dimpled with rage.

"Okay, thanks." Rachel backed away. She walked around the square because she didn't know what else to do. The stage stood empty, a couple of old crisp packets skittering their way across in a dance of their own. She thought of all the coincidences that had brought her to this place, wondered what it was that was pulling her, and smiled as she passed Alberto again, a familiar face at least. He had taken his cap off and was sat back on a fold-up chair, his rows of toffee apples gleaming with glassy sugar. He had quaffed a few drinks now and was slightly glazed himself.

He looked at her earnestly. "If you want a story, speak to Matías." He pointed. "Over there, look, with the black curly hair. He heard the ghost and he couldn't see for three days." Alberto touched his forehead in disbelief. "Three days," he said again starkly. "There were those who didn't believe... but we all saw what happened to him. There's something bad down there, something very bad. But be careful, if you investigate. Just be very careful."

"You think I should talk to him?" Rachel asked politely.

"Yes, go ahead, he speaks English, of course. Talk to him, but don't go down there. That's my advice."

"Surely, it could just have been a... timing thing. He heard... what he heard and then he got sick. It happens." The headache was splitting her skull in two now.

"I know... I know. We wanted to believe it was alcohol poisoning, they had all been drinking. But he's more sensible than the others and it went on too long for a hangover." Alberto regarded his apples, thoughtful. "And you know, there has been something strange about that cove for centuries; my grandmother used to talk about it and hers before that. We all heard the stories as children. Yes, you can say it is the ghost of his dead mother too if you like." He gestured as if Darim was still standing there. "Just one of many ghosts perhaps. But I think the old stories are true. You wouldn't catch me going there at night. Not me."

Rachel gripped her beer, weighing his words.

"Go on, go and talk to him, you'll see. You'll see. He knows what it is like to be cursed."

So do I, thought Rachel, smiling her thanks as the pain jabbed at her.

Matías was sitting with a small circle of friends. They'd pulled some chairs out of the main seating area so it looked as if the corner of a jigsaw had been undone. One of them had a guitar and was strumming lazily, others had their feet up and were smoking solid-looking cigarettes. Matías sat with his legs crossed, his arm on the back of an empty chair.

"Matías?"

The curly black head turned to look at Rachel, his eyes like waxy underwater rocks.

"Matías, hi."

He lifted his chin in response, it wasn't exactly a nod. The guitar player switched melodies.

"Um. Alberto suggested I talk to you." She waved her hand roughly in the direction of his stall.

"Yes?" There was a watermelon lilt in Matías voice, cool and sonorous.

"He told me to ask you what happened — when you got sick. Can you tell me?"

One of the other boys fired an aside to Matías — a splutter of Spanish — and he smiled but didn't take his attention from Rachel. "Why?" he asked. "Why do you want to know?"

"I'm... I'm interested."

"We already know you are a journalist." His eyes were like granite now. "Word gets around this village quicker than you might think. So, what's it to you?"

"Nothing, really. I mean, I'm just — I'm here for a different story — but I'm just curious."

"That's your job I suppose," he said philosophically.

"I'll tell you." A friend with a mop of flaxen hair interjected, he was cradling a bottle of wine and he took a swig. "We did it for a dare. It was his birthday. We have a little tradition of setting each other challenges for our birthdays." The boys all sniggered, remembering past misdemeanours. "It's just what we do. So we told him to go down there, to the cove. We thought now that he was twenty-one, he should face it — on his own."

"I was happy to go. I wasn't scared." Matías uncrossed his legs and kicked the blond boy's chair.

"Oh yeah?" The guitar player stopped strumming for a second.

"I wasn't. I was cool with it. And yeah, I heard the ghost. Whatever. It's a ghost. I was chilled." He shrugged and one of his curls bounced over his eye and back again.

"Ha! He was dying: I've never seen anyone so scared — ran all the way back — could hardly breathe."

"Whatever." Matías kicked his friend's chair again. "It took me by surprise I guess." He grinned. "But I was all right then. It was the next day that was weird. I guess I didn't sleep well and I woke up kind of cranky — but I thought it was the hangover — anyway, I went out for a meal in the evening and that's when it happened. I was starving, so I ate loads of *fabada* and I even had dessert, one of those berry tart things. I remember because my sister kept saying she wished she could have some of it but she's dieting, she's always dieting." (The guitarist nodded knowingly.) "So anyway — it was like I was okay, and then the next minute... I'm not sure what happened, I was sick, like really sick, drenched in sweat and throwing up and — it — it's all a bit of a blur."

"Yeah, nearly spewed over the whole of Mando's place," a small, spotty boy spoke up for the first time.

"I couldn't see properly, that was the scary part. I was hot and cold and shivering and I was in bed for three days. Don't remember that much of it really. Horrible nightmares. Apparently, I was screaming about the ghost, but I don't know whether my mama just says that to me to put me off drinking again." He smiled, fondling his beer.

"Mate, that wasn't a hangover, that was... creepy." The blond boy swigged his wine.

"Did you go to hospital? I mean, what did the doctor say?" Rachel wanted to know.

"Oh yeah, they called an ambulance and I went to A&E but the doctors had no idea and then, yeah, I kind of got better so they just sent me home."

"And you're okay now?"

"Yeah, yeah," he said dismissively, ducking his head down in a way that showed he was hiding something.

"How strange." Rachel thought of Joe and suddenly felt protective. "Your mother must have been terrified to see you like that."

"Furious more like. You don't know my mama."

The boy with the haystack hair laughed. "The only reason he's allowed out today is because she's here too." They all looked over to where the mayor was in serious conversation with a group of older ladies who took it in turns to nod furiously and move their hands from their hips to their hearts.

When Rachel turned back the friends had subtly regrouped, shifted their focus to each other in the casual and exclusive way of young men. The conversation was over. She thanked them and they gave a perfunctory wave as she left their circle.

Still thinking of Joe, Rachel checked her phone, and was surprised to see a message from Andy.

Good luck Rae, hope it's going well out there.

And he signed off with a kiss. It was the first time he'd messaged her about something that wasn't Joe-related for… she couldn't remember. A lightness spread across her chest, something like relief, or an old wound beginning to heal. She leaned against the worn church wall and messaged her reply, the ancient stones warm and solid against her back.

Thanks Andy, hope the off-roading is good and Joe is enjoying time with his grandparents. Thanks again for making this possible…

She closed her eyes, tilting her head to the wall as the conflicting thoughts came. There was love, but it was always mixed with something else — anger and resentment, hate and sorrow — the emotions competing and clashing. Her phone went again and her eyes darted down, but it wasn't him this time, it was Martin, demanding pictures for a preview, drawing her back to her job, to the task at hand. She pursed her lips, she could send him some snaps of the competition, for now… But she would not fail, there was more here. The feeling was like the sky just before it gets light: something lambent you can only guess at. *There is a story to uncover*, she thought, *I know it*, and a green and red parrot flapped over her head, calling and calling like he was saying yes.

51

Heart Lamp

𝒮he church was cool and dim and hidden. It was white on the outside and white on the inside — a glacial stillness throughout. Kezia was getting tired when she found it, tucked away up the hill, incongruous within of a loop of residential streets. The old wooden door was open and there was no one else inside.

Dark wooden pews lined up before the altar and there was a painted wooden statue of Mary and the baby Jesus on the back wall behind. They were wearing their hearts outside their robes; blue and white with red hearts blazing. Kezia stared at them as she slipped into one of the pews, glad to sit down, and she thought about what Darim had told her about the heart lamp; they needed to protect their hearts better.

The tears had stopped now, there was only the throb at the back of her throat, the sting in her eyes and the sense of failure she couldn't get away from, even in here. Kezia let the empty feeling of the church sink into her and she shut her eyes, because it was allowed. She didn't know how to pray, but she thought she would try. She put her hands into a small knot on her lap and made a silent supplication: *I pray to break the curse. I pray to break the curse. Uncurse me, God, everything is going wrong. I should not have messed up on stage, Darim should not be cross with me. James should not be here. Tell me how, and I'll do it. I need to break the curse. I was supposed to be the star on that stage...*

She opened her eyes and Mary and Jesus were looking at her but she wasn't sure they understood. In front of them, two candlesticks stood like soldiers guarding the solid stone altar wearing its plain white cloth. There were sprigs of carnations in vases placed lovingly on the windowsills and, all around, stations of the cross crept along the walls; Jesus standing and falling and carrying his cross.

A nun dressed in grey scurried from a side door to check a metal stand of votive candles perpendicular to the altar. Ignoring Kezia, she carefully took one of the tea-lights and used it to revive three others, extinguished by the breath of the church, before genuflecting and hurrying to the right aisle to attend to more candles there. Kezia stared numbly at the little flames, watching them dip and bob and flare. She didn't look around when she heard more hollow footsteps; she wasn't ready to see anyone, not now. She bowed her head.

"Hi Ron, how are you?" the nun whispered in parched English, breaking the protective peace of the church.

"*Hola* sister, very well thank you." The man's accent betrayed his Birmingham roots. "Did you go to the competition, Sister Jerónima?"

"No, I was needed here. How did it go? Did you see Matías? Were you able to tell him about how to break the curse? You said you were going to."

Kezia gripped the pew in front.

"Yes," said Ron, forgetting to whisper. "Well, I went to the library to find the place in the book, but—" He left a dramatic pause. "The page with the spell has gone — it's missing!"

The nun inhaled sharply.

"It's been years since I read that book and wrote about it for my blog, and well, since then, someone has taken the spell, so, you see, I didn't want to tell him that, to give him hope and just as quickly dash it."

The nun was silent for a moment, then she said, "Do you think it was Darim? There is a rumour that one of his dancing girls heard the ghost. Maybe he took it to cure them so they could take part today."

"Didn't work then, did it?" said Ron sardonically. "They were all over the place. Looked more like that routine was cursed than anything I've yet seen on that stage."

Kezia felt frustration and failure surge in her like a cardinal spike of mercury. The votive candles shivered as if they were laughing at her too. She looked up at the statue of Our Lady with her heart glowing red.

"Oh dear," said the nun. "Lord help them."

"I know, I know. But listen one way or another I'll find that spell, don't worry. Retired Ron is on the case, nothing gets past me in this place, nothing." The man settled himself down in a pew, picking up a missal, and flicking through its pages.

Too curious all of a sudden, Kezia risked a fleeting glimpse behind to see Ron: portly and tanned, his blond hair fading to white. He put the book down and rubbed his ample tummy, then a couple of elderly parishioners came clattering in on sticks and hobbled right to the front, followed by a festive looking woman wearing a big coat despite the heat of the day. The nun scuttled away to prepare for mass, giving Kezia a cursory and agitated glance.

Kezia shook her head, her thoughts floating and bursting and floating and bursting, like bubbles. She got up, unsteadily, as more people arrived for the service and she didn't look at Ron again as she left, feeling the eyes of the many Jesuses stumbling and dripping with blood.

***

When Kezia was near the house, she could hear all the other girls outside, their voices like confetti, pink sounds, full of life. She felt stunned, as if she'd been asleep in the church, and cold, aching for things to be different. She wanted her friends, needed to be with them now — hoped they could cheer her, hoped they could forget.

Tomi the cat limped over and stopped right at her feet. He issued one wiry miaow and then led her to the terrace, as if sure that's where she should be.

"Kezia!" They skipped to her, loose with alcohol, mouths and arms wide.

"Kezia, where have you been?"

"Are you okay?"

"Thank God you're okay."

"Where have you been?"

A volley of questions left her no space to answer until they finally stopped, and waited.

"I couldn't face it. I couldn't face you. I couldn't face him. I messed up, I messed everything up. I thought you'd hate me."

"No, no!" Rosa reached out, touching her arm. "No, what are you talking about?"

"I fell out of step, it's my fault we lost."

"No, it was my fault." Sue was flushed, her hair still stuck to one side of her head. "If I hadn't been so easily distracted, we would have all got right back on track."

"And me," said Java. "I couldn't concentrate with all those people, I was so nervous. You didn't see but I messed up before you — two times." She was smiling but she buried her head in Hady's sleeve.

"Look." Carmen draped her arm over Kezia's shoulder. "What you don't know is, we were never going to be voted the winners in a village that is against Darim. I hate to say it, but there you go — that is the truth. We did it for us. And we did it to say, 'up yours', we're going to do it anyway."

"Yeah!" cheered Rosa and Abril, raising their nearly empty cups, the dregs of the sun highlighting the dregs of the drink.

"So you don't need to worry," beamed Carmen.

"I'm so drunk," said Abril. "I'msodrunk." And they all laughed.

As the giggles waned, Kezia looked around tentatively. "Where is Darim?" she asked. "Do you really think he won't say it's all my fault?"

"Absolutely." Carmen nodded, serious now.

"No chance," Rosa agreed.

"Honestly, we just wanted to prove that we could do it, and we did, and that's all that matters," added Sue.

Kezia breathed out, they were all smiling at her. "So where is he?"

"He's out looking for you." Abril drained her cup.

"We'd better call him and tell him you're here." Rosa got out her phone, prodding at the screen with drunken alacrity. When Darim answered, Kezia could hear his curt replies. She watched Benja hop up onto the table and turn in small circles, smaller and smaller, until he finally settled, like water going down a plughole.

"Are you sure he's not angry?" she asked when Rosa hung up.

"It's not about what he thinks, it's about how you are." Sue was unequivocal. "We all just want you to be okay, okay? So stop worrying about this afternoon. A few stumbles in a few places, is not enough to get upset about."

"Yes!" Carmen slurred, raising her cup to Abril's again, empty now, apart from a few pebbles of ice at the bottom.

Kezia looked at her nails.

"Come on, just have a drink. Relax. Forget about it." Abril pressed a glass into her hand and poured from a vintage decanter. They'd been raiding Normando's special supply.

Kezia took a sip and the tang of the sangria spread in her mouth, citrus-sweet and hazy with the heat of the afternoon. She looked to the path for Darim, watching for him to come. The girls' chatter became the backdrop to her thoughts and, like standing by a fountain, she let it rise and drizzle, feeling its freshness but not its form.

Eventually she saw him, treading distractedly down to the house and even today, even when she knew he would be cross, it was like a curtain drawing back. She went to him.

"Just don't let him give you a hard time," Carmel shouted after her. "There will be other competitions... God knows he's won enough of them in his time — doesn't change anything — he knows that." Then she burbled something in Spanish Kezia didn't understand, so she just kept going, not knowing what she would say, how she was going to make it all right.

She walked slowly, giving herself time to think, focusing at first on the chipped pots and tangled weeds with the lame wheelbarrow by the path, but she felt his ineluctable pull, and as soon as she raised her eyes, she couldn't take them from him: his face, his figure, his fire. He was looking at her too, so it felt like the long, slow start of a dance. Steadily they drew together, a magnetic metre guiding their walk; they were in step, synchronised, waiting for the music to start.

When they got closer, he stopped, and stood, poised as a conquering conquistador, one hand on his hip, one leg straight in front. "I have been looking for you, my Kezarina."

Kezia halted too. "I'm sorry." The gap between them felt too wide. "Sorry?"

"I am." She stiffened. "I ruined the dance today. I'm so sorry."

Laughter from the girls billowed behind.

"No," he said, taking small steps, closing the space between them now. "You should only be sorry that you scared me by going missing. I have been looking for you all afternoon."

As he walked, he had thought of her and James together — touching and together — and his search was forensic, street by street; he knew how they mapped, he knew how they meshed and he left no corner, no alley, no side-shop unturned. He had needed to find her before the sun set and the moon rose and the ghosts came out at night. Then Rosa had called...

"I have spent more time with the people in that village than anyone should have to endure," he protested, with a beleaguered smile. "So, explain yourself. Where were you and why did you hide?"

Kezia looked down. A beetle was crawling over a stick, shining, coal-black. "I thought you'd be angry with me, for messing things up."

"You were afraid?"

She focused on the beetle, which stopped as if also waiting to hear what Darim might say.

"What do I always tell you, my Kezarina? You have got to face your fears. Only then can you get past them. You do not run. You do not hide. Do you understand?"

"Erm, I guess..."

The beetle started to move again.

"As for the dance," he said. "I saw you, Kezia, I saw it. You panicked. You are still letting others control you." The wind sallied around them. "I have told you. You only dance for you. For in here." Darim put a hand on his heart. "Not for me — not for anyone else — for you. And you didn't. You gave your power away."

"I'm sorry."

"No, no, no — that's what I am telling you. This is not about sorry." He reached out to lift her chin, his eyes sincere and his voice soft. "Look at me. You do not apologise. You learn. This was a lesson for you. You needed it." He paused, drawing his lips together, then he told her, "Look, it is a mistake I made for the first, oh, nearly ten years of my dancing career — that is why I can teach you — that is why I want to make sure you don't make it too. We have to stop making it about other people."

"I... I wanted to do it for you," she said. "Is that bad?"

Darim considered this, tilting back and turning to the trees as if they were an audience. "Because you think I will love you more if you dance better?"

"Yes, but... it sounds wrong when you put it like that."

"Because it is wrong. Love *is* a dance. But it is a dance of its own."

The trees murmured a swishy response.

"A dance of its own," she repeated. "So how do you learn those steps?" She hardly dared breathe.

He turned to face her fully again, eyes like ocean spray. "Now you are asking the right questions…" And he moved swiftly then and kissed her. All feelings of the competition melted, all feelings of loss took flight, there was only him, and the closeness she craved: strange and exciting. He pulled her waist to his hips and it put a warmth in the middle of her.

Time dissolved, she couldn't say how long they kissed, but too soon he pulled away, looking behind, watchful. "Come," he said quietly. "It has been a long day." And he stood straighter, adjusting his cravat.

He didn't take her hand as they went back down the track, he seemed suddenly tired, distracted, and the mesh of sound scratched by the cicadas eclipsed the need for talk. Only when they neared the house, Darim turned to her. "I must feed the animals. After the fiesta, the familiar — always." And he bowed, taking his leave.

Kezia smiled, watching him go, then, skirting the terrace, she went right to the end of the garden to savour the kiss, to keep the feeling undiluted. It was the trophy she craved, more than any competition, more than any other prize. She had won, on this day of losing, she had won.

The light was fading and the fairy lights were making constellations in the dusk. Through the trees the sea was talking to itself, telling stories in its deep and timeless way. She shivered, her thoughts ambushed by the unearthly music she had heard that night at the cove, the chill that went through her — the chill that returned, frequently, to haunt her. She could almost hear it now, the sweet, sweet sorrow — it pulled at her — it was the curse. She hugged her elbows and, looking out at the endless ocean, the presence of the ghost was like a snare on her soul.

Then. A cold hand on her shoulder. Ice that struck her core. She span around quickly to face her tormentor.

It was not the ghost.

It was Magdalena. Ethereal, pale and wan — but definitely human — Magdalena stood like a tortured spirit.

Kezia put her hand to her breast, breathless. "Magdalena. It's you… It's… You scared me."

The girl said nothing, casting her eyes down by way of an apology. When she looked up, there was something urgent there, something she was trying to convey.

"What is it, Magdalena? What's wrong?"

She shook her head to say nothing was wrong and then held out a crumpled piece of paper.

Kezia took it, unfolding carefully. It felt hot in her hands. It was hard to read in the dwindling light and she could only just make out the words.

Forever in the now, I offer you this gift,
Forever and all time, the curse for you to lift.
In passion and prayer and sorrow and sin
I wait in hope for your song to begin.

"*This gift? The curse*... Is this... Magdalena, this is the spell, isn't it? Is this the spell to break the curse?"

Magdalena nodded.

"But how... did you know where Normando hid the paper?"

She smiled, wilfully taciturn, feeling the power in her secrets.

Kezia looked at the paper again, this was no original, the spell seemed to have dripped onto the page in Magdalena's fluid handwriting. "You translated it for me?" she said, reading the words over and over. "Why? I mean, thank you, but you need to tell me more. What else did the book say? What gift do you think I should bring, do you think I should..."

But Magdalena was moving away.

"Don't go, please, I need to ask you about this."

She crossed her arms in a physical full stop and then turned gracefully, with the elegance of a dancer, away, away, leaving Kezia with the questions fizzing and her heart pounding.

She reread the words, repeatedly, as if the answers might materialise through the text. There was a rhythm to them she liked and they grew inside her head. She folded the paper and gripped it tight.

Herring gulls were flying over the cove, freewheeling and bold, painting the path of the invisible wind, confident the air would carry them. Kezia traced their course watching them dive and lift and wondered if she was brave enough to try — to break the curse. Her thoughts arched and eddied with their flight, vacillating, sinking and soaring, until, in the end, she turned back to the house, confused and unsure.

52

Ivy

𝒩ight was falling. Diminishing dusk brushing back with the breeze, colours smudging, deepening, shadows lengthening. Nobody spoke much at dinner. They listened as Normando told them stories about the early days — how he'd met Carlotta, how he'd started the bar — stories they'd heard before. Sue and Java were tired and went to bed willingly, to sleep off the heat and the drink and the dancing and the disappointment.

"Yes, rest," Darim had said, looking around. "Rest, tomorrow is waiting. Tomorrow is new."

But Kezia stayed, sitting on the little wooden bench, watching the moon paint the world pearl. Her thoughts flickered between the competition and the kiss; a doll with two heads, one leering, one smiling. The house felt listless. The animals were listless. Darim too, was listless. "This James has gone?"

"I don't know." She noted the apprehension in his face. "You know, I thought he was another hallucination at first, I didn't think he was real... And in some ways, he still doesn't seem real. My old life doesn't any more."

Darim stroked Rollo's head thoughtfully as the dog closed its eyes. "You are here now," he said, not looking up. "Maybe even he can see that."

There was a finality in his words which pleased her. Kezia knew she was due to go home after the competition, but she did not mention that; it was an old decision, a relic of the past. Still, as she listened to the restless snuffling and squawking of the animals, she wondered whether she should have spoken to James after all. He'd come all this way and she'd... she shook her head to get him out of it.

Darim's eyes whipped up, watching. "It is hard to shake off your past," he said knowingly. "I told you to confront it, but you would not listen. That is the only way. To speak with him. To tell him."

"But…" Kezia pulled her feet up onto the bench. "But I couldn't face it, Darim. I couldn't. Like you say, I am here now." She hesitated, then slowly, her words varnished with hope, she said, "Anyway, how do you know it's the only way? Being with you, is the way."

Darim looked thoughtful, reaching for his guitar. A peacock, somewhere in the bushes, made a noise like a bugle, calling. "Perhaps," he conceded. "Perhaps, there is more than one way." And he began to play; faint strains, pensive, plangent.

"Darim…" she wanted to tell him about the spell, the small scrap of paper in her pocket, the feeling that it gave her, something like stars coming out at night.

"Yes?" he said, looking at her sideways.

There was a sharpness in his features that held her back. He strummed lightly, obstinately now, edgy and wan. She knew this mood. She changed tack. "Um, thank you for bringing me here."

"Thank yourself," he said.

"Oh."

"Your soul desired it, or you would not have been at the cove that day. I saw it in you." He paused, letting the guitar speak for him in its morbid, minor tones.

Kezia looked firmly out to sea, feeling the notes like a net pulling.

"You wanted to come here to find freedom," Darim said, as though he was the narrator in a play. "And that's what we all want. That's what we all want, deep inside."

Kezia tried to remember how she had felt before she met Darim, but the memories were faded like old newspaper, the images bleached out with time.

"Clap with me," he said, abruptly. "Let us make music together, you can use Sami's shells, there on the wall."

Kezia fetched the shells, reassuringly sturdy in her hands, and adjusted her grip so she had them like castanets. As he played, she found the rhythm, letting them sing their solid song, hitting hard and soft: the song of the ocean — struggle and safety and surrender.

Eventually he stopped and stood up and she felt tiredness like a mist, settling.

"Let us go to bed," he looked anxiously down the garden. "It has been a long day."

Darim walked around the house with her, not taking the shortcut to his room, and there was something like a forcefield between them. She hoped he felt it too. When they got inside, he kissed her at the bottom of the stairs, leaning in close, looking into her eyes so that it was a meeting of minds and of lips, their hearts almost touching.

"Come to bed with me," she said, shocked at herself and suddenly scared that she'd said it. The statue of Mary snagged in her peripheral vision, blue and white and judging her.

Darim paused. He stroked her hair, smoothing it tenderly. "Not tonight," he said. "It wouldn't be right."

"Marry me then?" she tried to joke but his eyes went distant and sincere. He cupped her face in his hand and she reached out, holding his hips. Then he exhaled and kissed her on the forehead and it felt unbearably vague.

"I want—" she started to say, but he put his finger on her lips.

"Good night, Kezarina." He dropped his hand. "Goodnight." And he walked away, past the picture of the Last Supper, Judas with his sad and shifty eyes. She heard the door to his room close and she stood, not wanting the night to be over...

Until at last, she went upstairs, her hand dragging on the banister, her legs slow, feeling like a wind-up toy at the end of its cycle. She changed into the pink nightdress he'd given her, the satin cool against her skin, shaking it down to her knees.

Not tonight.

The curtain was fluttering at the window, the navy anchors in their sea of white. She went over, leaning on her elbows and looking out, trying to remember her first night here, how afraid she'd been, how lost. Everything looked different now, felt different. A new life, a new love. The waves tossed on a distant horizon and the ivy outside rippled, like many hands hugging the wall possessively.

She didn't see the shadow in the bushes.

Kezia sighed, looking up, feeling the alabaster light of the moon, big and full and weaving a braid of silver through the water. The stars, bright punctuation in the story of the sky, read for centuries, were speaking to her now. Esmeralda snorted and Tomi limped past, his marmalade coat sepia in the night. Clouds nestled into the moon, smothering its fulgent face, pushing the darkness further into the night.

James took a step closer.

Unaware, Kezia put her hands flat on the windowsill and began tapping out the rhythm of the tango: *uno dos tres cuatro*, one two three four... *Not tonight.* She could still see the sincerity in his face, the Virgin Mary with her peach mouth behind him. There was a sudden heat at the back of her eyes: the sharp stab of tears not yet cried.

James inched forwards, coming closer, blinking at the vision of Kezia, backlit in the room. He noticed the way the nightdress accentuated her shoulders, how the pink complemented her tan. He had wandered the streets all afternoon, dazed and desperate — backwards and forwards like the crazy flight of a bluebottle — with the ring, cold and unused in his pocket. He'd seen her on stage, and he'd seen her run away, so he knew he had a chance now; if she ran from Darim, she might run to him.

He lifted his hand but she didn't see him. He waved his arms, but she was looking at the sky. James frisked the floor for something to throw and found a small pebble in the shape of a shell. Then he realised, it was a shell. He took his aim and... the clouds swum away from the moon filling the terrace with a pewter light.

Kezia saw James. Her hand went to her mouth, the strap of her nightdress slipping down her arm. She hooked it up again.

"Kez," he whispered, dropping the shell, her name caught in his throat. "Kez."

"James?" she mouthed, and put her hand forward as if trying to touch him.

"It's me."

As they looked at each other, she began to move backwards, but James, desperate for her not to recede into the shadows and be out of reach again, took two steps forwards and began to sign. Secretly, silently, he spoke to her in the night. He held her attention and he told her many things.

He told her he was sorry. He told her he'd been wrong to put work first. He told her he couldn't live without her and it was obvious now. He told her he needed her, more than she knew. "Please," he said. "Come home with me. We can start again. I'll be different. I'll be better. I won't take you for granted, we will be happy. We were — happy."

"What?" she signed like a firework, incredulous.

"Please forgive me and we can start again. We're good together. Everyone says so."

"I don't... I can't..."

James dropped his arms, his shoulders slumped, and she thought he looked so meek, so weak, so compliant compared to Darim with his strong torso. She watched him feel for the ring in his pocket, he looked down at the stone slabs at his feet, he bent his knee slightly, but didn't go down. Instead, James looked up and signed, "I love you..." He said it softly, with his hands.

Kezia's breathing became shallow and fast. She gripped the windowsill, felt the smooth grain of the wood. The wind ushered in midnight; the diffuse bells of a church in the village, steeped with time and history. For a moment all was still and dark and they stood, speechlessly together as the stars crumbled between the clouds.

Then he was getting down on one knee, he was pulling out the ring box, he was fumbling to open it and Kezia was straining her eyes because she didn't think it could be real, not this.

"Kezia," he signed with the ring, holding her there. "Think about it — that's all I ask. Think about it." He focused on her forlornly.

"But you're not listening to me. What about what I want? I want to be me... without you. I told you..." Kezia thought hard as she remembered the words, her sign language had always been basic and now it was rusty too.

"You can't want to stay here?" James gestured towards the red and white striped house as if it was a fairground attraction.

"Don't tell me what I want. You don't know. You want to keep me small. Just because you don't understand something doesn't make it wrong!" She was pleased with that, it felt like something Darim would say.

"You can't stay here forever, you've got to come back. Come on. Your parents are worried. They want you back too."

He tried to say more but she was signing over him, more confident now, faster. "They encouraged me to stay here. They said it would do me good. It is doing me good. And now that it is doing me good you all don't want me to have it any more. You're making it about what you want — all of you. What about what I want... I need. It's not fair." She stared defiantly, "Go away. Leave me alone."

He stood up stiffly, unwilling to leave her. "You look so beautiful."

She said nothing.

James' heart was jarring in his chest and his cheeks and ears were burning. "I don't understand, I thought we had something special."

"We did. But maybe it's not for you to understand, maybe it's just that things have changed."

"I'll be waiting," James said, beginning to slouch away. "When you decide, I'll be waiting."

Just then the clouds cosseted the moon again, casting the terrace in an impenetrable glaze. Kezia glanced out to sea, to where the ocean was now just a black hole in the night. The plants murmured and one of the cats mewed, then, as the ivy trembled and the ashen light blew back over the garden, he was gone.

Kezia breathed out, long and slowly. She shut her eyes tight and put her hands on her head. Relief and guilt mingled in tangled strands of emotion, all tiredness abating as she tried to understand...

She needed Darim, wanted him now, to counsel and console her. Now she could arouse his jealousy. Now... It had to be now. So, impulsively, she turned, went to the door and pulled it. Locked. She pulled it again, kicked it in frustration. She wanted him now.

There was no response when she called Rollo's name from the window and she couldn't shout loudly in case James heard and came back. She tugged at her hair absent-mindedly, looking down, thinking longingly of the kiss with Darim, the pleasure and the uncertainty, the taste of his passion. Then the ivy clicked against the wall of the house like castanets and the moonlight illuminated the thick trunk with its structure of branches fanning out as if it was lighting the way. Kezia set her jaw in determination. "I will not be trapped, she said. "Not again. Not ever. I will rescue myself." And she climbed out of the window, feet first. Holding on tight, she squeezed out of the small frame and levered herself down until her foot found a wizened bough. She pressed and it was strong, so she stood there and steadied herself. Then she found the branch below and gripped the trunk as she sought the next bough and the next... it was easy; the foliage hid a climbing frame — a secret sinuous ladder — and she laughed a throaty laugh as she descended, step by step and rung by rung.

At the bottom, she felt for the firm flagstones and clambered to the floor, looking up as the leaves shimmied in appreciation, amazed at what she'd done. Tomi limped over, eyes shining with a peculiar alacrity, catching the colour of the moon.

Darim's door was shut. She stood outside and put her forehead close, wondering if she might hear him breathing, sleeping now maybe... imagining his chest, rising and falling, rising and falling like the sea. Then she straightened up and knocked, decisively, four times. She took a step back, waiting, deciding what to say.

There was no answer. Over in the shed, Hady yelled something chilling in his sleep and the restive trees murmured a rueful riposte.

Kezia counted to six in the *compas* of the sevillana and tried once more, just two taps now. Nothing. She leant forwards and her hand hovered over the handle. She hesitated, flexing her fingers, then pulled back, knocking again. When she got no reply the third time, she opened the door, just a crack.

The bedside light was on but the bed was empty. From his basket in the corner Rollo bounced up and flounced over, with his tongue flopping out. She stroked his happy head, "Hello Rollo. Where's Darim?" He looked at her in adulation but provided no clue. "Okay, back to bed then." And obediently he ambled away to dream of chasing chickens. Kezia shut the door, recollecting what Darim had said.

"Night walks, by myself. I told you, I sleep little, I sleep light."

She wandered into the garden. The scents of the flowers mingled with the night air, deep lavender, soft rose and bright azalea. She touched the petals as she passed and, as she felt their passive energy, the memory flashed like a flare: Magdalena, silent, holding out the piece of paper. The spell and the cure. She remembered the words and felt their possibilities. After the disaster of the competition, she could prove she was brave — prove it to him and be set free. The night was clear and calm and a certain sultriness was willing her on; it was the perfect time for magic. Kezia headed purposefully back towards the house.

53

Seaweed

𝔗here was a chink of clotted light at the back of the room in the stubby shape of a cross, denting the darkness. Kezia focused on the grate as her eyes adjusted. She was groping for the light switch and the little luminosity seeping in seemed viscous like candle wax, dripping slowly. A low buzz in the corner unnerved her, she had not noticed it before, and it was cold; the black wrapping round her and the chill creeping up on her. Mould and must percolated the air, thick with stories, as the fabrics rustled in an unseen draft.

It was a long time since she had been in the basement, it felt like a lifetime ago, and the old dresses and ballgowns hung like ghosts themselves — hideously they appeared, the way a black and white photograph develops — and they were watching her in the silence and stale air. So many costumes, he wouldn't miss one. She tried not to look at them as she kept reaching for the switch, feeling only brick, hard and blank, until—

The light snapped on — a painful yellow swab through her mind — a jolt. The bulb hung like an upside-down skull on a hairy piece of string and cast a curdled, bilious florescence, as if it had been sick all over the cellar. Now Kezia apprised the contents of the basement like an antique dealer, considering all the baleful gowns decorated by dust, the rows of fascinators splayed like peacock feathers and the decrepit shoes, going nowhere on the shelves. Again, she repeated the spell, again she felt for its power.

Forever in the now, I offer you this gift,
Forever and all time, the curse for you to lift.
In passion and prayer and sorrow and sin
I wait in hope for your song to begin.

It was no use. The dresses were judging her, the shoes had known wiser steps to take, the shawls sneered at her impudence: that she would even try. "I have to," she told them bitterly, and felt the taste of tears again. The costumes just stared, knowing the fullness of her stupidity in the texture of their velvet, silk and lace. Kezia moved forwards and bumped into a voluptuous skirt billowing gratuitously, layers and layers of damp material. She put her hand on the wall to steady herself. "I am cursed," she said pathetically and the fabric seemed to swell with consciousness at the comment. "This is my only way out, you have to help me. Please."

She walked along the rails, pulling out the garments one by one. The air was saturated with sadness and yet she needed to find something cherished and precious, something that was loved. She took out a red dress with black lace trimmings, held it high but wasn't sure, there was a humble black skirt, well used, but perhaps not well liked, and a green shawl, now loved by moths…

Kezia did another circuit of the basement and ended up back at the shoes. They appeared to look up at her, waiting, knowing. She ran her eyes along the line and there was one pair, right at the end, leather lax and faded, that held her gaze, that spoke of love in time-worn sincerity. They had to be the favourites, used more than all the others, ground down with the passion of her steps. Kezia took the shoes with such reverence the basement became a church — her own votive offering, never to go out — a sacrament among the silk and the chiffon and the twill. This pair had been loved by Carlotta, she could feel it in the creases and the thinness of the soles. She held them close as she left the cellar, inhaling their vintage magnetism and making her way to the back of the garden.

The sign for 'Carlotta's Flamenco School' seemed to be snoring, creaking over the gate and scratching out its pickled breathing. She waited for a moment, leaning against the side of the arch and looking down the path. *Don't go down to the water, don't go down to the sea…* the words washed in on a tide of thoughts… and with them, Darim's voice, so clear. *"You've got to face your fears, only then can you get past them."*

You've got to face your fears.

Looking down at the cove she remembered how powerful she had felt on the night she heard the ghost: spirit-soaked and free. *"This* is how

I break the curse," she said, out loud, to bolster her conviction. "No one else can do it. It has to be me. This time I will not run away and if — when — I hear her, I will make my offering and I will listen." The shoes felt hallowed in her hands, she gripped them tighter. "Then I will dance and dance and I will prove my power and I will be free." She glanced towards the statue of the lion, *I will prove it to them all.*

So she went. Through the gate, down the path, across the stones to the sea. Her steps were jumbled and her thoughts were jumbled too. She caught her nightdress on a thorn and it ripped, a tiny jagged tear.

The breeze picked up as she entered the cove, kidnapping clouds and smuggling in stars. Shadows reigned as they stalked across the moon, shifting and sewing adumbrated designs.

The cove, where it all started, where she first met Darim, when the wind blew and the gusts were swirling indecision... Not any more. She knew who she was now. That was why she was here. She was not afraid. Shapes morphed around the crescent of the bay; boulders grew and shrunk, broken bits of wood leered and leapt.

It was muggy now, close, like the time before rain and the air twanged with salt. The shrivelled seaweed crunched as she walked to the water, and the surf spoke of secrets as it caressed the sand, loving it, but always pulling back. There were boats out there, shifting hulks with no lights on, stalking their way to shore, almost invisible in the navy ink surrounding them. Emissary waves ran in ripples to her feet. Then the wind seemed to shudder and she heard a low moan.

She gasped, turning, clutching the shoes to her chest.

The groan came again, the low moan of singing. Unmistakable. Exquisitely sad.

Kezia looked towards the craggy rocks at the far end of the cove. She heard the ocean swell and with it her fear and her anger and her pent-up hate. She curled her fingers around the shoes and stood resolute; it was just her and the plaintive lament — long notes strung wide over the water. Resisting the urge to run, Kezia glanced to the top of the ridge, where the pine trees stood like centuries, faithful warriors, moving with the wind. *"What do the trees do, Kezia? They... react..."* The scent of pine, strong like the memory.

Kezia narrowed her eyes. "I've got to do this." She stood up tall. "I will *not* be afraid of you any more, I need to do this, I need more... *grit*." Gary's words came back to haunt her now too — all her ghosts, all at once... the bullies, the taunting, the shame. She was whipping her feelings around in a whirl, a dance of desires, and when she had built up enough momentum, and the beat and the rhythm were her own, she began to move... Towards the rock, towards the ghost, calling the power inside her, calling it into being, and as she summoned, it grew, bit by bit and step by step.

The singing shuddered over the cove, heart-breaking, sweet and strong. She felt the chill, the ice in her spine; it pierced her core and gripped her senses. She had to fight to go forwards, to get closer to it, fight to remember the words, remember the spell as the music took hold of her. "You can un-curse me now," she said through gritted teeth. "You can un-curse me." Steadily, and with a growing dread she went forwards.

The singing stopped.

Kezia wobbled where she was, her body tight, her breath shallow. She tried to revise the spell. *Forever in the now... Forever...* She could see a shape. The ghost was there and the ghost was looking at her — pale, blurred outline. *Forever in the now...* She crept nearer with the shoes, ready to speak, to say her part.

The ghost was gaining height and it was rising. It was moving backwards, sinking into the shadows, back and back, seeking to fade into the forever cold creases of the cove.

"No," Kezia shouted, stumbling over the rocks towards it, determined now to face her fears. She started to climb, but then she thought of Carlotta — of Carlotta falling — and she paused, steadying herself as she looked up.

There was the ghost and the ghost seemed to flicker as a cloud crossed the moon. It was shifting backwards, losing its footing or losing its form, she couldn't tell. Its arms were wide, held up high, ready to dissolve into a dilute umbra, to disappear discreetly into the realm of souls, but just before it could depart, just before its phantom shift, the cloud whipped away like a cloth, and she saw it, she actually saw it: the face of the ghost.

54

Sirens

ℐt was worse than she ever could have imagined. Her greatest fears were as nothing now. The shoes tumbled from her hands. "You..."

The ghost sank to its knees.

"You?" Kezia adjusted her position on the rock, unbalanced, unbelieving. "You are... the ghost?"

Seconds drizzled like cold rain. Was it a dream? Another hallucination, a mirage of the mind? She stared, taking in every detail, his face smeared silver in the moonlight. "Sami?"

The ghost stood and took a bow. It was Sami.

Before she had time to think, Darim was edging out from behind a bolder in a black fedora hat, his visage hidden by its shadow. He muttered something to Sami, who turned and scampered away, nimbly over the outcrop, down to the shore.

Kezia watched him go. "Darim? What's going on?"

"*Oh Leah*," he breathed, taking off the hat and clutching it to him. "All is not as it seems, Kezia."

"But the singing... it's... it's Sami?"

"All is not what it seems," he said again. "It's not... what it looks like." He put the hat back on and glanced away anxiously, picking out two stealthy boats slipping nearer to the shore. "I can explain, Kezarina."

The cove was closing in on her, the pines whispering like they had been warning her all along. Shock turned to anguish, fear turned to dismay; chameleon emotions transfiguring like the ghost. Kezia was dizzy. "But... why? Why would you..." She trailed off, lost for words.

Darim put his hands in prayer. "There are many things we do not understand. But I can explain, I will explain." His voice seemed to echo around the cove. "We do it in memory of Mama." He crossed himself then bowed his head.

"What?" Kezia wanted to sit down but the ground felt too far away.

"Mama," Darim moaned, casting his eyes to the heavens and saying it again. "For her." He looked around furtively. "She died here, she is here, we keep her memory alive."

Kezia began to back away, slowly down the rocks.

Darim focused intently on her. "This is our secret now, right? Our secret. It brings us closer together: no mysteries, no lies."

"No lies?" Kezia froze, incredulous.

Darim came towards her. "Don't you see? This is why I held back from you. I couldn't let you into... *this*. But now you know. Now..." he let out a puff of air. "I should have told you before, but I was protecting you. Out of love." He paused as Kezia stared, open mouthed, then he said, "Truth and illusion, Kezia. We find our own truths, we make our own illusions. Come into my world..."

The knowing water lapped at the shore, folding over darkly. Kezia started moving again, treading cautiously back down and onto the sand. "I don't... I don't know you..."

"Isn't that more exciting?" Darim's voice lifted. "You left boring behind."

She was sweating now, hot in the oppressive night. "But everyone believes... and it's just Sami..."

Darim picked his way forwards, stepping off the rocks too. "We believe what we want to believe, all of the time, Kezia. You and the rest of the village."

She was a sandcastle, destroyed by a sudden surge of the tide, the world that she knew crumpled around her. There were no words she could think of.

Darim scanned the beach. "You must go, it is not safe for you here." He held out his arms, pleading and pushing her away at the same time. "Go now, run, hide. Curses come in many forms, my Kezia, and you must not be discovered here now. Run." The boats were getting closer.

Kezia ran her hand over her hair, shaking her head, distraught.

"Please. Now. Go. I have told you, there is more than one way to be cursed. I should know." He looked up at the stars. "I should know."

She was trying to fathom what she was seeing, why she was seeing it, but there was a ringing in her ears and a ringing in her heart — a static in her senses — so she didn't hear the smooth grate of helms slicing the sand and she didn't notice the splash of men disembarking, or the pound of footsteps up the beach… There was only Darim until — she was aware of them — too late. An arm came from behind, a lock around her neck and Kezia was choked, unable to scream.

"Do not hurt her," said Darim.

Suddenly Omar appeared, walking in from the side, dressed all in black, clenching bulbous fists. "What is this?" he growled. "What is this? I warned you, Darim, I told you she was trouble. I told you. Now look where we are. If I hurt her, it is your fault, not mine."

Darim put his hand on his breast in a beatific pose. "She will not tell," he said solemnly. "She is in this too now. She is one of us. She can help."

"Pah! She can help? Have you lost your mind? A silly little girl in flamenco shoes?" He shoved the air as if shoving Kezia out of the way. "This is serious and it is dangerous, Darim, as well you know. But first things first, we have work to do. We need to get this lot stashed and we need to do it fast. Take her over there," he ordered the man at Kezia's back, who began dragging her, heels catching in the sand.

Darim stood helpless, watching. Omar turned to him and spat, "We will deal with you later as well. Come, let's get started."

Darim didn't move, he was looking into the fathomless ocean.

"Move!"

"Shh." It was Sami, back again, winding around them like a shark, moving nervously, staring at Darim and at Kezia. "Shh, too loud."

"Sami's right. We need to keep it down. Who knows who's still hanging around after the festival. Right boys, let's do this." His fists were still drawn tight — he brought them up, as if ready to punch.

Kezia had been hauled over to the boats and pushed to the ground where she sat, hurting. She watched as the men began unloading — crate after crate — in synergy with each other, like a mechanical engine.

"Guard her, Sami, make sure she doesn't get away," Omar ordered and then rolled up his sleeves to start lifting as well.

Sami looked down at Kezia. "See," he said. "You don't know anything. I sing for Darim. He needs me. He really needs me." He stood up proudly but there was a sadness in his smugness, something unsure under the surface.

A chill came through Kezia as she sat helpless on the sand, feeling all of the power go out of her. She shut her eyes and stifled a sob. She could hear the bash of boxes being moved, the forgotten gush of the sea, the jolt of the nearest boat slapping its mooring like a faulty heartbeat. Certainty frayed like an old rope, and she was somehow more deeply haunted now; now she knew the danger came from the living and not the dead. She opened her eyes: contours blurred as the men worked, five or six of them, busy and unfeeling.

"Get a move on, all of you." Omar was everywhere. "This is the biggest shipment we've had. It'll take longer to get up to the house."

Sami went forwards and picked up three crates. They were too heavy for him, too big and unwieldy. He staggered a few paces and had to stop.

"No, Sami. Just one for you." Omar strode over and pulled off the top two. "I told you to watch her anyway." He nodded towards Kezia. "Do as I say."

Sami started to protest but Omar was already taking the last of his load, so he affected a pout, was coming back to Kezia, was kicking up the sand, and then —

The night pulled apart at the seams.

An orange light exploded from above. Faces flashed, flooded with fire. Then a loud crack painted the colours with sound — a giant twig snapping — followed by a rushing like a plane taking off. Flames billowed with thoughts, crates dropped and voices hissed consternation. There was a violent stain, up through the trees where the house was, bleeding red, yellow, rust.

"Papa!" Darim's mouth and eyes opened so wide his face became a mask. For a few seconds he was stuck like this, then his whole body jolted and he ran, darting across the cove to the path. His fedora blew off and was tossed behind him, over the sand and onto a rock, where Sami retrieved it, holding it tenderly. Darim ran, fast, syncopated strides — so unlike his normal measured movements — he staggered up the path, his hand pressed tight to his ribcage, tripping as he went. Up and up...

Kezia didn't think. She followed. She let the force of her emotions propel her — away from the cove, away from the men and away from Sami, who wasn't watching her now anyway. Nothing made sense, except to run. When she got to the path, pebbles kicked loose and low leaves brushed her skin like phantoms as she left them behind.

The men watched, ashen — appalled and bewitched by a foreign force — theirs a dreamlike disaster. They stood, not knowing what to do, some of them still clinging to their crates, others putting them down, dazed. Omar had both hands on his head, staring at the faint light from the top of the hill. "Back in the boats," he said, after some time. "Put the boxes back in the boats." But he sounded uncertain and nobody moved. The tinge of fire on the horizon glowed and they stared, mesmerised. "I said, back in the boats," Omar ordered, hunched now and stalking between them. "Let's get out of here," he murmured morosely.

There was a shuffle and kerfuffle as the bewildered men rewound their ambitions and began to reload with the same speed, but a lot less zeal than before.

"Omar?" It was the rough man who had held Kezia. "Surely we can still take it up. It'll be all right, it'll be sorted soon. We can't risk going back with this. We need to shift it. You promised…"

Omar turned to him. "They will all be awake now, what do you think will happen? They will ignore us with all of this?" He gestured. "Is that what you want? To be arrested tonight?"

The man said nothing, turning back to help the others. Eventually they all clambered aboard, ready to retreat — except Sami — who didn't move, still clasping Darim's hat, holding it tight. "Come on," yelled Omar, impatient at the prow. "Time to go Sami. Get in."

But Sami stood, staring up towards the house.

Two of the men started to unhook the ropes from their moorings, a rhythmic unwinding. Sami turned, looking at the nearest rope like it was serpent, telling him lies.

"What are you waiting for? Come on," Omar howled. "We need to get out of here. Whatever has happened, tonight is not our night. We can't be caught with this lot. Come on Sami."

"But Darim needs me," Sami said, his words like water carried away in the wash of the sea.

"We're leaving. Your last chance, Sami." The boat began to bob away.

Sami looked back to where the nectarine glow on the hill was a faint blush now, the colour of his heart, broken open.

"Sami!" Omar's gruff voice was already being subsumed by the susurration of the ocean.

Sami turned to see his brother moving backwards, gliding into the waves. He hesitated a moment more, then he took one last glance up at the flames, before swinging around and planting the hat on his head. He staggered forwards, leaving all that had spilled from his heart behind, the feeling of an empty husk in his chest. "Darim, Darim," he said to himself. "Darim." As if the name alone could fill him up. "Darim, Darim," he chanted. "Darim." And he kept saying it as he waded into the cold and unforgiving water.

***

When Darim reached the top of the hill the moonlight was misty, the air foggy with fumes. He sprinted to the garden where the heat cut through the wind. "Papa?"

He could perceive the consternation — the rip through the night unmended — as he progressed… past the lion and its supplication in stone, turning through the flower beds until he could see where the fire cracked, illuminating the damage, showing the shards of the blast; the shattered windows, jagged teeth of glass glinting, the door blown off. The ivy above the kitchen was being eaten by voracious flames. He waded onwards — people were staring but he didn't register their stunned faces — he went right up to the hole in the side of the house and through the gap and no one stopped him.

The kitchen was all grey space and thick smoke. Concrete air. He couldn't see as soot surrounded him and it was hard to get through, hard to understand, hard to breathe. "Papa?" he choked as he peered through the charcoal haze to the black walls, smeared with the gizzards of the stove, which was now a mangled mess of metal, soiled with its own pink flesh. "Papa?" he wheezed, but there was nothing but the ominous quiet of drifting fog and flecks of fire floating. He trod on something soft and it didn't move. "Benja?" Darim bent down, shaking… but it wasn't the cat, it was his Papa's flat cap on the floor. He snatched it up and pulled it to him, backing out of the room.

As he withdrew, he gulped for air, still looking at the carnage in front of him.

Then, a voice from behind. "Carlotta?" Normando, hoarse, straining. "Carlotta?"

Darim hung his head. His heart was pounding. Slowly, he turned and held out his arms. "Papa, Papa. It's me. Don't worry. It's okay. It's me. Are you all right? Tell me you're all right?"

Normando's face crumpled in confusion.

"Papa. Are you okay? You're not hurt?"

Just then, a siren pierced the smoky air, shrieking its sonic nightmare, bewailing what it might soon see.

"Carlotta." Normando started to sink down into a chair that wasn't there. Darim ran and caught his arm, just in time.

"Papa. It's okay, Papa."

"No." Normando shook his head. "No." And the fire cackled like evil laughter.

55

Flames

There was a strange soupy heat and the smell of gas. Kezia swayed by the gate, catching her breath and her feelings. The fairy lights were eclipsed by the fire, which continued to consume the ivy above the kitchen like a raging parasite. The outlines of people were backlit by an eerie radiance — and it was quiet, too quiet. A group of people in nightclothes, not talking.

As she came closer, she saw Normando leaning on Darim's arm in devastation. They were inching over to the wall, where Darim helped him to sit. Rollo came padding up to his master, his liquid eyes urgent, his tail dropped low. Darim knelt, cradling him, burying his head in his fur and crooning; "Oh Rollo. My Rollo. My darling Rollo." He pulled back and they looked adoringly into each other's eyes.

Kezia could see Darim's face, open and unmasked, but now she knew the tenor of his lie the world shifted around her: silhouettes and shadows morphed yet again, this time into shapes even more startling. The season of secrets was gone, but underneath the fabric of the stories there was a darkness rustling, whispers she could only strain to hear. And even so, even now, with her belief broken and her faith fractured, she hoped for something with him; an unnamed, unknowable, ache.

Hady came over to her, topless, in just his jeans. "Everybody's out," he said grimly.

She saw Java leaning against the shed and, over by the camellia, she could make out Sue's blonde bob sticking up around her head. Magdalena was stood apart, arms folded, her hair falling down her face.

The sirens stabbed louder as the hulk of a fire engine came hurtling down the hill. It slowed at the top of the path, driving onto the verge, crushing a clump of chrysanthemum daisies, white-and-yellow heads bowing in stoic surrender. Burly men climbed out and unravelled large hoses with choreographed gymnastics. They came bounding forwards down the track and the night resounded with voices, words strung together with a gravity too great for punctuation.

They watched as water jets laced the smoke. Up, into the ivy, quenching the heat and filling the rapacious mouth of the flames. The fire succumbed gradually, like a wounded animal, falling to its knees, rolling over and then giving up in a puff of ash. When it was done the officers shouted more short words to each other, put their equipment down and filed towards the kitchen door.

Java came and rested her head on Hady's chest, unable to look at the destruction any longer. He stroked her hair tenderly, regarding the dying blaze with wan acceptance, the hollows in his eyes reflecting devastations past. It was getting light now, a discreet luminescence that spoke of dawn, and they shivered as more of the spectacle was revealed. Hady pulled Java closer to him.

Kezia moved to sit beside Normando on the wall, gently putting her hand on his shoulder, letting his comfort be comfort to her, and stunned, they contemplated the diabolical stains left by the fire together.

Next the police car came. It stopped at the verge and then drove precariously down the track, parking when the way became too narrow.

"You called the police?" Darim muttered.

"No," Hady replied, not looking at him.

Darim recognised the young policeman from the station, the one with the moustache like caterpillar's legs. Rollo growled at the police dog, a German shepherd with a hard, pointed face.

"Stand back," said the officer unnecessarily. "Nobody move." He went over to one of the fire officers and nodded in exaggerated movements at everything that was said.

Darim tried to walk around the group, to slip past to the front of the house.

"Stop! Where are you going?" The policeman lunged away from his conversation. "This is now a crime scene. You have to stay over there."

"It is not a crime scene," said Darim caustically. "It is my house, and I would like to see if everything is all right. My cats…"

"There is your cat," said the officer, pointing at Tomi, who was sat next to the lilies, licking his paw.

"I have several cats," countered Darim.

"It is not safe," said the police officer sardonically. "We need to make it safe. Explosions like this can shake things up more than you know. No one goes anywhere until we say. Go — over there," he dictated, while another two police officers went inside the house and he stood sentry outside, too afraid to enter.

So they waited. Time ticked like a metronome.

"I should be making breakfast…" Normando called out, perturbed. At his foot, the head of a geranium, blown off by the blast.

"No, not yet — not yet, Papa." Darim drifted back to him and pushed him down as he tried to stand. "Sit now, Papa. We wait." He didn't look at Kezia, instead his eyes were everywhere, darting around, unable to stop or focus.

Kezia stroked Normando's hand. She could feel Darim as he sat on the other side of the old man. The questions formed a mist inside her, nebulous and consuming… all she could do was fight the tears as she waited for Darim to speak, but he said nothing. He was watching, watching as more police came and were crawling over the house like bees in a honeycomb.

"What do you think happened?" Sue wandered over, still crumpled from sleep, her hair a messy halo around her face, like a child in a school nativity.

Kezia turned to Normando, but the old man was impassive, observing, so she stood up and hugged Sue and it was just another question, hanging in the air.

A lambent light permeated the day, the world coming into sharper focus, forms and shapes slowly saturating with colour. Plants tilted their heads in anticipation of the sun. The house drizzled with uniforms.

When the young police officer strode over, Rollo snarled protectively, taking him off guard. "Right," he said, slowly shifting his attention from the dog. "We have ascertained…" He paused, clearing his throat. "We have ascertained the explosion seems to have come from the Aga."

Darim rolled his eyes. "Isn't that obvious?"

The officer shot him a look and carried on. "We imagine some kind of fault with the stove — interesting colour choice by the way," he smirked. "But more likely… more likely someone left the gas on." He looked directly at Normando, who was mumbling something about orange juice and rotating his thumbs over and over each other in clasped hands, fingers bent inwards like claws. "We will of course check to see what else could have caused it." The officer regarded the fraught circumvolution of Normando's gnarled thumbs. "This is just an early-stage assessment. We will do all the necessary checks. But yes, from what we can see, this is purely a domestic fault, nothing suspicious."

"Of course it is nothing suspicious," Darim exploded.

The officer ignored him. "But you will need a new kitchen," he remarked snidely.

"A new kitchen?" Darim stood angrily. "My house blows up, my papa could have been killed, and you joke about needing a new kitchen? Why are you here anyway? You said yourself there was nothing to investigate. Go. Go away and tell your officers to leave us alone."

The officer bristled. "Oh. Well. I understand it's been a shock *Señor* de Santos. But my officers—"

"Your officers are meddling."

"No. My officers are doing a thorough job for the safely of all present, yourself included. This is what we do. I can understand your distress, of course," he pronounced in unctuous tones, "But need I remind you—" And he was just building to a pompous diatribe when one of his colleagues sidled up, conveying a message in energetic but hushed sentences. As he listened, his eyes widened and his lips pursed. "Excuse me," he said, ostentatiously, turning a full one hundred and eighty degrees and hurrying over to the house.

Shards of sharp sun filtered into the morning, illuminating a hairy leaf as it lay on the ground. Kezia looked at it, still close to Normando, following his line of sight as he stared fixedly at the floor. The breath of a breeze was blowing the hanging baskets and the rust on one of them made it scrape against its cast iron hook like a tuneless violin.

"What are they doing?" Sue nodded towards the police who were now pulling some packets out of the house and piling them up, carefully, one on top of the other, the dog ambling back and forth, sniffing and wagging its tail.

Darim began edging away, slowly, deliberately, like an invisible glue was tacking him to the air. Rollo made a brittle sound, teeth bared, and loyally reversed with him. Normando murmured something about making churros.

"Oh no." The officer with the scraggly moustache was coming back towards them now. "Oh no you don't. You're not going anywhere, Darim de Santos, *you* are under arrest."

Darim stopped moving, squaring his shoulders — contemptuous, proud — and somewhere, the first cockerel of the morning crowed.

***

They were putting the handcuffs on Darim when Rachel came into view. Restless at the hotel, she'd heard the sirens running through the village and she didn't think about it — she knew — she was about to get her story. As she hurried down the path, Darim lifted his arm to hide his face in a limp arabesque, but he couldn't avoid the photographs.

"What's happened?" she asked the officer with the moustache who was only too happy to brief her, chest puffed out as she noted down the details. "So, what do you think it is then?" Rachel nodded to the packets, closely guarded, stacked against the red and white sides of the house.

"Cocaine. Marijuana. Lots of it," he told her, satisfied. "Hector has a nose for these kinds of things." He was pointing a vain finger at himself. "They don't call me 'Hector the Hound' for nothing. You can put that in your report."

The officers took Darim to the police car, and he stood, poised, refusing to be folded into it. One of the detectives was pushing at his shoulders, fussing about and being ignored. Darim was surveying the activity around him like it was a dance, out of kilter and out of beat. Kezia half expected him to shout at them to go faster, or put more meaning into their moves.

"Tell me how these drugs came to be in your possession." Rachel had her microphone plugged into her phone now, recording. She scraped strands of tangled hair off her face, towards the messy bun at the back of her head.

"You are assuming that they were," Darim replied.

"So you didn't know anything about the drugs then? You think they were planted?"

"Do any of us have intimate knowledge of our own hearts, let alone our own houses?" Darim looked wistfully to the sky, like an actor in the final scene of a play.

Rachel took more pictures, zooming in on Darim's face, her mind whirring with potential headlines. She was about to ask another question when Magdalena came towards them, herself like a ghost in her nightdress. She trod slowly, softly, her arms at her sides, before stopping and angling her pale face to the officer. No one breathed.

Then she spoke. For the first time they heard her voice, delicate like pink peony petals. "He didn't do it," she said. "He wouldn't do it. He's a dancer, not a drug dealer. You're wrong, all of you."

"Silence," growled the officer, unaware of the momentous event he had just witnessed and determined to have the upper hand.

Magdalena drew back.

"You will have your chance to give a statement. You all will. But now... now is not that time."

Magdalena opened her mouth again but before she could speak the brusque officer who was trying to squeeze Darim into the car addressed her. "If he's so innocent then where have all these bags come from... and why are they on his premises?"

Magdalena stepped to the side and was quiet once more.

"Thank you, my darling," Darim sung out to her. "Thank you, precious one. You see? You need to listen to her. She does not waste her words." His own utterance rang out to no one and only Rollo stood dutifully by Darim's side, ears cocked, alert.

"I'm afraid you won't be able to take your dog to the police station." Hector leaned over with a sanctimonious smile.

Darim bent down gently, "Rollo," he said. "Go and take care of Mando. Go now. Go on." Rollo looked between his master and Normando. "Go on." Rollo's brow creased and he whimpered slightly, but, looking behind him periodically, he trotted over to the old man. "That's it," Darim said encouragingly. "Good boy. I'll be back soon. Go on." Normando made a fuss of Rollo, whose tail wagged cautiously at first, and then in abject delight.

"Er, Inspector?" A tall officer, who had been continuing to search the house, came over to the car, wearing blue plastic gloves.

"What is it?" Hector kept his eyes on Darim.

"Sir. We've found another… substance."

Rachel turned to look at the lofty officer, feeling a sudden sense of déjà vu, the same feeling she'd had when she had seen the flamenco poster on that rainy day in Leicester Square, the woman with the skirts rushing out like a waterfall of blood. She instinctively recognised something in the timbre of his voice — the professional surprise — something that told her there was more to this, more than just a conventional drugs bust. She had found it, she had her scoop.

"What is it?" Hector asked quickly.

The man held up a small vial full of murky liquid. "This, and some poisonous looking berries. Not anything I recognise but I think, err, considering, perhaps we should investigate?"

"I don't suppose you'd care to enlighten us, would you?" Hector rounded on Darim.

Assuming the pose of a damsel in distress, Darim leant against the side of the police car. "What else have you found in my house?"

"This will go a lot better for you if you cooperate with our inquiries. Go on, get in the car."

Darim did not move.

The young officer rubbed his scant moustache just as Pedro swooped over in a dash of green and red. "Erk. Belladonna. Belladonna," he screeched. "Belladonna."

Hector swatted, irritated, but the parrot had risen far out of reach. "Yes, send it off to the lab," he instructed his gloved colleague curtly, and the man nodded and walked away.

The sun had burnt through the clouds now and its sterile light made everything seem like an overexposed photograph. Kezia blinked, wanting to look at Darim and not wanting to look at him at the same time. When she did, she found he was regarding her sadly, still propping himself up on the side of the police car. She felt that look like a cloak, heavy, but warming — until someone shouted something at Darim and he turned — the moment was gone.

Feeling the shock of tears, Kezia wiped her eyes before they could betray her, looking instead to the house, a picture of loss and burnt-out happiness. The charred walls and her charred heart felt the same.

Esmerelda made a throaty bleat, sensing the sadness there, and it seemed as if everything had peeled away, like the memory of a dream. If the ghost wasn't real, then why had she got sick? Suddenly dizzy she leant forwards, focusing on the tiny lines on the flagstones, which seemed, to her, like the contours on human skin. She let them swirl and blur with her vision... *Who are you, Darim de Santos?* The questions kept swirling too, and all she knew was that she did not want them to take him away.

Beside her there was a shuffling and a low moan. Normando had woken from a doze and was reassessing the damage, rubbing his feet on the floor in distress. Kezia took his hand again and squeezed it tight.

At that moment, Darim was at last forced into the back of the police car, a haunted, contorted look on his face as though he had finally seen the ghost of his own making. The door slammed hard and the wheels stuttered, trying to get traction on the ground; the green grass buckling, submitting, showing the brown face it hides. The engine revved harder, the tyres turned, and eventually, the car shot up the hill and out of sight.

Nobody spoke, not yet — they sat, listening, feeling the weight of things they were yet to understand. The village clock struck, distant and hazy, the trees swayed to the tempo of another day, and the birds were singing as if nothing had changed.

56

Lemon and Sugar

$\mathcal{H}$er body twisted and curved, spiralling with the music — it flowed through her — until the force found her feet and she stamped down on the hard wood floor, pelting and pounding with the insistence of rain and the modulation of metal. She fired off a volley, a defiant salvo, beats too quick to count, arms reaching up and pulling the heavens towards her. Rosa's head turned and turned, her skirts swung, her fingers flexed. The old sound system in the corner thumped out the tunes and she danced for the tourists who sat nervously, sipping their beers, self-conscious at witnessing such a display of passion.

"*Olé!*"

They clapped and an old man at the back, who was bent over like a bishop's staff, stood up to show his curved appreciation. Flushed, Rosa bowed, flourishing her shawl and then clattering off to the side to sit with Sue and Java, blowing the air up her face so her fringe lifted.

Normando was behind the bar, beaming, while Hady took charge — taking orders and making sure they were delivered — leaving the old man to talk and move glasses unhelpfully. Gone were the tarts, the berries shining in glycerine complicity, instead, Normando had baked some *magdalenas*, light and lemony, with sugar on top. "For Magdalena," he had said.

"How is it going?" Sue was asking Java. "You guys running this place?"

"Good! Hard work." Java crossed her eyes and giggled. "But we love it." She gazed adoringly over to Hady, who winked back at her whilst pouring a drink.

"Show me then. Where is it?" Sue waved the back of her left hand.

"Oh." Java blushed. "I don't have a ring. Not yet. He wanted to give me his grandmama's but it got lost in the move after the earthquake and

352

they haven't found it yet." She faltered, envisaging the devastation, then brightened. "But we're going to go to the market, get something else second-hand, something we can afford, but something we love. We think if it's been loved before that's even better, even more love."

"Ahh, that's a nice way to see it."

Dreamily, Java put her head in her hands.

Then Hady came over and pulled up a chair. "Gossiping are you girls?"

"Absolutely," declared Sue. "I've never seen you both happier. It's wonderful."

Hady smiled and there was something very peaceful about it. He and Java shared a contented glance. "It's true — I'm finally sleeping inside again, at the bar here. It's like I faced my demons that night — we all did in some ways, I guess. I still have my nightmares occasionally, but that's okay, that's okay. I started some counselling and it's helping, so... I'm okay." Hady was still gazing at Java.

"Good for you, I'm so glad." Sue clasped her hands. "Although, I suppose you could say it was a strange godsend you were having nightmares before the explosion, or Mando might have been in the kitchen, you know how he tends to fall asleep in the rocking chair."

They pictured him snoring, with Benja on his lap.

"Bless him." Rosa made the sign of the cross. "Coming out to see if you were all right. Thank God."

"That's him all over." Sue nodded approvingly as they looked over to the bar where Normando was chuckling heartily with a customer. "I suppose in a funny way it's a good thing Darim wasn't there either, really. He might have been too wrapped up in his own world to smell the gas, we know what he's like, and he's always there fussing about Mando..." Sue trailed off, pushing her glasses up her nose, and for a moment, they were all back in the moon-soaked night: the bang, the siren, the shock.

"He didn't get bail, no?" Rosa asked.

Sue shook her head but Java wanted to be the one with the story. "You can't when you're accused of poisoning the mayor's son."

"God. Matías." Rosa crossed herself again, with more fervour this time. "And Kezia too. No shame. No shame. And we all fell for it."

"Isn't it true you see what you want to see, most of the time?" said Sue. "And if everyone believes something, doesn't that make it stronger as well? I mean, surely even the cynics have to question themselves then — they have to at least ask themselves why everyone else believes."

"I suppose you hear the singing on the beach and you're too scared to go any closer — and then you fall sick… and you tell everyone what happened…" Rosa shivered.

"In a way, the real story is even more amazing," said Hady, shaking his head. "That it was Sami all along and they managed to pull off poisoning anyone who heard him."

"Talk about taking it too far," agreed Sue. "I mean, I'm sure Darim was being bullied by Omar to do it — I can't imagine him wanting to get involved in that — the music and the mystery, yes, maybe, that kind of thing is him all over, but not the rest, and to be fair we don't know which one of them was putting the substance on the food."

"Substance?" Rosa's brows furrowed. "Yes, what was it, what were they using exactly?"

"Belladonna," Hady said, articulating very precisely. "From Morocco. It's a plant — makes you deranged and hallucinating and sick. Very sick."

"How do you know?" Rosa asked.

"The police told me at interview. That one with the thin moustache. He was relishing all the details. Showed me some berries and asked if I'd ever seen any around the house. I had, but only in a back room — had no idea what they were, but I didn't think to ask. I'd have guessed at blackcurrants but they seemed a bit old and decaying to be honest, I wasn't tempted to eat any, thankfully!"

"Belladonna. *Bella donna*," said Rosa, enjoying the sound. "Doesn't that mean 'beautiful lady', in Italian?"

"I think so, I'll look it up." Java got out her phone. "Okay, let's see… Ahh, here we are… 'Belladonna, or Atropa Belladonna, is a poisonous plant that has been used in medicine since ancient times…' blah, blah, blah…" She scanned forwards. "Ooh, here we go: 'It is named 'Belladonna' for the 'beautiful women' of the Renaissance, who took it to enlarge their pupils and make them more alluring'."

"What? They used to drip it in their eyes?" Rosa's own eyes widened.

"That's what it says, and listen to this, here are the effects of taking it: 'headache, nausea, confusion, vomiting, dry mouth, blurred vision, hallucinations, madness...'" Java looked up and they were all silent around the table, then she turned back to her phone, quietly clicking on another article.

"What else does it say?" Sue tried to peer across.

"It says, 'Belladonna is often seen as a gateway, a passage that can take you to places deep inside yourself, thus even while enslaving you it can set you free'. I don't understand."

"Hmm. Bizarre. Well, I guess we'll have to ask Kezia about that one." Sue blanched. "Poor thing. And all that to smuggle a few drugs."

"A few drugs? Quite a lot by the sounds of it." Hady sat up straight. "Lucrative business from what I heard. It's the money, isn't it?" he contemplated. "People get greedy, then they'll do anything."

"Money, money, money," said Rosa, clicking her tongue. "And, no one's seen the brothers since all this happened? Omar and Sami?"

"Nope." Java brought her fists down emphatically. "Nowhere to be seen. Done a runner. Didn't even take any of their stuff; it's all out the back."

"The police officer told me he thinks they've gone back to Morocco, at the very least. Maybe even further, to get away."

"It's kind of sad, isn't it? Darim left to pick up the pieces," said Sue.

"I feel sorry for Sami too," Rosa mused. "He obviously had a great talent, an amazing voice, but his brother would only let him use it to haunt the bay. It's a waste, and now who knows what will happen to them?" Rosa looked down and turned her bracelet over and over on her wrist.

"It's hard to know who was singing whose tune here," said Sue, pleased with her pun. "I mean, Darim was obsessed with the stories, we know that, right? So I honestly do think it *could* have been Darim's idea, that part, at least, but as I say, not the rest."

"It was a distraction that worked," said Hady philosophically. "I can hardly believe this place was a drug den and we didn't even know it." He gestured to the bar. "We still get people coming in, looking shifty, asking for Omar and getting panicky when we tell them he's moved on."

"Yeah, you can tell the ones. They're not tourists and they're not from the village," Java added. "They quietly seethe with rage when we tell them."

"They don't get violent, do they?" asked Sue.

"No, they mostly storm out."

"Thank God." Rosa put her hands in prayer. "So, no drugs, no ghosts, no hallucinations." She curled her fingers together as if grasping this new reality.

"And how's Magdalena?" Sue addressed Hady.

"Yeah, she came to me after Darim was taken away, feeling abandoned again. The girl was traumatised about her parents, and now this. But we talked — you see, it's strange, but something was uncorked in her that day."

"Do you think she knew? She did watch everything," Sue asked.

"That's for her to tell you herself," said Hady. "One day... one day soon." He smiled. "I'm confident she's going to be fine. Next step we need to get her dancing, she's amazing apparently. Rosa, do you think you could take her under your wing?"

Rosa agreed readily. "Yes, oh, she'll be on that stage before long." She motioned, assured.

"Magdalena is talking to Hady," Java chipped in, "because she knew out of everybody he would understand."

"Yeah, you just need that affinity sometimes." Hady looked to the bar to check he wasn't needed. "I mean, we've been though different types of trauma, but we've been having some good conversations and I can see things shifting in her."

"Dancing will be the next step," said Rosa, with maternal warmth.

"Whatever the problem, flamenco is the answer," Java said, parroting Darim without thinking, jutting one finger in the air.

"Oh dear," said Sue, making the connection. "I hope Darim is going to be all right."

"I still don't get why he did it." Rosa blew up on her fringe again, lifting it momentarily off her forehead.

"Revenge on the village maybe?" said Sue. "His mama died after an argument with the mayor and it was never an easy relationship, was it? Also, he was probably sucked into the performance, the drama of it, making those stories come to life." She stopped for a moment, thinking, and then added, "Plus, he wanted to be free to do the thing he loved — dancing — but we know there wasn't any money and the school was making a loss and the bar was making a loss... so he needed a way out, he didn't want to get another job..."

"Can you imagine Darim doing anything else?" Java crinkled her nose.

"But he could have, he could have gone to teach in Almería," said Rosa. "Surely that would have been better, he could have got in with one of the big academies."

"He wouldn't leave Mando and Mando wouldn't leave the house," Hady said with certainty.

"Oh," Rosa breathed.

"So the important thing now is that we look after Mando until he comes out." Hady glanced back to the bar where Normando was tittering quietly with a group of tourists.

"Do you think he'll be different, do you think this will change him?" asked Rosa.

"I doubt it," mused Sue. "Darim is Darim, he'll find his own spin on it."

"I know it's bad, but I miss him," said Java. "I can't help it. Even after all of this, I miss him."

The others nodded and they were all lost for a moment in their own little worlds of memories and doubts... Conversations clattered, cutlery clinked and the bar moved on around them. The people of Parños with another story to add to their archive, another tale to pass down the generations, gather dust, and gain new life each time it would be told.

57

Clouds

𝒮he gaudy fan was unfurled like the precocious plumage of a peacock and a tiny hand with tiny painted-on nails held it aloft, her arm at an agile angle above her head. Her dress — red and white in the pattern of an enchanted mushroom — flowed over her hips, foaming in frills at her feet. The miniature dancer was looking at James with nonchalant painted eyes and he stared back at the puckered lips and the finely drawn eyebrows.

It was an early morning flight and puffy people drifted around Almería airport, wan and drawn. Insular, they queued for coffee and huddled in silent family clumps. The pallid light infused the glass walls, speaking of sunshine in its pale hope.

There were shelves and shelves of souvenirs and it all seemed so pointless, so plastic. James had wanted to distract himself by getting something for Hannah, but as he scanned the rows of mementos, all he could think about was Kezia. He had seen it, the way she looked at him, even as the sirens shrieked and the drugs were piling up outside the house.

James hadn't gone to bed... he'd been walking and walking and replaying the conversation over and over in his mind: Kezia at the window, Kezia in the pink nightdress, there with the light behind her, glowing, like an apparition. She had never looked more dazzling. Then, he had heard the explosion and sprinted back, her name like a rubber ball bouncing in his head. But when he arrived, all he could do was watch, he stood back; it was a place he did not belong. She was with the old man, holding his hand and there were too many people he didn't know — nothing for him to do now, anyway. An unnatural cold came over him, he rubbed his arms but it wouldn't let him go. He saw it — even as Darim was being pushed into the back of the police car. Even then, there was love in her for him. That was how he knew, for certain, that it was over — and he should have seen it sooner.

He felt so stupid. He had slunk away and he hadn't slept. It was the feeling of a tree, dying, the leaves falling slowly, one by one. They gathered at the bottom of his mind, decaying and rotting with the rest of this thoughts. The leaves were falling again now as he looked at a black and white picture of a couple tangoing together, entwined, their bodies fusing. When he turned away a flamenca on a pottery mug gave him a derisory look, even trapped beneath the glaze she was more powerful than him.

James wondered abstractly if he might ever be happy again. After winter, must come spring, they said, but there was no feeling to his thoughts, which, like the wooden castanets on the next shelf along, needed action to make them work. He ambled aimlessly to a rail of T-shirts, where shouty suns surfed over bulbous palm trees and psychedelic seas.

"James? James is that you?"

Behind him, Rachel stood in her high heels, not wearing any lipstick.

"Oh, hi, er... hi."

"We meet again! How are you?"

"Fine." He tried to smile but felt his face might crack like it too was pottery.

"Did you see my article?"

James nodded. He'd read it online that morning. He knew all about the 'Flamenco Felon', and the drugs ring operating from Mando's bar. He'd seen the picture: Darim being arrested and Kezia's face, blurry, in the background. "That was fast work," he said.

"Yeah." Rachel lifted her shoulders as if embarrassed. "Needed to get it out there. I was going to go with the 'Cocaine Dame', for the ghost, but my editor preferred 'Flamenco Felon'." She attempted a laugh but stopped when she saw his serious demeanour. "So, er, how is Kezia in all of this? Exciting stuff but not what she expected, right?"

James frowned. "Yeah, I guess." He shrugged. "I... we... we haven't spoken since."

"Oh. Are you okay?" She put one hand on her heart, thinking of her own break-up, the ache still there.

"Yes. No. Give me two years?"

She smiled. "Anything I can do?"

"Yeah, don't print that. Anywhere. I've had enough publicity for a lifetime after a little cameo on the royal Instagram recently and I prefer... I prefer to keep it low key."

Rachel nodded. "I wasn't sure you knew about that, to be honest."

"You did?" James rubbed at his eye. "Seems I was the last to know."

"It's my job to be across stuff like that, don't worry... I don't suppose many people saw it."

James glanced over to the wooden fridge magnets, tiny patent shoes in rows.

"Um. Are you on the nine thirty-five to Gatwick?" she asked.

"Yeah." James looked at his watch. "It's probably time to go to the gate."

They walked in silence through the airport, steering past suitcases and navigating darting passengers. All James could think about was Kezia. Kezia laughing and the way her dimples sang with the sound of it. He was looking for her everywhere, every solo traveller, every head that turned, around every corner. She had to fly home, didn't she?

Rachel was dwelling on Andy — the congratulations text, the feeling something had shifted between them — now she had done something for her. They could be friends now, really, not just for Joe, she was sure of it. She had been wanting too much from him, and when she couldn't get it she resented him; she'd wanted him to fulfil her, but he could never do that. So, if it was just friends, just that, well, they could all go forwards together. She looked across at James, so beaten and tired. "James. I'm sorry. I know you were hoping for a different sort of weekend, a different sort of outcome, and Kezia—"

James' cheeks flushed and he staggered slightly, catching the sole of his shoe on the compact carpet.

"Sometimes it just doesn't work out between people," she said sympathetically. "I... I know how that feels."

They arrived at the gate and James double-checked the flight number on the board, pushing the hair out of his eyes, looking like he might speak again, but then saying nothing.

Rachel put her head to one side. "You'll be okay, James."

James flinched, peering down at his laces. "I still want her back, even though..." he said, unable to finish, his voice suddenly saturated, damp.

"Of course, I know how that feels too. Look, if there's anything I can do, if you need a friend, someone to talk to, then… here's my card, it might be nice to keep in touch."

James raised his eyes and bit his lip. He regarded Rachel, and past the heavy eyeliner and the clumps of mascara there was a sincerity he hadn't seen before. "Thank you," he said quietly, taking the card. "Thank you, and if I can help you, then I will too. I can't get you an interview with the Queen though," he quipped.

Rachel laughed. "Actually, I've already started thinking about my next project and it's not about the royalty. If… if it's not too much information… I got so mad when that man Darim told me he could cure my endometriosis with flamenco. He actually said that. He kind of shouted it at me — he hasn't got a clue — and it made me realise just how much ignorance is out there, and well, if I don't do something, that won't change, will it? So I'm going to pitch a feature — I think I've been too scared to tell my story before, but I'm not now, I don't have to pretend. Why should I?"

James smiled earnestly. "Yes. Good for you. I confess I am ignorant too so I will read it and learn." He glanced towards the gate, thinking. "I suppose you could say that's something good to have come out of all of this then — it will really help people — and it's funny because you said, 'if it's not too much information', well, it's not too much information that's the problem, is it? It's not enough information."

Rachel relaxed, nodding. "When you put it like that, it's very simple, isn't it?"

A man in a Hawaiian shirt got up, manoeuvring a huge suitcase on wheels towards the front desk, illustrious, ushering other passengers out of his way. A ripple went through the waiting room as everyone turned to see… Then a squabbling family stood, still pointing fingers at each other, and followed, so that more people started to move, unsure, joining the queue just because it was there. After a while a woman in uniform shuffled into position and took up the microphone, calling them onto the plane in a frail voice made loud.

"Well, I suppose I might see you on the other side?" Rachel said to James.

"Yeah, Chris is picking me up from the airport, he's the one who put that post on Instagram so he's got a bit of making up to do."

"Ha — it's his round for the next six months, surely?"

"Something like that." James managed a grin.

They filed onto the aircraft and found their seats — alone again — adjusting seat belts and adjusting to their new reality, listening as the air hostess told them to fix their own oxygen mask before anyone else's. When the safety briefing was over, they settled back, making polite conversation with strangers, letting other people's stories relieve them of their own.

***

The rhythm was still in her step. *Ta dah taka da.* Into the airport and up the stairs. *Ta dah taka da.* Darim, breaking her heart, breaking everything apart. *Taka taka da.* He haunted her now, the feeling of his last look always there and a hollow sensation in her stomach, where the sickness had never really gone away.

"You've still got the dancing, Pet. You can find a class over here. It wasn't going to last forever in Spain anyway, now was it?" *Was it?* Her dad, on the mobile; she'd had the screen fixed at the airport. "You've had your adventures now you can come home. We'll have shepherd's pie for tea."

The pang of the familiar hit like grief. Then there was her mum. "He seemed like such a nice man," she said, for the third time. "He did seem so nice."

They'd taken Darim's phone so she couldn't talk to him. They'd taken his life too if he wasn't dancing, she knew that. She'd made Java promise to tell her everything — every detail, every piece of news — no matter how much it hurt: everything. "It wasn't his fault," she told her dad. "They made him do it. I'm sure they did. I'm sure."

Pat wasn't interested. "All that matters is that you come home now, Pet. Just come back and we'll go from there."

But go where? She had changed. There was something stronger in the middle of her now and she wanted to keep it. She was afraid they would force her back to the old Kezia, the easy one for them... and yet, she craved their hugs and their strong cups of tea.

Kezia focused her eyes on the beer in duty free, trying to decide whether her parents would really prefer wine. The stickers shouted brands in bright colours and there were too many to choose from, so she shifted back to the bottles of red and found the one with the Spanish insignia they liked.

The man looked at her thoughtfully as she paid for it. "Good choice," he said, like it mattered. Like anything mattered now. The feeling wasn't of going home, it was of leaving Darim, but... which Darim? Love and lies, everything mixed with poison now.

It was three thirty. Twenty minutes until boarding. She moved past perfumes in sculpted glass diffusing the light with labels full of flowers. The rush of scent was hopeful, but fake.

"You can't still love him."

People who said that didn't understand love. Her friend Lucy was one of them. *"But you can't!"* Kezia hadn't tried to explain, she just held the love like a rare and expensive perfume, like those behind the glass, the bottle the shape of her heart.

When it was time, she boarded the plane, scarcely noticing the grey seats and the plastic overhead luggage holders, the chill air conditioning or the people like zombies, locating their seats. The place next to her was empty and she imagined Darim there, free. She wanted to pretend she was taking him home but the image wouldn't stay, it was like he belonged in Spain, belonged in his own world, and if you took him out of it, would slowly fade, like a mirage.

The aircraft began to taxi along the tarmac, following the lines straight and sure. They stopped. Then the plane started again, faster and faster this time and — suddenly — the feeling of no feeling inside as they lifted off and into the air. Kezia watched Spain receding, the crinkle of the coast and the great sweep of sea. Hues diluted and shapes blurred and the plane turned, heading over great mountains. She watched them shrinking, like abandoned swathes of brown and green cloth.

Clouds billowed and blocked the view — the fog in her mind made real. Kezia leant back, closing her eyes, and for a moment, all she could see was the fog... then, the darkness came, and out of the darkness, the flamencas, bending and twisting against the black curtain of her mind. They danced to the hazy thrum of the plane's engine, stamping down in angst and agony. One of them turned and it was Sue and she was saying,

"It's not your fault." And she was dancing with her hands over her eyes and then Java came and they twirled together.

"You were poisoned." It was Abril, swinging in from the side.

"What were you supposed to believe?" Rosa and Carmen were there too, dancing, all dancing, dancing... *It's not your fault;* a strange and faraway concept... and then she came up, swimming along a charcoal tunnel, everything rushing past her, surprising and sudden.

The sleep had caught her unawares. She hadn't realised how tired she was. Remembering the dream, she put her hand on her heart. *Heart lamp*, she thought, shifting uncomfortably, crossing and recrossing her legs. An air hostess with slightly smudged lipstick was pulling a trolley down the aisle, dishing out smiles and capsules of water. When she glided next to Kezia, she pulled the tray table down for her and laid a small packet on a tiny serviette.

"Thank you," said Kezia, but the woman was already gone. Kezia picked up the small flat pastry and turned it over in her hands, watching the crumbs come off and stick to the inside of the wrapper. *To find freedom you need to be healed from the past, trust the future and live completely in the present.* That's what he'd said, when the music overlapped the words and she played the shell castanets, striking the night into stars. Now, the sentence seemed to turn with her hands, over and over, everything crumbling like pastry behind the transparent film of his lie. Did one lie make everything else untrue? "He gave me something," she'd told Sue. "Something I haven't had before."

Sue had adjusted herself on the bench, brooding. "But he couldn't give you something you didn't already have. It was inside of you, otherwise, well, you wouldn't have stayed past that first night. So don't make this about anyone else now. It is about you. Forget the disappointment and make it about what you have learnt — and keep dancing, the magic will stay with you. You'll be surprised. Remember, Darim doesn't have exclusive rights on *duende* — that comes from you and always will."

They'd hugged after that and Kezia had hoped some of Sue's wisdom might rub off on her. She cried as she said goodbye.

"Now don't forget — no more unhappy men telling you what to do. No more men who are only pretending to have it all together dictating your moods, not any more!"

Kezia had let the words percolate as she got into the taxi. Sue was going back to her own family next week, time for her to live her own lessons. She'd promised to keep in touch and Kezia had promised to let Sue know what happened with Gary as well. They'd sent the email together. It had felt good in the end and Kezia wondered why she had resisted for so long. "You had to do it when you were ready," Sue told her, and she was right because Kezia wasn't scared any more, and she could understand: she did it not just for herself but for other girls in other offices that she would never know and never meet. She did it for justice.

Kezia looked out at the startling saturation of the sky. The clouds had transformed into a bulbous carpet underneath them, spreading out, away and forever. Her hopes and dreams were drifting too, with her emotions all snarled up together. She loved him and she hated what he'd done... she hated him and she loved what he'd given her. Their last kiss still burnt in her mind, at the bottom of the stairs. *Not tonight, Kezia... Not tonight...* It wasn't what she'd wanted but now she was glad it had ended there. Less to regret. A man started coughing three rows back, the sound catching in the back of his throat and again she wondered if she should have known, if the signs were there, or if love had made her myopic. The plane buffeted and the seat belt sign flashed. Kezia gripped her elbows across her chest.

"Just a bit of turbulence," chimed the air hostess as she bustled past; she had fixed her lipstick and was smiling out of habit.

Just a bit of turbulence. Kezia looked down at a scratch in the armrest as the aircraft juddered. A free magazine was tucked into the seat pocket in front, she could see the legs of a woman in a swimsuit, her head and torso hidden by the sick bag.

What if she never saw him again? The notion settled in-between the cracks made by the pain, cementing it, making it worse. She pictured Darim playing the guitar, the image piercing like a shaft of sunlight. He was on the low brick wall outside the house, the sky a blaze of blue at his back, the notes weaving out into the garden, his necktie at an angle and his purple jacket as vivid as the music... his eyes glazed with the ecstasy of playing, carrying him to some far distant place. She would never reach him now. Did she ever reach him then? Her thoughts were stifling, romance and remorse, curdling.

Kezia felt for the spell, still in her pocket, the paper tired and soft now, the meaning faded with the words. She wanted to scream. He taught her that. Darim, the cure and the curse. She pictured him again and her eyes swelled with tears, purple tears, the colour he wore reflected and refracted over and over, extracted from her memories and preserved in salt; an indelible emotion she could never cry out. Purple — the colour of mourning, of absence, of Lent; a forever fast, just beginning — the idea of him and her together an illusion now, like everything else.

The turbulence sign pinged again and a man across the aisle looked up from his book, over his glasses, not really seeing.

Kezia blinked back the tears. She clasped her hands into fists and turned back to the window — tiny crescents of dirt rippled across the pane, showing the scars of journeys past. The clouds were closer now, jostling and drawing pictures in the sky. A white drift morphed into a mask and grimaced in slow motion before it was wiped away by the wind. Another cloud turned into a horse, running, with its tail out straight behind. Softly it disintegrated, leaving her with the recollection of the horse's hooves she'd seen from the train. Hooves, no horse, stranded on the path like a discarded pair of shoes. *I've left my shoes behind, but I can still dance,* she thought dimly, reaching for a sense of hope even as it evanesced like one of the clouds. *I will dance.* For a moment she counted the beats in her head, letting them carry the current of her despair. *Okay Sue, no more unhappy men telling me what to do because it makes them feel better.*

Her stomach dipped — they were coming in to land — the woods and fields of England like a knitted patchwork, fuzzy from above, with crocheted trees and windy wool roads — grey greens and green greys. Closer they came, getting more distinct, and yet, when the plane touched-down decisively on the tarmac, Kezia felt unprepared.

Everyone scurried to get off, arms reaching for bags and babies kicking out fat legs. She let them go, filing out in a raggedy line, until it was her turn, stepping out under a bruised sky, ripe for rain.

It was as she descended the steps it came to her. *Always forwards, never back.* The words of the saint with the small mouth and the circle of yellow around his head. *Forwards.* From now on she would carry her church in her own hands, like he did.

Epilogue

Don't go down to the water, don't go down to the sea.
He's there, and he stares, with the haunted look of the dead.
Don't go down to the water, don't go there alone.
He wails and he wails for his long dead mama, screams of torment
raging down to the waves.
They locked him up, but it didn't last long...
He danced with the shadows and now he lives with them, side by side
and step by step.
Just him. His friends took south in a boat and were never to be seen
again.
He did their favours and he did their sentence and now he is all alone...
He sits and he waits, and there is no telling which ghosts come to him
now.
He had his turn pretending but illusions can't last forever.
The dawn yawns, the light leans in and the mists won't hold his secret.
The sun picks out a man who is more afraid than the people he was
trying to scare.
They cross themselves when they tell his story, shiver in disdain...
But holy water won't wash them clean because they know we are all
pretending somewhere, deep inside... deep where the darkness meets
our soul.
Somewhere we are all stained with the stories we tell ourselves.
The deceitful dark holds many secrets — his and yours — and they run
together, the way ghosts play with form.
So don't go down to the water, don't go down to the sea. You'll find the
truth is there, if you know how to undress it — and most people don't
want to see that...
Because hearts break in a thousand different ways.

****